"*End Game* has all the makings of a major bestseller—a close look at the unique world of chess champions, great and sympathetic characters, and a plot that just doesn't let go. Watch for a smash movie to be made of this."
—Ed Gorman, author of *The Marilyn Tapes*

"Stryker is the joint pseudonym of a husband-and-wife writing team who are expert at putting the fate of the world in the balance and making the pages fly. [*Deathright*] is wild, preposterous, and very hard to put aside."
—*Ellery Queen Mystery Magazine*

"Dev Stryker is billed as the pseudonym of a pair of bestselling thriller writers who have combined sales of thirty million books and three Edgar Awards. The talent is evident. *Deathright* is a smooth, accomplished thriller that begins with a methodical, drawn-out tease and rapidly accelerates to roller-coaster velocity. The action is driving and relentless. A highly entertaining thriller."
—*Mystery News*

"Two bestselling authors combine forces under a pseudonym to write a fast-paced, bloody, and exciting terrorist thriller. Readers will want to stay the course."
—*Booklist* on *Deathright*

ALSO BY DEV STRYKER

Deathright

END GAME

Dev Stryker

FORGE®

A TOM DOHERTY ASSOCIATES BOOK
NEW YORK

This is a work of fiction. All the characters and events portrayed in this book are fictitious, and any resemblance to real people or events is purely coincidental.

END GAME

A Forge Book
Published by Tom Doherty Associates, Inc.
175 Fifth Avenue
New York, NY 10010

Forge® is a registered trademark of Tom Doherty Associates, Inc.

ISBN: 0-812-51597-8

First edition: April 1994
First mass market edition: August 1996

Printed in the United States of America

0 9 8 7 6 5 4 3 2 1

For Michael Seidman
Who Keeps Us Living the Dream

Acknowledgments

Special thanks to the members of the Bethlehem (PA) chess club, for both their technical assistance and their pertinacity at staying with an endeavor which I find increasingly bewildering.

Dev Stryker

1

He...

...ignored the escalator—he had never trusted them—and walked down the wide marble steps of the Port Authority Bus Terminal, pretending to be a tourist, looking around as if he had never seen the place before.

But he was very familiar with the building, and while it was well lit and bright, especially compared to Manhattan's ancient subway stations, he was sure it was the most depressing place in America. *It's the creatures who infest this sewer*, he thought.

He had once written a long poem about it for school. He called it "Terminal, Land of the Losers," and in it, he had identified three distinct populations who inhabited the huge but squat stone building. In the morning and evening, there were the commuters, heading intently to their platforms, ignoring the littered floors in their hurry, first to get to their jobs and then to get home and leave Manhattan behind them.

The terminal also had a second, permanent population of retail personnel, the store clerks and cashiers and cooks and waitresses who worked in the building and then headed thankfully home at the end of their shifts.

And at all times, but especially at night, the building had a third population ... skid row alcoholics begging for handouts, apprentice con artists selling expensive "gold Swiss watches" for five dollars, shaved-head religious cultists dunning people for contributions, roving gangs of hostile youths distinguishable from each other only by their brand of sneakers, and a wide variety of eccentrics, the spaced out, the drug dealers, the addicts, the downright crazy ... all those who lived on the edge of civilization, on the fringe of the law.

He thought, *Tonight there's a fourth population. Me. And there are no others here like me.*

He stepped off the stairs and walked through the main lobby, gawking with bemused astonishment at the late-evening assortment of life's losers on display. He stared with open curiosity at a tall, rail-thin black woman in a long black dress who was striding ahead of him toward the entrance. She was dragging a small cherubic boy, neatly dressed in a sailor suit, who could barely keep up with her long paces. It took him a moment to figure out what was unusual about the woman.

It was her bushy black mustache. Apparently, "she" was a man. But nobody else in the terminal even seemed to notice, not even the uniformed policewoman who stood at a fast-food counter, drinking a can of soda.

He wore a tight contemptuous smile as he neared the entrance door. He shifted a small valise from one hand to the other and ignored all the outstretched hands and pushed through the revolving door onto Ninth Avenue.

The July heat of the city slapped him in the face like a barber's steamed towel. He took a deep breath and paused for a moment to examine the street people.

Walking slowly now, he moved down toward the corner of Fortieth Street, pausing again as a man of indeterminate age, sitting on an old army duffel bag, wearily asked, "Spare some change, mister?" and lazily extended his hand.

He stopped and looked at the man carefully before asking, "Are you one of those homeless people I keep hearing about?"

The unshaven dirty man blinked. He was not used to being asked questions.

"Yeah. I'm out of work and I lost my apartment. I'm trying to get back on my feet."

"That's terrible," he said earnestly, then leaned back from the smell of cheap wine on the man's breath. "Something should be done about this. Aren't there shelters to go to?"

"Not very safe to spend the night in. Wake up dead in the morning," the man said, then cackled when he realized he had made a joke.

"Dear, that's awful. There's nothing like this back in Salt Lake City," he said. Perspiration was trickling down the sides of his face.

"Salt Lake? You a Mormon or something?"

"Yes," he said. "I'm here to do missionary work. And maybe I'll just start with you. Would you like a safe place to spend the night? And a meal?"

The disheveled man blinked and tried to focus his thoughts. He saw a big smile beaming down at him and answered, "That'd be great. But I ain't no Mormon."

"That doesn't matter. We're all brothers," he said. "What's your name?"

"Joe."

"Mine's Hiram. Hiram Walker."

He stared down at the man for a few seconds, waiting, then shrugged and began to walk away. After a moment's hesitation, Joe grabbed his duffel bag, lurched to his feet and staggered after him. He did not much like leaving his regular spot on the sidewalk but who could tell when good luck was going to turn up. Perhaps he would be able to beat this Holy Roller out of a few bucks. Christmas in July. Why not? He remembered just today telling someone that things had to get better because they couldn't get any worse. Or maybe it was yesterday. No matter, he *definitely* remembered saying it to someone some time or other.

The man who called himself Hiram Walker got into a dark blue sedan that was parked at the corner, then opened the front passenger door and said cheerfully, "Hop in."

Joe got in, hugging his duffel bag between his knees. He frowned at a large plastic garbage can that took up much of the rear seat. What could that be for? Taking up collections at the services? Joe tried to remember what he knew about Mormons. Were they the ones who didn't like drinking? Joe remembered the half-filled pint bottle of wine inside his jacket and decided that if this Mormon tried to take it away from him, he would fight him for it.

The car pulled away and drove down Ninth Avenue for a few blocks, then over to Twelfth Avenue, where it turned north to run beside the Hudson River. Traffic was light at this time of night.

Hiram said what a pleasure it was to do the Lord's work. Joe thought that maybe he was a fag.

Eventually the sedan veered abruptly off the parkway, made several turns and ended up heading southbound on the same road. A minute later, it turned into an empty parking lot beside the Hudson River and came to a stop.

"Well, here we are," he announced cheerfully.

Joe looked around, confused. "Where? There's nothing here. There's just the river."

"We're going to have a short prayer meeting," he said and walked around the car, opened the passenger door and pulled Joe effortlessly from his seat. "Say your prayers."

As Joe straightened up, an abrupt punch in the stomach made him gasp and double over. Hiram pulled a weighted sap from his jacket pocket and hit him several times in the face, then began kicking him when Joe fell to the ground.

Joe lay in a fetal position, trying to cover himself up

from injury, and Hiram straddled him from behind, looped one arm around his throat and lifted him to his feet.

Then Joe saw the glint of a knife in front of him. He saw it, then felt it plunge into his stomach. Joe groaned and tried feebly to ward off the knife, waving his arms wildly in front of him. He caught many of the strikes on his forearms and wrists, but Hiram was too big and too strong and finally Joe's strength gave out and the knife kept plunging in and out of his stomach, over and over, in and out, many wounds, until finally it lodged in his heart. Joe stiffened, then went limp.

An automobile turned into the parking lot. Screened by his own car, Hiram looked up, but the other vehicle parked at the far end of the lot and the driver walked away.

There was a faint groan from the ground, almost a bubbling sound, and he reached down, grabbed Joe's hair, lifted his head and cut his throat.

He dropped into a crouch next to Joe and, holding the knife as if it were a pen, carved the letter P deeply into the man's forehead. He paused, then spitefully slashed Joe's cheeks and throat several more times before finally closing the knife, wiping it on Joe's grimy shirt, and putting it away.

He opened the rear door of the car, pulled out the plastic garbage can and stuffed Joe's body into it, then hoisted it back onto the rear seat, closed the door and drove out of the parking lot.

At the first exit, he left the parkway to veer east. A few blocks later, the car entered the northwest corner of Central Park, continuing east and south to emerge at Seventy-second Street and Fifth Avenue.

It was after midnight and the streets of Manhattan's posh Upper East Side were almost empty.

He came back on Seventy-first Street, and between Second and Third Avenues, he stopped in front of a hydrant outside a trim four-story townhouse and waited for an approaching car to pass.

When the car had gone and he was sure there were no pedestrians on either sidewalk, he wrestled the trash can from the backseat and placed it beside several others awaiting the next morning's garbage pickup. He made sure both of Joe's legs were dangling out of the can and that the lid was neatly balanced on his knees.

Then he drove away, idly wondering how many pedestrians would pass the garbage can before someone noticed the dead man's protruding legs . . . and then whether that sharp-eyed pedestrian would call the police or simply hurry on home, chanting to himself New York City's famous theme song: "I didn't want to get involved."

Although savage, the killing was just another New York City murder and would not have rated any news space, had it not been for the wealthy neighborhood where the body was found. That made it worth three paragraphs a day later in the *New York Post*. Neither the *New York Times* nor any of the local television stations carried anything.

The police did not mention the letter which had been carved in the dead man's forehead.

2

Six men moved silently up the dimly lit stairs of a tenement in Spanish Harlem. They walked single file, sticking to the outside edges of the stairway, where the bare wooden steps were less likely to creak. Using hand signals, they positioned themselves on both sides of a third-floor door.

One of the men tried the doorknob gingerly. He shook his head, shrugged, stepped back, raised his foot and kicked as hard as he could just above the doorknob.

The door crashed open; the kicker yelled, "Police! Freeze! Don't anybody move!" and the other men swept by him, each, by prearrangement, aiming his gun at a different corner of the room.

Police Inspector Paul Regal, the man who had kicked in the door, stepped in last, his gaze and his gun aimed at the ceiling. It was not meant to be a joke. Regal had once busted into a South Bronx apartment and been shot at by a suspect who was hiding atop a sleeping deck he had built high up on the wall of the room. It did not happen often but you only had to die once. Well-trained cops looked up, down and to all four points of the compass.

But the apartment was empty, empty to the point of being bare. They were in the kitchen but it held not one stick of furniture, not a table, not a chair.

"Damn," Inspector Regal said. "Another waste of time." He huffed a sign. "Give it a toss. See if anybody's left anything behind."

The rest of the men moved through the shabby little apartment to dismember it in search of evidence, but one of the men, a worried look on his face, stayed with Regal. He was Lieutenant Tony Bolda, Regal's second-in-command.

Bolda was fifty but looked older. His thinning sandy hair that he combed straight back, light blue eyes, and a mouth that, even in repose, turned down at the corners, gave him naturally the constant expression of sarcastic disdain that other policemen worked to attain. Bolda was wearing an expensive-looking gray pinstripe suit, but as always, his pockets were stuffed with newspapers, crumpled waxpaper from sandwiches, and he looked like what he was: a man with an eye for good suits but with absolutely no business ever wearing one.

"This was supposed to be a live one, Paul," Bolda complained. "I'm starting to wonder about us."

Regal shrugged. He was tall with an ordinarily handsome face, except for his eyes, which were shopworn and wary. "Wonder what?" he asked.

Bolda moved closer so he could lower his voice. "I don't want to think what I'm thinking," he said, "but I'm still thinking it. And it's always up here with the Latinos that things seem to go wrong."

Regal looked away as a younger detective with a scowl on his tawny face walked toward him. He was as agitated as Bolda was laconic.

"No good, Inspector. The damned place's been cleaned out. I'm gonna rip the tongue right out of that kid's face," he snarled. "He swore that they were working up here."

"Take it easy, Pete. These things happen," Regal consoled him. "Land of the free and home of the brave. People move all the time. Maybe they found a better apartment."

Detective Pete Muniz snorted and Regal said, "Go talk with the super, if you can find him. See what he can tell us."

Muniz nodded and left and Regal glanced at his watch.

"Tony," he told Lieutenant Bolda, "I'm going home. You finish up here and we'll talk about it in the morning. But don't go repeating what you said to me. No sense getting any tongues wagging."

"You're the boss," Bolda said, raising his hands to his sides, palms upward. "We'll talk to some neighbors. Maybe somebody saw something."

"Don't count on it. But try anyway and then leave. This is a dry hole."

Regal drove back to his apartment in Manhattan, thinking without pleasure about the conversation he would have the next morning with Police Commissioner Richard J. Gallagher. The old man seemed to regard fruitless drug raids by Regal's squad as a personal insult, even though he understood enough about police work to know that cops often had to work on the basis of dubious information and flimsy rumors.

More to the point, though, he was sure to want to know why the raid was held in the first place. Regal commanded only six detectives, and the mission of the small, elite unit—which worked directly out of the commissioner's office—was to find out when and where large drug shipments would arrive in the city. It was certainly not, as Gallagher often reminded Regal, to waste time trying to bust small-time street dealers in Spanish Harlem apartments.

It would just be a day for catching hell.

It was almost 2 A.M. when Regal arrived home. He opened the door to the main bedroom and looked inside. His wife was huddled at the side of the bed, snoring gently, one hand dangling limply over the edge of the mattress.

He closed the door quietly and went to his own room. He always slept better when he knew Patrice was home. It was a jungle out there.

Regal entered the office of Police Commissioner Gallagher the next morning looking more calm and self-assured than he felt. Bolda's suspicion—that last night's raid might have been tipped off—had kept him tossing and turning before he finally fell asleep, and when he woke in the morning, the possibility was the first thing on his mind.

As usual, Gallagher was crouched behind his desk as if he expected to have to leap over it at any moment. He was scowling at the litter of papers in front of him, and by way of greeting, he just transferred the scowl to Regal.

"It better be fast and it better be good."

"Why don't I come back, Commissioner? Say, next year?" Regal said, taking pleasure in the easy, almost informal relationship he had developed with the department's top civilian boss.

Gallagher looked at him for a few long seconds, then smiled and said, "Sit down, Paul. It'll be a pleasure to deal with someone sane for a moment. What's going on?"

Quickly, Regal briefed him on the previous night's non-event. When he was done, he hesitated just a moment, then added Lieutenant Bolda's half-formed suspicion.

Gallagher's scowl returned, deeper this time, dropping the corners of his mouth almost to his chin. "What do you think? Anything to it?"

"I don't know. I doubt it. We were acting on a pretty thin rumor that Pete Muniz came up with from one of his informers—something about a new bunch of dealers moving in from Panama to set up shop. It was an iffy thing but we thought it was worth moving on. As I said, the apartment was empty. But, you know, Commissioner, it was too empty. They didn't even leave dirt behind. You could still see the broom marks on the floor."

"So?" Gallagher said.

Regal shook his head. "People in Spanish Harlem who move out without telling the superintendent don't spend time sweeping up, at least not to get rid of dust. I think they were maybe just making sure they left no traces. So maybe they were tipped off." He shrugged. "But who knows? If it weren't for the sweeping, I'd say maybe they spotted us coming or maybe they found a better apartment. I don't know but it's possible they got advance word of the raid. I don't want to overreact but I've got to think about this one carefully. And I hate it."

Gallagher leaned back in his huge leather swivel chair, his index finger absentmindedly twirling one of the few strands of white hair on his head. His eyes were focused somewhere above the ceiling and Regal guessed the commissioner's mind was racing through a series of convoluted schemes.

Finally, Gallagher sat straight up in his chair and pierced Regal with his stare. "I don't have to be a career cop to know that drugs mean money and whenever there's a big enough pot of money, somebody might try to get his hands on it. It's a problem with the regular narcotics squad and it could be a problem with your gang. So you just think about it some more and let me know what you come up with. But don't discuss it with anyone in the department except me. No one at all. Not even Bolda. For the time being, we'll leave it with you."

Regal nodded, keeping his face impassive, but he did not believe for a moment that the police commissioner was going to let the matter rest with Regal.

While Gallagher had never been a cop himself, he was the son and grandson of New York City policemen. After Fordham and Yale Law School, he had graduated from army intelligence into the CIA and later into a fortune on Wall Street. He had come out of retirement three years earlier to take the post as police commissioner for the city's new mayor, whose campaign committee Gallagher had headed. He had told friends that he was bored by retirement; Regal guessed that the truth was the man could not stay away from the cut and thrust of day-to-day politics.

Regal thought he knew the commissioner as well as any other man in the department, and if there was one thing the man always did, it was to play both sides against the middle. So he was sure that as soon as he left the room Gallagher would be on the phone with Deputy Inspector Vincent Flaherty, head of the Internal Affairs Division, to tell him about the possible corruption in the commissioner's elite drug task force.

Well, maybe that's the right way to handle it, Regal thought, *but I don't like the thought of any of those IAD bastards harassing my men.*

Regal stood. "Then I'll get back to the salt mine, unless there's anything else."

"Not unless you can tell me why a homeless wino was stabbed thirty-seven times and dumped in a garbage can in front of the house of a retired admiral on East Seventy-first Street."

Regal pretended to think for a moment. "Someone didn't like him?"

"Very funny," Gallagher said. "Your friend Inspector Burton was on the phone bright and early wondering if we've got ourselves a real nasty psycho on the loose. That's all the mayor needs—a nice new crime scare in the Upper East Side."

"Commissioner, there are knife killings every day in this town. Is this a big deal just because of where the body was dumped?"

"You don't even have to ask that question. But since you did, yes. The Upper East Side is special. Everybody who runs a paper or a TV station lives up there and I'll be damned if I'll have the streets running with blood. I told Burton to start a new Homicide North unit up there and pull in some manpower but clear up this slicing real fast. There's an election next year, in case you forgot."

"Oh," Regal said.

"Don't be smug. Politicians pay our salary." He paused and looked out the window toward the Empire State Building. "Burton says the guy was almost cut to ribbons and he'd been beaten up first. And it looked as if the letter P had been carved on his forehead. Shit, with my luck, it's going to be some kind of goddam zombie voodoo ritual thing and everybody in the city's gonna have to wear garlic around their necks." He paused. "Why the hell would anyone carve a letter on somebody's face for? And whoever did it supplied his own garbage can, too. Who does that?"

He looked at Regal as if demanding an answer and the lanky inspector just shrugged.

"It *has* to be a psycho," Gallagher said. "And I hate psychos. The press gets all excited and the politicians start peeing their pants and it's all a big mess. Tell your guys to keep their eyes peeled for any nut with a knife. Now get out of here and let me do some work."

Regal nodded and left. He could sympathize with Gallagher, whose friendship with the city's black mayor extended back many years. There was nothing like some kind of highly publicized crime wave to screw up an election campaign and the mayor was planning to run again in less than a year. *Better Gallagher than me*, Regal thought. *I hate politics.*

His squad's office was in a little-used corridor in the basement of the big police headquarters building, behind a door bearing only the legend: PRIVATE. KEEP OUT.

Inside, Tony Bolda sat with his feet up on a desk, reading the racing form. In front of him was a cardboard container of coffee, leaking on the green desk blotter, and a half-eaten bagel. On a corner of the desktop, a small hand-lettered sign printed on cardboard read: CAUTION. TOXIC WASTE AREA. The sign had been put on Bolda's desk by some other member of the squad, but if they had thought to shame him or make him change his ways, it had not worked. He still lived in litter. Regal noticed he was wearing the same suit he had been wearing last night.

Bolda nodded to him and, without saying anything, followed the inspector into Regal's private office.

"The apartment was clean and nobody knew nothing, as usual. Mostly blacks live on that floor and all they knew was that some Latinos moved in a couple of weeks ago. But nobody knew where they were from. They couldn't tell a Puerto Rican from a Mexican, much less a Panamanian."

When he grinned, Regal said, "What's so funny?"

"I don't know," Bolda said. "I just think it's funny that blacks think all Hispanics look alike. Anyway, it looked like even the walls were washed but we picked up a couple of prints anyway. We've sent them off to the FBI, but you know what the odds are."

"Got to try though," Regal said. "Any descriptions?"

"Sure. All short or medium height, all in their twenties or thirties, all had black hair."

"And you mean, with that much to go on, you haven't picked them up yet?" Regal said sourly. Without waiting for an answer, he said, "Where's Pete Muniz?"

"Out looking for that dippy kid who gave him the tip."

"Tell him to see me when he comes back."

"Got it." Bolda began talking about the latest rumors of new drug action in the city. Almost always, they were nonsense, far removed from reality, but Regal liked to know the talk that was circulating on the street. He thought it helped him keep a feel for things. Neither man seemed anxious to discuss Bolda's suspicion of the night before.

They stopped talking when Detective Second Grade Jane Cole stuck her head into the office. She was a stunningly pretty redhead with light hedge-green eyes who had joined the squad only six months earlier and had found herself stuck with all the office's paperwork, not just because she was the newest member of the squad but also because she was a woman and Regal did not know quite what to do with her.

Bolda leered openly and twirled the end of an imaginary mustache.

"Put a cork in it, Tony," she said. "Sorry for interrupting, Inspector, but did you order any fish?"

"Fish? Jane, what are you talking about?"

The young woman's face seemed to flush a little. "You just got a call. For you by name. And the voice said something about prawns. Like '*P* is for prawn.'"

Regal shook his head in consternation. "I don't know what that's all about. Did you get the call on tape?"

"No, dammit. The tape machine is down and I'm waiting for the repair guy. This was like one of those taped messages though." She began to imitate a computer talking. "This-is-a-message-for-Inspector-Regal. P-is-for-prawn."

"Was it on the private line or through the switchboard?" Regal asked.

"Private line."

"I don't know. Must be some cop with a weird sense of humor. Who the hell else has the private line?"

"I guess so," the woman responded.

"But if anybody sends me a box labeled shrimp and you hear it ticking, call the bomb squad first."

Detective Cole grinned back. "Yes, sir," she said.

Almost every day, Regal ate the same lunch, a tuna salad on toast delivered to his desk by the delicatessen just a block away from One Police Plaza.

But this day, still annoyed by last night's worthless waste of manpower, he decided to trek to the Galway Bar and relax with a bottle of beer. He wanted a chance to think about the possibility of a turncoat in his squad, and when he ate in the office, there was precious little time for thinking because the telephones were always ringing. But as soon as he walked in and settled at the bar, he realized he had made a mistake.

"Well, well, Inspector Hollywood," he heard a voice

roar and he turned to face Inspector Joe Burton, who commanded detectives in one of the Upper East Side precincts. Burton's unit, now tagged "Homicide North," was handling the murder of the wino found in the garbage can.

"Hello, Joe," Regal said. He added, "Nice seeing you," in a forlorn attempt to cut off the conversation but he knew that it would never work.

Burton was sitting at a table across from the bar with three other men, obviously policemen and probably officers under his command. Regal did not know any of them. Burton rose from his seat with a grin and walked toward Regal. He was a big, burly cop, and in the past he had enjoyed sneering at Regal as an overeducated liberal who was soft on criminals. He gave grudging respect to Regal's Vietnam War record but scoffed at his college education and hard-won night law school degree.

The root of his resentment though, as the department's top brass all knew, was that he saw Regal as his prime opponent for eventual promotion to chief inspector, the highest uniformed post in the New York City Police Department. Ten years older than Regal, Burton clearly dreaded the thought of being passed over in favor of the younger man when the position became vacant next year with the retirement of the current chief, Aloysius Riley.

"I'd rather see some flame-o get it than that overeducated headline hunter," Burton had been heard to grouse. Like everything else said in the department, the remark had gotten to the subject's ears even before the echo of Burton's voice had died out.

So Regal knew he was not in for a pleasant luncheon conversation with Joe Burton.

"So what are you doing here, Regal?" Burton demanded at the top of his voice. "Isn't the Stork Club open yet?"

"Just slumming with you poor folks," Regal said.

"Hey, bartender," Burton called out. "My table will

have another round. And give my friend here his usual sarsaparilla."

The bartender looked at Regal, who mouthed the word "beer." The barkeep nodded and Regal tried again to deflect Burton.

"Anything doing with that body in the ashcan?" he asked.

"What do you care? That's police work. You know . . . the stuff that gets dirt under your fingernails."

"Go away, Joe, you're giving me a headache," Regal said softly. He turned back and hunkered down over the beer the bartender had put in front of him.

But Burton pressed on. "I'll tell you what. If we get a break on the case, I'll let you know. I'll call the Twenty One Club first thing. If you're not there, your wife can take the message."

Regal wheeled on his seat. "What the hell do you mean by that?" he said coldly.

"Hey, every time I open the paper, there's a picture of your wife at some nightclub. Don't blame me for what the newspapers print. You hang out with celebrities, you get your picture taken. That's how it works, right? Don't knock it. It got you promoted to inspector, didn't it?"

"Joe?"

"What?"

"Go fuck yourself."

3

So Regal wound up back in his office, eating tuna salad on toast, when Pete Muniz entered the office with his usual worried frown.

He sat down, without apologizing for disturbing Regal's lunch, and said, "It looks like Hector's among the missing."

"Hector was last night's informant?"

Muniz nodded. "Hector Guzman."

"He gave you a bad tip. You surprised he's hiding out?"

Muniz waved his hands to his sides in an intentionally comic gesture of ignorance. "If he fed me a line of crap the other day about knowing where these alleged Panamanians were holed up, okay, he might be hiding out 'cause he's afraid I'll lean on him. But his kid brother told me some guys were looking for him yesterday. Said they had business with him, whatever that means. And then he didn't come home last night. So I don't know what it's all about, Inspector. Your guess is as good as mine."

"Any description of the men who were looking for Hector?"

"Sure. They all looked like me," Muniz said with a sour smile. "It could have been the guys who had that apartment or it could be half the people in New York."

"Let's hope Hector's just hiding out," Regal said.

"Yeah, because then he'll surface sooner or later and I'll hear about it. But I told the brother anyway to watch his step and keep his eyes open."

"Will he call us if he hears anything?"

"I doubt it," Muniz said. "But I got a guy I know on the block to keep an eye on things."

Regal didn't ask who the guy on the block was. Muniz was young and relatively inexperienced as a detective but he had a strong grapevine of friends and informants through the Latin areas of Manhattan. Not all of them were law-abiding and some were even small-time dealers themselves. Basically they got a safe conduct pass from Muniz in return for letting him know about any major new players showing up in the city's narcotics trade. That was how Hector Guzman, a very small-time dealer himself, had come to tell Muniz about the three Panamanians who he'd said were planning to open a major drug factory in Spanish Harlem.

Cops had to do it—trade off petty arrests for the chance at big arrests—and superior officers lived by the unspoken rule that they did not ask for the identity of any tipsters. What you didn't know wouldn't get you indicted for corruption . . . or get an informant shot.

It was not the kind of police work that Regal wanted to see analyzed on *Sixty Minutes* but it was the only way to work on the streets.

"You've done what you can do, Pete. Just keep looking for Hector, I guess."

"I hope I find him before those Panamanians do—if there are any. But I've got a bad feeling about this whole thing. Something's wrong. I don't know what it is but I can feel it and I don't like it. I think we're gonna find Hector in the river."

"Or in a garbage can," Regal said, drawing a surprised look from the young detective. He sighed and explained about the overnight murder up on the East Side. *Odd that it should come into my mind*, he thought.

Regal moodily stirred cream into his coffee and looked across the table at his wife. "What have you got against this restaurant?"

They were in a small neighborhood Italian eatery, just down the block from their Seventy-fifth Street apartment.

"It's all right for a snack, I guess, but I prefer a tablecloth when I'm eating dinner," she sniffed.

"It's a real wood table, not formica," he said. "And the napkins are cloth, not paper."

"Polyester. Not linen or cotton. Even paper napkins pick up spills better than polyester."

"Why should you care? You never spill anything. Anyway, I like this place. Good food. If we have to eat out all the time, I'd just as soon do it here. Next time, we'll just remember to bring our own napkins."

"Let's face it, Paul. You're hopelessly déclassé. If a restaurant is above Sixtieth or below Fortieth, it's not a restaurant, it's a diner. And it doesn't matter what kind of napkins it has."

Patrice laughed at her own remark and Regal could not help admiring the perfect beauty of her perfect smile. She was a tall whippet of a blonde, sleek and elegant, with amazingly large gray eyes. At five foot ten, she was only three inches shorter than Regal, who was used to towering over women, and she looked as if she were in her late twenties, instead of her early forties. He remembered with a pang how wrapped up in her he had been when they were first married. Even his police career came second and he would have left the force then, if she had insisted.

But that was twenty years ago, when the former Patsy Pickett of Buffalo, Missouri, newly arrived in New York City, was just beginning the process of transforming herself into Patrice, the elegant fashion model. For three years she had been at the top of her profession, and then, in one of those bewilderingly instantaneous shifts of taste among the Beautiful People, elegant whippetlike blondes were out and natural-looking brunettes with scraggy hair and moles that they called beauty marks were in.

She had taken that sea change badly. He remembered one night she had come home and burst into angry tears.

"The bitch they hired instead of me? She's got stretch marks. You could use her thighs for an accordion. Fucking stretch marks."

"Get some," Regal suggested with a smile. "I know how to do it."

She stared at him coldly and stomped from the room. It was the first time Regal suspected the depth of his wife's determination not to have children.

Patrice had continued to work, although she put in longer hours to earn less money, and slowly the two had drifted away from each other, until now his police career was all Regal had left and that just wasn't enough. Not without children.

He had always wanted kids, but whenever he raised the subject, Patrice found a way to put it off. Eventually, she informed him that her gynecologist had warned that a pregnancy might prove dangerous to her health and that they should forget about having children.

"We could adopt," he pointed out.

"It wouldn't be the same," Patrice said. "I wouldn't feel the same about them as I would if they were really our own. It just wouldn't work."

Regal did not argue with her. As Patrice had segued gracefully from modeling into a new career in interior designing, it grew increasingly clear to him that she had never really intended to clutter her life with children.

Arguing with her about it seemed unlikely to make her think more warmly about motherhood of any type. In truth, if the role were forced upon her, he doubted that she would be up to it. He shuddered at the thought of a young child being the object of her frequent temper tantrums.

But he did wish she would stop referring to each of her interior design assignments as "my new baby."

"So what's the latest with your apartment building?" he asked idly, waving to the waiter for their check.

"Don't I wish it *were* mine," she sighed. "Storm Mountain is going to be the best address in Manhattan . . . in the entire damned world. God, I'd give anything to be able to live there."

"Not on my salary, you won't," he commented mildly.

"I'm very well aware of that," she said, her lips tightening. "If we had to live on your salary, we couldn't even afford to eat at this place."

"Sure we could," Regal said. "Especially since we only eat here on Mondays 'cause that's the only night in the week you can spare for me."

"Somebody's got to be thinking of our future."

"I don't know," he responded wearily. "I make a good salary, more than enough for two people to live on, even in Manhattan."

"And you would have doubled your salary if you had taken that chief-of-security position that Oliver Storm offered you," she snapped.

"I don't need to trade in my shield for a tin badge and a fancy office," he said coldly. "Being a cop was good enough for my father; it'll do for me. I'm not going to spend my life running errands for people like your dear Oliver Storm. I don't care how many millions he's stolen."

"Oh, God, my dear Oliver Storm. We're not going to have to go through this jealousy routine again, are we? Why can't you just accept that Oliver is just a very wealthy client who happens to appreciate my talents?"

"I'm sure he does," Regal murmured, sipping his coffee.

"Obviously more than you do," she responded and her remarkable eyes narrowed. "At least when we go to dinner, it's to a real restaurant, not some grubby neighborhood pizzeria."

"Happens more and more often, it seems to me."

"And every time is money in the bank. Let me point out to you, my fine flat-footed friend, that not only am I being *extremely* well paid for the work I am doing for one of the wealthiest real estate developers in the world, I am also making a reputation as a top designer. Being seen with Oliver Storm is the best public relations I can get in my work."

"You're sure people won't think you're just another of Ollie's pretty faces?"

"Don't call him Ollie," she snapped. "And petty people can think what they want. That's their tough luck. Wait until Storm Mountain opens. Every designer in the country will eat their heart out."

"And then you'll stop having dinner with Ollie every night?"

"I hope there will be a long line of future projects. But even if I never do anything more with Oliver, this job is worth *anything* it takes. It will make me as a designer."

"So why do I get the feeling you've already been made?" he wondered aloud, bracing himself for a nasty flare-up, but unable to resist the jibe.

However, Patrice simply looked at him with a pitying smile.

"Why, darling, I didn't think you cared."

He looked at her somberly. "I care."

"Then care quietly. I would hate it if you started carrying on and embarrassing me."

"It's you who's doing the carrying on. And smiling sweetly for the newspaper photographers while you're doing it," Regal said. "Joe Burton was sneering at me today, rubbing it in that I've got a wife who spreads herself around town like a jar of marmalade."

"Who cares what that ghastly man thinks? He's got hair growing out of his ears. Just ignore people like him. You know I wouldn't do anything to embarrass you.

And you certainly don't have to be suspicious of Oliver. He's years too old for me."

She looked at him blandly, with the bright shining eyes of a practiced liar and Regal said, "Let's get out of here."

They walked silently the block back to their apartment building, but Regal noticed the glances they drew on the street. He knew they made an attractive couple. Tall and dark, he set off her stylishly slim figure and shining blonde hair. He thought of how proud he had been to walk down the street with her when they were newly in love, how he had enjoyed the envious looks from other men, and he felt again the deep sadness that seemed to be all that was left of their earlier passion.

And then a curious thought struck him. He should have had prawns for dinner. *P is for prawn. The whole world is going nuts.* He remembered that the slashed wino's body had been found only a half dozen blocks from where they were now.

So what? There's a broken heart for every light on Broadway and a dead bum everywhere you turn in this city.

He dismissed the thought. That killing was none of his business. And neither, he guessed, was Oliver Storm. And probably, neither was Patrice.

He . . .

. . . stood in front of a mirror, naked, carefully examining his bulky, almost hairless, body.

"What was it like?"

"It was wonderful. Every time the knife went in, blood spurted out. It was like jabbing pins into a water balloon."

"Ooooh. Did he scream?"

"No. I didn't think of that before. The old bastard didn't scream."

"I hope the next one screams."

"He will. He will."

4

Oliver Storm sat behind a vast marble-topped desk in his penthouse apartment on Central Park South, smiling affably at a reporter from the *New York Times*.

"But that's just the point," he said earnestly. "I know that crime isn't just a New York City problem. It's on the rise all across the country. There's not one small town that doesn't have problems that were unheard of twenty ... even ten ... years ago."

He paused to sip herbal tea from a vaguely pink porcelain cup.

"This is an age of personal insecurity. Who knows when some drug addict is going to rob him? What woman isn't afraid to walk down a street alone at night? Even the homeless, even the underclass, are at risk. Why, just today the body of some poor drifter was found stuffed into a trash can only a few blocks from here. Stabbed repeatedly, I'm told. Savage and senseless. We're in the nineties now and this is the Decade of Terror."

He repeated the phrase, rolling it around in his mouth

with obvious pleasure and lifting his chin defiantly. "The Decade of Terror. And that is why Storm Mountain is a breakthrough in residential real estate development. This complex has been planned from the start to emphasize personal security. Of course, it will be elegant. We're sparing no expense on the decor and we don't apologize for it. But the main selling point for our clients will be their personal security. And that doesn't come cheap. It costs money, my friend."

He leaned forward and shook his head sadly at the young journalist who had touched off the speech by suggesting diffidently that the asking prices for apartments in the luxurious Storm Mountain complex might seem "obscenely high" to the average New Yorker.

"All of us are at risk. But those who are well known are at greater risk," Storm intoned gravely. "No sensible person would condemn them for voluntarily spending their own money to safeguard themselves and their loved ones. *Any* parent, rich or poor, would sympathize with someone who is determined to prevent his children from being kidnapped or murdered." He stared at the reporter until the young man blinked. "Go ask the average New Yorker if he or she would like to live in Storm Mountain and the answer you'll get is 'Hell, yes.' " He leaned back triumphantly. "And the tax revenues from this complex are going to make an appreciable contribution to the city's finances and that goes to the benefit of every citizen. Don't forget to point *that* out to your readers."

"You don't think the average New Yorker might think your new apartment building is . . . well, rather ostentatious?"

"In what way?" asked Storm, frowning.

"There was an item somewhere about gold bathroom fittings, for instance."

"Only at the request of the client," Storm said evenly. "And at their own expense. People can do whatever they want with their homes, after all. This *is* America. But we're not just selling luxury. We're selling safety.

Safety in the Decade of Terror." He stood up to indicate that the interview was over. "Wouldn't you pay well for that, if you had the money?"

He waited until the writer reluctantly agreed. "Could be," he said, his liberal antipathy for Storm overcome for the moment by memories of the last time he had been mugged while living in trendy Brooklyn Heights, before he moved his family to a peaceful Connecticut suburb.

"Sure you would. And it would be worth every penny you spent," Storm said. "Maybe it's not the way things should be but it's the way they are now, and the way they will stay until this city gets back on track and can provide safety for everyone, rich and poor alike." He came around the desk to bid the journalist good-bye. His jacket was off and he was wearing a vertical-striped, highly starched shirt that was tailored tight to his obviously muscular torso. His sleeves were rolled up and his hands and forearms looked powerful.

The reporter stood up and took Storm's handshake, then asked almost as an afterthought, "Are you thinking of running for mayor?"

"You know I've thought about it," Storm said, with what he hoped was disarming candor. "That's not news. In truth, I'd rather support someone else and spend my time rebuilding this city with bricks and mortar. But if no one comes along who can do the job and that means I should run for mayor . . . well, I'll cross that bridge when I come to it."

He had his left hand on the young man's shoulder and was already steering him toward the office door and into the hands of a waiting assistant.

When the door closed, he walked back to his desk, rolling down his sleeves and refastening his cufflinks and then putting his pin-striped suit jacket back on.

He smiled at his lawyer and public relations consultant who had been sitting quietly in a corner of the office during the entire interview. "What do you think? I thought it went pretty well."

The lawyer pursed his lips judiciously and rubbed his chin, but Dave Thornton, a former presidential speech-writer now comfortably running his own public relations firm, smiled enthusiastically. "You hit every one of the right buttons, Oliver. Hell, I can see all those straphangers dreaming about hitting the lottery and first thing, buying an apartment in Storm Mountain. Pour it on. You can't go wrong with safety on the streets."

"I suppose so . . . but what if the writer had asked for hard figures on what security is costing?" the lawyer fretted.

"He should have," Storm said. "I was going to hit him over the head with TV surveillance cameras and private police and everything else we've built into the complex. I couldn't ask for better advertising than the *Times* running off at the mouth about our 'obscenely expensive' security."

"He's right," Thornton assured the lawyer with practiced conviction. "Personal security will sell Storm Mountain and it'll sell Oliver Storm, too. If the governor wasn't so good at peddling the same line, I'd recommend taking a shot at him, instead of going for City Hall. But the timing's right for the run for mayor." He paused and smiled at Storm. "Anyway, it's can't lose. Even if some freak should happen and you lost, you'd win because no one would have expected you to win in the first place. And the next run, for the U.S. Senate, would be a lock. And then, who knows what's next?"

"One campaign at a time, Dave," Storm said, but the pink flush and repressed smile on his face told his true feelings.

The lawyer rose and left the meeting. When he was gone, Storm said, "He's got no feel for politics."

"No," the public relations man agreed. "The mayor's going to have a shit fit when he reads the story."

"Good. Keep him worried," Storm said. "Now, any problems with the opening of the Mountain?"

"No, everything's right on schedule. Just three more

weeks and we're going to get enormous coverage.
Maybe even in Europe and Japan. Hell of an idea, if I
do say so myself, combining the first look at the world's
ritziest condominium complex with a glitzy charity ball
to help the homeless."

"That's what I pay you for. Bad ideas I can get for
free."

"There's still an outside chance the vice president
might come. And, of course, half the Senate *and* Wall
Street *and* Broadway *and* Hollywood and all the jet-set
twits, of course."

"Shame on you, Dave," Storm chided him, with a
smile. "Those *twits* are our future tenants. They'll want
to live there just to convince people that they *are* important enough to worry about terrorists. They'll wet
their pants when they see all those Saudi sheiks and our
guards carrying Uzis. I don't know why I didn't think of
this years ago."

"Because years ago, it wasn't the Decade of Terror,"
the public relations man said with a smile and Storm
nodded.

"Oh, one more thing you might want to peddle to the
decorating magazines," Storm said. "Patrice came up
with some gold lamé curtains three stories high for the
atrium. Hell of an effect."

"Jesus, talk about conspicuous consumption," Thornton responded cautiously. "You're sure that's not just a
little too grand? I don't want a story with some bastard
reporter figuring out how many turkey dinners those
curtains would pay for."

"Not to worry, my friend. We're renting them from
the Met. They're from some opera they did a few years
ago, so we save money and we help the Met make a few
bucks. It was Patrice's idea. Or that fag partner of hers,
probably. But I like it."

"Good. The *Times* won't dump on you for helping the
Met. They don't care how much the Met spends on curtains. They may even give you a medal."

"I'll take it," Storm grinned, raising an imaginary glass. "Here's to civic responsibility."

Dave Thornton raised his own imaginary glass. "Here's to the next mayor."

5

If the New York City police arrested as many career criminals as it issued departmental directives, the city would be as safe as a convent, Regal reflected as he sat at his desk, burrowing through a pile of paperwork.

After a hesitant knock, Detective Jane Cole peeked in the door.

"Am I interrupting you?" she asked with a cautious smile.

"Yes, thank God. Come on in."

She walked inside, then said, "Would you like some coffee?"

"No. Is that why you wanted to see me?"

"Not really." She sat down warily, looking concerned. "I bumped into a guy I used to know when I was on bunco and he had quite a few questions about our squad and what we do and how we do it."

"So?"

"I didn't tell him anything but I happen to know that he works in Internal Affairs now. I don't think he knows I know that. I just thought you ought to know."

Regal blinked, trying to sort out the past few sentences. "I should know what? That you know he's one of Flaherty's guys? Or that he doesn't know that you know?"

She looked at him, apparently as confused as he was, but it was evident that her confusion stemmed from the fact that Inspector Paul Regal could not understand a very simple, straightforward statement.

"I'll try again," she said. "I thought you ought to know that he was asking questions about our squad. What business is that of his? Is something going on? is what I was wondering."

"It's Flaherty's job to know what everybody's doing, Jane. You know that. But in this case, I think you ought to just forget it. I think your friend was probably just angling for a date."

She shook her head. "No, that wasn't it. He was after something. And I can tell you're not surprised and to me that means that there *is* something going on. And since I asked you about it, Inspector, I think you ought to tell me. I'm on the squad too, you know. And I hate it when the shooflies start buzzing around. They give me the creeps."

Regal laughed. "Relax, Jane. IAD can look until doomsday and we've got nothing to hide. Hell, you know we always take some of the regular Narcotics guys with us when we make a raid. And if we come up with some junk we turn it over to them on the spot, just so nobody gets any ideas that we're holding back. We're clean as a whistle and everybody knows it. If Flaherty's snooping around, it's probably something routine. He's as devious as the commissioner. I wouldn't put it past him to have sent that friend of yours knowing that you'd finger him, just to keep us on our toes."

Her green eyes opened wide in astonishment and Regal thought, *Her eyes are as big as Patrice's. But hers are alive. Patrice's look like a statue's eyes.*

"You think he knew that I knew?"

Regal laughed. "You're doing it again. Talking funny.

But to answer your question, I don't know."

She thought it over, then shook her head, red curls tossing vigorously. "He didn't know I knew," she said firmly. "I'd have known."

Regal felt a headache coming on. *Maybe this woman is a ditz.*

"Don't worry about it," he said. "Just keep doing your job. That's what they pay us for."

"Not enough. I guess what I want to know is this. This guy from Flaherty's squad was pumping me. Not anybody else. Not Bolda or Pete. Me. So maybe I'm in trouble?"

"Not likely," Regal said. "But go ask Flaherty."

"That'll be the day," Cole snapped. "I'd rather talk to the devil than Inspector Flaherty. It's bad luck even to mention his name."

"Then stop mentioning his name. Go answer a phone."

"I'm on my coffee break."

"Where's your coffee?"

"I don't want any right now," she said distractedly, rubbing her chin with her fist. Her red hair surrounded her face like an aura.

Regal sighed. "Jane, what do you want from me?"

"All right," she said with resignation. "I know I'm not in any trouble. Is Pete in any trouble?"

It was his turn to look surprised. "Pete Muniz? Why should he be in trouble with Internal Affairs?"

"That's what I'm asking you, Inspector."

"Dammit, Jane, you're beating around the bush. Why don't you just get to it and say it? Why should they be sniffing around Pete?"

"Because he's bothered about something. He wouldn't tell me what it is. He just said something was wrong and he looked worried. He's as bad as you are. I can't get a straight answer out of either of you."

She scowled and crossed her arms and legs simultaneously, looking indignant. She had fine legs, Regal thought, as he leaned back in his chair and smiled despite himself. Jane Cole was thirty-two years old. He knew that from her personnel file, but at the moment she looked more like a petulant teenager, hardly old enough to be the divorced mother of a five-year-old girl.

She came from a police family and had been on the force for seven years now. Six months ago, Commissioner Gallagher asked him to take her on the squad, the only such request he had ever made. At the beginning, Regal had assumed that she was reporting back to the commissioner privately—that was how Gallagher liked to do things—but he had never seen any sign of that and had finally abandoned the idea. He had saddled her with the desk work for the squad because he did not feel comfortable about involving a woman in streetwork and shoot-outs. He knew a big portion of society regarded that as a sexist attitude; he was convinced it reflected a man's compassionate concern for a woman.

She had never complained though, at least not in his hearing. She was efficient and cheerful. He had heard that she and Pete Muniz had become an item sometime recently but it still startled him that she would interfere so boldly on his behalf.

"Jane," he said, "as a friend, don't you think maybe you're getting a little out of line?" His voice was gentle, unthreatening.

She flushed a little and seemed to have to force the words out of herself. "Pete is a good, clean cop and one of the nicest guys I've ever known. But he's no good at speaking up for himself. And I want to know why he's worried."

"It might just be his informant. The kid gave Pete a tip about new Panamanian drug runners and then they weren't there and now the informant's gone. You know all that."

"Yes, Inspector," she said patiently. "I know all that. But I'm not stupid. I know Flaherty's sniffing around for a reason. I've been around the department my whole life, you know. Even my husband was a cop. A lousy cop but a cop."

Regal had been brought up to respect loyalty and he could not help admiring her for standing up for Muniz, even if she was being foolish about it.

"Jane, has it ever occurred to you that maybe it's me and not Pete that Flaherty is checking on?"

"The dirty devil," she gasped in a broad Irish accent. "Is there no end to the man's wickedness?"

Regal burst out laughing. "You sound like Barry Fitzgerald."

"Hell. I was trying for Maureen O'Hara."

"Her too." Regal stood up behind the desk. "Look, Jane. I am telling you the absolute truth. I don't know what Flaherty or his man may be up to. Probably nothing. I have absolute faith in the integrity of every man in this squad. Especially Pete Muniz. I think you should stop worrying and go drink coffee."

She nodded and rose. "Thanks, Inspector. You've made me feel better."

"My pleasure." He held his smile until the woman left the office and closed the door behind her and then his face soured over.

So Gallagher *had* called in Inspector Flaherty's bloodhounds, just on the basis of Tony Bolda's offhand comment about a leak in the squad.

Petty bullshit, he said to himself, before realizing he had only himself to blame. He was the one who had relayed Bolda's suspicion to the commissioner. What had he expected Gallagher to do? Forget it?

To hell with it and to hell with bureaucrats. He sat back behind the desk and started rummaging through the pile of papers again, but he could not help thinking that Jane Cole had worked for him for six months and that was the first time they had ever said more than a couple of sentences to each other. And it really had been kind of pleasant.

He found himself comparing the younger woman's forthright manner and obvious sense of humor with his wife's studied coolness and rigid control. They were like fire and ice, utterly unalike, he decided. Generally, he thought, he liked fire better.

With a conscious effort, he put both women out of his mind and picked up the department directives again. *Better to read the unreadable than to think the unthinkable.*

6

Hector Guzman was dead. The news came from Pete Muniz when he caught Regal outside the squad's office door the next morning.

Muniz looked shaken. He needed a shave and his clothing, usually spit-shine neat, was wrinkled and dusty.

"I was looking for him all night but somebody found him this morning in a cellar up in the Bronx. Dead maybe twenty-four hours.

"How?" Regal asked.

"Knifed. Once in the back. Whoever did it had experience or luck. One plug was all he needed."

Regal could tell from Muniz's face that the young detective was taking the death hard, as if it had been his fault somehow. Words did not help at a time like this, Regal knew. The only thing that could lessen the hurt was doing something about it.

"Have you got any leads? Anybody see anything?"

"No. Deaf, dumb, and blind, the whole neighborhood. But I'm looking for this girl Hector was seeing. Estrellita something. The way I hear it, she's Panamanian so she might have been the real source of the tip Hector gave me. Who knows? Maybe I'll get lucky and find her and maybe real lucky and she'll know something. I may have a lead on her."

"Okay. But be careful and no risks. There's not a word out on the street about any drug dealers from Panama but that doesn't mean that they're not out there. You just make sure that Tony or I know where you are and what you're doing, understand?"

"You got it, Inspector."

"But before you do a damned thing, go home, take a shower and get some sleep. You put in too many night hours. Don't you and Jane ever go dancing or to the movies or anything?"

"Not too much," Muniz admitted. "I've got my night classes a couple of days a week and then the job. Mostly I sit around in front of the tube, trying to cool out, and drink beer."

"Careful," Regal said. "That's what drives cops to eat their gun."

"Nerves?" Muniz asked.

"No. Too much television."

Muniz laughed. "Maybe *that's* why Jane won't marry me. She hates television."

"I thought you two were an item."

Muniz shrugged and blinked and Regal could see the weariness in his dark eyes.

"Jane said she wants to keep things more . . . informal."

"What does that mean?" Regal asked, realizing it was precisely none of his business but finding himself curiously interested anyway.

"She wanted me to move in with her, but she isn't sure about getting married again. She was married before, you know, and her first husband was a bum."

"Sounds like a good offer."

"I wasn't raised that way, Inspector. My folks would have a fit if I started living with a girl and I'm not so sure it'd be good for Jane's little kid."

"Maybe Jane's had it with cops as husbands."

"Not really. She told me once she'd never marry anybody again except a cop. Civilians just don't understand what it's like being on the job."

"That's true enough," Regal said. He thought of his own wife. "Would it help if I dropped a word in Jane's ear?"

"Thanks, no," Muniz said somberly. "We'll work it out ourselves."

"Good enough. Go home and get to sleep."

Muniz sighed. "Okay. Big test tonight at school anyway. It might help if I had my brains on straight."

"It never helped me any," Regal joked, "but go ahead."

Shortly after noon, Lieutenant Tony Bolda, rumpled as usual and holding in his hand a particularly vile-looking bagel sandwich, stuck his head in Regal's door.

"Paul, I just got the precinct report on Hector Guzman. You want us to put some of our guys on it?"

"No," Regal said. "Let Joe Burton's gang handle it. Pete'll keep watching too. He's got a lead on a girlfriend of Guzman's. Somebody named Estrellita."

Bolda paused a moment, then grinned. "Estrellita, huh? Cha, cha, cha." He waved his arms through the air, simulating a woman's curvy body. Droplets of moisture sprayed from his sandwich.

"Clear out, Tony," Regal said with a chuckle. "Let us working stiffs . . ."

"Work?"

"Get stiff."

Every day, all the department's reports that dealt in any way with narcotics—whether from the citywide narcotics squad or from uniformed patrolmen in neighborhood precincts—were copied to Regal's desk. Anything that involved even so little as one marijuana cigarette he wanted to know about, so the reports came in daily by the dozens and Regal scanned each one, trying to find familiar names, looking for a pattern that might be a tip-off to what was happening out there day by day.

He read the reports with extra diligence this day, looking for any trace of the elusive Panamanians who had probably killed Hector Guzman, but when he closed up the folders at 5 P.M., there had not been a sign, not a hint, not a word, and all he had to show for his day's work was a headache and eyes that throbbed from the strain of reading so much bad typing.

Another day, another dollar, he told himself as he put on his jacket in his darkened office and then walked outside into the still-bright sunlight of the day.

As he waited for a policeman to stop the maze of traffic and let pedestrians cross, he wondered what he was going to do with himself for the next hour. Patrice had announced that she would make one of her rare evening appearances at their apartment and he planned to be home by seven and it was now only a few minutes after five. He had time to kill and nothing to kill it with.

The fact was that Regal was basically a loner. He knew that among the men who had served under him in his command years in the department were men who swore by him, might even kill for him. But it wasn't possible for a full inspector to hang out with detectives or patrolmen or even low-ranking officers. In the tight hierarchy of the New York City Police Department, it just wasn't done.

And Regal had no friends among top brass of his own rank. At forty-six, Regal was younger than most of them and represented a different generation. It explained his personal problems with his rival, Inspector Joe Burton. Burton was, despite being a blowhard, a good cop, loyal to his men, honest on the job. But he distrusted Regal for the simple reason that Regal was one of "the new college boys," and was not likely to enjoy sitting around for an evening swapping stories about suspects they had brutalized during questioning.

There had also been talk in the department that Commissioner Gallagher was soon going to appoint a new personal assistant. The post, which would probably call for inspector rank, could well be the stepping stone to the chief's job when the present chief, Aloysius Riley, retired next year. Burton had made it clear that he wanted the job and just as noisily clear that he thought Regal was his chief competition. That kind of rivalry was never going to build friendships.

Shut out from department camaraderie, but forced by the job to work long hours, often seven days a week, Regal had little chance to meet people who were not policemen too. The only social circle he was vaguely familiar with was Patrice's, and with the exception of her wildly queenish partner in the interior design business, whose company Regal always found curiously pleasant, her friends weren't worth a pail of spit.

And he had no family. It always came back to that. His parents were dead and he had no children.

It always comes back to that, he thought, and decided idly he would be glad to trade his personal problems for Pete Muniz's. He had been Pete's first precinct commander and had liked the young man from the start. A native New Yorker, street-smart, Pete nevertheless had a fresh-scrubbed innocence about him and Regal knew he came from a close-knit, highly religious Puerto Rican family. They were proud that he was a policeman. Like Pete, they believed it to be a worthy career for a young man—and so did Regal.

He had always been proud to be a cop, and when he was courting Patrice he thought she felt the same way. It was only after they were married that he realized she had always expected him to use his hard-earned law degree as a stepping stone to political appointment or corporate affluence. Now she seemed slightly contemptuous of him for remaining on the force when he could be doing something "worthwhile" with his life. At least Pete didn't have that problem with Jane Cole, who restricted her social relationships to fellow police officers.

Maybe that's what they mean by "Misery loves company."

The traffic patrolman finally blew his whistle and then

waved the waiting pedestrians across the street. Before Regal could move, he was elbowed politely but firmly out of the way by a woman in a hurry. Amused, he followed docilely behind her across the intersection, noticing the firm strong stride that was so different from Patrice's languid glide. Then, with a start of surprise, he realized it was Jane Cole herself.

He reached forward to tap her on the shoulder. "Watch it, lady, or I'll bust you for shouldering with intent to pass," he growled.

She looked around, wary as policemen always were at touches and surprises, then smiled as she recognized him. "Hi, Inspector. Sorry, didn't realize that was you dawdling back there."

"Some of my happiest hours are spent dawdling," Regal said. "I can tell that's not one of your problems."

"Can't help it. Just a fast walker," she admitted.

"Care to gallop over to the Galway and have a drink?"

Her eyebrows shot up. "Inspector Regal. And you a married man." She grinned. "Well, maybe one quickie. I have to get home to Sarah."

"Lucky you," he said, meaning it, but before she could ask him why, he took her arm and led her down the street toward the tavern.

They found a corner table and both ordered draft beer but Jane also asked for a nip of Guinness and poured some into her glass.

"Gives it more body," she said. "Try it?"

He shrugged and she poured some into his drink. The small amount of stout darkened the beer markedly and changed the flavor. "Not bad," he admitted. "Where'd you pick that up?"

"One of the few things my husband gave me—except for the occasional black eye. He couldn't deal with the booze, the poor son of a bitch. That's what eventually got him thrown off the force."

"Thank God that's one problem I don't have yet,"

Regal said, knocking three times on the polyurethaned wooden tabletop.

"No, you don't have the reputation. I don't know anyone who's ever seen you drunk."

"Not my speed," he admitted. "I don't even like hanging around drunks. If I wanted to slobber and babble, I would have become a professional wrestler."

Jane giggled. "You're like my family. We've got a couple who can't handle it but they know it, so they lay off. Not a woman-beater among them," she added with enduring bitterness.

"You don't have that problem with Pete, either," he said.

"No. He's a lamb. I was just thinking of my first husband, the bum. Pete is too nice. Sometimes I think he should have been a priest."

Regal cocked an eyebrow at her and she reddened. "You can put that thought right out of your mind," she said. "Pete's all man when it's time to be all man."

"I never doubted it," he said.

"You know, he thinks the sun rises and sets on you," she said. "He wants to finish college and go to law school, just like you did."

"Maybe you can talk him out of it. I don't know if it's worth the time and effort, especially with a wife and kids."

"Pete's not married. You know that."

"But he wants to get married," Regal said quietly.

Jane pursed her lips. "You two have been talking."

There was a moment of strained silence and he regretted having raised the subject.

"My apologies," he finally said. "What do you think about the Mets this year?"

"Screw the Mets. And the Rangers and the Yankees and the Knicks too."

"All right. I can live with that. Seen any good operas lately?"

"I hate the opera. Fat people yelling at each other. Are you an opera fan?"

"No," he lied. "I like rap music. Hip-hop is my life."

She laughed. "Pete is too damned nice, that's the trouble."

"I don't want to hear this."

"You brought it up."

"I do a lot of dumb things. I'm supposed to. I'm an inspector."

She took a huge gulp from her glass, emptying it, and handed it to him. "One more and I'm out of here."

He finished his drink and went for refills. Waiting for them at the bar, he watched her sitting at the table, her chin propped on one fist, her eyes fixed on the opposite wall.

She was a very attractive woman, Regal decided. Pete was right. This was a woman to marry and to laugh with and to fight with and cherish and enjoy all the days of your life. He would be happy to dance at their wedding. *If I can find a date for the night*, he thought sourly, *since Patrice likes being with policemen so very much.*

When he returned, she silently sipped some of her beer, added more stout and poured the rest into his glass. Then she fixed her eyes on his, her chin lifted defiantly.

"Because you're Pete's friend and because you're my boss and we both trust you and like to work with you, even if you haven't given me real police work to do and that pisses me off, and even though you're right, it's none of your business, I'm going to tell you anyway about Pete and me." He started to protest and she put a finger across his lips to silence him. "I like Pete. I like him fine. I like the way he treats me. But I don't know if I love him and want to live with him for the rest of my life. And I'm never going to get married again unless I know it's for good and forever."

She shrugged expansively. "Pete's the best man I know—kind, tolerant, caring. Sometimes, I feel like a bitch alongside him."

Regal put on a studiously blank expression and she glowered at him. "Real clever, Inspector. It's easy for you with the good job and the beautiful wife with her picture in the paper all the time, but a lot of us don't have it like that."

He choked on his drink and wiped his mouth with a napkin.

"Down the wrong pipe?" she asked.

He nodded.

"What I'm saying is I've had a bad marriage and I don't want another one and I don't think Pete and I are right for each other. There's just a little softness in him and I'm afraid I'd cut him up if we were in close quarters all the time. Cut him up and make something sour out of him. I won't have that." She sighed. "All marriages aren't made in heaven. But you wouldn't know that."

"I'm learning."

Jane finished her drink in one long swallow. "Done. Got to get home to Sarah. Sorry if I bent your ear out of shape."

"Thanks for the company. You cheered me up. When do you bring your little girl around for a tour of where Mommy works?"

"One of these days. See you tomorrow," she said.

"I'll walk you to the subway. There are crazies out there. Remember *P*-is-for-prawn?"

"Hell with crazies. I'll just blow them away."

"You *would* too, wouldn't you?"

"Believe it, Inspector. Believe it."

She turned and sauntered out of the tavern, leaving Regal to watch her. He found himself wondering if her hips were moving with somewhat more insolence than he had noticed before—or if it was simply that he was noticing Jane more closely than he had before.

Maybe it's a little of both, he decided and went to the bar for another beer.

Late that night, Pete Muniz stood at a street corner in Spanish Harlem, glancing occasionally at his wristwatch and wondering when Inspector Regal would show up.

A car pulled up with its windows down. Muniz peered inside and said, "Hey, how you doing?"

"Anybody here yet?" the other man replied as he got out of the car.

"No, I'm just waiting. Now it's you and me and the rats. This is one lousy neighborhood, you know. Say, I wanted to talk to you. You know a little chickie named Estrellita? She says she knows you."

"I was afraid she might," the other man said somberly. He looked across the street. "Shit, look at that." As Muniz turned, his companion pulled a blackjack from his pocket and tapped the detective expertly at the base of the skull. The young man slumped to the ground without a word.

After a glance around, the other man knelt, pulled a small plastic envelope from his pocket, extracted a soft piece of paper and carefully pressed the first two fingers of Muniz's right hand against it. He lifted Muniz's head, pulled his mouth open and touched the paper against the unconscious man's tongue.

Finally, he replaced the paper into the envelope, put it in his pocket and produced a snub-nosed .22-caliber revolver—a gun so small it was almost hidden in his hand.

A single shot to the back of the head completed the job, but he pulled the trigger twice to make sure. The noise was hardly louder than a balloon popping.

The man bent over Muniz's body to search his pockets, but then he heard a sound and he bolted back to his car. He drove away quickly, keeping his lights off for the first half block.

By the time the body was discovered twenty minutes later, the rats had already begun to nibble on it.

7

When Paul Regal arrived at the scene, three patrol cars, lights flashing, were blockading the street in both directions. An unnecessary ambulance was parked by the curb, with the driver and the attendant leaning against the front fender watching the policemen work. A crime lab van had pulled partially onto the sidewalk. Two private autos with portable blinkers on their roofs were nearby.

And on the sidewalk, covered by an olive drab woolen blanket, was a body.

Inspector Joe Burton was in the middle of the activity, a scowl on his beefy face and a thick cigar clenched between his teeth. When Regal strode up, he rumbled, "Hope we didn't drag you away from anything important."

Regal's lips tightened but he did not reply. He walked over to the blanketed figure on the sidewalk, raised the corner of the blanket and looked silently at the blown-apart face of the murdered man. He winced.

"It is Muniz, right?" asked Burton.

Regal covered up the young man's face again, stood and nodded silently.

"Any idea what he was doing here?"

"This is an area he's been working a lot, but he wasn't on assignment," Regal said.

"On duty?"

"Shouldn't have been. He had class tonight. Night school."

"So why was he here?" Burton demanded.

"I don't know."

"When'd you see him last?"

"This morning in my office. We talked about work and . . . other things."

"What other things?"

"His love life."

"What's his love life's name?" Burton said, taking a notebook from his right jacket pocket. "Maybe she's involved."

"I doubt that," Regal said. "It was Jane Cole."

"Jane?" Burton was startled. "She was going out with Muniz?"

"Yeah."

"Well, she wouldn't be involved. Any chance Muniz was up here to pick up some floozy señorita?"

"No. Not a chance. Not Pete," Regal said. "Was he robbed?"

"No. Still had his gun and his tin. His wallet too. That's how we identified him."

"Then this was no street killing," Regal said.

"I already figured that out," Burton said.

A small group of detectives around them listened silently, their faces hard. None of them had ever met Pete Muniz but each understood it could just as easily have been one of them under the scratchy wool blanket.

"I want to know what Muniz was working on," Burton said crisply. "I want to know everything he's been doing that could have put him here tonight. I want to know who he's been seeing, who he's had any contacts with. I need that information from you and your squad right away tonight. And then I want you to stay out of this case. It's homicide and Homicide North'll take care of it."

Pete's not even cold yet and this son of a bitch is using him to empire-build, Regal thought. *Him and his goddam Homicide North.*

He glared at Burton but was saved from making an answer by Tony Bolda, who came out of a nearby building and moved up to stand beside his commander. "It's our case too, Inspector," he said, his voice quiet but firm. "Pete was one of us. We can't walk away from this. You know that."

Burton stared hard at him. "It's homicide," he repeated. "It's ours. You're out of it."

Bolda shook his head. "You're in charge but we'll be on it too. Even if it's off-duty time. You don't expect us to turn our backs, do you?"

There was a murmur of agreement from several of the men clustered about them. Burton glowered at Bolda, then visibly relaxed. "Okay. But you know the rules. Any help you can give us, we'll be glad to have it. But no going around behind our backs or holding anything back. You understand that."

Bolda nodded and Burton said, "Lieutenant Davis will run the investigation—under me." He nodded toward a stocky black officer in crisp police uniform. "You give him everything you come up with and you give it to him right away. No cowboy tricks. And if you come up with anything that indicates Muniz might have been dirty, you pass that along too. Understand?"

Bolda bristled. "Pete wasn't dirty," he snapped. "He was the cleanest kid in the department. This has got to be a drug killing from somebody he was getting close to."

Burton nodded curtly, but there was understanding and sympathy in the look he gave Bolda. A cop all his adult life, Burton knew that a slain officer's partners could not be kept out of the hunt for his killer. He would have felt contempt for Regal and his squad if they had not insisted on being in on the investigation.

"Give everything you have to Davis," he said again. "We're going to jump all over this."

"Was he shot here?" Regal asked.

Burton nodded. "Blood on the sidewalk says so. Someone down the block said she might have heard a shot about an hour ago but she didn't even look out the window to see. Said it might have just been a car backfiring. And anyway, she was afraid that if it was a shooting and somebody saw her, they'd shoot her too. Some neighborhood."

He paused a moment, then asked, almost reluctantly, "Jane Cole doesn't live around this way, does she?"

"No," Regal said. "She's out in Queens."

"Don't give me that fish stare. I've got my job to do and you know it. You just make sure you give Davis everything you know about Muniz and why he might have been here tonight."

"Who's going to tell his parents?"

"I've got men on the way there now. We have to question them anyway, see if they have any leads." The burly homicide officer turned on his heel and stomped over to his sedan, waving at one of his men to follow him.

Regal turned back to Bolda, who had now put a toothpick in his mouth and was chewing it furiously. "When'd you hear about it, Tony?"

"I was hanging around one of the precincts where I used to work, the Eight-Seven, and I heard it come over the radio. When they said Muniz, I borrowed a squad car and zipped up here. I got here the same time Burton did. He must have been working late."

"Quick response," Regal said, just making conversation.

Bolda shrugged. "A cop down."

"But what was Pete doing here anyway?"

"Don't know. I saw him in the office around six tonight. I guess after you left. He stopped in on his way to school. Then he made a couple of phone calls and then he left. I don't know."

"Find out if he showed up at school," Regal said automatically, but his mind was far away. He was thinking that if he had not tried to help Muniz's career by selecting him for the special drug task force, the young man might well be alive right now. He put the thought out of his head. That kind of thinking would not help anything.

Another vehicle arrived, dark blue, with just the medical examiner's identification on its front doors. The morgue wagon. Regal looked away as two attendants expertly put Pete Muniz's corpse into a body bag, unfolded a metal stretcher and gently lifted the bag onto it. When he turned back, they were sliding the gurney into the back of their van. As they drove away, a detective instantly began gathering up samples of blood and brain matter that lay pooled together on the sidewalk.

"I'm going to go back to the office, Tony," Regal said. "I want to look through Pete's files."

"I'll meet you there," Bolda said, nodding.

"I'll be a little late. I have to talk to Jane first."

"I'll do it if you want, Paul."

"No." Regal sighed. "Burton's right about one thing. He has his job to do and I have mine and this is part of it. I have to talk with Pete's folks too, but that'll wait until tomorrow."

Bolda touched Regal compassionately on the shoulder. "If you need any help, just let me know."

Regal walked off without responding, stopping to look down at the chalk-marked outline of a body on the sidewalk. He said a few words to Lieutenant Davis, who nodded back sympathetically, then walked across the street to his own car.

From down the block, Regal saw a long black limousine approaching. That would be either the mayor or Commissioner Gallagher. He did not want to see either of them now, so he started his engine and drove quickly away.

*   *   *

Jane Cole was deeply asleep when she heard the door-bell buzzer ringing from downstairs.

She scurried out of bed, wearing only men's-style pajamas, ran into the living room and spoke into the intercom.

"Who is it?"

"Jane, it's Inspector Regal. Can I come up?"

She sucked in cold breath over suddenly clenched teeth. Whatever it was was bad because Regal had automatically identified himself by his rank. Without speaking, she pressed the buzzer to unlock the front door.

When Regal reached her apartment door, she was standing inside, a heavy woolen robe over her pajamas, her face anxious and worried.

"Pete?" she said simply.

Regal nodded. "He was shot tonight."

"And he's dead." It was a flat declarative statement.

"I'm sorry, Jane."

The woman took several deep breaths and Regal stepped inside the apartment, swinging the door shut behind him, and put his arms around the red-haired cop.

"It's okay, Inspector. I'm not going to cry."

"I wish I could," he said.

"How did it happen?"

"Spanish Harlem. He was shot at close range in the head. They left his badge and his gun. Cabbie saw the body and called his dispatcher, who sent it in. We guess it happened right after midnight, but nobody knows yet what he was doing there."

Jane took another deep breath and stepped back one pace from Regal to search his face with her eyes.

"What do you mean, you don't know? Weren't you with him?"

"No," Regal said.

"But he was on assignment with you tonight," Jane said.

"What are you talking about? Pete didn't have any assignments tonight. He had night class."

Jane Cole shook her head. "He called me about ten, when class was usually over, and told me he wouldn't be coming over tonight because you had called him and asked him to meet you uptown on a job."

There was a moment of silence before Regal asked, "Did he say when I called him? Or anything about the assignment?"

"No. He was in a hurry. He just wanted to apologize and tell me not to wait up for him. He said he'd try to give me a call if it didn't get too late. I told him not to bother, we could talk about it tomorrow." She suppressed a sudden sob and fought to regain control of her emotions.

"Jane. There's something very wrong here," Regal said in a leaden voice. "The last time I talked with Pete was this morning. I told you about that at the Galway after work. But I didn't call him about any assignment. There wasn't any assignment."

"But . . ."

"I want you to call Joe Burton at Homicide North right away and tell him everything you've told me. If you can't get him, talk to Lieutenant Davis. He's in charge of the case. This is important, Jane. Somebody set Pete up. This wasn't any street killing. It was a deliberate assassination."

"But why, Inspector? Why?"

"I don't know. It may have been those Panamanians we've been chasing. It looks like they took care of the kid who gave Pete the tip. Maybe they got Pete too. I don't know. You call Burton now. If he wants me, I'll be back in my office."

"All right," she agreed, her eyes beginning to tear.

"And then maybe you should try to get back to sleep."

"Fat chance," she said bitterly.

"Jane . . . what can I say? I'm really sorry for you . . . for Pete."

They looked at each other for a moment and then Jane emitted a choking sob and the tears she had been holding back flooded down her face.

As Regal stepped forward to comfort her, he saw a motion in the corner of the room and looked past Jane to see a little girl standing in front of the open door of one of the bedrooms. She had wildly curly red hair and a band of freckles across her face and nose. She looked like Jane Cole, reduced in size and then her features exaggerated to an almost unbearable cuteness that would be appropriate on the face of a child's doll.

To Regal's quizzical look, the girl stared back dispassionately and asked, "Why are you making my mommy cry?"

Jane turned at the voice but Regal had already walked past her toward the girl. He squatted low on the floor in front of her and touched her hands.

Shaking his head, he said, "I didn't make her cry, Sarah. She just got some bad news and I was trying to make her feel better."

Jane, wiping her eyes on her sleeve, stood alongside him. "I'm all right, honey. This is Inspector Regal. He's a policeman too."

"Oh," Sarah said. "All right." Regal was still holding her hands and now she squeezed his.

"Come on, honey," Jane said. "I'll put you back in bed." She turned back to Regal. "Go to work," she said. "I'll call Burton."

Regal hesitated, then nodded and stood up. "Bye, Sarah," he said, before turning and striding swiftly from the apartment. He made sure the door locked solidly behind him.

Inside the apartment, Jane put Sarah back into bed and stroked the girl's temples for a few moments until she was back asleep. For a moment, she remembered the happy times Sarah had often enjoyed with Pete and she wondered if, in later years, the girl would remember the kindly man who had wanted to become her daddy.

Then she sighed deeply, stood up and marched determinedly to the kitchen telephone even as tears continued to stream down her cheeks.

When he got back to his office, the door was open and the lights on and Bolda was inside, just hanging up a telephone. Butts overflowed his ashtray onto his grimy desk.

"Pete didn't make it to his class tonight," he told Regal.

"Then where the hell was he from the time you saw him last?"

Bolda shrugged. He shoved aside the sports section of the *New York Post* that was open on his desk and began looking through his Rolodex.

Regal nodded. "Call Fred and Joe and let them know what happened to Pete. I want to know where he was tonight. I'm going to start looking through his report folders."

"Did you talk to Jane?" Bolda asked as he jotted two phone numbers on a small yellow pad.

"Yeah."

"How'd she take it?"

"She's tough. She's holding up. But she said that Pete told her on the phone that he was supposed to meet me up there on a job tonight."

The lieutenant's eyes narrowed. "What the hell is that all about?"

"I don't know," Regal said. "But I'm damned sure going to find out."

He . . .

. . . . stopped and wiped the sweat off his forehead.

It was swelteringly hot that night, the kind of blistering heat that spurs parents in poor neighborhoods to turn on fire hydrants for their children and to hell with the fire department and its problems and then, at night, to sit on the front stoops of their sweaty tenements and let cold beer start heated arguments.

The Pits, a dimly lit bar on the fringe of the West

Village, was like a sauna. It had no air-conditioning and all the doors and windows were kept closed. Despite the temperature inside, most of its customers wore heavy black leather jackets over sweaty tee shirts. Most also wore heavy boots and some had chains wrapped around their waists. At a glance, they looked like bikers, and in fact, there were a number of motorcycles parked in the street outside, chained to meters.

But the resemblance to bikers was only superficial. The Pits was one of the city's best-known leather bars— a saloon for homosexual rough trade who enjoyed violence and esoteric forms of sex that would make the average Hell's Angel vomit. But the Marquis de Sade would have loved it.

Wearing a mustache and dark aviator glasses, he entered shortly before midnight, looking out-of-place with his prewashed denim jeans and jacket. He seemed aware of it, approaching the bar hesitantly and being careful not to stare directly at any of the other patrons.

He asked for a bottle of beer and paid for it with a fifty dollar bill, leaving the change on the bar for everyone to see.

After only two minutes, a tall thin man with a drooping Fu Manchu mustache stalked over to stand beside the newcomer.

"You looking for someone?" he asked in a menacing tone of voice.

"I wouldn't mind finding someone," he answered in a whisper.

The biker smiled grimly. "You better watch your step or someone is liable to pull down your pants and ram a fist up your ass."

He smiled. "I've heard it can be wonderful."

"What's your name, asshole?"

"John. John Begg. What's yours?"

"None of your fuckin' business. Come into the back room with me."

He shook his head. "I'd rather go to my place. I've got lots of very good stuff there."

The biker hesitated, then reached over and picked up the other's change and stuffed the money into the pocket of his studded black vest. Then he strode to the door without looking back. The man who called himself John Begg followed meekly.

Outside, the biker glared at him. "Where do you live, pissface?"

"Uptown. My car is around the corner."

"Move your ass," the biker snarled.

He led the way to a dark blue sedan, unlocked the passenger door and politely waited for the biker to be seated before closing the door gently and going around to get behind the wheel. He started the engine but did not pull away immediately. "Do you do this kind of thing often?" he asked softly.

"What's it to you?"

John Begg smiled. "I just thought you might enjoy knowing that I don't like fags. Like that one walking over there. Look at him."

The biker turned his head to look out the window, and as he did, John Begg slapped the lead-packed sap against the side of his head and the biker slumped forward against the dashboard.

"You were easy," he said. "You're all easy."

He went back to the same parking lot off the Henry Hudson Parkway and waited. When the biker awoke, he found himself in the backseat. His hands were tied behind him. Another rope bound his boots together at the ankles.

He saw the man with the aviator glasses leaning over him into the car. He had a knife in one hand, a small tape recorder in the other.

"What do you want?" the biker said, squirming frantically.

"I want to hear you scream," he said.

8

Regal had not gone home, so when the summons to Commissioner Gallagher's office came shortly after 10 A.M., he splashed water on his face in the basement men's room and then walked swiftly up the three flights of steps, rather than wait for the elevator. New building or not, elevators were always sluggish when you were in a hurry.

He could tell immediately that Gallagher was upset. Instead of crouching behind his desk, the commissioner was sitting back, slumped in his huge black leather swivel chair, and in place of his normal expression of outraged irascibility, he wore a puzzled and almost sad expression. Usually he barked at Regal when the policeman entered; today, Gallagher simply looked at him and dolefully shook his head.

"Bad business, all this," the commissioner said.

"I know."

"Have you seen the lab report on Muniz?"

"No. They said they wouldn't have it until this afternoon."

"They rushed it. The fuckers always rush bad news. They found traces of drugs in his body."

Regal was stunned. Without being invited, he sat down heavily in the chair across from the commissioner's desk.

Gallagher waited silently. The sad expression was still on his face but his eyes were sharp and steady.

"Are they sure?" Regal finally stammered.

"They didn't say 'maybe' or 'perhaps.' " He looked at a green sheet of paper on his desk. "You know how usually the first thing the M.E. does is wash a corpse. Well, one of the attendants saw some powder on Muniz's face as he was getting ready to scrub it down. They tested it right away. Cocaine on two fingers and tongue, flat and final."

"They're wrong," Regal said flatly.

"Why?" Gallagher asked, his eyes suddenly narrowing.

"Because Pete Muniz was an altar boy. He was as clean a cop as any on my squad."

"Then I'd say your squad is in a lot of trouble. The autopsy found traces of some drug in Muniz's urine too."

"More cocaine?"

Gallagher shrugged. "Maybe. Just a trace."

Regal dropped his head and stared at his chest for a moment.

"It's wrong, Commissioner. It's wrong. I'd stake my life on it."

"I appreciate your loyalty to your men, but—"

"This doesn't have anything to do with loyalty to my men," Regal interrupted. "This has to do with facts."

The commissioner's face reddened slightly and he picked up the green autopsy report and shook it at Regal.

"Dammit, these are facts, too. Not hearsay, not good thoughts. Facts. And they say Muniz was a user."

"I will never believe that," Regal said flatly.

"Right now, it's not your beliefs that I have to worry about."

Regal waited, suddenly knowing what was coming.

"I've got to worry about what the public thinks. Do you know we had another one of those knifings last night?" He did not wait for an answer. "Some motorcycle nut got himself all carved up and tossed into a doorway on the Upper East Side with a pretty little *K* carved in his head." ·

"I didn't see the paper."

"It was a little late for the morning papers but you'll see plenty of it later. And now we've got a dead cop with a cloud over his head and people already talking about a goddam 'Decade of Terror' on our streets. Real life is real life, Paul. There's an election less than a year away and the mayor's not going to beat anybody if the people buy into this terror crap."

He's after something, Regal thought. *And I think I know what it is. He wants a scapegoat.*

"Are you going to suspend me?" Regal asked in a flat voice.

"For Christ's sakes, Paul. Of course not." The commissioner shook his head vigorously, the loose flesh under his throat jellying back and forth. "Why the hell would you think of that?"

Because it'd be convenient for you, Regal thought, but he said, "You ought to think about it, Commissioner. You know, there's a hell of a mystery about why Pete was out there last night anyway. He told Jane Cole that I had asked him to meet me on an assignment, but I didn't do any such thing."

"I know. I talked to Burton just before you came in. He had Cole in his office. She can't remember if Muniz said he actually talked to you or it was just a message."

"Of course it was just a message. I never talked to him last night."

Now there was the expectant look from Gallagher and Regal began to feel that he was being coached through some sort of test.

"You see, that causes us another problem. If it wasn't you . . ."

"It wasn't me," Regal snapped.

"Then somebody just got hold of one of your cops and imitated you and the cop got killed. It doesn't sound like we're running a very tight ship and if the papers get hold of it, well, you can guess the consequences."

Suddenly, Regal was weary of the whole cat and mouse game. "Just tell me what you want me to do, Commissioner."

"I want you to lay low for a while. Stay out of the press. Keep a low profile around this building. I see that two of your men—what're their names . . . ?" He looked down at a sheet of paper on his desk while Regal sat, stubbornly silent.

I'll be damned if I make it easy for this son of a bitch, he thought.

The commissioner looked up. "Kane and Kaler. They're due to go on vacation."

"They came in last night," Regal said. "They're planning to postpone their leave."

"No," Gallagher answered quickly. "No need for that. Let them go. As I said, we'll want to keep a low profile."

"So naturally, there'll be no replacement for Pete Muniz either."

The commissioner shrugged. "Certainly not now. Maybe later on."

"So it's down to me and Tony Bolda and Jane Cole."

"Right," Gallagher said, his face brightening like a teacher whose most stupid student had just figured something out on his own. "And if you want to move all three of you out of the building into a precinct somewhere, okay by me. The three of you can keep working on those Panamanians. If they killed Muniz, the sooner we get them, the better. I'm talking to the press today and I'm going to tell them that it's our belief that a drug ring killed him. And I want you to tell anybody who asks that we think Muniz was lured to that spot in the performance of his duty. No details though. And as far as the public's concerned, he died a hero's death."

Regal nodded but the bile was rising in his throat.

"Meanwhile, I want you to cooperate with Joe Burton."

"You know there's no love lost between us."

"Keep it to your personal lives. Don't let it affect the job. I've already told Burton the same thing."

"Joe is good at his job," Regal said with reluctant honesty. "He'll play it straight."

"He doesn't speak quite that highly of you, but I think you're right. So it's clear. You lay low. Work on the Panamanians. Burton handles the Muniz murder. You help any way you can."

"With just the three of us, there's not much help we can be," Regal said.

"Naturally, Paul, but I know you'll do your best." Gallagher was silent for a moment and Regal stood. The commissioner added, "By the way, Inspector Flaherty will be continuing his investigation, of course. Please give him your full cooperation too."

"Oh? Was Internal Affairs investigating us?" Regal asked with studied innocence.

"As you well know, I'm sure, so don't get pissy. You're the one who brought up the possibility of there being a leak on your squad. I hate to say it but maybe last night the leak got plugged."

"Pete Muniz was clean," Regal said again.

"Fine. You work on proving that. It's important that we get this situation explained and cleared up. But, quietly, for everyone's sake."

For the sake of the mayor's reelection campaign, you mean, Regal thought bitterly, wondering if the mayor knew how hard his police commissioner was working to keep his reputation untarnished, even at the expense of people who used to count him among their friends.

"Anything else, sir?"

"No. There will be a full departmental funeral for young Muniz," the commissioner continued. "I'm sure the mayor will attend if his schedule permits."

It will permit, Regal thought. *You're getting ready to give a hero's funeral to somebody you thought was a dirty cop, just to get the mayor reelected. You bet he'll be there.*

Wordlessly, Regal turned and left the commissioner's office.

Back in his office, Regal fumbled his way through the agony of speaking with Muniz's bereaved parents, both of whom had marked Hispanic accents.

"You fin' the man that keel our son?" the mother asked him urgently.

"The entire department is working on it," Regal assured her. "The commissioner asked me to give you his personal condolences. He knew Pedro and thought highly of him. He called him a fallen warrior," he said, annoyed at finding himself protecting the commissioner just as Gallagher had been working to protect the mayor.

"Fallen warrior?" the woman repeated slowly, obviously confused by the phrase.

"He was a hero, Mrs. Muniz," Regal explained patiently. "Like a soldier in wartime."

The woman began to cry again and her husband took the phone from her. After a few more minutes of confused questions and face-saving answers, Regal managed to end the conversation and hung up, feeling emotionally exhausted.

There was a tap on his door and Tony Bolda entered, looking even more rumpled than usual.

"Anything going on, Paul, that I should know about?"

"Close the door, Tony," Regal said. When his assistant did, he continued, "They found traces of narcotics on Pete's hands and mouth and in his urine."

"Horseshit," Bolda snapped.

"That's what I said but it looks firm."

"Somebody planted it on him some way."

"Yeah. Any ideas?"

Bolda shook his head. "He never made it to his law class but I don't have any idea where he went. We checked all his stoolies, everybody he talked to, and nobody saw him. All we can do is keep trying."

"You might want to rethink that," Regal said.

"What do you mean?" Bolda asked.

From the moment Bolda had walked in, Regal had wrestled with telling him about his meeting with the commissioner and what it meant—that Regal had already been cut loose by the commissioner, stamped permanently as a bad manager at best, a corrupt cop at worst. In the end, he realized that if he didn't tell him, Bolda would still find out before he left the building; the police grapevine was remorseless and heard everything.

Quickly he recounted what had just happened in Commissioner Gallagher's office.

"Those cheapshot bastards," Bolda said angrily. "So what's next?"

"Kane and Kaler are going on their furlough. Pete won't be replaced. It's just you, me, and Jane. And the commissioner made it clear he wouldn't care if the three of us vanished off the face of the earth."

Bolda's face paled as he immediately understood the significance of Regal's words. "They're cutting you loose?" he said. "They're looking for a sacrificial lamb and they pick you?"

"It looks that way, Tony. And I'm afraid you and Jane are in the soup with me. We may all be marked rotten."

"That's a bad rap, Paul."

"I know. But if you want a reassignment or you want to get out while the getting's good, I'll understand."

"Not in this world," Bolda snapped. "Screw the commissioner, screw Burton. We're not going anywhere. The way I see it, Burton's got himself a serial killer up there and Pete's killing's going to get the short end of the stick. So I'm going to keep looking and I'll cooperate with Burton and his goddam *Homicide North* and cross every *T* and dot every *I*, but Pete was one of ours and we'll be the ones who find those goddam Panamanian bastards who killed him. And Gallagher can just stick it up his ass."

Regal started to speak but Bolda silenced him by raising his hand.

"I'm with you," he said. "All the way."

It was almost 1 P.M. before Regal realized that he had not eaten since the previous evening. He had ordered Chinese food delivered for Patrice and himself, but after eating, she had decided that she wanted to go back to the design shop to do some more work on the plans for Storm Mountain's opening, now less than three weeks away.

Regal had been disappointed but had said nothing. He had sat home alone, watching television, and had been trying to ignore some insanely stupid late-night show when he'd gotten the phone call about Pete's death.

He got up from his desk and went into the outer office where he saw Jane Cole sitting wan and disconsolate, staring at her phone. He walked over to her.

"Are you hungry?"

She considered the question, then shrugged.

"Let's get some lunch," he said. "We ought to talk."

"I don't know," she said apathetically. All her usual spark seemed to have drained away. Her face looked ashy pale and she wore no lipstick. Regal realized for the first time that she had a light dusting of freckles across her nose that were normally hidden by makeup.

"Misery needs company, Jane," Regal said.

She shrugged again. "Sure. Why not? Life goes on, right?"

"Right."

"But not for Pete," she said, her eyes beginning to fill. "Oh, damn. I'll be right back." She fled for the ladies' room.

9

Because it was after one o'clock, the Galway Bar was only half full and not nearly so noisy and cheerful as usual. The diners from police headquarters were well aware that one of their own had been taken out the night before and many of them recognized Regal and Jane and came over to offer condolences.

They don't know yet that Pete was supposed to be dirty or that my ass is in the wringer, Regal thought. *If they did, they wouldn't come near me with a ten-foot pole.*

Eventually, the crowd thinned and they were left alone at their booth.

"No new developments, I guess," Jane said sadly.

"None that I've heard of. But we do have to talk."

"That's why I'm here."

"This is a tough question. I trust you to answer it honestly."

She only nodded, staring at him across the top of her coffee.

"Did you ever see Pete use drugs? Anything. Even marijuana?" Regal asked.

Anger stormed across her face, but for a fleeting moment, Regal had the idea that there was something wrong with her reaction. There was anger but there did not seem to be surprise.

"Just what are you getting at?"

"My question first. Then I'll answer yours."

"Pete never took a drug in his life," she said. "Nothing. No cocaine. No grass. He hated drugs. His older brother died a junkie with a needle in his arm. It's why Pete became a cop." She bit out the answer, one staccato word at a time, and then snapped, "Now why are you asking that?"

"Because the coroner's report said that Pete had traces of cocaine on his fingers and his mouth and there was some kind of drug in his urine."

"Well, they've been sucking formaldehyde down there for too long," she said, "and it's affected their goddam brains. And yours too, Inspector, for asking a question like that."

"Jane, please. The commissioner hit me with the damned report this morning. I told him that it was absolutely, totally wrong; that Pete Muniz was the cleanest cop in the department. But I had to ask you anyway, just to be sure."

"Well, be sure," she said. "Never once, never one single drug. Never. And you can tell the commissioner that for me."

"I don't think I'll be telling him too much of anything for a while."

"What do you mean?"

"I think I'm off his Christmas card list. I either run a leaky ship or I'm a crooked cop. He did everything but tell me to go on an ocean cruise and get lost. You and Tony, too."

"I always thought he was your buddy," Jane said evenly. "That's the word in the whole department."

"I always thought so too. But I guess they're afraid I might be an embarrassment in the mayor's reelection campaign. I'm only telling you this because I'm sure you're going to hear it through the grapevine and I want you to know what it's about. I don't want you stamped rotten with me."

"That sucks," she said with sudden vehemence. "You're the best and straightest squad commander in the department. And everybody knows it."

Regal sipped his beer. "Thanks, Jane, that helps. Maybe when I'm looking for work, I'll list you as a reference."

Abruptly, she reached out and touched his hand. "It's a bad rap on you, Inspector. What can I do to help?"

"Joe Burton's in charge of the investigation into Pete's ... death. But nothing can stop us from working on it too. I think it was those Panamanians that got away the other night. Maybe if we get them we can put this whole thing to rest."

Their orders arrived—an open-faced roast beef sandwich for him, a Taylor's ham sandwich for Jane. Regal discovered he was even hungrier than he had thought, but Jane nibbled disinterestedly at her sandwich and sipped her cup of coffee pensively, the corners of her mouth occasionally turning down as if the brew were bitter.

It wasn't the coffee, Regal knew.

"Jane, I'd like to hear that business about Pete getting a call to meet me for an assignment."

She jerked her head up from her coffee cup. "I went over that two dozen times last night and again this morning with Inspector Burton. Pete told me you wanted him to meet you uptown. I thought that meant you had called him. Maybe you did, I don't know. But I talked to his mother today. She told me someone called before he got home from class and left the message. You say it wasn't you so I guess it wasn't, but whoever it was told her to tell Pete to meet Inspector Regal at midnight. And he gave the street address.

"She thought it was you calling, but when Burton's men questioned her, she realized whoever it was never actually said 'I'm Inspector Regal' so it must have been someone else. She was sure it was an Anglo voice but it was muffled and she couldn't recognize it. Then Pete telephoned and she gave him the message. I guess he called me right after that to tell me he wasn't coming over 'cause he had to meet you." Jane shrugged. "And that was that."

"I talked to Mrs. Muniz about an hour ago to tell her how sorry I was but I didn't have the nerve to ask her about the call."

"I guess not," she said blandly, then, "I believe you, Inspector."

"Thanks," he said bitterly, the food he had just eaten lying like a lump in his stomach. If Jane Cole thought it was necessary to reassure him that she didn't believe he had assisted in the murder of one of his own men, God only knew what suspicions would be raging through Joe Burton's thick skull. And maybe not just Burton. Others in the department might be wondering too and that was the way careers ended. Not necessarily by doing anything wrong but by being suspected of it.

Another thought came into his mind. *And another way to have your career ended is to be shot like a dog on a street corner, so stop feeling sorry for yourself.*

"We've got to find those Panamanian druggies. Hector Guzman—that was Pete's snitch. They found him dead in a cellar. And now Pete. That's connected and we've got to find them."

Her eyes slitted. "Let me know when you do."

"And check you out a few hand grenades?"

She nodded. "That would be nice."

"You'll have to stand in line," he told her grimly.

Their conversation was interrupted by a big body pushing into the booth. "Move over," Joe Burton harshly ordered Jane. Before she even had time to comply, he plopped his body on the seat, crowding beside her, and fixed Regal with a stony look.

"You think of anything that could give us a lead?"

Regal shook his head and Burton turned toward Jane. "You?" She shook her head too and Burton rubbed his eyes wearily. "I hate cop killings. Routine always goes out the window when one of ours buys it. I do it myself. I want to get the bastard so bad that it affects my thinking. It looks to me like this was some kind of drug deal that went bad. I don't understand why Muniz would be making a buy at midnight without some kind of backup but I can't think of anything else."

"Pete didn't use drugs," Jane said.

"So I'm told," Burton said.

"By whom?"

"By everybody. You know things like that. People talk; everybody knows everybody else's business. Muniz was no user, that was the word."

He turned back to Regal. "If you or the real narcotics squad can get me a line on these mysterious Panamanians, maybe we'll get lucky and make a case. And find out why there were drugs in Muniz's body." Again he rubbed his eyes tiredly, obviously feeling the strain of a long night without sleep. "What I don't understand is how somebody could call Muniz's house with a phony message. Who the hell has a cop's private phone number?"

Regal shrugged. "Every one of his snitches probably. Every cop in the city. It wouldn't be hard to find out. Our squad even has business cards with our office phone on it. Pete may have been passing them out and writing his home number on it." A thought popped into his mind and he turned to Jane. "Did you ever hear Pete mention someone named Estrellita?"

"No," she said as Burton demanded, "Who's that?"

"She's the girlfriend of that Hector Guzman. He was Pete's snitch who told us about the Panamanians."

"The one they found dead in a cellar?"

"Yes," Regal said, and found himself impressed that Burton knew about it. The man had obviously done his homework.

"Well, what about her?"

"With Hector dead, Pete was going to try to find her to see if she knew anything about them. According to

Pete, she was a Panamanian herself and most likely was the one who gave Hector the information in the first place. She might have some answers to all of this."

"We'll just keep looking for her," Burton said, then wearily shook his head. "Christ, what a job. We got another one of those garbage pail murders last night with the bastard carving his initials in somebody's head."

"What's the tie to the first killing?" Regal asked, and before Burton could answer, Jane rose to her feet and said, "I've got to get out of here." She fumbled in her purse and threw a five dollar bill on the table, then pushed past Burton and walked quickly out the tavern door.

"What the hell was that all about?" Burton said.

"I don't know. I think maybe she's heard enough talk about murders already today."

"Yeah, probably," Burton said. "Women aren't cut out for this kind of work. Anyway, no connection between the two victims, except the killings themselves. One was a homeless bum; the one last night was some motorcycle fag. Both times, they were killed somewhere else and dumped up on the East Side."

"Sounds like you've got yourself a crazy," Regal said.

"Just what I needed to make my day. Listen. Check out everybody that Muniz talked to or dealt with. Maybe somebody knows something. Especially this Estrellita."

"We're already doing it."

"Good. And if you find anything, it comes to me. It's my investigation."

"I know. The commissioner told me." He looked at Burton but could see no trace of gloating in the man's face.

All Burton said was, "Then make sure you do it."

When Regal got back to his office, the outside door was locked and he had to let himself in with the key. The top of Jane's desk had been cleaned off, as it was every night, and there was no sign of her.

He went inside his private office and found a note on his desk.

> Dear Inspector:
> I left early because I'm not feeling well.
> You got another call from your weird mechanical friend.
> Something about Kay is tonight. It's on the tape if you want to play it back.

She signed the note with her full rank and name: Detective Jane Cole.

Regal went to the telephone console on her desk and pressed the replay button on the built-in tape recorder. It automatically reversed to the last message. He pressed the play button and heard a very mechanical voice say in a tone devoid of inflection or accent: "This-is-for-Inspector-Paul-Regal. Kay-is-for-night."

First prawns, then night. *Who's Kay? What the hell is going on?* he wondered.

"It must be a full moon," he mumbled under his breath.

Patrice was not home and she had left him neither a note nor a telephone message.

Just as well, he decided, as he made himself an elaborately awful sandwich from butt ends of ham and hardened pieces of cheese he found in the refrigerator. He didn't want to bicker about anything tonight. All he wanted to do was to get some sleep.

When he was done building the sandwich, he popped the whole thing into the microwave for twenty seconds to warm the ham and to soften the stale cheese. He ate it at the dining room table while reading the late afternoon edition of the *Post*, which he had picked up on his way home.

A picture of Pete Muniz smiled at him from Page One. The headline read: HERO COP GUNNED DOWN.

The story was on the second page and, allowing for the reporter's gee-whiz style of writing, was a straight-forward account of the murder of Muniz, whom it identified as a member of the commissioner's "personal crack antinarcotics squad."

Joe Burton was quoted as saying that police suspected that Muniz was gunned down by drug dealers he was investigating but he refused to make any further comment and Regal was relieved to see that the story did not hint at anything beyond that.

There was no innuendo that Muniz was a user himself or that there was any hint of corruption in the city's drug-fighting apparatus. And Regal's name was not mentioned at all, about which he felt very pleased. He wondered what all of Burton's grudging good will would cost him.

He worked his way through the sandwich and the newspaper simultaneously.

On a page toward the back of the paper, he found a report on the dead biker who had been found last night on Seventy-first Street between First and Second Avenues. The story was only a few inches long. It mentioned that the man had been stabbed and that his was the second body of a stabbing victim to be found in the area in the last few days.

But the paper failed to make any connection between the two killings. Regal knew that Burton had suppressed the information about the initials carved in the victims' foreheads, and without something like that to tie them together, the two slayings were just two separate random killings.

Good enough, Regal thought. *At least for now. Maybe Burton'll nab this nut-with-a-knife before anybody's even aware of what's going on.*

He looked again at the newspaper story. Both bodies were found on Seventy-first Street. And he lived on Seventy-fifth Street.

The neighborhood was just going to hell.

10

After nearly three hours of very earnest discussion in the basement of St. Dymphna's Episcopal Church, the chairlady summed up: "I believe we have a clear consensus that a committee be formed to speak with the city administration and make clear our deep concern regarding the deplorable lack of safety on our city streets."

She looked around for approval. One woman stood and said somberly, "I think we should call the committee The Concerned Citizens of Chelsea."

"Very good." The chairlady smiled and glanced about with smooth confidence. "Do I hear any objections?"

"You damn right you hear an objection," a voice bellowed from the rear of the meeting room.

As one, the nearly one hundred heads turned to look in astonishment as a short, fat, middle-aged black man with glossy, straight, shoulder-length hair bustled determinedly to the front of the room. His light blue suit was so shiny it seemed to spark as he passed under an overhead bank of fluorescent lights. A three-inch diameter golden sun pendant hung around his neck, flopping against his dark blue turtleneck sweater as he walked.

When he reached the front of the room, he yanked the microphone away from the startled chairlady and spat out angrily, "You call this a con-sen-sus?" He dragged the last word out mockingly. "What kind of con-sen-sus is it when the black people of this community aren't represented? Or did you forget you have black folks here in Chelsea? You just forget to invite them?"

"We invited everyone in the community to attend," the chairlady stammered, leaning back from his index finger, which pointed accusingly at her. "There *are* a number of Afro-Americans present, I believe."

"That's African-Americans, not Afro-Americans. If you gonna abuse us, at least get our names right. And anyway, they don't count," the fat man said. "I count and I count a lot of white people here and a couple of black people who probably haven't said one word tonight because they have to live with you racists and they want you to like them. So I'm gonna talk for them and all the other black people in Chelsea, 'cause I don't give a damn whether you like me or not."

"Exactly who are you?" interjected a tall lanky man in a gray suit with a clerical collar.

"The Reverend Benedictus Keane and I speak for all the people of color in this city," the man shouted, thrusting his chin toward the man in the gray suit. "Who you?"

"I am the rector of this church. Where is your church, Reverend Keane? It's not here in Chelsea, is it?"

"*My* church is the Church of the Holy Spirit of God-in-Man and my congregation is everyone in this city, especially if they don't have blue eyes. I speak for the poor, for the disenfranchised, for all the people that you always trample underfoot."

He glared until the man in the gray suit glanced away, then turned back to the crowd. "I'm Keane and I'm mean but I'm not very lean. I'm a BIG muthah," he bellowed.

With the audiences he was accustomed to, this declaration always brought a roar. This time it was met with deafening silence until a voice shouted from the rear of the room.

"Tell 'em, Big Ben," a black man called out from the back doorway, where he stood keeping an eye out for the police. Suddenly, the audience all recognized the name. Big Ben. One of the city's prominent new activists whose sole goal in life seemed to be to force confrontation. The chairlady tittered nervously and looked around for assistance.

"Really, sir," the rector began, but Keane turned his back on him and began haranguing the audience with practiced authority, even while noting with disappointment that there appeared to be no newspaper reporters at the meeting, much less the television coverage he had been hoping for.

"This here lily-white Chelsea that you think is yours is worse than South Africa," he shouted. "And I got news for you. Chelsea ain't yours. Chelsea belongs to the people. All the people. Chelsea belongs to me."

"Tell 'em, Big Ben," shouted the lonely cheerleader in the back of the room.

"And now you making up lies about black people assaulting you on the streets and stealing your measly little tight-assed purses where you keep the money you stole from the black man. And you got the nerve to tell all these lies in a church basement. Well, maybe Jesus Christ forgive you for what you do, but Big Ben don't. No way no how."

He . . .

. . . sat in a quiet corner of the back row, watching the black man ramble on. *You are perfect for me, Big Ben*, he thought, and once in a while he smiled as Keane began screaming obscenities at the audience.

Tonight you are really going to do something to make the city streets better, he thought. *You're going to be lying on one.*

* * *

Keane had just finished calling them "a gang of no-count racist and Tom motherjumpers," and the rector said, "Now, really. That's too much." He extended a hand to touch Keane's shoulder.

"You touch me, white devil, I call the law."

"Right on, Big Ben," shouted the cheerleader in the back. "Clergical brutality."

"Shall I call the police?" an elderly man in the front row asked aloud.

"Yes, please do," the chairlady said, and the rector nodded agreement. The man in the front row left the room through a side door, searching for a phone.

"Go ahead, arrest me for speaking the truth," Keane shrieked, his saliva dampening the first two rows of seats. "I been arrested before by you rednecks. So was the Reverend Doctor Martin Luther King Junior and I stand with him against your apartheid."

He struck a martyred pose and looked scornfully at the rector. "You racists can arrest me but you can't silence me because I'm free at last, free at last, thank God Almighty, I'm free at last."

The rector, who had wandered late into the meeting after having performed a half dozen homosexual weddings in the main church, was taken aback. He had been called many things before, notably "a slack-jawed, mush-brained left-wing moron" by the *New York Post*, but never a racist. He wondered if people would misunderstand if he had Big Ben arrested, although in truth, Keane was no stranger to arrest. When Martin Luther King led the march on Selma, Alabama, Keane had been in jail on a bookmaking charge. When King was assassinated, Keane was serving two-to-five years for procuring. He had become a minister only two years before this night, ordaining himself one evening in a ceremony that consisted primarily of swinging a chicken around his head three times in a rented storefront in the Bronx.

The rector did not know any of that. What he did know was that he had to go slowly and really think over his own beliefs. Perhaps he *was* a racist. Yes, the rector really had to consider that possibility about himself. After all, Big Ben was black and should certainly be able to recognize a racist when he saw one. In confusion, the rector sat down and Keane began haranguing the crowd anew.

Quietly in the back, *he* stood and walked toward the exit door. The fun was over in here for the evening. The rest would take place elsewhere.

Two uniformed patrolmen entered the church. When he saw them, Big Ben's one-man cheering section remembered there was a warrant out for his arrest on rape charges and bolted out the side door of the church hall.

"Well, well, Atlanta Slim," one of the cops said as he approached Keane.

The rector of the church meanwhile had decided that Big Ben was right: the rector was, in his innermost heart, nothing more than a racist.

He heard the policeman speak and jumped to his feet. "This is not any Atlanta Slim. This is the Reverend Benedictus Keane."

"*Now* he is," one of the cops said in a bored voice. "But when he used to be a pimp, we called him Atlanta Slim." He turned back to Keane. "Come on, Slim. Time to go home and stop bothering people."

One on each side, they grabbed him firmly by the arms and started to escort him to the door.

"Police brutality!" Big Ben shouted. "Brutality!"

"Come on, Slim. Time to go back to Brooklyn," one of the cops said.

In the front of the church, the rector began screaming too, "Brutality! Brutality! Police brutality!" until he was silenced by a wicked glance from the meeting's chairlady, who was not so quick to forgive anyone who called her a motherjumper.

Outside the church hall, Keane looked around for the man he had driven in with, but he was gone and so was the car that had been parked across the street.

"Damn chicken-livered mother," he growled, then turned to the policemen with a smile. "How about giving me a ride up to Harlem?"

"Come on, we don't run a taxi service. Take the subway."

"This damned neighborhood's not safe," Keane protested.

"But nobody would attack you, Rev-e-rend," the cop said with a grin. "You be their man."

"Argggh," Keane growled, spat on the sidewalk and strutted away, thick legs rubbing together from the knee up. All in all, he thought, not such a bad evening. It would have been better if the television cameras had been there, but when he got back up to Harlem, he'd be sure to call the stations and report how the police had brutally silenced him. That charge would be sure to get air time.

As he reached the corner, a slim blonde girl in faded jeans and a loose men's-style shirt sauntered out from between two parked cars.

"You really told them where to get off, Brother," she said admiringly in a low throaty voice.

"Who you?" he asked suspiciously.

"I was at the meeting. It was a real drag until you came along. You really told those mothers where to go."

"I don't take no shit from nobody," he told her. " 'Specifically not those whitebreads."

"I know. I'm so ashamed of what white people have done to men like yourself . . . well, I just wish there was something I could do about it. Myself."

Keane's eyes widened. *God moves in mysterious ways*, he reminded himself.

"Can I give you a ride?" she asked. "Where are you going?"

"Heading up to Harlem to see some people, say a few prayers, maybe mess around a little."

"I'm right around the corner," she said. "Maybe I can

show you that not all white people are like those in there tonight."

"Sheeit, them folks don't know nothing about giving people a hard time. They just get all constipated when somebody yells at them. They don't know how to deal with a *man*." He emphasized the last word and the young woman snorted with appreciation.

"God, I've never met anyone like you before close up," she said. "You make the boys I know seem like they belong in kindergarten."

"Pretty thing like you, I guess you have lots of boy-friends."

"Enough. I like action," she said. She unlocked the passenger door for him, then hurried around to get behind the wheel. "Just tell me where you want to go. I'm good at following instructions."

Keane licked his upper lip. "Let's just head uptown and we'll figure out the best way to spend the next few hours."

"Anything you say, sir." The thin blonde turned and smiled at him and drove away from the curb.

He . . .

. . . saw them driving away. He touched his mustache nervously, then pulled out from the parking spot a half block down the street and followed them. He hummed tunelessly to himself. Everything was right on schedule.

Big Ben Keane would have loved it, had he lived to see it. He made the front page not only of the *New York Times* but of most other major newspapers across the nation. His slaying drew attention even in the European press.

At last, although too late, he was getting the media attention he had craved—and even a little respect for a change. A number of black leaders who previously had refused even to shake his hand, sneering with open contempt at his circus antics, now bemoaned "America's tragic loss" and deplored the continuing racial hostility that obviously gripped New York City and imperiled the lives of all African-Americans.

They did not push the point too hard, however, being well aware that not only an overwhelming majority of New York's white citizens but an equal percentage of black citizens had viewed Keane with undisguised loathing.

The police this time had not been able to conceal the fact that a letter—*B*—had been carved into Keane's

d, although they still held back the infor-
ut the two previous killings.

cision not to announce that the three killings
tied together had come after some heavy dis-
n that morning at City Hall.

he mayor had pointed out that the fact that the first
wo victims were white would be enough to cool down
any black hotheads who might see racism in Reverend
Keane's murder. "Why don't we just explain what's happening before people start killing each other?" the
mayor asked.

"Nobody's going to kill each other over Big Ben,"
Police Commissioner Gallagher answered. "Hell, the
fact that he was seen walking away from church with a
white woman would put the squash on that. We're not
talking about some saint, you know."

The commissioner leaned forward over the mayor's
desk. "Keane's dead and we can live with that problem.
But if the public finds out we've got a serial killer running around loose, it's going to hit the fan. I think we're
better off keeping it quiet as long as we can. There's got
to be some damned significance to those letters. *P* and
K and *B*. Even nuts doing nutty things make some kind
of nutty sense. Let us try to track down this killer. I've
given Inspector Burton a green light to do anything he
needs to close down this case."

"I hope you're right, Richard," the mayor sighed.
"Remember, if Keane's death does lead to a bunch of
street violence, your cops will be out there in the middle
of it."

"It's a calculated risk," Gallagher said. "But I think
there'll be some noise for a while but that's all. Until
the next killing if we don't get the guy . . . or woman . . .
before then."

The noise level threatened to go a lot higher and last
a lot longer than the commissioner expected. Something
about Keane's untimely and undignified death—he was
found on East Sixty-ninth Street, between Lexington
and Third Avenues, stuffed into a giant plastic leaf bag

with a Halloween pumpkin face on it—seemed to capture the public's imagination.

Everybody wanted to get into the act.

Keane was hardly cold before Beatrice Belle, a fading actress who had recently lost her role in a television soap opera and was having trouble finding work, called a press conference to announce shrilly that obviously the initial *B* carved into Keane's forehead was the work of a madman, out to kill people whose names started with a *B*.

As a double *B*, she pointed out, it was clear that she would be high on this maniac's list and she denounced the mayor for not giving her around-the-clock police protection until she could complete her arrangements to move to the safety of Southern California.

"But Keane's name started with a *K*," one incredulous reporter observed at the press conference.

She looked at him in astonishment. "But you're forgetting. Big. And Ben. And he was black. *B* for black, you know. He was a triple *B*."

The morning radio disc jockeys talked about little else that morning, each trying to outdo all the others in bad jokes and tastelessness. That prompted the governor to "view with alarm" from Albany and reveal that he might appoint a task force to look into the "racist" murder. And then again, he revealed, he might not.

The public school system was closed for the summer so the incidents were only sporadic, but some of the town's ever-inventive teenagers immediately started walking around the streets with their initials painted on their foreheads with red nail polish.

The capper came when Oliver Storm wound up on a morning talk show, ostensibly to promote his new complex, Storm Mountain. But instead, he dropped the bombshell of announcing his mayoral candidacy and wound up talking for twenty minutes about why he was going to have to run.

"We've had enough," he roared. "Our city is becoming a laughing stock for the whole nation, and a sick, dangerous laughing stock at that. We have been betrayed by this mayor and his administration. We need more police on the streets so that the citizens of this great city, black and white alike, can walk about without fear of being stabbed and mutilated."

The mayor folded.

At 1 P.M., the very day that Keane's body was found and less than three hours after his meeting with Commissioner Gallagher, the mayor called a press conference and revealed that two previous killings, both of white men, were linked by police to the slaying of Reverend Keane. "We've put into this all the resources of the greatest police department in the world and I can assure you that an arrest is imminent. But I can also assure you of one very important thing—that the Reverend Keane's lamentable death was not racially motivated."

The reporters, eager as sharks with the smell of blood in the water, cared not one damn about racial motivations. They pressed the mayor to explain what it was that tied all three deaths together, but the mayor, belatedly realizing that he had screwed things up by acknowledging the existence of a mass murderer, said any further comment would have to come from the police.

And Paul Regal's office got another telephone call.

He had been standing in the doorway when the phone rang, and as Jane Cole picked it up, she frantically signaled to Regal to pick up an extension.

He got the phone to his ear just in time to hear a mechanical voice say: ". . . for-bishop." Then the click of a disconnected line was followed by a dial tone.

"What did he say?" Regal asked Jane as he hung up the phone.

She pressed the tape playback button on her desk. The eerie mechanical voice droned into the room: "For-Inspector-Paul-Regal. *B*-is-for-bishop."

"Prawns, bishops, somebody out there is a real

wacko," Jane said. But when she looked up, Regal was already striding into his own office. The door slammed closed behind him.

Regal stood in front of the huge plastic city street map that covered half a wall in his office, and with a wipeable marker, he placed an X on the spot where the Reverend Keane's body had been found.

He looked at it for a moment, then walked to the telephone and called Inspector Joe Burton. A clerk had him wait for a while, before coming back with the news that Burton was busy and unable to talk to Regal. Perhaps Lieutenant Davis might be able to help?

Regal waited for Davis with a sour smile on his face. *Nobody is as dead as a cop cut loose by the New York City police brass*, he thought. *They can't even raise somebody to talk to them on the telephone.*

Lieutenant Davis eventually came onto the wire. Apparently expecting Regal to ask about the investigation into the murder of Pete Muniz, he said, without prompting, that there was nothing new, and then was surprised when Regal just grunted and asked where the bodies of the two earlier knifing victims were found.

"It's not my case, Inspector. But let me look," Davis said. A moment later he was back. "The wino was on Seventy-first Street between Second and Third. The motorcycle fag was Seventy-first between First and Second."

"What side of the street did they find the wino's body?" Regal asked.

"Let's see." Regal heard Davis mumbling to himself as he checked a building number. "South side of the street."

"And the biker?"

Davis, who had been at that scene, answered immediately. "He was north side."

"Thanks a lot," Regal said and hung up without explanation. He walked back to the map and put two more Xs where the other two bodies had been found.

He stared at the map for a long time and then hissed a sigh. "Jesus Christ," he said.

"I'm sorry, Commissioner. Maybe I'm thick but I don't know what the mayor was thinking of."

Joe Burton had just poured a cup of coffee for Commissioner Gallagher, who had strolled into the temporary headquarters of Homicide North, above a police precinct building near Central Park.

The telephone had been ringing wildly in Gallagher's office with reporters trying to get more information on the serial killings that the mayor had revealed and, faced with the dilemma of dodging reporters' questions or telling them more than he should, the commissioner had relied on that most traditional of politicians' reactions: he fled.

Finally he had lighted at Inspector Burton's offices and gone in to check on the progress of the investigation. Burton, as usual, had started complaining immediately . . . about the low quality of rookie policemen, about the weather, New York baseball teams and about the mayor's press conference, which he had watched on an old black-and-white television in a corner of the office.

"Now that they know it's probably a serial killer, we're going to have reporters coming out our ass, pardon my French."

"I know, Joe," the commissioner said. "I guess the mayor had a reason for tipping them off, but I don't mind telling you I wish he hadn't either."

Burton nodded, his own good judgment confirmed by his boss.

"Any new leads?" Gallagher asked as he took the coffee that Burton had poured from an electric pot kept on his office table. He noted idly that the cup was dirty. Policemen were the same all over, he thought. He had been commissioner for three years and had not yet once found a clean coffee cup in any police facility in the city. It was as if the cops had yet to discover running water.

"No new ones and no old ones. Nothing," Burton said. "Those damned alphabet letters make no sense at all, and we can't find a thing that ties the three victims together."

"What about this woman that Keane walked away with last night?"

Burton shrugged. "A thin blonde in blue jeans. They drove off in her car. It was blue. No description of her, no license number, not a damned thing. Somebody thought they saw her at the church meeting but nobody's sure. We're up against a stone wall."

"So what are you doing?"

Burton sighed and it turned into a cigarette-induced cough. "What we always do. We've got all the locales flooded. We're going back to requestion the people we questioned before. Somebody somewhere saw something. They always do and we've just got to find it."

Gallagher nodded. He hesitated, then asked, "Is there any possibility that the connection is where the bodies were dumped? They were all found pretty close to each other. Is it possible all the properties where they were found are owned by the same person? Something like that."

"Pretty good, Commissioner. Most people wouldn't think of that."

"And?"

"We thought of it," Burton said. "No connection that we can find. I've got more men still working on that though."

He looked up when he heard a tapping on the door.

Burton frowned and said, "Sorry, Commissioner," then shouted angrily, "Yeah?"

The door opened for Lieutenant Tony Bolda, who looked rumpled and tired. He seemed shocked to see the commissioner sitting in front of Burton's desk and said quickly, "Sorry, Inspector, I'll come back."

"No, come in," Gallagher said. "It's not personal, is it?"

"No, sir," Bolda said, still obviously discomfited at

Gallagher's presence, but he stepped inside and closed the door behind him.

"So what is it?" Burton asked gruffly.

"These alphabet killings . . ."

"Yeah?"

"I think I know what the letters mean," Bolda said.

He paused and Burton snapped, "Out with it, Bolda, for Christ's sake." Gallagher just looked at the visibly uncomfortable lieutenant.

"I think they're chess moves. Like a game of chess," Bolda said.

"What are you talking about?"

"That's how they abbreviate the names of pieces in a chess game. *P* is for pawn. *K* is the knight. *B* is the bishop. Think about it, Inspector. The *P* was a homeless bum and the knight was a biker. Somebody mounted . . . you get it? And the bishop, well, that was Atlanta Sli—— sorry, Commissioner, Reverend Keane. A minister . . . you see, a bishop?"

"Aaaaah," Burton snarled in disgust, but Gallagher silenced him by holding up his hand.

"Hold on, Joe. I think the lieutenant . . . it's Bolda, isn't it?" Bolda nodded and the commissioner said, "I think maybe he's on to something."

"Thank you, Commissioner," Bolda said. "You can really see it on this map of Manhattan." He pointed to the usual police street map hanging on Burton's wall. He looked back at the commissioner hopefully, noticing though that Burton was leaned back in his desk chair, arms folded across his chest in a posture that said "show me" as clearly as if he had been wearing a sign.

"Explain that, Lieutenant," the commissioner said.

Bolda walked over to the map. He leaned over to look at it closely, then pointed to a small quadrant of one square block. "See, this is where the wino was found. That was the pawn. And then the knight was found here. And then the bishop here. Those are moves on a chess-board."

He looked back at the two other men, as if soliciting

encouragement, but they only stared silently at the map.

Bolda cleared his throat nervously and continued. "And if you figure it out, well, a chessboard is eight squares by eight squares. You put it on a map and it means the board runs from Sixty-seventh Street to Seventy-fifth Street and from the river to Fifth Avenue. That's an eight-by-eight grid, the same as a chessboard. And the killer's playing like a game. It's called..." Bolda thought but could not summon up the words he wanted so he fished a piece of paper from his pocket.

"Sorry, Commissioner, Inspector, I like to write things down. It's called the Roy Lopez opening. Pawn to king four and knight to king bishop three and bishop to queen knight five." He looked up from his notes and added, "I think."

Burton was watching him carefully now, switching his glance from Bolda to the map and then back. Finally he stood and walked to the map and said, "Show me again." As Bolda pointed out the spots where the bodies had been found, Burton started nodding. The commissioner just watched and listened.

Finally Burton said, "This is good, Tony. Real good. I think you've got something."

"Well, thanks. I just thought about it and I . . . well, I wanted to pass it on right away." He shoved his hands nervously into his baggy pockets, then pulled them out when he remembered the commissioner in the room, and finally said awkwardly, "I think I'll go now."

Commissioner Gallagher stood up. "Joe," he said to Burton, "I'd like to talk to the lieutenant privately for a moment. Would you excuse us?"

Burton nodded and moved toward the door of the room, still looking at the map.

When the office door had closed behind him, Gallagher looked at Bolda sharply and said, "When did Regal figure this out about the chess game?"

"When he got the . . ." Bolda caught himself. "He didn't, sir. I figured it out."

"Lieutenant, no offense intended but you wouldn't

know a chess piece from a bowling pin. It's not Roy Lopez. He's a bandleader, I think. The chess opening is the *Ruy* Lopez. So spare me the flapdoodle. I know this was Paul's idea. I know the man. What gave him the clue?"

For a brief second, Bolda looked trapped between loyalty to Regal and having to lie to the commissioner. He finally shrugged and said, "The office has been getting some strange phone calls. Today, the inspector finally put it all together that they were talking about the killings."

"And then sent you up here to tell Joe because he knew Joe wouldn't listen to anything that came from him. Is that right?"

Some things Bolda obviously drew the line at revealing. He said stiffly, "Sorry, Commissioner, but I don't know about that. You'll have to ask the inspector himself."

"I think I'll do just that," Gallagher said. He saw the look on Bolda's face and said, "Stop worrying. He's not in any trouble and let me tell you, you've got balls coming up here this way."

"I try to do my job, sir."

"Okay. You can go now. I'll handle it from here."

Bolda nodded, obviously happy that he had survived the session, and almost fled from the room. When Inspector Burton returned, the commissioner was on the telephone.

"Paul. I'm in Joe Burton's office. Get up here right away, will you?"

He paused, listening, then said—obviously referring to Tony Bolda—"He tried his best, Paul. Hurry up. We're waiting for you."

12

"You mean you got three phone calls from the killer and you didn't tell us till now?" Joe Burton's face was red as he glared from behind his desk at Paul Regal.

"I *still* don't know if the calls came from the killer or not," Regal said evenly. "But I dug out the tapes. Maybe the lab boys can figure out something." He tossed a pair of small cassettes onto Burton's desk. "We only got two on tape. And, yes, three calls came to the office. One I didn't hear and people in my office said it was about prawns and they thought it came from a fish store. The second one didn't register on me. When the third one came today, I connected the *B* to Keane's body."

"And sent Bolda up here to tell Joe?" the commissioner asked from his seat in the corner of the room.

"Yes, sir."

"Why not do it yourself?" Gallagher asked.

"Why don't you tell the commissioner, Joe?" Regal said.

"Because I don't know the answer," Burton snapped.

"Yeah, you do. If I had called you with some cock-

and-bull story about chess pieces and a chessboard on the city streets, you would have told me I was playing with myself too much and hung up on me. That's why I sent Tony. And I figured once he got the idea into your head, then I could talk sense to you."

"That sounds to me like you're trying to shove blame on me for your own incompetence," Burton snapped.

"Well, not to me," the commissioner growled angrily. "I've listened to you two badmouth each other for so damned long, I'm sick of it, and yeah, Joe, I believe you would have laughed in Paul's face. And I've told you both before and I'm telling you both again, knock off the shit. We've got a crazy out there and we'd better stop him before he kills half the town."

He looked viciously at both men, first Burton, then Regal. The officers, buffaloed by his vehemence, nodded.

"All right. We understand each other," Gallagher said. "Now what's next? Paul, you've had these phone calls on your mind longer than we have. Do you have any ideas?"

"A couple, sir," Regal answered. "First, Joe should have the lab check those tapes. The voice on them . . . I'm no expert . . . but the voice seems mechanically made. Maybe our guys can figure out the machine or where it came from or something about it. Second, the messages come to me personally. They all start 'for Inspector Paul Regal' and they come in on the office's private line."

"Anybody can get the private line," Burton said. "It's in every precinct house in the city."

"Right. So that doesn't mean much. But why would whoever-it-is call me by name?"

He looked at both men and the commissioner said, "Any ideas?"

"I've been thinking about it. Maybe he wants me to play chess with him," Regal said.

"Why?" Burton sneered. "I figured you were a big man in ballet circles. You a big chess expert too?"

"That's enough, Joe," Gallagher snapped. He told Regal, "Maybe you're right. It makes as much sense as anything else. But how can we do it?"

"How does this sound, sir? Do you think you could get the *Times* to save us space for one of those little classified ads that they run at the bottom of Page 1 most days?"

"I think so," the commissioner said. "Why?"

"Well, I think if I put the killer's opening moves there and my own moves and then just signed the ad with my initials, there's a good chance that he'd see it and know it was me."

"Suppose he doesn't read the *Times*?" Burton said.

"Then you give me his name and address and I'll send him a letter," Regal snapped. "Maybe he doesn't read the *Times* but I don't know of any better chance. If he calls again, I can try to talk to him. But if he doesn't, how else can I get a message to him?"

"You don't think we ought to announce this to the press?" the commissioner said.

Both inspectors answered in unison, "No," and despite the tension between them, each grinned.

"Your turn, Joe," Regal said.

"Commissioner," Burton said, "announce this to the public and we'll have six thousand nuts coming out of the woodwork with chess sets under their arms and the whole investigation will go up the chimney. Right now, the only people who know about this are us and the killer. The longer we can keep it like that, the better chance we have of getting him."

As the commissioner looked at him, Regal nodded.

"Who else knows about this?" Gallagher asked.

"In my office," Regal said, "I've only got Tony Bolda and Jane Cole and they won't say a word."

"Did you tell anybody, Joe?"

"No."

"Okay. Then it's just us three and the two on Paul's squad. Let's try to handle it on a need-to-know basis for a while. And as far as I'm concerned, *no one* needs to know."

"Good by me," Burton said. Again Regal nodded.

"Paul, I'll set up the advertising for tomorrow's *Times*. Do you know anything about chess?"

"I played a lot when I was a kid before I discovered girls. I haven't played for years but I know enough to fake it for a while. It's a Ruy Lopez opening by white. I can make the first half dozen moves out of any decent chess book, just to get things going. But if this guy *wants* to play and is a *real* chess player, pretty soon I'll be over my head."

"We'll cross that bridge when we come to it," Gallagher said. "Let's find out first if we can make contact."

"How long's it take to play a chess game?" Burton asked.

Regal shrugged. "A move a day . . . I don't know. Chess games go fifty . . . sixty moves sometimes, I think."

"Balls. You'll be playing till winter," Burton said.

"No. You'll catch him before then," Regal said easily. "There's one other thing, Commissioner," he added. "I don't know if it means anything, but maybe this nut has picked me out to call because I live in that target area."

Gallagher considered that for a moment, then shrugged. "So do a lot of people. It'll give you extra incentive, knowing you may be walking past this killer on your way to work. Who knows? Maybe it's your next-door neighbor."

"Thanks a lot," Regal said.

"Think nothing of it. I'm getting out of here and I'll leave you two alone. Nothing has changed. Joe is in charge. Paul, you handle the chess end of it. It means you're going to have to work together so no crap. I want to know what both of you are doing every day. As for me, I'm not even going to mention this to the mayor, so if there's a leak, it comes right back to both of you." He looked sharply at the two men, just to make sure they understood, and then walked quickly from the office.

"Sit down, Regal," snapped Burton. "You really think you can pull off this chess game?"

"As I said, a few moves. Maybe we won't even get a response."

"Somehow I think you will. Think back. Has anybody talked to you about playing chess recently?"

"I wish it were that simple. I've been racking my brain and I can't think of anyone. I just get the usual poker invitations like you do."

"Then why would this yahoo challenge you to a game, do you think?"

"Beats the shit out of me. Maybe because he's crazy as a loon?"

"That's for sure," Burton grunted. "How many chess players do you suppose there are in New York?"

"A million at a guess. Most people know a little bit about the game, I think. The newspapers run chess columns so somebody must read them."

"Christ, a million people, every fucking one of them a suspect. Don't you have any good news for me?"

"Not today," Regal said. "I don't seem to remember your asking me for advice before this."

"I didn't but I'll take all the help I can get," Burton admitted. "The mayor is shooting off his mouth, the silly old bastard, and the press is yapping around like a bunch of dogs chasing a bitch in heat. You'll talk to our phone guys or should I?"

Despite the animosity between the two men, Regal was pleased that Burton respected his police ability enough to assume that Regal would know what he meant by the reference to the telephone.

"I already did. We'll have a tracer gizmo on the phone first thing in the morning. I don't know if it'll do any good but at least we'll cover that base."

"All right. Then I guess I just better think about this some more," Burton said.

"And I've got to go buy me a chess book," Regal said. "Anything new on Pete Muniz?"

Burton shook his head. "I know that you and everybody else thinks he was clean, so I made them recheck those lab tests. Paul, there's no question about it. He had cocaine on his fingers and tongue, but the drug trace they found in his urine *wasn't* cocaine. But it was so damned small they really couldn't swear about it. Maybe morphine or heroin. Does that make any sense to you?"

"I didn't believe he used one drug. I sure as shit won't believe that he used two."

"They checked the body again for me. No needle marks. Nothing. Stomach just held some kind of bread. I don't know. Davis has a lot of guys looking for this Estrellita that Muniz was trying to track down. What was his name, Hector's, girlfriend. No luck so far. And I'm afraid I'm going to have to start to yank some of them off to work on this alphabet nut."

"We'll keep looking for Estrellita," Regal said calmly.

"I know that," Burton said. "And officially I disapprove."

"And I know *that*," Regal said. "So we understand each other."

"Maybe for the first time," Burton said.

"Maybe."

The midtown traffic was ferocious so Regal passed up the big stores on Fifth Avenue and stopped in a used bookshop near his apartment where he found a beaten-up old copy of a book called *New Techniques for Winning with the Ruy Lopez*. He also bought a cheap plastic chess set with a cardboard playing board.

When he got home, Patrice was not there. Again, she had left no message, and again, Regal did not mind the solitude. He had a lot of work to do tonight.

But when Regal opened the brittle yellowed pages of the chess book, his heart sank into his stomach.

The book was filled with page after page of seemingly incomprehensible numbers and letters. It covered scores of possible variations of the chess opening, along with a blizzard of footnotes that mentioned even more variations.

How the hell does anyone learn to play chess well? Regal asked himself. He hunkered down at the dining table with a pot of coffee, set up the white and black plastic chess pieces on the board, and with a lined yellow pad and a red ballpoint pen, he started to trace the moves throughout the book.

After a while, he found that it was starting to make some sense to him. Not that he had even a clue to what all the analysis in the book meant, but at least he was able to understand the notations used and what they signified.

He was startled for a moment when he noted that the book he was consulting used the initial *N* to stand for the knight. The killer had used the letter *K*.

He went back and skimmed through the introduction and found the author writing that many people still used *Kt* as an abbreviation for the knight piece, but he was using the more modern *N*.

So it's just an option, he thought. *Use what you want.* He considered it for a moment and decided that in placing his move in the newspaper he would use the letter *N*. *Let's see if it gets a rise out of this lunatic.*

He had finally found a fairly clear listing of white and black moves in one of the variations and was jotting them down on the pad when the telephone rang.

Commissioner Gallagher, with the sound of dance music blasting in the background, said that he had worked out an arrangement with the *New York Times.*

"You call them any night before eleven P.M. and they'll put a small classified ad at the bottom of Page One for you."

"And no one's going to ask any questions? I don't want to be explaining this to reporters, Commissioner."

"No questions. You just call this number." He read off a local phone number. "That's the night line of the advertising department and there's always someone there. You give them your code word so they know it's you. And then tell them what you want in the ad."

"Sounds good, sir. What's the code word?"

"Alphabet," Gallagher said. "Sorry, Paul, but it's all I could think of on the spur of the moment."

"It'll do fine."

"When are you going to place the first ad?"

"Right away, I think. And then if he responds somehow, we'll figure out what to do next."

"Good. Good night, Paul. And Paul?"

"Yes, sir."

"I'm glad you're in this," the commissioner said before hanging up.

As Regal replaced the telephone, he thought bitterly, *Sure, you're glad. Until you or Inspector Flaherty and his IAD shooflies make your minds up that I'm either an incompetent or a crook or somehow dangerous to the mayor's reelection campaign. Don't do me any favors.*

Regal had trouble sleeping. He was still awake when Patrice came home and he glanced at the illuminated face of the alarm clock next to his bed. Three A.M. She went into her own bedroom without looking in on him.

He finally fell asleep, but his rest was fitful, and he was up and out of the house before 6:30. At a hotel near his apartment, he bought a *Times* and read the ad while walking toward his subway stop.

The ad was in the lower left-hand corner of Page One. It consisted of four simple lines of type:

P-K4	P-K4
N-KB3	N-QB3
B-N5	P-QR3
	P.R.

Using the traditional method of recording chess moves, the first three lines showed the killer's initial three moves and Regal's—the black player's—response to them. The *P.R.* in the corner was Regal's initials. If the killer saw the ad, he should be able to understand that the moves came from Paul Regal and that the policeman was accepting the tacit challenge to play.

Now it was white's—the killer's—move . . . and only time would tell.

Regal folded up the newspaper without even glancing at the rest of it, jammed it into his jacket and strode off briskly to catch his train. He was in the office well before it opened at 8 A.M. He called one of the building maintenance workers and when the man, yawning from having his sleep interrupted, came to the office, Regal asked him if he could reactivate the bell on Regal's phone. Generally the phones only rang in the outer office, and Regal could tell when they were in use only by visually checking the blinking lights on the various lines. But now he wanted to hear the phones ring, he said.

"Sure, Inspector," the maintenance man said. He unscrewed the base of Regal's desk phone and removed a small clip.

"There. It'll ring now," he said and scurried toward the door before Regal thought of anything else to do.

When Jane Cole came in—early as usual—Regal called her into his office.

"Jane, I want to handle all the calls today on the private line. I've had the phone activated in here and I've swiped the tape machine from your desk."

"Anything special going on, Inspector?"

"As a matter of fact, yes. Those nutty phone calls we've been getting from the mechanical man?"

"Yes."

"I think they may be from the one who killed Reverend Keane and those other two men."

"The Monogram Murderer?"

"What?"

"The Monogram Murderer. That's what the *Post* called him this morning."

"Monogram? Like initials carved in somebody's head?"

"Yeah," Jane answered. "They had that. And they had a field day. Paper was filled with pictures of kids with letters scrawled on their heads. Like Halloween masks."

Regal winced. As far as he knew, neither Gallagher nor the mayor had mentioned that the thing which connected all three killings had been the initials carved into the victims' forehead. But the press had it already. Some son of a bitch had already started leaking on the story.

Feeling a little stupid for worrying about what was obviously already a lost cause, Regal said, "Jane, this is important. Don't tell anybody about these phone calls. Not a soul. You understand?"

His tone was hectoring and her response was a little chilly. "Yes, Inspector, I understand."

Regal had no desire to be sympathetic to her mood. "Fine," he said. "Just remember that."

"I will. Is there anything else?"

"No. Thank you."

She walked toward the door, the stiff walk of an angry woman, and Regal called to her, "Jane, I talked to Burton last night. Still no leads on Pete's murder."

She nodded curtly and walked outside.

It was just after ten when the private line rang for the first time that day.

Regal picked up the receiver carefully and saw the reel on the tape machine start to revolve.

"Inspector Regal here," he said.

A shudder went up his neck when he heard the mechanical voice: "For-Inspector-Paul-Regal. I-am-glad-my-challenge-has-been-accepted. White's-next-move-is-bishop-takes-knight. As-longs-as-the-game-stays-interesting-there-will-be-no-more-killings."

The metallic voice stopped and Regal said, "Hello. Listen to me. Can you hear me? Let's talk about this."

But all he heard back was a click and a dial tone.

He hung up the telephone and sat back in his chair and heaved a sigh of relief.

Okay, he thought, *no more murders. At least for a while. If I can keep this damned game interesting and that's a big if.* Ten minutes later, the telephone company's lineman who was assigned regularly to the police headquarters building showed up at Regal's office to attach call-tracing equipment to his telephone.

Regal watched him work and thought, *Too late for this call. But next time we get you, you bastard.*

13

Whoever it was who said that no news is good news had never been a cop, Regal decided, because there was no news this day and all of it was bad.

First, Tony Bolda came into the office to report that there was still no trace of the mysterious Estrellita whom Pete Muniz had been trying to find. "Not a trace," he said. "It's like she dropped off the earth."

"Then *look* off the earth," Regal grumbled. "Keep searching."

"Yes, sir," Bolda said with a hint of sarcasm, as if annoyed that Regal had ordered him to do what he was going to do anyway. But Regal was hunched over, head down, studying reports on his desk and he did not even notice.

After receiving the killer's latest message, Regal had phoned the commissioner's office—he did not want to go up there in person lest he be made to wait in an outer office like somebody who had just wandered in off the street—and told Gallagher that the murderer had responded to his chess game.

"Good, Paul," Gallagher said. "Keep me posted if you need anything."

Then Regal had called Inspector Burton's office to give him the same news, but Burton was out and he left a message to call back.

By midafternoon, when Burton still had not called, Regal phoned him again. Burton answered the phone himself.

Regal briefed him quickly on the new message, then asked, "Hear anything about the earlier phone tapes?"

Burton hesitated just a split second before answering, as if wondering whether he should share his information with his fellow inspector, then said, "Nothing good. The lab went over them and said it's some kind of computerized voice, which is just telling us what we already knew."

Regal remained silent.

"Did you know, Regal, that people now can buy programs for their home computers and then the computers will speak anything you type?"

"No," Regal said, "but I don't know anything about computers."

"Well, they can. The lab said a half dozen companies sell the program and it doesn't even cost two hundred dollars. No way of telling how many there are in New York City."

"Well, maybe that's a break," Regal said.

"How so?"

"If this guy is using his computer to call me, he's probably doing it from his home or his office . . . some fixed location. That might make it easier for us to trace the call."

"No such luck," Burton said. "The lab said the voice was recorded from a computer onto a little tape recorder. Probably one of those handheld battery jobs. And I suspect the bastard carried it to a phone booth to call you from there. The lab can tell all this stuff by the quality of the sound or something . . . some bullshit that I don't know anything about. But they analyzed street traffic in the background noise. Probably a phone booth but no knowing where."

"So the tapes are a dead end," Regal said.

"Yeah."

"I'll keep making them anyway when he calls."

"Naturally," Burton said.

" 'Cause he might make a mistake. A fire siren or something in the background might tip us on location."

"Exactly," Burton said. "Your phone trace in yet?"

"Yeah. This morning. Unfortunately right after he called."

"What'd he say exactly?"

"He said no more deaths as long as I give him an interesting game," Regal answered.

"Then you'd better get home and start studying the chess books," Burton said. "And send that new tape straight to the lab."

"I already did," Regal said. "I just hope they can keep their mouths shut about it. Looks like somebody's already been yapping to the papers. Monogram Murders and that crap."

"Yeah," Burton agreed sourly. "It busts you, doesn't it? But we were stuck. Too many cops knew about those carved-up bodies for it to stay secret for long. Especially with the mayor shooting his yap off. But the chess game. That's all ours and nobody knows."

"Let's hope it stays all ours," Regal said.

"It better. Or you and I are in big trouble."

There did not seem to be much to say after that and Regal took Burton's advice and went home to study the chess book and to prepare his response to go into the *Times*.

As he sat at his dining room table, looking through the chess book he had semi-figured out, a chilling thought wormed into Regal's mind. It was true that this was a chess game and he was just thinking of what piece to move. But it was more than that. It was life and death and who knew what the crazy son-of-a-bitch killer was likely to do; who could guess what was going to trigger his violence again?

The mechanical message had said no more killings as long as the game stayed interesting. But what defined "interesting"? The awful truth was that the life of some innocent person or persons might right now rest in Regal's hands and he did not know what the murderer required of him. It wasn't bad enough that he had to worry about playing a game at which he was just the rankest of amateurs; he had to worry about people's lives too.

Another thought gripped him, so forcibly that Regal bolted from the table to the nearest telephone.

He found Burton just about to leave his office.

"What is it, Regal?"

"Joe, you have men out on street patrols in the chess-board area?"

"Yeah. I've got squads all over."

"Have them keep an extra eye on Sixty-ninth to Seventieth between Park and Lexington."

"Why?" Burton said. "You hear something?"

"No," Regal said. "But today when he called in his move, he played white bishop takes knight. My knight was in that square block. I just thought that he might use his move to put on another demonstration of a dead knight."

Burton was silent for a moment before he said, "He told you no more killing if the game stays interesting, though."

"That's right, Joe, that's what he said. But do you trust him?"

"You're right, Paul. The bastard's nuts. He's liable to say anything. I'll flood that area tonight with plainclothesmen. If he shows up to deliver a body, we'll have him."

"Good, Joe. Sorry to throw this at you at the last minute but it just popped into my mind."

"No problem. Good thinking. Now you'd better get back to the chessboard."

And, as always, Burton abruptly hung up. And Regal,

with a sigh, took his advice and went back to the chess book.

But the murderer did not show up; no bodies were found, and the next morning, Regal sat in his crisp, rarely used dress uniform, in a Bronx church at the departmental funeral for Pete Muniz.

He had seen the mayor and Commissioner Gallagher walking in together and, despite the surroundings, had been silently amused by the fact that the mayor was wearing one black sock and one brown one.

Regal wondered whether the mayor's personal staff were so dumb they hadn't noticed or if they simply didn't give a damn. They were civilians; maybe that's how they thought a politician dressed for a cop's funeral.

On the other side of the church, Jane Cole and her daughter, Sarah, sat in a front row beside the small Muniz family. Jane had her arm around Pete's youngest sister, a twelve-year-old girl who looked dazed and uncomprehending. Everyone else in the row was crying unashamedly, as were many others in the large old Roman Catholic church. Regal caught Sarah's eye and the girl smiled at him.

He was glad Patrice had declined to accompany him to the service. "Sorry, darling, I don't do funerals," she had told him. "And frankly, I'm too busy. It's simply a madhouse at Storm Mountain, getting ready for the opening. It's just a couple of weeks now and if you don't watch those workmen like a hawk, they make every kind of stupid mistake you could imagine. You have to stay on top of them all the time."

"You're good at that," he had observed quietly.

"Yes, I am," she agreed, patting his cheek. "Have a nice time, dear, and do give my regards to the moron mayor if you happen to speak to him."

"Nice time? Dammit, Patrice, it's a cop's funeral."

"Well, life goes on, doesn't it?" she said blithely. "And don't forget, we've got a charity ball tonight. We should get there about eight. Don't eat. There'll be lots of food."

"Charity at eight," he had sighed. "Got it. Is Oliver going to be there?"

"Better believe it, Buster. He's running for mayor publicly now. He'll be everywhere. And besides, he's the chairman of this one. It's to save Central Park."

"Oliver Storm *and* Central Park too. Oh, joy," Regal had said, but Patrice either did not hear him or chose not to respond to his sarcasm.

Life was strange, he thought, as the elderly red-faced priest gravely performed his solemn ritual. Here he sat, mourning the untimely death of a young friend and trusted fellow policeman. In a short while, he would see Pete's casket lowered into the ground, while on a nearby hillside one of the department's bagpipers would play "Amazing Grace" and the rifle squad would fire a final volley over Muniz's body. And then it would be back to the office and business-as-usual, dirty fingernail-breaking police business.

But then tonight, he'd be in a sumptuous hotel ballroom, surrounded by some of the richest men and most beautifully adorned women in the world, and not one of them would give a damn about poor Pete Muniz.

And would he? Would he be thinking of Peter then or would he be caught up in the glitter and gaiety of the occasion, exchanging laughing banalities with the men and perfunctory innuendos with the women?

He knelt and bowed his head with the rest of the congregation, banishing the thought, focusing instead on good memories of Pete Muniz. Sufficient unto tonight was the drivel thereof.

The advertisement appeared again in the next morning's *Times*. A single line, again signed with Regal's initials *P.R.*:

BxN   QPxB

It repeated the move the caller had recited to Regal yesterday and the response the policeman had found from his book of chess openings. Black's queen pawn takes white's bishop. Regal had inspected the ad carefully to make sure there were no typographical errors.

The ad was fine, but this time the killer did not call. Regal waited until almost 6 P.M.—as long as he could— but there was no sign of the Monogram Murderer.

He wondered if he should have made arrangements to have his office phone transferred after hours to his home number. *No,* he decided. *Whoever it is hasn't had any trouble reaching me here during office hours. He knows it's my office and if he doesn't call before five, he's just not calling that day.*

That thought made him feel a little better and he left for his apartment. But he hoped that there would not be another killing tonight.

Regal considered himself a quiet and modest man, not given to ostentation or display. But he freely admitted to himself that he had a weakness for good clothes and liked to look well dressed in an understated, modest way. In fact, he often thought that one of the reasons that Joe Burton detested him was that Burton always looked like an unmade bed. He and Tony Bolda must have gone to the same finishing school.

This came to mind as he dressed in his tuxedo at his apartment. It was a good suit that he had had for eight years, and he thought if he was lucky he might be able to wear it for another eight.

Just another clotheshorse, he thought wryly. But when he entered the ballroom of the Centurion Hotel with Patrice, he knew that no one was looking at his tuxedo. All eyes went to his lovely wife—not only those of the men, who admired her beauty, but also those of the women, who envied everything about her . . . her beauty, her makeup, her poise and confidence.

She strolled almost arrogantly beside him, looking around and nodding at her many friends and acquaintances. Regal almost laughed aloud when he noticed one middle-aged man, wearing a flamboyant red plaid cummerbund much too youthful for his portly frame, stare so intently at Patrice that when he absentmindedly raised his cocktail for a sip, he spilled most of it down the front of his ruffled shirt.

They found Pierre LeBlanc, Patrice's business partner, waiting for them at their table.

"Oh, you look absolutely divine," Pierre gushed. "Oh, God, if only I were straight, I'd kiss your hands and feet and all points in between. Especially your belly button."

"Now, Pete, don't act like a fool tonight," Patrice scolded in a tone that said she was very pleased. "Anyway, being kissed on the belly button doesn't sound very romantic."

"Ah, but from the inside?" giggled LeBlanc. He nodded to Regal. "We have champagne, sent over by Oliver Storm. Shall I open it?"

"Go ahead, Pete," Regal told him. "But watch out with that cork. The last time I saw you open a bottle, you bounced it off two walls and nailed a woman in the back of the head."

"A remarkable carom shot, executed with the skill I developed playing pool for money as a child back in dear old Cicero, Illinois," LeBlanc boasted as he expertly loosened the wiring, then covered the top of the bottle with a thick cloth napkin. "And besides, that dreadful woman deserved it. I knew the moment she walked into the party that I wanted to do something violent to her."

He poured the champagne into three glasses with a flourish. "Not the best of brands but one must forgive. When one has as much money as Oliver Storm, one doesn't need also to have taste. He can simply buy it from more gifted people like Patrice and myself."

She looked at him sharply, even as she accepted the glass. "I'm not for sale, Pete."

"Then you're the only person here who isn't," LeBlanc said blandly. "Do you think all these people are here because they share Oliver Storm's wonderful vision of saving Central Park for future generations? For shame, child. I thought I taught you better than that. They are here because they are hoping that Oliver Storm will want to buy them body and soul. Right, Paul?"

Regal, determined not to be drawn into the middle of an argument, said mildly, "Damned if I know. I'm here because Patrice told me I'd better be."

"I stand corrected," LeBlanc said. "And I'm glad you're here. Just in the event that someone shows up with a machine gun. I will hide behind you."

"Not too close behind," Regal said. "Flamer."

As LeBlanc chuckled, Patrice said, "I see someone. You two stay right here. I'll be back in two minutes."

"We've both heard that before," LeBlanc said, but he seemed almost relieved to see her go.

Regal eyed LeBlanc with amusement as the younger man watched Patrice sweep across the floor to embrace two women on the other side of the dance floor, and then he let his eyes methodically look over the rapidly filling hall. In truth, Regal was glad LeBlanc was there; once he got past his obligatory impersonation of a homosexual queen, he always turned out to be good company.

The policeman wondered how many people in the room would believe that Pierre LeBlanc was born plain Peter White back in Illinois. Regal knew that LeBlanc was considered in these circles to be the cutting edge of French fashion and tonight he was wearing an avant-garde blue tuxedo that looked as if it might glow in the dark. The man was tall and skeletally thin, with a death's-head face—prominent cheekbones and a nose like a knife—and in the suit he looked like a demented Hollywood version of a high school prom ax murderer. It never seemed to matter. LeBlanc had élan and his flamboyant style made most men and women find him charming, except for the handful that loathed him on sight.

And Regal knew that LeBlanc was not as brazenly homosexual as he claimed to be. Where there was constantly smoke, surely there must be some fire, but he often saw LeBlanc looking at women with a gaze that was nothing but lustful and he had finally decided that LeBlanc's almost excessive swishiness was an artifice, a persona adopted for business reasons to conceal his real personality.

He had no problem, though, in admitting to himself that, gay or straight or bisexual or whatever, he liked the man. He was talented, hard working, witty and considerate, and in a curious way, Regal regarded him as a man he might trust in a time of trouble.

"Is that true about the pool hall days?" Regal asked.

"You wound me, Paul. Would I lie to you?"

"To me and everyone else, you rascal."

"Ahhh, so quickly you learn all my secrets, no doubt because of my own big mouth. Actually, it is true. There was a period in my teens when I practically lived in a pool hall, and I made a lot of money at it." He sipped his drink and Regal saw that he was wearing a light blue eyeliner. "Pool is, I suspect, like police work. Luck will get you through once in a while but to succeed consistently requires talent."

"Hear, hear," Regal said.

"But, alas, pool is behind me now. It no longer fits my image."

"And image is all, right?"

"Wrong as usual, Paul. Not all, but much. Clothing, uniforms, the way teenagers dress. It's all involved with one's image. For instance, I can tell by the way that suit fits you that you gave its selection and tailoring a great deal of attention. Because you want it to reinforce your own image of yourself."

Regal laughed. "You're shrewd, Pete. I give up. Image is important. And thank God for that. Isn't it what you and Patrice sell? Giving people an image, through your designs, that they couldn't give themselves?"

"Exactly, my friend. We're con artists and we charge

people to help them con the rest of the world."

"Are you charging them enough? How's business?"

"I'll be glad when this Storm Mountain business is over. Your dear wife has been driving me crazy. She has gotten too personally involved in this assignment. Nothing is ever good enough. Everything has to be better." He took a healthy swallow of his champagne, then made a face at its taste.

"Will things be better after the opening?"

"One certainly hopes so."

Regal studied him. "Are you and Patrice having business troubles?"

"Aren't we always?"

Regal shook his head. "You've always bickered and had a few spats but no real troubles. At least that's what I thought."

"That was then," LeBlanc said. "Now . . . well, she's changed."

"Since she met Oliver Storm?"

The other man glanced at him sharply, then turned away to study the people still arriving. "I don't know if that's a factor or not. Maybe she just feels that she's outgrown me and doesn't need me anymore."

"I don't like hearing that, Pete," Regal said with a frown. "I know Patrice feels a lot more confident about her abilities now than she did when you two first got together, but I think she'd be a damn fool to break up the act. You two are good together. And you're still the brains of the operation."

"Thank you, Paul. I have to confess that I think you're right but you know how headstrong Patrice can be."

"A whim of iron," Regal agreed. "Who knows? Maybe she thinks she's outgrowing both of us."

"You say that very calmly, Paul. Like a man who doesn't care."

Regal sighed. "Who knows anymore? I think Patrice has got something going with Storm and I think about it and I guess, you're right, I just don't give a damn any more. I'm just waiting for the other shoe to drop."

LeBlanc shook his head. "Life's a bitch, isn't it? For what it's worth, I can't swear that there's anything going on there—although if I did know, I probably wouldn't say anything to you anyway. I like you, Paul, and I wouldn't want to see you get hurt. But the truth is, Patrice is more and more secretive these days. A lot of the time, I don't know where she is or what she's doing. It's playing hell with the shop's operation."

"You shouldn't care, Pete," Regal said. "You don't need Patrice as much as she needs you. If you two split, you'd probably be better off in the long run."

"You're a sweetheart," LeBlanc said. "And you might be right, but let's face it, I was small-time until Patrice and I got together. Her contacts from modeling were great then and she has even more now. She's the best front man in the world." Mockingly, he licked his finger and wiped his eyebrow and affected a bizarre English accent. "I don't know why but some people become ridiculously affronted when I tell them that their taste is shit and they should shut their stupid mouths."

Regal laughed. "Well, maybe you *do* come on just a little strong. You know, perhaps you're right. Maybe you do need Patrice. Why don't you talk her into divorcing me and marrying you?"

A look of horror swept over LeBlanc's face and he clutched dramatically at his throat, started to speak, then froze. "Speak of the devil," he said softly. "Here comes the King of Kitsch himself."

14

Regal looked up to see Oliver Storm approaching, walking amidst a gaggle of teenagers.

In his early fifties, Storm was tall enough to carry his considerable bulk with authority. He was dressed conservatively—in a handmade suit, Regal saw—and he radiated the confidence of what he was: a pampered only-child who had taken a substantial family fortune and enlarged it.

Storm's father, one of the city's leading slumlords, had sent his son to Groton and Princeton, where he had majored in business and pleasure. His first wife, the mother of his twin children, had died in a boating accident ten years ago and Storm had gone through two brief marriages since then, both times to busty blonde screen starlets.

The first had committed suicide and the second marriage had ended in a quick expensive divorce. Since them, Storm referred to himself in the press as a three-time loser, but he was still often seen and photographed in the company of beautiful women, among whom, lately, Patrice Regal had been the most prominent.

Regal knew him only from the press but he would have guessed that Storm's only real love was the relentless promotion of his personal wealth and renown. He had moved the family real estate firm into glitzy office buildings and high-priced apartments. And now everything had been put aside to make way for his latest monument to bad taste, unlimited credit and an avalanche of self-promotion—Storm Mountain, a sixty-story condominium occupying an entire block on East Sixty-eighth Street, with options on surrounding property already in hand for possible future expansion. It was literally a blockbuster of a real estate deal and the total cost was now talked about as "near a billion dollars."

The selling theme for the residence—as Regal had heard often enough in the past few months to make his eyes glaze over—was safety. All the building's personnel—even the doormen and custodial staff—were former policemen, and at higher levels were retired FBI and CIA people, all well trained in counterterrorism. Regal had once heard Storm boast on television that even the maids would be licensed to carry weapons.

The huge building itself was promoted as a gold-plated fortress, all shrewdly designed to attract the ultrawealthy who wanted a New York City address but feared—or perhaps even hoped—that "they" were out to get them and that they needed and deserved the maximum in personal protection.

Even at exorbitant prices, most of the units had sold quickly, establishing a new standard for successful avarice in the real estate business, and while no one had yet mentioned it publicly, Regal thought it was uproarious that mixed in among the Japanese business tycoons and Arab oil sheiks who had purchased early were a large number of Mafia bosses, apparently willing to pay the price for the luxury of being able to sleep at night without being awakened by a bomb outside the bedroom window.

Who was it that said, "He who creates the deluge often gets wet," Regal wondered.

And while gangland thugs might be considered a little crude for Storm's usual social circles, the man might not have much choice, Regal thought, because rumors had been circulating that he was now so highly leveraged that his entire financial structure could come crashing down at any time.

One cynical newspaper columnist had even suggested that Storm's sudden announcement of his candidacy for mayor might have had less to do with his desire to clean up the city than it did with finding a way to protect himself from sudden bank foreclosures on his property. After all, what New York City bank would want to foreclose on a man who might just be the city's mayor in another year?

Regal saw Patrice hustling across the floor toward their table from a different direction. She got there before Storm and sat down, but not in her earlier seat where she was flanked by Regal and LeBlanc. With a wry expression, LeBlanc silently picked up his glass and moved over next to Regal and the two men exchanged knowing smiles.

Storm's progress across the ballroom floor was slow, interrupted by dozens of handshakes and political cheek kisses. Already, a bodyguard had stationed himself near the table, Regal noted.

Finally Storm arrived and greeted Patrice and her two escorts with gusto. "Hello, you gorgeous animal. How are you? Inspector! Glad you could make it. LeBlanc, you're a genius. Great work you and Patrice are doing on Storm Mountain."

In the meanwhile, the four teenagers behind Storm were shifting uncomfortably from foot to foot, and finally Storm turned around and waved toward them.

"You've all met my twins, Tim and Marcie. And their dates and I'm sorry I don't know their names, but since they're not old enough to vote yet, I don't think it'll hurt." He smiled. "The kids are probably leaving early but I wanted them here for a while tonight. I think it's a good part of their education to be exposed to charity fund-raisers like this, don't you think?"

"I couldn't agree more," Patrice said with solemn conviction, and Regal wanted to kick her under the table for her patently phony attack of civic sensibility. "It's essential for young people," she said.

It also didn't hurt Storm's image as a family man despite his three marriages, Regal thought. And there was no bimbo on his arm tonight. *He really is serious about running for mayor.*

Regal had met the two Storm youngsters once before and Patrice seemed well acquainted with them, having often taken Marcie shopping. Until that moment, Regal had never realized they were twins, and looking at them now, the only similarity they seemed to share was a bored, uninterested expression. Tim was as tall as his father but weight lifter beefy with a bland impassive expression and dark bovine eyes. His tuxedo was wrinkled across his huge shoulders and not any too clean and Regal wondered what seventeen-year-old wore a tuxedo often enough for it to look threadbare. Marcie was tallish too for a girl, although not as big as Tim, and had lighter hair surrounding a lean and angular face with bright shining eyes and a wide mouth that frequently twisted nervously in odd ways.

Storm nudged Tim to introduce their dates. Tim was with a plain-faced but expensively dressed girl and Regal recognized her last name as that of one of the state's leading political brokers. Marcie's date was a twittery but good-looking young man who seemed to freeze solid when Marcie glanced at him, as if he was afraid of her. Regal noticed LeBlanc eyeing the young man speculatively and muttered out of the corner of his mouth, "Jail bait." LeBlanc responded with a surprise sputter of champagne and a hiccup and Paul said, "Two points for me."

The five people sat, with Storm directly across the table from Regal. His twins were together on his left and on his right were, oddly enough, their dates. Tim's date sat next to Patrice with a contented expression on her face and Patrice, disappointed at not having Storm by her side, turned away from her. The orchestra struck up a medley of 1920s hits.

Regal had imagined that a lot of people who had bought tickets months ago for this fund-raiser might be annoyed that Storm had announced his mayoral candidacy and, in essence, had changed it to a political rally. But no one *seemed* annoyed and a steady procession of people came to the table to wish the real estate man well.

Eventually Patrice became bored with leaning forward, pretending interest in Storm's political discussions, and she turned swiftly toward Regal and said brightly, "Let's dance, Paul."

"I wanted to wait for 'Happy Days Are Here Again,' " he said, but Oliver Storm did not hear the jibe so Regal nodded and led her to the floor. As they circled, he noticed Pierre LeBlanc talking to Marcie's date, who seemed fascinated. Marcie and Tim were both staring at their father, and the plain girl who was Tim's date sat smiling at nothing in particular, trying to look at ease and not succeeding very well.

"I feel sorry for those kids, being dragged to a thing like this," Regal commented as he danced Patrice smoothly through the crowd. "Oh, sorry, I forgot. It's 'essential for young people,' isn't it?" he said, in a voice that mocked her earlier comment.

She had obviously forgotten making the statement. "I don't know if it's essential or not but I would have given my eyeteeth to be able to go to dances like this when I was growing up."

"They're bored out of their skulls. If this keeps up, they'll be happy to get back to Groton or wherever the hell they go to school."

"Groton is right. And you're wrong. The top people in New York are here tonight and those kids are lucky."

The music stopped and they strolled back to their table, where Regal asked Storm, "Did you take notes on all the good advice you got in the last fifteen minutes?"

"All up here," Storm said, tapping his temple. "When I get home, I'll write it all down. On the head of a pin." He paused. "How about you, Paul? You have any good advice for me?"

"Sure. Promise the police a hefty raise. Tell those overpaid pinochle-playing firemen that parity is finished. Promise to cut taxes and lower the subway fare. And swear that you'll never allow George Steinbrenner in the city again. Do that, and I'll even vote for you."

"You could do more than vote," Storm said in an obvious political probe.

"Afraid not, Oliver," Regal said in a politely regretful voice. "I've never been involved in politics at any level and I have no desire to start. But if I did, my first loyalty would be to Commissioner Gallagher. Get his endorsement and you and I can talk business."

"Paul!" gasped Patrice.

Storm laughed. "He's right, Patsy. He has to be loyal to Gallagher. If he said otherwise, I wouldn't trust him or have any respect for him. But you never know. Gallagher's a good man. We might find him aboard someday."

When hell freezes over, Regal thought. He leaned forward. "As long as we're on politics, do you mind if I ask if you have any plans for Patrice to take a public role in your campaign?"

His wife's head snapped toward him as if pulled on a spring. She looked flustered and yet somehow pleased.

Storm said, "I hadn't thought about it, but now that you mention it, I can see why you might be concerned. No, I won't do anything that would put you in an embarrassing position, Paul."

"Thank you. That's considerate," Regal said.

Patrice exhibited alarm. "But we have so much to do," she protested to Storm. "All those plans we discussed."

"Relax, darling," LeBlanc cooed from across the table. "They're talking politics, not business."

"He's right," Storm said as Patrice turned to glare at her partner. "You and Pierre figure very largely in my future business plans. But it could be an embarrassment for Paul if you played any obvious role in my campaign."

"They can't do anything to Paul. He's Civil Service," she protested.

Both men laughed at that and Storm explained gently, "Dear, if Paul wound up on the hit list in the department, they could find ways to make him very uncomfortable indeed, Civil Service or no Civil Service."

They already have, Regal thought. *My squad has been gutted. The commissioner's office door is closed to me and the ratsquad is trying to figure out if I'm a crook. Maybe I should hit them with my Civil Service certification form. And we'll see what tomorrow brings after Gallagher finds out—and he will—that I was sitting with the mayor's leading political opponent.*

He yearned for the old days when life was simple and uncomplicated—like maybe a week ago.

"I'll be Patrice's substitute on the campaign trail," LeBlanc volunteered with girlish enthusiasm. "I twirl a mean baton and I just adore leading parades."

Marcie tittered and Tim snorted, but Storm said, "Why not? Just deliver all your friends' votes to me, Pete."

"And then I can twirl my baton?"

"Have you really got one?" Marcie asked.

LeBlanc nodded. "You better believe it. A really big one. I twirl it like an airplane propeller."

"Stop it, Pierre," Patrice ordered. "You're impossible."

"You're just jealous because at last you will stay behind the scenes while I get a chance to scintillate in front of an adoring public."

Patrice gave him a tight-lipped smile while Marcie sniggered. Regal wondered idly if perhaps LeBlanc had already had too much to drink.

The music started again and Storm stood. "Paul, may I borrow your wife for a dance?"

"Be my guest."

They walked away and Regal looked at Tim and Marcie. "Why don't you young folks get out there too? Or is this music too awful for you?"

Tim looked at his sister. "Might as well," she shrugged, giving her date a poke in the side with her elbow. The four young people rose and left Regal with LeBlanc.

"Are you aware that several photographers have been snapping away at us?" Pete asked.

"I saw them," Regal shrugged. "I just didn't think it would look too good if I tried to pull my coat over my head. But I wish she'd have told me we were sitting with Storm. I hate surprises."

"If I were you, I wouldn't have been surprised," LeBlanc said.

The two men glanced at each other again and Regal said, "She's going to have your ass for breakfast the next time you two are alone. You and your damned baton." He chuckled.

"I don't care," LeBlanc said. "It was worth it. And those two drippy kids of his ate it up. I don't think they like her very much."

"I didn't notice. But do me a favor. Pick fights with Patrice on your own time, okay?"

"I promise. She's had a tough enough night. After all, she set this whole thing up so that we had a nice table for eight and she arranges everything to sit next to Storm and instead she gets little Miss Pudgy Face from Scarsdale. No wonder she's feeling testy."

Regal glanced out at the dance floor, now well crowded with swaying couples. Storm and Patrice were at a corner of the floor, dancing close together. He suddenly felt remote and weary and oddly guilty.

Guilty because he was supposed to care but he didn't. If it made Patrice happy to dance with Oliver Storm or sleep with him or whatever, then let her have her fun.

Their marriage had eroded to the point where it existed in name only, a legal fiction and a social habit.

He still wished her well but he realized that he did not love her anymore and he wondered idly if she had ever loved him—or anyone but herself.

He took a swallow of the champagne. It was bitter and the bubbles stung his tongue and Pete Muniz was dead.

Regal excused himself and got up to call his office to see if there were any messages.

15

As he had every night for the last two weeks, Paul Regal, after calling in his chess move to the *New York Times*, went for a walk around the Upper East Side.

Unless there was another killing, his day's work was over. Sometime tomorrow, the killer would see the chess move in the *Times* and call in his response.

Within no more than a minute after the brief tape-recorded message was received, police who monitored Regal's private line in the basement communications center would have the location of the calling phone. The routine was well developed now and squad cars would race to the location and find exactly what they had found for the past two weeks—nothing but an empty phone booth. The calls were made from all over Manhattan, which made it impossible to stake out all the booths in any geographical area, and almost always the booths were in busy hotel lobbies or on almost deserted street corners where no one ever saw who had been using the telephone only minutes before. The few reports the police had gotten about the caller's identity had not helped at all. Some thought a man might have made the call; some thought a woman. None of the sightings came with anything that even resembled a description.

The tapes of the calls themselves, analyzed scrupulously every day at the police and FBI laboratories, contained no clues either.

The sad truth, Regal realized, was that the police were no closer to finding out the killer's identity than they had been when the first derelict was found almost a month earlier stuffed into a garbage pail.

He wondered if that was why he had started these nightly prowls through his neighborhood, just in the hope of stumbling on, by luck, what he and the rest of the police could not discover by hard work.

The first few times he had ventured out, he had pretended to be surprised when he found himself walking past the spots where the three victims of the Monogram Murderer had been found. He no longer tried to convince himself he was doing something else, but instead he walked briskly right to the three locations. The farthest away—where Big Ben Keane had been found—was on Sixty-ninth between Lexington and Third Avenues, fewer than ten blocks from Regal's apartment, and he now had a routine of going there first, then coming back along Seventy-first Street where the bodies of the vagrant and the biker had been found, only a block apart but on separate sides of the street.

The criminal always comes back to the scene of the crime. But he did not expect that, not for a second. In the first place, all three killings had been committed somewhere else. This neighborhood was just the dumping ground for bodies.

But even more than that, Regal believed that the killer was not the normal garden-variety psychopath, driven by lusts he could not control.

This one has a plan. These killings have a meaning. And I've just got to find out what it is.

It was a searing steambath of a July evening, and although it was just past eleven o'clock, the streets were almost empty of pedestrians as Regal walked again past the brownstone outside which Keane's body had been found.

Why?

Why in a leaf bag?

Why in this neighborhood?

And why's the son of a bitch calling me about it?

Regal had no answer to that. He stopped and pretended to be looking for a cigarette in his shirt pocket. There was no one to be seen in either direction along the darkened block and he realized that the public had begun to lose interest in the killings. When he had first started these nightly walks two weeks earlier, he often saw people gawking on the sidewalk, pointing out the sites where the bodies had been found, but that interest seemed to be dying.

It helped, he guessed, that the schools were closed for summer vacation. If they had been open, with the herd-like instinct of the young, every kid in the city school system by now would be walking around with initials painted on his head. But that little fad too had died out. So had the late night television jokes about New York City as the home of "thoughtful murderers who monogram your body before stuffing it into a garbage can."

Even the governor had stopped "viewing with alarm." The press coverage had tailed off and a casual observer might have thought that the police had even slowed down on the investigation.

And that casual observer would have been very wrong.

Joe Burton was driving his men mercilessly through the dismal slogging that most detective work actually was. Neighborhoods had been canvassed three and four times but the answer was always the same: no one had seen anything. The garbage pails that the bodies were found in had been tracked down, but they were three different brands, common objects sold in most big grocery and hardware stores, and had been a dead end.

The background of the victims had been checked and

rechecked but there was no connection between any of them, except the obvious one that each had had the bad luck to drift into the path of a homicidal maniac.

Nothing on the tapes. Nothing on the nature of the initials carved into the victims' bodies. Everywhere the police investigated, they turned up nothing.

It had all gotten so dismal that just five days earlier Joe Burton had reluctantly agreed to call in the behavioral science unit of the FBI.

Commissioner Gallagher had decided on it and Burton groused about the decision in a phone call to Regal.

"They're a bunch of shrinks, for Christ's sake. What do they know?"

"I don't know," Regal had said blandly. "You know, they do come up with good profiles, especially in motiveless stuff like this."

"Yeah? You like them so much, you deal with them."

"Sorry, Joe. This is your case. As you keep reminding me."

Regal had wondered why Burton had such a loathing for any new methods in police work. Was that a sign of getting old, when you didn't want anything to change so that you didn't have to learn anything new?

Or maybe it's just from knowing you're right in the first place, Regal thought.

At any rate, the FBI men had come in, three of them, professorial, well dressed, and coolly efficient, and had met with Burton in his office. One of them came down to interview Regal. Another had gone to talk to the coroner. The third went to the places where the bodies were found.

They hung around for two days but they were already out of Regal's mind when Burton had telephoned again.

"They're so freaking smart, they should give me his freaking phone number," he had snarled.

Regal knew immediately that the older policeman was talking about the FBI.

"What did they say?"

"That's the trouble," Burton said. "They said everything. It's what you always get from these scientific types. It's why I hate you and all the rest of the computer nerds just like you. Wait a minute, I have their notes here. Did you know, Regal, that we have an organized killer and not a disorganized killer on our hands?"

Regal mumbled noncommittally.

"It takes strength to kill somebody with a knife and lug his body around in a garbage pail, so our killer's probably a man. That's what they say. I say maybe she's a freaking lady wrestler. But he's organized even if he is a lady wrestler because he brought along his own weapon, which makes him a stalker. Maybe even cunning. Probably comes from a broken home. Probably right-handed because of the way the bodies were cut. Probably intelligent and skilled in his job and maybe depressed and under stress. I hope you're writing all this down, Regal. Depressed? The son of a bitch ought to be depressed 'cause when I get him, I'm gonna rip his freaking throat out."

"That might account for his stress too," Regal offered.

"No jokes from you. You're responsible for these guys."

"Me?"

"Yeah. People like you with your freaking computers and your psychological horseshit and pretty soon everybody believes it's on the level instead of just being a crock. There's more. The killer apparently doesn't take souvenirs from the bodies—nothing's been missing that we know of—and that doesn't quite fit the pattern. But maybe if the press writes a lot of stories, it'll make him jumpy and change his behavior. Screw that, I said. Let him stick with the same behavior 'cause right now he's not killing anybody. And probably, they said, he didn't know any of the victims."

"How'd they know that?"

"Something about the wounds. Nutsos, I guess, carve out the eyeballs or something of people they know. Anyway, they guess this guy likes to read about himself in the paper and they said he might maybe change jobs and leave town."

Burton paused and Regal said, "That was it?"

"That was it. Oh, they said the whole thing was a little unusual because serial killers usually kill women or children and not men and they said maybe we should keep an eye on the place where the bodies were dropped because sometimes killers like to go back to the scene of the crime, and I told them nobody goes back to the scenes of these crimes except you when you're wandering around the streets at night."

Regal was surprised. "You know about that?"

"I know everything you do, Regal, and don't forget it. So do me a favor, will you. Take all your modern methods of criminology and the FBI too and stick them where the sun don't shine."

"Gee, Joe, sure thing," Regal said mockingly. But into a dead phone.

Regal found himself walking into his own apartment building. As he rode up to his floor, he thought there wasn't much point in his nightly patrols if he performed them as if he were sleepwalking, hardly noticing the streets at all.

We're all sleepwalkers. The whole damned department. And there's a murderer out there stuffing corpses into garbage pails and he's laughing at us. And there are others who killed poor Pete Muniz and that investigation is dead in the water too.

Why did I ever sign on to be a cop?

When the twin investigations had started, Burton had called in a lot of additional manpower from other police units in the city. Now he was under increasing pressure to send the men back to their regular jobs. The constant complaints were doing nothing for his disposition.

Oliver Storm kept peddling his Decade of Terror mayoral campaign speech whenever he could, but even he seemed to have put his campaign mostly on hold while he tended to the plans for the grand opening of Storm

Mountain, now less than two weeks away. Patrice Regal also seemed to regard it as the greatest event since Columbus discovered America and she now spent even less time at home.

And Paul Regal just didn't care. He had other things to worry about.

The next morning, he went into the neighborhood branch of his bank to make a deposit and the branch manager, who recognized him, asked if he had gotten the reports he requested.

"Reports? Which reports?"

"On all yours and Mrs. Regal's deposits and withdrawals. For your IRS audit." When he still looked blank, the manager said, "I gave them to the man from your office."

"Oh, yes. I remember now," Regal said. "Thanks."

He knew immediately what it meant. Inspector Vincent Flaherty's men from Internal Affairs were checking Regal's bank records to see if there were any signs of activity that might indicate Regal was playing around with dirty drug money.

Well, let them look. They'll find nothing there.

He had heard nothing directly from Flaherty or his investigators. That could mean one of two things: they had already dropped their investigation into a possible leak in Regal's squad; or they were still looking but had not yet been able to find anything to implicate Regal or his men. Unfortunately, a third possibility was not so promising: they had already compiled enough of a case against Regal or someone in his squad and were preparing to present it to a grand jury to seek indictments.

And the bastards will never tell you which scenario is correct, Regal thought, *but they're still sniffing around my bank so I don't think that means that they're done with us. Not just yet.*

He sat at his desk later that day, feeling sorry for himself. With a conscious effort of will, he pushed the IAD probe from his mind and went back to worriedly studying the chess book he had bought, trying to decide on his next move. Now he was clearly out of his element. He needed assistance and even though Commissioner Gallagher was even more resolutely dodging him—had it been because of his attendance at Oliver Storm's Save-the-Park fund-raiser?—he had to get help at the chess-board.

He decided cautiously on his next move, jotted it down on paper, then walked outside partly to get coffee, mostly to talk to Jane Cole. In the last two frustrating weeks, a sort of mild boss-employee friendship had grown between the two. Regal knew now about her family, her friends, her background, and as his own marriage chilled and he found himself more alone, more friendless, he had started to look forward to the conversations, the occasional shared cup of coffee with the pretty red-haired detective.

"The usual on the phone trace?" he asked, referring to the killer's call earlier that day.

She nodded. "Phone booth in Soho. Nobody saw anything."

"Well, we just keep trying."

"Why even bother?" she groused. "It's not doing any good."

"You're right, Jane, but we keep doing it so that nobody can jump on us for not doing it. And we might just get lucky," Regal explained patiently.

"Make-work," she snorted.

"Self-defense," he said.

She walked over to Bolda's desk and swept some of the litter on it into a wastebasket. "Still nothing new on Pete?"

Regal shook his head. "A complete dead end so far. Tony has been running all over Spanish Harlem looking for Estrellita, and Narcotics is working on it too. We keep hearing rumors about some new drug guys in town and maybe those are our Panamanians but we can't nail it down. Meanwhile, Homicide is helpless. They're just going through the motions, waiting for us or Narcotics to give them a lead."

"Inspector Burton must be pleasant these days," she said.

"He's not happy," Regal agreed, "but who can blame him? Nobody's feeling real good. He's stalled on Pete and he's stalled on the alphabet killings. It's quiet now, but who the hell knows. Somebody decides to run a memorial for Big Ben or some zany tattoos his own head with a butcher knife and decides to shoot up a Gristede's and the press is all over him again. It'd make me antsy too."

The young detective visibly started as the telephone rang. She answered the call, spoke briefly, and then hung up.

"I've been taking some strolls uptown," she told Regal casually.

He frowned at her. "How far uptown?"

"The Spanish area."

"Why?"

"Pete."

"Jane, Burton has dozens of guys moving through there—guys who know how to handle themselves and not get hurt. You don't even know how to speak Spanish. Do you?"

"I know a few words. Anyway, I bring an interpreter."

"Who?"

"A guy," she said evasively.

"If he was a friend of yours, he wouldn't take you up there. Jane, stay out of this."

"Just sit and wait and wonder if they're ever going to find the bastard that killed Pete? Forget it," she flared. "I can do what I want on my own time. So should I tell you about it or just keep my mouth shut about what I find?"

He hesitated, at a loss for words. "I guess the first thing is that I don't want you to get hurt, Jane," he said finally. "I don't want to go to your funeral too. I don't want Sarah to lose her mother."

Her face softened. "I'll be careful. And I'm well protected, believe me. But I have to do something . . . make some kind of an effort. I told Pete's parents that I would and they said the same thing you just did, but I know what I'm doing, Inspector."

"Then, naturally, you're going to let me know if you come up with anything. Who'd you say you were with?"

"I didn't say," she answered with a slight smile. "But a very nice guy. Not a cop, but he speaks Spanish and he's competent. I'm well protected."

"Sure. You going to give me his name?"

"No."

"Why not?"

"I have my reasons."

"Just remember. This is no game."

"And maybe you should just remember that I am an experienced detective and not some kind of secretary."

Regal shrugged and walked back to his office. Before he reached his desk, the telephone rang. The commissioner wanted him up there right away.

"You wanted to see me, Commissioner?" Regal was studiously polite as he entered Gallagher's office after waiting almost thirty minutes outside in the anteroom.

"Yes. They also told me that you called. Sorry, I didn't get the message. What's on your mind first?"

Gallagher had spoken without looking up from the papers on his desk and Regal thought, *The bastard is such a bad liar, he can't meet my eyes. Sure, nobody told him I wanted to see him, just like nobody's told him that I've been trying to reach him for a week.*

He held his tongue. He was good at holding his temper, he realized. It was probably one of the least attractive by-products of being a civil servant.

"This chess game, Commissioner."

"I see the moves every day in the paper but Joe tells me we're just not getting any closer to the nut."

"That's right. I want to remind you, sir, when he agreed to play with me, his message said there would be no killings as long as the game remained interesting. I don't know if I can keep it interesting anymore. I don't know enough about chess and I need help. I've lost a couple of pawns, I don't like the looks of the board and it may already be too late."

Gallagher nodded. "You understand, Paul, that I had hoped to keep as tight a rein on this as possible with only the minimum number of people knowing about it. We've been lucky on that score. Nobody has figured out what was going on. If we bring in someone else, the chances increase that there'll be a leak."

"That's possibly true," Regal said, "and I don't have any answer for you, sir. All I know is what the killer's tape said about an interesting game and all else I know is that I'm out of my depth now. There are no rules about something like this, but I just sense that we'd be better off dragging this game out and maybe winning, than losing in a hurry and that's what I'm liable to do."

"All right. Just so you understand the difficulties," Gallagher said and Regal realized, *This bastard is going to try to put the blame for this decision on me. If he's my friend, Lord, please don't give my enemies my home address.*

Regal nodded and the commissioner said, "There's a police department chess club. I guess you know that."

"Yes, sir. It was my first thought, but I held off contacting them when you told me to keep everything secret."

"Well, forget that. The head of the chess club is a Lieutenant Needham. He works on the dock squad. From what I gather, he's got a master's rating, whatever the hell that is, and he knows how to keep his mouth closed. Work with him on the chess game."

"Does he know I'll be calling him?"

"No. I haven't spoken to him, but just tell him you cleared it through me."

This fox is being very careful to leave no trail at all, Regal thought. *It'll turn out to be my idea to call Needham and if the story leaks, it'll be my problem to deal with. Politicians suck.*

"I'll talk to him today," Regal said stiffly. "You had something for me, sir?"

"Yes. Do you know a reporter from the *Daily News* named Jack Ferguson?"

"I've met him a few times. He hangs around here a lot."

"When was the last time you talked to him?"

"A year ago, I guess. As I remember, it was a slow news day and he was calling everybody to try to scare up a story. I didn't have anything for him."

"You haven't talked to him in the past week?"

"No, sir."

"Well, somebody did. He called Joe Burton a little while ago and asked whether the letters *P, K* and *B* carved on the bodies could stand for pawn, knight and bishop.

"Shit," Regal blurted instinctively. "I knew it was too good to last. Did he mention me?"

"No. Not that I know of."

But naturally you suspected me immediately, you worthless scumsucker.

"The leak—if it is a leak—didn't come from me or my people," Regal said firmly. "It may just be a bright idea in his city room. Can we talk him out of it?"

"I don't know. If somebody brainstormed the idea, it wasn't him. I've met him and he's not too swift. I just feel political fingerprints on this one."

Regal shrugged. "I don't know about that. What did Joe say to him?"

"He said how the hell would he know if the letters stood for pawn or knight or bishop. They could stand for Poughkeepsie and Baltimore and Kentucky for all he knew. Joe said he yelled at him to stop wasting his time and hung up. Then Joe called here to warn me."

"And told you that I'd probably been running off at the mouth," Regal said. "Not guilty, Commissioner."

"Okay. Well, if Ferguson gives you a call, at least you won't be surprised."

"I sure will," Regal said. "Because there's not a reason in the world for him to call me about this unless someone has tipped him off and told him I'm involved."

"It might happen though."

"If it does, I'll tell him I don't know what he's talking about and tell him it's Burton's case."

"I hope you can pull it off," Gallagher said in a tone of voice that implied, *You'd better pull it off.*

When Regal got back to his office, he found a short, heavy-set man with wildly gnarled white hair waiting for him—Jack Ferguson of the *Daily News*. Jane was watching him with the distrust policemen feel for all reporters, as if expecting them to steal something off a desk if they were left unsupervised for a moment.

They shook hands in Regal's inner office and the policeman resisted the impulse to wipe his hand on his jacket pocket. Ferguson always seemed to him to be covered by an invisibly thin head-to-foot coating of oil. He oozed his way about police headquarters.

"Just stopped in, Inspector, to see if there's anything new on Detective Muniz's killing."

Sure you did. And I buy swamp land in Florida. "You'll have to talk to Joe Burton about that, Jack. He's in charge of the investigation. Homicide, you know."

"Have a heart, Inspector. You know what Burton is like. He won't give you the right time unless he's already made an arrest." Ferguson clutched his heart dramatically to express anguish.

"Sometimes that's not a bad rule to follow," Regal said mildly. "Couple of years ago I opened my yap before a case was finished up and wished later I'd kept my mouth shut. I know you've got your job to do, but I just don't have anything for you."

"You know I'm on your side," Ferguson said, giving his head an odd sidewise shake to indicate his total commitment.

"I know that. But really it's Burton's case. I'm a lot more anxious than you are to hear that we've got the bastard who killed Pete, but what Burton says goes."

"But it was your man who got shot. Can't you tell me

anything about progress?" He looked pleadingly at Regal.

" 'Can't' is the right word, Jack. You're asking the impossible. I haven't any real information for you, and even if I did, I couldn't release it. It's Joe's."

"Okay," the reporter said with a sigh, his shoulders slumping as if he had just lost his final death row appeal. "Just trying to do my job the best I can. I figured that, well, Joe Burton is so tight with the administration that maybe you might have a different outlook."

The word has already gotten to this slug that I'm out of favor, Regal thought. *He expects me to tell him that the commissioner is a back-stabbing lowlife and Joe Burton would like to arrest me for Pete's murder. Not this week, Binky.*

Regal just shrugged. "Sorry," he repeated.

"If you hear anything," Ferguson said, "I'd appreciate your letting me know."

"You can count on this: when Burton has something to say, I'll ask him to talk to you first."

Ferguson stood and walked toward Regal's door.

One, two, three, Regal counted mentally. *Time for the Colombo "by the way."*

"By the way, Inspector. As long as I'm here, you hear anything new about the Monogram Murders?"

"Joe Burton's case too, Jack. Sorry."

"I hear it might have something to do with a chess game," Ferguson said, watching Regal carefully for a reaction.

"You hear all kinds of things in a cop house," Regal said. He stared at Ferguson until the reporter backed off and said, "See you, Inspector."

"Sure thing. Always a pleasure."

Regal stared at the closed office door. Somebody knew something and somebody had leaked it. But who?

16

Regal was finally able to track down the chess-playing dock squad member, but when Lieutenant Francis X. Needham came to his apartment, he brought nothing but gloom.

"I'm sorry, Inspector," he said, after he had carefully replayed Regal's and the killer's moves on the cheap plastic chessboard in Regal's apartment, and then spent fifteen minutes studying the position. "You've got a lost game."

"You sure?" Regal said.

Needham nodded. He was a smallish wiry man with short wavy hair and intelligent eyes.

"I just tried to play the move from a book of openings," he said. "I figured that would keep me out of trouble."

"This book?" Needham asked. Regal nodded and the other policeman shook his head sadly.

"Your tough luck, Inspector. You managed to find a book that was not only too old but one that didn't make a lot of sense the day it was written. Nowadays, there's so much opening analysis that if you don't take the exact right path through the minefield, you're going to get blown up." He paused and asked Regal if he minded Needham smoking.

"No, go ahead," Regal said, still staring at the chessboard.

When he looked back up, there was a faint smile on Needham's face. "If you don't mind my saying so, Inspector, it seems pretty odd that you went and got the commissioner's okay so that I could analyze a chess game for you. Is this something I'm allowed to know about? Because I'd sure as hell be interested."

"Let me think about that for a few minutes, Lieutenant. You say this is a lost game. Is it a quick loss or a long drawn-out loss?"

"Pretty quick, I'm afraid. All this stuff you've been doing here . . . it's allowed white to mass up his forces. He's going to go through you like a dose of salts. A dozen moves or so and it's probably all over."

"Shit," Regal snapped. He did not know whether it would be better for him to win or to lose the game. The killer had never mentioned that. But Regal had the feeling that the longer he could keep the game going, keep it almost equal, the better chance they had of holding off any further killings and maybe even getting a line on the killer himself.

And now this game's down the toilet and I may have just helped put somebody else's body into a garbage can.

"Lieutenant, can you keep your mouth shut?"

"You work on the docks, it's the first thing you learn," Needham said.

"I mean shut. I mean I tell you something and it doesn't go past this room . . . not even to the men on your squad or your chess club or your wife. If you can promise me that, I'll tell you what's going on. If you can't promise me that, fine too. No hard feelings and I appreciate your honesty with me. Think about it. I'll make us a drink."

"No drink for me, thanks," the lieutenant said. "I'm

retired. And I don't have to think about it. Whatever you tell me stops here."

"All right," Regal said. "But I'm going to have a drink anyway." He poured himself a vodka on the rocks, then sat down and told Needham the whole story about the alphabet killings and the mutilated bodies and the chess game he'd been playing through the *Times*.

When he finished, Needham was shaking his head. "Man, Inspector, you've got yourself a pail of problems."

"Now you know why I don't want this game to end. If I don't keep it interesting enough, somebody else might die."

"I wish I could help you but I can't. The chessboard's one of the few places in the world where you can find absolute truth. And the truth is you've got nothing left. Everything I know about the game says you're dead in the water."

"Don't take this personally but would there be any point in my talking to somebody else? Maybe somebody with a higher ranking than you?"

"It's called rating," Needham said, "and my feelings aren't hurt but I don't think it'd do any good. An opening like this has been analyzed to death and we all know what we know about it." He shrugged. "It's lost. Maybe Kasparov could make something out of it," he said, looking up to make sure that Regal knew he was referring to the Russian who was the chess champion of the world. Satisfied that he did, Needham added, "Like I said, maybe Kasparov. Maybe Bobby Fischer or Billy Abbott . . . somebody like that . . . maybe *they* could make a game out of this but probably not even them."

"Jesus, you're a bundle of optimism," Regal said. Needham lit a second cigarette from the butt of the first. "Is there anything you can tell me about my opponent from the way that he's played so far?"

"Only that he's better than you, Inspector. Sorry but you're looking at a loss."

*   *   *

The bad news was compounded when Jack Ferguson's story appeared in the next day's *Daily News*. It speculated that the Monogram Murders might have been committed by a demented chess player and that the initials inscribed on the dead bodies might stand for chess pieces.

It was a long rambling article that seemed to stop just short of suggesting that anyone crazy enough to play chess might just be crazy enough to kill people too.

Joe Burton was quoted as saying nothing and denying everything except that the killer would soon be apprehended. And Ferguson wrote that Regal "refused" to comment on the case because Burton was in charge but there was a clear implication that Regal knew more than he was saying. The story never mentioned, however, why Ferguson had bothered to interview Regal at all, since technically Regal worked on a special drug squad and was not concerned at all with the Monogram investigation.

Regal read the story at the coffee shop near his apartment and then again in his office. Where the hell had the leak come from?

His first instinct was to blame the chess-playing cop, Needham, but that quickly passed. Even if he was a loose-lip, which Regal doubted, Needham would hardly be stupid enough to spill the story minutes after he heard it.

Who else then? Joe Burton? It wasn't Burton's style. As much as Burton disliked Regal, he probably disliked the press more and he was just too good a cop to conduct a sabotage operation against Regal that might contaminate his own murder investigation. Jane Cole and Tony Bolda wouldn't have said anything either and there was no one else left in his squad.

Could it have been Commissioner Gallagher himself, trying to curry favor with one member of the press corps? Not very likely, Regal decided. The answer was probably something pretty prosaic, like Burton had made the mistake of confiding in one of his own men who, as it usually happened, turned out to be some kind of shirttail cousin of Jack Ferguson.

He closed the paper, satisfied that he had probably solved the riddle of the leak, when he paused with a chilling thought. Perhaps Ferguson had been tipped off by the killer himself. And he might then know something that would help the police.

When the private phone rang, Regal expected to hear the mechanical voice of his chess opponent; instead it was Joe Burton.

"What the fuck is this dipshit Ferguson up to?" Burton demanded in his usual bullying voice, as if Regal had already been read his Miranda rights and was about to get a fist in the stomach.

"I'd sure like to know," Regal said and related Ferguson's visit to his office the previous afternoon. "Truth, Joe, at first I thought he was carrying water for you."

"Me? Why the hell would I want to deal with a garden slug like that?"

"I discounted it after a while, but I thought you were trying to make me look bad by getting me involved. Make it look like I leaked something. Give me a kick in the shins sort of."

"Shit, I'm not worried about you. You're a lightweight," Burton said. "And I'd be a lot more likely to punch you in the nose than kick you in the shins. You've been hanging around with too many fag interior decorators."

"I'll let that slide," Regal said. "Anyway, I couldn't see you playing games with Ferguson."

"Believe it. He's hinted around before that if the money was right, he'd write puff pieces about me. He tried that on me once and I told him to take a flying fuck on a rolling doughnut. Most reporters are pains in the ass but some are just shit and Ferguson is one of them."

"When I saw my name in the story—and there just wasn't any reason for him to talk to me about it—I thought maybe somebody was trying to set me up. More likely me than you anyway."

"Of course," Burton said in surprise. "I'm a real cop, not a political flunky like you. Why would anyone want to take a shot at me?"

Regal grinned. Burton had all the tact of a Philadelphia Eagles football coach.

"So who spilled it?" Regal said.

"I don't know. You been talking to anybody?"

"Just my own people. And a dock cop named Needham who's a chess player."

"Forget him. I know Needham and he wouldn't say spit," Burton said. "And I trust my own guys, and some of them I had to let know what we were doing. Hell, we've been scouring every damned chess club in the city . . . but not one of them would say a word," Burton insisted.

"You don't think it could have been the FBI men who were in, do you?"

"No. Not since Hoover died. They used to travel around in the old days with a public relations man and you couldn't shut them up if you sewed their lips together. But nowadays they play it straight. It wasn't them."

"Then maybe you ought to have someone try to reach Ferguson. Because maybe he got his tip from the killer."

There was a momentary pause. "Dammit, Paul, you might be right."

"Yeah," Regal agreed.

"I'll work on that. About Pete Muniz, not a thing is new."

"Thanks for telling me."

"Why not? Pete was one of your guys. You've got a right to know."

Regal was stunned. Could this be the Joe Burton he had known for twenty years? Was the man finally mellowing?

"How's your chess game going?" Burton asked suddenly.

"I'm going to lose."

"I figured that. You're a pussy." Burton hung up.

Well, so much for Joe Burton mellowing.

Five minutes later, the phone rang again. When Regal answered, the mechanical voice intoned: "For-Inspector-Paul-Regal. Pawn-to-queen-rook-four." There was a brief pause before the voice added, "This-game-is-getting-dull."

"Hold on a minute," Regal shouted. "Let's talk."

Click. Dial tone. Regal lowered his head to his desk. Of all the words he had not ever wanted to hear, those were the scariest: *This game is getting dull.*

Someone was going to die.

He walked outside to Jane Cole's desk. She was on the telephone and he waited until she hung up. She looked at him and said, "A phone booth near the World Trade Center. On their way there now."

He nodded and went to pour himself a cup of coffee. He saw Jane's cup was empty and poured her one too, and her eyes at first blinked her surprise and then she nodded.

The departmental switchboard line rang. Jane answered it, listened and said, "Thanks."

"Nobody at the phone booth, of course," she told Regal. "The cops will see if anybody saw anything." She sighed. "But of course, nobody will have."

He patted her on the shoulder. She looked up quickly at the contact and he dropped his hand just as quickly.

"Don't get discouraged," he said. "We'll get this bastard yet." He thought of Pete Muniz. "We'll get all the bastards."

Five minutes later, he was surprised to get another phone call from Joe Burton.

"I was just going to call you," Regal said.

"All right. You first."

"That bastard told me today that the chess game is getting dull."

"And?"

"I don't know," Regal said. "But he said he wouldn't kill as long as the game was interesting. You might want your guys to tighten up things tonight."

Burton sighed. "All right. Maybe we should thank God for small favors. By playing him, you've kept him in his cage for a couple of extra weeks. I'll put extra men out tonight."

"All right. Now it's your turn," Regal said.

"I was just talking with somebody who wanted to talk to whoever was playing chess in the *Times*."

"What? Who was it? Did he give a name?"

"No, dammit. He asked for me and told the clerk it was about the Monogram Murders. Davis wasn't here so I took the call and the first thing he asked was whether I was the one putting the chess moves in the *Times*. I said I didn't know what he was talking about and asked him his name but he said he didn't want to give it to me. I tried to keep him on the line but he got nervous and hung up. He sounded like a flake but I thought you ought to know."

"Do you think this is some kind of stunt that Ferguson is pulling on us?"

Burton snorted in disgust. "My thought, too. I'm busting my balls and driving people crazy trying to handle two separate murder investigations and I have to worry about swamp slime like Ferguson getting cute. I'm thinking about having somebody lean into him a little."

"Careful, Joe. Reporters can be vicious."

"This one can be had," Burton said coldly. "Guys like him are always afraid that somebody's going to do to them what they're always doing to other people. If he thinks I've decided to frame him for something, he won't go all noble and indignant, standing on his First Amendment rights and all that shit. He'll run for cover."

"But you wouldn't do that, would you, Joe?"

"Whether I'd do it or not doesn't matter. What matters is that he'll think that I'd do it. And—"

"Hold on," Regal said. He looked up. Jane Cole was

waving frantically at him from the doorway. "Take the call on six," she said urgently. "It's something about that chess game."

"Call Communications. Trace it if you can," he snapped. "Joe, I think that guy is on the phone to me right now. I'll call you back in a few minutes."

"Trace it!" Burton bellowed.

"It's being done," Regal said, then cut off Burton and reached to the telephone to pick up the other call.

"Hello," he said casually. "This is Inspector Paul Regal. May I help you?"

"Are you the one putting those stupid chess moves in the *New York Times*?" The voice was thin and querulous, an odd combination of apprehension and arrogance.

"What moves do you mean?"

"The ones on Page One, the little ads at the bottom."

Regal leaned forward eagerly over his desk. *A break at last. I've just got to keep this guy talking.*

In what he hoped was his reasonable gentle voice, Regal said, "Well, I really couldn't talk about that over the telephone. But I know some people who've been following that game and they didn't think the moves were stupid. They told me they were right out of the book."

"What book? Doctor Seuss?" the caller demanded. "Look, I don't know that it matters any to anybody but if that's your game, you're going to lose it."

"Well, it must matter to someone," Regal said evenly. "But why are you so sure it's a losing game? And what makes you think the police department has anything to do with it?"

Blessing Burton for having called to tip him off, Regal refrained from asking the man's name in order not to scare him off the line.

"I know how to play chess and I read the *Times* every day and I happened to spot that game, so naturally I followed it. Then I saw the story in the *News* today about the three people that were killed . . . you know, those Monogram Murders . . . and I had a hunch. So I checked that old story ... I keep old papers ... about that minister that got killed and then I was reading where the three bodies were found and when I looked at a map of the city, it was obvious that if the blocks from Sixty-seventh to Seventy-fifth were the sides of a chessboard, the bodies were left at the spots marking the first three moves in a Ruy opening by white. And that was the game that was being played in the *Times*."

"My God, is that so?" Regal exclaimed. "We never even realized it."

"How could you have missed it? It was staring you right in the eye." The man sounded puzzled and annoyed, as if talking with someone surprised to hear that two and two equaled four.

Jane Cole appeared in the doorway. A broad smile was on her face and she nodded and made a thumbs-up gesture. Regal grinned back.

"I think I'm wasting my time talking to you," his caller said.

"Oh no, sir. Not at all. I'd really like to know more about this chess game. And with your broad knowledge of all these things, it's possible that you could be very helpful to us in this murder investigation. Would you be willing to assist us?"

"I don't want to get involved," the man said instantly, alarm clear in his voice. "I don't care about murder cases. I just care about chess. If you are playing black, then you're a terrible patzer and you're going to get your clock cleaned real fast. Listen, I gotta go. I'll call you back later maybe."

"But sir," Regal began, but the man had hung up.

He replaced the receiver slowly. This did not sound like someone calling to confess a crime. His instinct was to take the man at his word: he was a chess nut and somehow he had guessed what was going on.

Unless it's a trick by that goddam Jack Ferguson. Regal thought back. Had he said too much? No. He had been careful. He could always claim that he had just been trying to stall the caller. He had never admitted that the police department was playing that game of chess with a mass murderer.

He grew clammy at the thought that the call might have been traced to the *News'* editorial office.

"So?" he said to Jane.

"Dunno. The whizzes will let us know in a few minutes."

Regal closed his eyes and said a silent prayer. *Please, Lord, don't let it be Jack Ferguson busting our chops. Let it be a homicidal maniac chess player. Please, Lord, please.*

A young man in shirtsleeves walked up behind Jane and Regal nodded to the two of them to come into the office. The man had shoulder-length hair and wore a flowered sports shirt. Ten years ago, that would have meant that he was definitely not a policeman. Now it didn't prove anything.

"We got a complete trace," the man said cheerfully. He was a cop, Regal realized. "It's out in Brooklyn and the cops in the neighborhood are rolling on it."

"Thanks. Keep us posted," Regal said.

The man nodded and left and Regal said to Jane, "Do you have a cigarette?"

"Do I look like a smoker to you?"

"I didn't ask that. You got a smoke?"

"Yes."

"I want one," Regal said.

She looked startled and left, returning several hours later, it seemed, with a cigarette and a lighter.

"I thought you didn't smoke," she said.

"Not in four years. But this seems like a good day to start."

He lit the cigarette and promptly went into a choking fit.

"These things are killers, you know."

"You told me the other day that coffee was a killer," he reminded her when he had gotten his breath back.

"Well, it is. Kills your stomach. Eats holes in it the size of a fried egg."

"Good. Get me a cup of coffee and I'll sit here huffing and puffing and blow my brains out."

When she reappeared with the coffee, so did the policeman in the flowered shirt.

"Pay phone in Brooklyn," the man said. "The squad cars didn't find anybody." He handed Regal a slip of paper with a Brooklyn address written on it.

"Okay," Regal said, even though he was disappointed. "Good work."

"Thanks, Inspector," the man said with a tone that indicated that he always did good work.

After he left, Regal asked Jane, "Is Tony around?"

"No. He's mooching around uptown, still looking for Estrellita. He should call in later."

"Damn," Regal snapped. "It's tough running a unit without personnel."

"In case you hadn't noticed, Inspector, I'm personnel," Jane said briskly.

He hesitated, then said quickly, "Okay, we've got some work to do. Want to come along?"

"Of course I do," she said. She spun and ran from the office as he dialed Joe Burton's number, then quickly described his phone conversation.

"My hunch is that the guy isn't involved, he's just a chess freak, but we're going to check it out right now. Even if he's clean, I want to find him and sit on him. I don't want him spreading the news about what's going on."

"I want in," Burton said flatly.

"Just you or some of your people?"

"I'll bring a few men."

"Fine. Meet me in my office first. I managed to tape the call so I'll play the tape and everybody will know what he sounds like. By the way, no uniforms."

"Of course not," Burton snorted. "I was doing this kind of work when you were majoring in flower arrangement in high school."

"Grade school," Regal said softly. "You're forty years older than me, Joe, not twenty. In fact, some people say you're already way past retirement age. See you here in a few minutes."

He had the satisfaction of hanging up before Burton could get another word in. It felt good to sit back and relax for a moment and sip his coffee with the prospect of real police work ahead of him. He took another drag on the cigarette, coughed again and looked around for some place to put it out.

From outside, Jane yelled, "Smoking kills!"

<u>17</u>

The two unmarked cars turned onto Avenue M in Brooklyn and moved quietly down the street, the passengers staring intently at a row of retail shops. The public telephone was at the end of a block beside a gasoline station. They found parking spots nearby, got out and split into four groups of two.

Paul Regal and Jane Cole paired off, strolling down one side of the street, with Joe Burton and one of his men close behind. They took turns wandering into shops and questioning store personnel. The other two teams were working the other side of the street.

The operation took several hours and covered both sides of two blocks in both directions from the gas station, but it all drew a blank. Nobody remembered anybody who had used a nearby phone or who had wanted to use their phone or who spoke nervously like Regal's caller.

When they reassembled at the service station, Burton surprised Regal by ordering the rest of his group back to their car but pulling him off to one side.

"What do you think, Regal?"

"I think we should put a tap on this phone for a while in case this guy uses it regularly. If we hear his voice again, we might be able to get some line on who he is."

Burton nodded. "That's basic. Anything else?"

"It might pay to drop into the local precinct and see if anyone there recognizes the voice. We don't have to play them enough of it for anyone to know what's going."

"I buy that," Burton said. "Frank Razoni is the captain at the Eight-Eight and he's an old friend of mine. We can do that on the way back to headquarters. Anything else?"

Regal was reminded of a time in his youth when he was quizzed by his high school science teacher about the steps he had taken in carrying out a laboratory experiment.

"Well, coach," he said drily, "the only other thing I can think of is putting a camera on that phone. Maybe with a van across the street. If we can afford it, let's stake the place out for a couple of days."

Burton nodded again. "That's the way I see it too," he said with reluctant agreement. "Maybe I've misjudged you, Regal. You seem to know something about police work after all. Not much, but a little. Let's get over to the precinct. You know, this guy sounds young. If he's a high school kid, maybe we should check the nearest schools."

"A long shot," Regal said, "but worth trying. I kind of think that maybe it was just somebody driving by. It might not hurt to check on anyone who had car service this morning. Maybe take a look at the receipts for gas credit cards too."

Burton looked at him as if he had just crawled from under a rock. "My guys already did that," he said with obviously vast satisfaction.

"Took them long enough," Regal growled. "Let's go."

Captain Frank Razoni at the Eighty-eighth Precinct was offered no information and asked no questions. He agreed to play an edited copy of the tape to his men at roll call.

"And tell your cars and uniforms not to hang around that phone for a few days, Frank," Burton said in a tone that bade ill for his old friend if he disobeyed. "We don't want to spook this geek."

"I know the drill," Razoni responded in an annoyed voice. "That box has been bugged three times in the last couple of years by my narcotics guys."

Burton rode back to headquarters with Regal and Cole, unchivalrously commandeering the front passenger seat as a matter of course.

"I'll ride in back, Inspector," Jane Cole commented brightly after Burton had already taken the front seat. "Okay?" Burton looked at her in puzzlement as Regal suppressed a snicker.

When Regal and Jane got back to the office, Tony Bolda was waiting impatiently, eating a chicken salad sandwich three inches thick, while flipping through the pages of a racing paper. He was annoyed that he had missed the action. "You could have had me beeped," he told Regal. "I would have hotfooted it over."

"No need, Tony. Turned out to be a waste of time anyway. You just stay on Pete's investigation. That's more important to me than all the damned monogram killers in the world."

"Nothing on Pete. Not a sniff. All we know is that he was moving around, talking with people up there, looking for new guys on the block. What must have happened is he ran into Hector and his girlfriend, this Estrellita, got a clue from them and followed it up. The Panamanians, if that's who it was, heard about it, whacked Pete, finished off Hector and the girl for good measure, and skipped back to the Canal Zone." He shrugged. "At least that's all that seems to make sense now."

"Just keep looking," Regal ordered. "I don't think anybody who comes to town to sell drugs ever leaves without selling any. We keep hearing the Panamanians are around. Well, if they are, they're going to have to hit the streets eventually if they're going to get any action. And I want to be there to greet them."

"Everybody's trying. Narcotics is busting their nuts over this one. Some of those guys were Pete's friends, and anyway, Inspector Franco is no friend of Joe Burton. He'd love to have his guys be the ones to make the collar."

"Dammit, we don't sound like cops. We sound like the freaking Middle East with everybody digging at each other. Why can't we all just do our jobs and get along?"

"Because we're a bunch of rotten human beings, Paul," Bolda said. "That's how normal people are. Nobody claims to be a saint. We're just cops. The only reason I stopped beating my wife is that she divorced me. That doesn't make me a bad person, does it?"

"Ask Phil Donahue," Regal said. "He's in charge of talking to weirdos."

"I'll do that today. Right after I talk to a man about a horse." He waved the rolled up racing paper in his hand and then walked from the office.

On Regal's desk was a message from Patrice, and when he called her at the office, she said, "Pete and I are going to be working late over at the Mountain, supervising the painters. I don't know when I'll be home. These idiots wouldn't even use a drop cloth if I didn't stay on their backs all the time."

Their backs okay; your back not so good, Regal thought, but said mildly, "Have fun. I'll see you when I see you."

"Ciao."

He hated people who said "Ciao."

He called Lieutenant Needham at the dock squad and told him the move the killer had called in that day.

"Pawn to queen rook four," Regal said.

"I expected that. I've been fooling with this game all day here in the office. If it were my game, I think I'd move my own pawn-queen rook four. It might cost another pawn but it might slow him down some."

"You don't sound hopeful," Regal said, as he jotted down Needham's suggested move.

"I'm not."

He...

... stood in front of the closet door, looking at himself in the full-length mirror. He spoke in a dull monotone while staring at his reflection.

"The game is getting dull," he said. "I warned him what would happen if the game got dull."

He was wearing a flowered cowboy shirt, open at the neck. He undid another button to show more of his chest.

"Good. Tonight the queen?"

He shook his head. It was too early for the queen.

"Something small tonight. Maybe another pawn."

He opened still another button of his shirt.

"Bring the recorder. Let's hear screams."

Regal was just turning out the office light when the telephone rang again. The switchboard line. Cole had already left and Regal thought about it for a moment, exhaled and picked up the phone. "Paul Regal."

"What's your next move and why?" demanded the thin anxious voice he had heard earlier that day. His heart leaped.

"I'm not sure. I haven't figured it out yet but he's moved pawn to queen rook four. I've been thinking about doing the same thing."

"Don't do that!" the voice screamed. "That's drek and double drek."

Paul Regal's mind raced. Could he notify someone to trace this call? Should he ask the man's name and risk scaring him off again? Was he calling again from Brooklyn? Had Burton's men already staked out the phone booth in case he was calling from there? He thought of all those questions but not one answer, so he just said, "I thought it was a book position."

"What do you know about a book position? You've

already lost one pawn and you're going to give him another one? Screw what he's doing. You get your horse out of the center and try to get some play."

"Are you sure? That doesn't sound right to me," Regal bluffed. "I think I can stop him."

"You can't stop spit," the caller insisted. "You've got to ... what? ... you'll have to wait a minute ... I'm making a call ... find your own phone ... you have to wait until ..."

There was a strangled noise and Regal heard a sharp thump as his caller apparently let the handset drop. The policeman waited, a smile on his face. Finally a voice asked gruffly, "Who is this?"

"Inspector Regal at headquarters," he answered.

"Detective Newmeyer, Homicide North, Inspector. We've got him. We'll send this guy back as soon as the precinct sends a car over."

"Why don't you bring him back yourself? You won't be needed there anymore."

"Not until Inspector Burton tells us to leave, sir. He says stay here and watch, we stay here and watch."

"Good enough. Good work, Newmeyer. I never thought he'd call me again today. Just goes to show you can never take people for granted."

"That's for sure, Inspector. He looks harmless anyway. Wasn't carrying anything."

"Does he have a name?"

"His driver's license says he's William F. Abbott, age twenty-six. He says he drives a delivery truck for a florist here in the neighborhood."

"You'll send him to Joe's office?"

"Of course," the detective answered in a shocked tone.

"Thanks again. If we ever meet in the Galway, the drinks are on me."

"I'll take you up on that, Inspector. See you around."

Regal hung up and found himself rubbing his hands together in anticipation. At last.

*   *   *

Struggling feebly in the arms of two hulking policemen, William Abbott was ushered into the interrogation room. He was a tall, gangly young man wearing jeans and a Tampa Bay Buccaneers jacket. His mouse-colored hair was a little scraggly and a lock of it kept falling forward into his eyes and he kept swiping at it with the back of his wrist.

Regal and Burton were waiting for him, along with a stenographer and two Homicide detectives. The two uniformed patrolmen steered Abbott into a soft armchair in the corner of the room.

"Has he been advised of his rights?" asked Burton quietly.

"Yes, sir," one of the uniformed policeman said, before leaving the room.

"Mr. Abbott, you understand that you don't have to talk to us without having your lawyer present."

"I don't have a lawyer. Why should I have a lawyer?"

Regal's heart threw in an extra beat as a bonus. The voice was the one he had heard twice over the phone that day.

"You might want a lawyer because you've got yourself involved in a murder investigation," Burton told the young man gently.

"Am I under arrest?"

"No. We brought you in just for questioning. We could hold you on a charge of assaulting the police but I hope we don't have to bother with that. All we want to know is why you called me and Inspector Regal about these so-called Monogram Murders."

"I don't know anything about any murders," the young man protested. "I thought I made that clear to that patzer, Regal. I know about chess and he's making an ass of himself, you know. I'm sorry now that I got myself involved. Tell him he can go to hell with that stupid game he's playing."

Burton covered up his laugh by coughing into his handkerchief. Regal glowered at the young man in the chair.

"We know your name now, Mr. Abbott. Do you live at the address on your driver's license?" Burton asked.

"That's right."

"And where were you born?"

"Right here in New York. In Red Hook. That's Brooklyn, you know."

Regal sat back on the far side of the room as Burton quietly and calmly continued the interrogation. The older man surprised him. He had just presumed that Burton would rant and yell at a suspect, even louder than he did at his own men, trying to bully out information. But Burton was cool and dispassionate, methodically extracting information and listening politely when Abbott would zig off on tangents.

"Would you mind, Mr. Abbott, if I called you Bill?" Burton asked.

The thin young man said, "You're going to beat me, aren't you?"

"No one's going to beat you, Mr. Abbott."

Abbott's eyes narrowed and he seemed to be considering Burton's answer. Finally, he nodded. "People used to call me nicknames but I don't like it. You can call me William."

Nicknames? Billy Abbott. The name hit Regal like a hammer thudding onto a thumb. He looked at Burton but obviously the name meant nothing to him at all.

Billy Abbott. Abbott had been a high school dropout who became the national junior chess champion of the United States when he was only twelve years old. He was an international grandmaster at thirteen—the youngest ever to be awarded that rating. In the press of the late seventies and early eighties, he was hailed as perhaps the greatest chess prodigy of all time, an automatic cinch to become world chess champion.

Through the early eighties, he played in a string of international tournaments, cutting through the other players like a diver's hand through water.

And then he had disappeared. At nineteen, he walked out of a tournament one day and never came back. His father, a retired bank clerk, had refused to give any information about his son, other than to say that he was "pursuing other endeavors."

The press followed the story avidly for a few months and then, because there was nothing new in it, they dropped it and forgot about it. Once every three or four years, someone would do a "whatever happened to so-and-so" story about Abbott, but no one seemed to know anything about him and there was a lot of speculation that he had probably wound up in an insane asylum.

Regal remembered a famous news photo of Abbott. The boy was young then, maybe twelve, crewcut and cherubic, and the picture showed him looking up across the chessboard at his opponent just before finishing him off in a game, and the smile on his face was that of a hired killer.

Regal cursed himself for not having recognized the name immediately. Hell, Lieutenant Needham just the night before had told Regal that only someone like Billy Abbott would have a chance to salvage his losing chess game.

And now, here was Abbott in the flesh, as it turned out, a delivery-truck driver for a florist, sitting in an interrogation room in homicide headquarters. It seemed an unbelievable coincidence.

Burton was gently leading Abbott through his life story but all Abbott would say was that he had played a lot of chess when he was young but then quit "and decided to leave New York and see what life is really like, you know." He had gone to Florida and held a variety of jobs, including working on a shrimp boat out of Tampa for a year. Two years ago he had come back to New York and was attending St. John's College at night.

Driving the delivery truck for the Brooklyn florist earned him all the money he needed and didn't interfere with his studies, he told Burton earnestly.

He had not decided on a college major yet but was leaning toward astronomy, even though his father wanted him to become an accountant. "Math comes easy to me," he explained. "An accountant can always make a good living. You know? But astronomy sounds like it might be more interesting. What do you think, Inspector Burton?"

Burton said, "I think you'll be a success in whatever you choose to do." He looked down at a notebook. "You told Inspector Regal that you had seen the chess game being played in the *Times* and figured out it was related to the Monogram Murders. Is that correct?"

"It was obvious," Abbott said, looking affronted. "I mean, if I hadn't happened to see the *Daily News* story that said something about those letters standing for pawn, knight and bishop, it might not have occurred to me, you know. I don't usually read murder stories in the newspaper. I don't believe much of what I read in the newspapers anyway. All the papers are owned by a handful of people who are out to hoodwink the public about what's really going on, you know. The television stations too. Everybody knows that." He sat back, crossed his arms over his scrawny chest and nodded knowingly.

"And so you called me and Inspector Regal in an effort to be of some help?"

Abbott frowned. "I wish I hadn't called you people," he complained. "I've never been arrested before, you know. I don't like being hauled down here getting the third degree. I don't give a damn about those murders. I don't know anything about them except what I happened to notice in the newspapers or hear on television and I don't believe any of that stuff. All those reporters lie, you know. That's what they're paid to do. But the chess game caught my eye and I thought I'd be a good guy and give you a little advice. So much for being a nice guy. Never again."

Burton asked Abbott if he could account for his whereabouts on the nights of the three Monogram Murders. He was hazy about the first night but said he was in class on the nights of the other two killings. The night the biker was killed, he had gone straight home from class, but he had gone with several classmates to a pizzeria after class on the night that the Reverend Keane met his untimely end.

He supplied the classmates' names and Burton nodded to one of his detectives who quietly left the room to check them out.

Burton regarded the man with mild annoyance. "I'm beginning to think you've been telling us the truth. I was hoping at first that you were the killer we're looking for, but if your story checks out, it looks like you're in the clear."

"Of course I am," Abbott said, surprised. "Why would I want to go around killing people?"

"You've never been mad enough at someone to kill them?"

"Of course not. And if I were, I wouldn't use a knife. That's stupid. I'd get a gun or something. How can anybody stick a knife into somebody else? You'd have to be crazy to do something like that, you know?"

"Unfortunately, there are a lot of crazy people in the world, William . . . especially here in New York."

"You can say that again. And most of them drive cars. Listen. Have you ever thought of giving a sanity test to people before you give them a driving license? Especially cab drivers. They're really nuts. They'd just as soon cut you off as look at you. In fact, that's the trouble. They don't look at you. They just go ahead and drive like you're not there. Aren't there any laws against that?"

"Yes, there are."

"Well, why don't you enforce them, instead of picking on me because I make a little phone call? I haven't done anything wrong. Why pick on me? Are you Russian?"

Burton seemed to lean back. "No, I'm an American. Why do you ask?"

"Because they're behind it all, you know. The drugs and the tobacco business and the newspapers and the crazy driving and everything. Half of the cab drivers live in Brighton Beach, you know. They come over here from Russia and they're all in the Mafia and right away they start driving cabs like a bunch of maniacs. They were put up to it, you know. It's part of the plot."

Burton eyed him with increasing wariness.

"You play a lot of chess, William, so I—"

The young man cut him off. "I don't play chess any more," he said firmly. "I quit the game, you know. I'm through with it. I have better things to do with my life. To hell with chess."

Burton blinked in surprise and pondered the response. He pulled a cigar from inside his jacket.

"No smoking," Abbott announced firmly. "Especially cigars. Tobacco is the leading cause of death in the world, you know. Even cigarette smoke can give cancer to nonsmokers and cigar smoke is deadly. You have no right to endanger my life by blowing smoke at me."

Regal choked back a laugh, earning a sour look from Burton, who snapped, "You say that the black moves in the newspaper game aren't very good, William?"

"No, I didn't say that. I said they were ridiculous. I know five-year-olds who can play better than that."

Burton turned to Regal with elaborate courtesy. "Inspector Regal, do you have any questions to ask our young friend here?"

Abbott jumped to his feet, startling the detective who was sitting near him. The man moved forward hurriedly to restrain the youth from violence.

"You're the one making those moves?" Abbott said, staring at Regal. "Boy, are you stupid. How did you ever pass the Civil Service test? I bet you must have had political pull to get on the force. That's how the Russians run their police force, you know. Everybody's a friend of somebody else."

Burton's beefy face wore a smile of vast satisfaction. "Your move, Inspector Regal," he purred.

It took all kinds. If there was one thing that Larry Fifer had learned in thirty years of driving a horsedrawn around Central Park, it was that people were weird and the weirdest of them all always seemed to find their way to his carriage.

Like the guy sitting alone in the backseat right now.

Here it was, the hottest night of the year and this guy was wearing a jacket with the collar pulled up, a scarf that covered most of his face, a hat pulled down low over his eyes. And sunglasses. *Ten o'clock at night and he's wearing sunglasses.*

And jabbering.

Talking nonstop.

Crazy talk too. About people not really being people but just pieces in a game. Everybody was a pawn.

Larry Fifer thought, *Sure. Everybody's a pawn except him. And he's the king of Siam.*

"That's why nobody really misses anybody when they die. Because who would miss a pawn?"

Sure, right. I'll be happy to get rid of this nutcake. And I'll be happy to get out of this park too. I'm surrounded by nutcakes.

Now, what's he doing?

Strange sounds started to come out of the backseat. Larry Fifer turned around and saw that his passenger was holding a small tape recorder in one hand. From it came the sounds of screaming. Somebody screaming.

What the hell is this?

Is this lunatic smiling at me?

"This was a pawn too. This is what he sounded like just before he died. Do you ever wonder what you'll sound like just before you die?"

The passenger lunged forward. As he did, he reached under his jacket and pulled out a long evil-looking knife. Larry Fifer saw it glint in the overhead light from one of the park's old-fashioned streetlamps.

Just before the passenger could get his arm around Fifer's throat, the driver bent forward out of reach, then jumped down from the cab.

The passenger was standing in the back of the cab

now, with the knife extended in front of him, toward the driver.

Larry Fifer never ran so fast in his life.

He ran back along the roadway toward the park entrance. As he ran, he screamed.

"Help, police! Murder! Help, police! Murder!"

He ran as fast as he could, as far as he could. It felt like his heart was going to explode inside his chest.

But he heard no footsteps behind him.

Finally, he could not help it anymore. Still screaming, he slowed down and glanced over his shoulder. His passenger was not chasing him. All Fifer could see was the cab stopped in the roadway. He couldn't see his passenger at all.

That doesn't mean he's not chasing me. Maybe he's in the bushes coming after me.

Larry Fifer kept running.

And screaming.

"Help, police! Murder!"

But no one heard him until he came out of the park onto Central Park South a few minutes later.

And by that time, *he* was gone.

18

"Sit down, son," Regal ordered. "You're making people nervous."

Abbott muttered something inaudible but lowered himself back into the padded armchair. The detective took his hands off the young man's shoulders and backed away from the seat.

"This chess game is real important to me, Mr. Abbott," Regal said calmly. "Are you sure it's lost?"

"Of course I'm sure. You botched up everything. Now you're dead as a doornail. If you were a real chess player, you'd know that."

Regal noticed the corners of Joe Burton's mouth crinkling in suppressed pleasure but ignored it.

"You sound like you know a little bit about the game," Regal said.

Abbott looked down at the floor. "A little," he conceded.

Regal waited until Abbott looked up. "More than a little. Isn't that the truth . . . Billy?"

Abbott reacted to the name as if hit with an electric

prod. He jumped to his feet and said, "I've got to get out of here."

"Why?" Regal asked, even as he reached out to gently restrain the younger man.

"Because Billy Abbott's dead. I'm not Billy Abbott anymore. I'm William Abbott. That's the way I want it."

His eyes met Regal's and the policeman was stunned to see in them not anger but the wild, unreasoning fear of a trapped animal. Billy Abbott was afraid of chess.

"All right," Regal said. "You're William Abbott." He gently guided the young man back into his seat for what seemed like the hundredth time. There was perspiration on Abbott's brow and the youth wiped it off by running his shirtsleeve across his forehead. "But you've got to tell me why Billy Abbott died," Regal said.

Without looking up, staring at his shoes, the young man answered in a voice so soft that Regal had to lean forward to hear him.

"It's a funny thing," Abbott said. "You know the two greatest chess champions who ever lived were both Americans. Paul Morphy and Bobby Fischer and they both tried to get away, you know. Morphy stopped playing but it was too late. He died nuts, drowned in his bathtub. Fischer stopped playing too. He just walked away from the world's championship. People used to say he had a mouthful of cavities because he was afraid that dentists would put radio transmitters in his teeth. Then he finally shows up to play some dumb exhibition and he's talking nothing but crazy talk."

He finally looked up. "You know why Billy Abbott is dead? Because it was happening to him too. It wasn't a game anymore. All of a sudden, it was his life. It's a drug, you know. Chess is worse than alcohol or cocaine or anything. It just takes you over and you can't ever get away."

"You could have been world champion," Regal said.

"And I could have been crazy as a bedbug and I saw it coming and I ran away and I buried Billy Abbott and I became William Abbott again."

"But don't you ever think about it . . . about chess?"

"Sometimes," Abbott admitted. "Okay, a lot. But I just don't play anymore. I read the chess column in the *Times* and I read the chess magazines. And sometimes I'll waste an hour or so fooling around in my head, thinking of opening variations. But I don't try to keep up with it anymore, you know. That's all behind me now. It can't get me anymore."

"You've reformed?"

Abbott considered the phrase, then nodded. "Yup, I reformed." He felt good enough now to even try a little smile.

"But you *are* still interested."

"There are lots of things I'm interested in, now that I've got time to think about something besides chess moves. Like reading. I do a lot of reading now."

"Who's your favorite writer?"

Without hesitation, Abbott answered, "Dean Koontz."

"Why?"

"Because he writes about how things outside can make you crazy inside. He knows about that."

"And you read the chess columns too," Regal said.

"But I don't play. As long as I don't sit down and play, you know, I'll be all right."

"Billy, you've—"

"William," Abbott corrected.

"All right, William. You've been very critical of the way I've been playing this game in the *Times*."

"Sure. You stink."

"I know. I haven't played more than a half dozen games of chess since I was a teenager and I wasn't very good then either. I've been trying to get someone with some ability to take over this game but for one reason or another, it hasn't worked out yet."

"Well, it's too late," Abbott snapped. "If I had a chessboard, I could show you."

"I've got a chessboard," Joe Burton rumbled. Regal looked over in surprise but Burton's head was down. He was leaning over his desk drawer and he pulled out a cheap paper chessboard with plastic pieces on it. For a moment, Regal felt a strange sympathy stirring inside him for the grizzled old inspector. He could imagine him sitting in this office, late at night, staring at the pieces and board of a game he knew nothing about, trying desperately to find in there the key to a killer's identity. He understood the hopeless feeling.

Abbott was out of his chair and over to Burton's desk. He swept all the pieces off the cheap board, and then with hands that were astonishingly fast, he snapped up pieces and placed them in different locations. He looked at Regal.

"Now this is your position now, see? And you said white moved pawn to queen rook four."

"That's right," Regal said.

"Well now, he's got all this, see?" Abbott began to talk almost as quickly as his hands were moving over the board. "If you move your own pawn like this, see, first he picks it off. Then your bishop goes. And if you try to run, he opens with this next pawn, then his queen, and no matter what you do, he's going to finish you off on the back rank." He was moving the pieces, demonstrating the lecture, and then in a flash the pieces were back to the initial position again. "And if you just try moving your rook back now, it's too late. The pawn push comes first and then the queen and you're on your way out." He snapped pieces back onto the board again. "And if you. . . ."

His voice trailed off, his fingers lingered in the air over the board, motionless now, but continuing to exude an almost electric crackle of energy.

Finally, as if it took a deliberate act of will, Abbott let his hands drop to his side.

"And so forth," he said mildly, all the excitement squeezed from his voice. "You've lost. Forget it. Why don't you just quit? It's only a game," Abbott said. There was a soft undertone in his voice, almost a note of triumph, as if he had just that moment achieved the ultimate victory of being able to say that chess was "only a game." He smiled and went back to his armchair and sat down again. "It's only a game," he repeated. "Quit."

Regal decided to tell the truth.

"Because if I quit, people will get killed," he said.

"Why?"

"Because we think my opponent is a deranged killer. He's ordered us to play this game, and play it well, or we'll find more bodies with letters carved into their heads. Until we track him down, we just have to go along with this madman. But we don't want the public to know about it. You've seen the publicity these killings have gotten already. Can you imagine what the public reaction will be if they hear that somebody is using bodies as pieces in a chess game? That the Upper East Side is one deadly chessboard?"

Abbott considered the possibility. "Yeah, people would go ape," he agreed. "But what happens when you lose?"

"It's already lost? You're sure?"

"Yeah. You've got a bad position already. If you play strict defense, you're going to get chewed up by pawns. But you're not in any position to launch a counterattack. You've got nothing going for you."

"You're wrong," Regal said. "I've got one thing."

"What's that?"

"I've got Billy Abbott."

"No . . . no . . ."

"I want you to take over for me. I want you to play this death game. I want you to win it."

"No. No!" Abbott's hands tightened on the arms of the chair. "I can't."

"Why not?"

"Because I can't get started again," he shouted, banging his clenched fists on his knees. "It's like asking a retired alcoholic to have just one drink, you know. I can't let chess get hold of me and take over my life again, the way it used to. I've got my life to live. I've even got a girlfriend and she doesn't even know how to play checkers and she never heard of Billy Abbott. I've been thinking that when I finish school, we'll get married and have kids like normal people do. You know any great chess players who have families? Who have kids? If I get started playing chess again, God only knows what will happen to me."

It hurt Regal but he steeled himself to be ruthless.

"Dammit, do you want to live out your life knowing that you caused innocent people to get killed?"

"I'm not killing anyone."

"But someone is and he's kept his word so far. We haven't found any more bodies since I started playing the game with him. But if we play badly, then we can expect bodies to start showing up. Inspector Burton is working night and day on this case and he's going to nail this madman sooner or later. But in the meantime we've got to play for time—and that means playing the game." He glanced at Burton without turning his head and saw the disgusted look the other inspector was giving him. Flattery obviously was not the way to Joe Burton's heart.

"Billy . . ."

"William," Abbott corrected.

"I don't need William. I need Billy. As far as I'm concerned, William Abbott is a delivery boy. Billy Abbott is a great chess genius and he can help me save lives. You said that Billy Abbott is dead? I don't believe it. I just saw Billy Abbott standing at that cheap chessboard over there on the inspector's desk and he was alive for the first time in ten years. Don't you see why I need you?"

"And don't you see why you can't have me?" Abbott answered softly.

But Regal ignored his answer and kept speaking. "Other than a handful of men in the police department, you're the only person in New York City who knows about this chess game. We thought of enlisting some top player but we were afraid to let anyone know for fear they might talk. Since you already figured out for yourself what's going on, you're the logical person to help us."

He leaned forward until his face was no more than a foot away from Abbott's.

"You said this maniac chess player is beating me and I've got a losing game. Tell me, is he better than you? Is he better than the Billy Abbott that everybody in the world was afraid of ten years ago? Is he? Or could you save this game? I don't even need a win. I need the game to last. Could you get me a draw?"

Abbott managed to look tearful and affronted at the same time. "It's a bad position," he muttered, lowering his head and talking toward his lap. "But I think he might be a no-talent patzer just like you, you know. I'm not sure, but I think you're playing against a machine."

"A machine? Why do you think that?" Regal asked, thinking of the otherworldly mechanical voice that telephoned in his opponent's chess moves each day. For a moment, his mind even sparked with the thought that maybe this killer wasn't a human being but just a chess automaton running amok, but that was science fiction and crazy and he forced his mind back to Abbott whose face, lifted now, seemed no longer able to suppress its energy.

"Two reasons," Abbott said. "First, those initials."

"What about them?" Regal asked.

"Real chess players wouldn't use them. The *P* and the *B* are all right. For pawn and bishop. But a real chess player wouldn't use the *K* to mean knight. *K* stands for king in chess notation. We use *N* for knight. That's one reason. And the other is the way the game is being played."

"I'd say my opponent's playing pretty well," Regal said.

"I've seen these computers and their programs and I was on vacation once and I played with one of them at a college before I put all that behind me too. A couple of times in this game you played, white had a chance to really open up on you with some chancy combinations.

But every time that happened, white just put a little more pressure on you, squeezed just a little harder. That's the way computers play. They beat you to death with feathers. Just a hunch, I said, but you're playing something like *Mind Game*. That's a computer."

Regal paused to consider that a moment.

"Does that mean if we got a copy of *Mind Game*'s program, it could play our side of the game for us?"

"Sure."

"Would we win then?"

"Nope. Too late for that now. White's got an advantage and it'll hold on. You have to get outside the books they fed into the program and come up with an attack that the computer doesn't recognize. Originality confuses the machines. They fall back on standard defenses and they dither around, waiting for a pattern they do recognize to show up."

"Then what if I just make crazy moves?" Regal asked.

"It'll rip your ass off. The machines are dull but some of them're good, you know. They can beat any average player. You're in trouble any way you look at it."

"Could you win this game?"

The question hung silently in the air like a palpable object.

Abbott's hands worked restlessly in his lap. "I've had a few thoughts," he confessed, almost in a whisper, as if ashamed of himself, like a young boy in a church confessional admitting to masturbating.

"I don't want to mess up your life," Regal said, leaning forward intently, "but three people so far have had *their* lives taken away from them for no reason that we have been able to discover and we're afraid more will die if I can't keep this game going. Will you help us?"

Abbott scowled at his clenched hands. "No. I can't," he said, almost choking out the words. "If I help you, people will remember me again. I've thought about changing my name, you know. I don't want the chess people climbing all over me and hounding me again.

They've forgotten I'm alive and that's the way I want it."

Regal sank back on the edge of the desk. That was his best shot and it had failed. And there was just no way he could force Billy Abbott to play if he didn't want to.

Before he could say anything though, a detective stepped into the room and handed Joe Burton a note. The burly inspector glanced at it, nodded, then rose from his seat.

"Good enough for me, Regal," he said. "Let's take this kid home."

"I'll pass," Regal said disconsolately.

"No. You've got to come along," Burton said, and when Regal glanced at him sharply, Burton winked.

Five minutes later, the two policemen, with Billy Abbott in the backseat, were driving through Central Park in Burton's unmarked police sedan.

As Burton swung around one of the wide sweeping curves in the park, Regal saw police cruisers and flashing lights ahead.

"What's going on?" he asked.

Abbott leaned forward from the rear seat to look.

"Our chess-playing lunatic was out again tonight," Burton said.

"What?" Regal snapped.

"Don't worry. He missed. But I thought Mister Abbott would like to see some of his handiwork."

Burton pulled the car up onto the grass and parked. When he and Regal got out of the car, Abbott followed them. Regal saw Burton's top aide, Lieutenant Davis, standing in a group of policemen across the wide roadway.

Behind them was one of the old horse-drawn carriages that prowled the edges of the park on pleasant nights.

Davis was, as ever, impeccably dressed in a crisply pressed blue uniform. He looked up as the three men approached.

"What happened, Will?" Burton asked.

"It was our cuckoo, Inspector," Davis answered. "He tried to cut up the hack driver but the guy got away. Then he did this."

He gestured with his arm as he moved aside and suddenly Regal could see on the ground behind the carriage a horse lying on its side.

Abbott followed the two inspectors closely as they walked toward the fallen animal.

As they neared it, they could see that the animal was dead. Its eyes were open but its throat was covered with blood.

"Best I can tell," Lieutenant Davis said, "is that he busted its leg somehow and then cut its throat."

"Jesus Christ," Burton said.

They were standing next to the animal now, looking down at it. On its broad flank, Regal could see the initial *P* cut into the flesh.

"Anybody could have carved that. You sure it was our guy?" he asked.

Davis nodded. "The driver's over there in one of the cars talking to our detectives. He picked the ride up near the Plaza and turned into the park here. He said the guy was talking crazy about how everybody was just a pawn in a chess game. Then he said he heard some kind of soft screaming and when he turned around, the guy was holding a little tape recorder in his hand. It was playing somebody's screams. Then the guy lunged at him. All of a sudden, he said, the guy had a knife in his hand, but the driver jumped off the cab and ran like hell back to the park entrance. The nut stayed here and did the horse."

"Any description?" Burton asked. "Maybe for once we get lucky?"

"Don't count on it. Sunglasses, a baseball hat pulled down over his eyes, his jacket collar turned up. All the guy knows for sure is that he was big," Davis said.

Burton grunted in disgust. He turned and took Abbott's elbow and pulled the slight young man forward.

"Here's what we work with, Mister Abbott. It might

have been a person instead of a horse. Next time, it probably will be."

Abbott was silent, staring down at the horse. He finally looked up at Burton and said, "I want to go home."

"Life ain't all chess pieces, is it, kid?" Burton said. "Get one of the uniforms to drive him home, Paul. There's no way I'd let this kid play a game for me where lives depended on it."

"Joe," Regal said seriously, "this is Billy Abbott."

"No, it's not," Burton snapped. "He said it himself. Billy Abbott is dead. This is William Abbott, delivery boy. And we're playing a life-and-death game against a killer and a chess machine, probably one of those smart Russian machines, and this kid isn't in that league."

Regal saw Abbott's head snap up in anger. "Not in that league?" he said. "Not in that league? You clown, what do you know about chess? I can beat any machine that was ever put together. And I can beat any damned player who ever lived." The words poured out of him, angry, impassioned.

"Forget it. You're a delivery boy. We're dealing with a killer . . . probably a smart Russian killer. We don't need you."

Abbott glared at Burton for a moment, then spun toward Regal. "I'm your man, Inspector."

"You sure?" Regal asked.

"No," Abbott said, "I'm not sure. But people shouldn't be allowed to do things like this." He waved his hand toward the horse. "I'll take over that game for you."

Burton said, in a voice tinged with awe, "You're not afraid to take on the Russians?"

"I'm not afraid to take on anybody."

Burton gripped the young man by the shoulder. "Win it for us. Win it for America." He turned to Regal and added solemnly, "Now see about getting Mister Abbott home."

Regal nodded and led Abbott across the street to

where a covey of squad cars were parked. He glanced at his watch.

"It's ten-thirty. I've got only a half hour to call my next move in to the *Times*."

Abbott said instantly, "Advance your knight. King knight to king knight three. Let's attack."

"But..." Regal began and then was silenced as the young man held up an index finger. There was a smile on his face now, the smile of a cat at a cornered crippled mouse... the killer smile that had once terrified the opponents of Billy Abbott, the greatest attacking genius the chess world had ever known.

"I'm sorry, William," Regal said. "That's the last time I'll open my mouth."

"It's okay," Abbott said. He reached out a hand to Regal's shoulder and patted him comfortingly. "And you can call me Billy."

Regal arranged for a uniformed cop to drive Abbott back to his home in Brooklyn, after first reminding the young man forcefully that he was to tell no one at all, not even his father, not even the cop driving the squad car, about the chess game and its connection to the Monogram Murders.

Then Regal used a police radio to patch into a phone line and called his chess move into the *Times*.

He walked back across the road to Joe Burton.

"Inspector, sir, may I humbly request that you give me advance notice before going into your George M. Cohan routine. I almost ruined your act by breaking into tears."

"I figured that might happen so I toned it down," Burton chuckled, obviously pleased with himself. "Are all chess players as nutty as him?"

"I don't think so. I met a top international player on a cruise once and he seemed sensible enough. I think Billy Abbott is just a wild card. I read once that he'd only go to doctors who belonged to the American Legion because he was afraid the others might be Russian agents. He's around the corner, no doubt about that. But for me, Joe, he's heaven's gift. I knew damned well I was over my head in that game but the commissioner wouldn't let me find an outside expert. Maybe I was lucky. If Billy is half as good as he was ten years ago, he's still better than anybody else we could get."

"Do you think he's right about you playing against a computer?"

"Christ, how would I know? That never even occurred to me. If it had, I would have let a machine make all my moves right from the start."

"Screwed up again, huh, Regal?"

"Probably."

"Well, Mister Monogram didn't score tonight. Now if your kid can make the game interesting again, maybe it'll just buy us enough time to catch the bastard. By the time I get finished, I'm going to know everything that goes on twenty-four hours a day in those blocks up on the East Side. Maybe the nut'll kill again, but if he does, I'm going to get him."

"Good luck," Regal said. "But how are you going to monitor sixty-four square blocks?" Regal asked. "They're already trying to take your manpower away."

"I'm not going to let them," Burton growled. "I can give them a fight, you know."

Regal thought a moment. "A stakeout team on every block? No way, Joe. Too many men. Why not use cameras? Put all those blocks on videotape. Night and day electronic surveillance."

"Regal, just butt out, will you?" snapped Burton. "I can just see fifty cops standing around shooting movies twenty-four hours a day. Take care of your chess game and leave the police work to me, okay?"

"I'd have some people on the streets too," Regal said stubbornly, "especially at night, just to be safe. But the bodies have been brought in from outside, obviously by car or truck. If cameras could pick up every single car that drives on those blocks, you could check back the day after a killing and pinpoint the vehicle. Maybe even get a recognizable picture of the driver."

"Regal, it's late. I'm standing here next to a dead freaking horse and I haven't got time for this chitchat. Go home. Call me when you have something worth talking about."

And Burton stomped away.

Regal took his advice and went home, even though he was annoyed at Burton for so cavalierly dismissing Regal's idea of using TV cameras.

It would work, Regal thought. And it would be a sensational way to solve the Monogram Murders. And if Burton did it, that might very well make Burton the next chief inspector of the police department.

Well, if that's the price to find this killer, I'll pay it. If Burton pulls this off, he deserves the prize.

Back in his apartment, Regal opened Patrice's door and peered inside. There was no sound that he could hear but she seemed to be huddled at the edge of the big bed. He eased the door shut, wondering what he would have felt or done if her bed had been empty. Would he even have cared? Or would he simply have shrugged his shoulders and continued on to his own bed?

He was astonished to find himself overwhelmed with an abrupt surge of longing to see Jane Cole. He had not given her a thought since the day's trip to Brooklyn, but suddenly he could feel her presence, almost as if she were in the room, almost as if he had only to reach out his hand to touch her.

He stopped short, did an about-face, and poured himself a stiff drink at the living room bar, feeling all the while as if his life was spinning faster and faster. If this kept up, he would surely fly apart into a million pieces.

Jane Cole. He barely knew the young woman. Why would she be so vivid in his head? She was nothing to him except a fellow cop—an attractive and charming fellow cop—and surely he was nothing to her. She was still Pete Muniz's girl.

But Pete was dead, and perhaps even at this moment, she was prowling the streets of Spanish Harlem seeking his killers, while Regal stood drinking before toddling off to bed.

Regal thought about that for a while and then poured the Finlandia vodka down the sink. With a sigh, he started toward his apartment door. Time to walk the neighborhood.

19

Jane Cole was not, in fact, prowling the streets. She was seated at a table in a small grimy nightspot, listening to a rather plump maiden wail of love in words Jane only occasionally recognized.

"Her heart breaks because her man has left her," the man beside her whispered. "She will light a candle for his soul. And then she will track him down, carve out his liver and feed it to the dogs."

"His liver?" Jane giggled.

"Shhh. If she hears you laughing, it may be *your* liver."

Jane bit back a snort of amusement and fumbled for another cigarette. Her pack was almost empty, she realized with dismay. She had quit smoking three years ago after deciding that she hated the way it made her hair and clothing smell. Still, perhaps out of some sort of twisted I'm-not-an-alcoholic egotism, she had always carried cigarettes in her purse . . . smoking one only once in a while in a tense moment. But lately the tense moments seemed to be coming with great frequency and now it was clear that the only thing to do was to quit totally, which was exactly what she was going to do. Someday.

Someday lots of things, she thought, suddenly feeling tired and morose. Someday Prince Charming would come riding up. Someday Sarah would be attending her first prom and someday Sarah would go off to college. And Jane Cole would be left alone. Just her and her nerves and the cigarettes she didn't really want.

Someday, too, she would find out who killed Pete Muniz . . . but not tonight, she realized. It was late and she was getting sleepy, lulled by too much smoke and one or, perhaps, two drinks too many and too much conversation in a language she did not really understand, beyond the occasional "por favor" or "muchas gracias" or "mira, mira, mira."

She smiled sleepily at her companion. Jose Colon was a cousin by marriage of Pete Muniz. He was also a sergeant in the army military police and he was spending precious furlough time with her in an effort to find a lead to Pete's killer.

Jane puzzled over why she hadn't told Paul Regal about Colon when the subject first came up. There was nothing to hide. Why make a mystery of it?

To punish Regal, she decided. To punish him for being Pete's boss and still being alive when Pete was in the ground. To punish him for having even speculated about whether Pete was taking drugs or not or whether he might have been on the take. Regal probably deserved better treatment than that. After all, he wasn't the only one who had those same questions about Pete. She knew that, painfully and firsthand.

Oh well, if he didn't deserve it for that, he probably deserves it for some other very good reason. Everyone fucks up all the time. Especially me. Oh God, especially me with this game I'm playing. Paul Regal isn't perfect. Let him suffer. I suffer. They say it's good for the soul.

So why do I feel soul-dead?

Starting to nod off, despite the singer's heel-stomping

yowls and the noise of the small band, she forgot for a moment that Pete was dead and that it was his cousin beside her. She reached out her hand, touched his arm, and almost said, "Let's go home to bed, Pete," before she caught herself.

Her eyes teared as she remembered the look of delight on Pete's face when she would say that to him.

She pulled a tissue from her purse and dabbed her eyes. "Too smoky in here," she explained to Jose.

He looked back at her and said, "Better than the last two places we were in."

"It must all be catching up with me. I'm getting a little woozy. Maybe it's time to leave."

"Stick it out for just a few more minutes. She should be finished any time now."

As if on cue, the singer gave a last wail of shuddering despair, clutched at her bosom with both hands and crumpled to the floor—only to rise beaming at the smattering of applause from the small audience.

A minute later, she was seated between Jane and Jose, looking back and forth from one to the other with suspicious metronomic regularity.

Jose Colon talked low and insistently, hands moving with fluent grace to emphasize his remarks, sometimes resting briefly, but respectfully, on the singer's fleshy upper arm. Once when the woman tossed her head and made a curt remark—not a word of which Jane understood—Jose's fingers tightened for a moment and his voice took on a hard edge, but for most of the talk, his tone was soft and lulling. His large brown eyes were fixed on the singer's face as if he were trying to hypnotize her and Jane saw the woman begin to bask and preen under that steady look. Her glances in Jane's direction grew farther and farther apart.

Whoever Jose winds up marrying better keep a close watch on him, she thought. This one handles women like a train handles a tunnel.

Eventually, Jose indicated Jane with an upturned, beseeching hand. She recognized the words "amor" and "corazon" and seized her chance when the singer looked at her again, this time with a softer expression on her face.

"I loved him," Jane said in a low voice. "He loved me too and we were to marry. Now he is dead and I light candles to his memory." She slumped her head dramatically onto her folded hands, thankful to close her eyes for a moment.

She felt the singer's sweaty hand on the back of her neck. "Eeet ees hard," the woman said, a catch in her throat. "You suffer."

Jane nodded mutely, willing herself to stay awake and be of help to Jose.

He had produced a color photograph of Pete. It was one of her favorites, showing him grinning shyly at the camera. The singer studied it with fascination and then handed it back.

She glanced around with elaborate casualness, then spoke for a moment in light-speed Spanish to Jose. Jane thought she heard several names mentioned but was not sure. Then the singer turned to Jane and advised in a kindly voice, "Pray to God. He ees the only help." She patted Jane on the shoulder, then stood and hurried away.

"Gracias," Jane called after her softly. Then she asked Jose, "What did she say?"

"She didn't want to get mixed up in anything, naturally . . ."

"They all say that," Jane responded.

"Who all?" Jose asked lightly.

"All all. Nobody wants to get involved."

Jose nodded. "Pete was here a couple of weeks ago. She's not sure but it might have been the night he got shot. She remembers him because he was so good looking. He was looking for a Panamanian girl named Estrellita but he had just missed her. He may have found out or he may not have found out that Estrellita had an apartment on 107th Street."

"Who may he have found out from? Or not found out from, as the case may be?" Jane asked.

Jose grinned. "Not from our singing friend. Of course, she knows nothing. And even if she did know something, she would deny everything. She would not even remember that Estrellita used to come in here pretty often with her boyfriend, whose name she remembers as Hector."

"Bingo," Jane said. "Hector Guzman, the one who got killed."

"Right."

"Is there any point in sending the regular narcs up here to lean on her?"

"No," Jose said, shaking his head. "I think she's done us a big favor. She's given us the right Estrellita, Guzman's girlfriend, and tied in that Pete was looking for her. And she gave us the street where Estrellita lives. I think it's all she knows and it's a pretty good contribution." He saw Jane rub her tired eyes again. "And a pretty good night's work."

"Okay," Jane agreed. "Let's get out of here." She looked around. "And let's hurry. I think she's going to sing again."

Jane tapped perfunctorily on Paul Regal's open office door and entered hesitantly. "Are you busy?"

He looked up from the pile of reports on his desk. "I'll live. Come on in."

She sat down and eyed him shrewdly. "Something's up. I can tell by your eyes."

"I left the report on your desk," Regal said. "The nut case tried to kill a hack driver last night in Central Park. Guy got away and he took it out on a horse instead. We managed to keep it out of the papers."

"Any ID? Prints? Anything?" Jane asked.

Regal shook his head. "We came up empty."

"Damn," Jane snapped. "Well, at least you know it was a guy now . . . . it was a guy, right?"

"Yeah."

"Not some crazed feminist anyway. Give us women a

bad name." Her eyes sparkled. "I was hoping you caught the guy who called you and Burton."

"Oh, yeah, that too," Regal said blandly. "We did."

"And?"

"He didn't know anything about the murders. But he's a chess player. He may be able to help. Any help is good help."

"And Inspector Burton? Is he happy with that too?"

" 'Happy' is never the word for Joe Burton," Regal said. " 'Snarling less' might be a more accurate description."

"He's a lot more bark than bite," Jane said. "Sometimes he's even human."

"I'll keep that in mind the next time he's sucking blood from my jugular."

"He's okay. He did me a big favor once. At least, I thought it was a big favor at the time."

"What was that?"

"He got me out of bunco and into this office. I was desperate to get away from bunco and all my ex-husband's snide, thieving, lecherous cronies. My Uncle George at the One-Six spoke with Burton and he talked to the commissioner and I wound up here. By and large, this isn't quite as hateful."

"Thanks a lot," Regal said.

"Of course, it would be a lot better if I were treated as an experienced cop rather than a gofer. But one can't have everything, can one?" She sighed theatrically and gazed pensively at her fingernails.

"Now that this is a no-man's-land in the department, without staff and without prestige, you've got a clear road to the top," Regal said. "See? If you wait long enough, everything comes around."

Jane nodded, and that should have ended the conversation, Regal knew. Instead, the young woman remained seated, still examining her nails.

"All right, Jane. Come across. What's on your mind?"

"You see right through me, huh? I thought I was being unfathomable."

"Today, you're fathomable," Regal said. "What did you come in to say?"

"Just that I'm getting closer to Estrellita. We ran into a nightclub singer last night who remembered Pete being in there, asking about this Estrellita. We've got a clue on her neighborhood."

"Who's 'we,' Jane?"

"A friend," Jane said airily and again wondered why she was still playing this game with Regal. "A friend of the family. Not someone in the department."

"Fair enough," Regal said. "Did you give it to Burton's people yet?"

She shook her head, annoyed by his lack of reaction. "There's not really anything to give yet. I think we need another night of looking before we call in the cavalry."

"Jane, I understand it, but I don't like it," Regal said, "so this is your last night. Tomorrow, I want a report made to Burton's men and a copy to me. And don't leave anything out."

She nodded, rose and walked toward the door. "Not anything?" she asked in the doorway.

"Absolutely," Regal said. "Don't leave anything . . ."

Too late. She was gone and Paul Regal scratched his head, wondering for perhaps the ten thousandth time in his life why women were so stunningly different from men. Even women cops didn't think like cops. They thought like . . . well, like women, for God's sake.

20

The killer never mentioned the butchery of the horse when he continued to call in his chess moves. But neither did he strike again and Regal was willing to settle for that. Perhaps, he was like a covered kettle and every so often the steam had to blow out.

If it takes a dead horse to save a human's life, then bring on the ponies, Regal thought.

He knew it was not logical but he had expected some kind of major change to occur instantly, once Billy Abbott took over playing the chess game with the killer. But nothing had happened—at least nothing Regal could understand. The killer—or his computer—still called in every morning, reciting his move with his mechanical voice.

True to his word to trust no one with the identity of Billy Abbott, Regal then personally telephoned the move to Abbott at his Brooklyn home. If the young man was out, Regal left a message on his answering machine and the chess master would call him back in the afternoon with his move. If Abbott was at home—as he usually was—he would listen to Regal, grunting almost impatiently, and then immediately give Regal the next move for the black pieces.

"Shouldn't you think about this before deciding?" Regal asked him. "Study the position or something?"

"Remember our deal, Inspector? No questions and no second-guessing."

"Okay," Regal said reluctantly.

"But because you sound worried, let me tell you something. I played my first big tournament game when I was nine. I was white in a French defense. The game was pretty even but then on the twenty-third move, my opponent moved his knight to king three and I took him apart. He should have moved the bishop to king bishop one. You understand what I'm getting at, don't you?"

"That I should butt out and that you already have this game memorized in your head?" Regal offered.

"Something like that," Abbott said.

"Tell me. Do you really remember every game you ever played?"

"Of course. Doesn't everybody?"

"No, Billy. Everybody doesn't."

"Well, I do, so stop worrying about it. And so far, this guy is making just the moves we expected from the communist creep and I'm ready for all of them. The only time I'll have to think about it is if he does something I'm not expecting."

"I trust you, Billy."

"Good. You should, 'cause I'm going to own this bastard soon. By the way, Inspector. We *are* playing a computer."

"How do you know?" Regal asked quickly, hoping perhaps that if Abbott recognized the program or the specific computer, police might be able to trace it to the killer.

"Because he's got no vision. He's just chewing away, trying to gum us to death. It's not a very good computer either. Don't worry about a thing."

"Just keep the game interesting," Regal said.

"It's going to get more interesting soon," Abbott said, and it was hard not to recognize his apparent glee even over the telephone.

He obviously had some serious plan in mind but when Regal, in the evenings, alone in his apartment, set up the chess pieces and tried to see where Abbott was going and what he was doing, he came up empty. The policeman was himself such a low-quality player that he always assumed chess to be slashing, cutting brilliant moves with flags flying and guns firing. But Abbott was playing on a different level because his moves were quiet, almost nondescript, and Regal could not see where the black pieces—Regal's own—were any better off or more threatening than they had been when the policeman himself was playing the game. He thought about it for a long time and then created some solace for himself by deciding that some things just had to be taken on faith.

After Jack Ferguson's story about the possibility of a chess-playing killer had appeared in the *Daily News*, there had been a brief flurry of stories in the other papers. But Joe Burton had been as good as his word. None of his people talked to the press and Regal's staff stayed quiet too. Commissioner Gallagher had still not let the mayor know about the chess game, and so no one had anything to say. Burton stonewalled it against all questions and, without new bodies being found to keep up interest, the story quickly died—pushed off the front pages by the other tragedies, the other disasters, the other lunacies that made up an average news day in New York City.

From all Regal could tell, even the teenagers around the city had tired of writing messages on their own heads with nail polish. Now, from what he could gather, they were more interested in a newer fad—that of wearing underwear outside and over their regular garments, in imitation of some rock singer or other. The *Post*, in particular, seemed to find this trend an item of major news value and managed to run a photo of some underdressed swollen-breasted teenager on Page One every day, and

Regal decided that America had gone bad when it failed to institute a national policy of shooting rock-and-rollers on sight. But at least the chess killer was off Page One. That was worth something.

Regal had just hung up after getting the next game move from Abbott when his private office telephone rang.

Joe Burton said, "One of my men has finally gotten to Ferguson about that chess story."

"Yeah? And?"

"An anonymous tip," Burton said. "Someone called his city desk and Ferguson just happened to be there to get the call. It was just luck on his part."

Regal thought for a second, then said, "What do you think?"

"I think Ferguson's telling the truth. Even if he doesn't have much practice at it."

"So that means it wasn't one of our guys," Regal said.

"Probably not. When a cop leaks a story, he doesn't do it anonymously because he'll want a favor back sometime."

"Ferguson didn't recognize the caller or remember anything about him?"

"No. Just a man's voice, he said. Muffled," Burton related.

"It was our killer then."

"It looks that way. But why? Why would he want the press involved?"

"Maybe he wants to read about himself," Regal said. "A lot of them do." He paused. "I just hope the bastard isn't getting bored."

He heard Burton sigh. "You and all the horses in town. I'm dead-ended. I hate to say it but I don't know if we've got a hope at this guy unless he kills again." Burton coughed, then asked, "Did you hear from the commissioner yet?"

"No," Regal said.

"You will. Let me know if anything happens."

"I will."

"By the way, I got that report from Jane Cole about Estrellita. I've got men checking out the neighborhood."

"My men too," Regal said.

"Good. Maybe we'll get lucky."

"Be the first time this year."

"That's 'cause you always hang out with fags," Burton said as he hung up and the telephone clicked dead in Regal's ear.

Five minutes later, the commissioner's office called and Regal was summoned upstairs.

Gallagher waved him to an empty chair in the office, and as Regal sat down, he realized that only a few short weeks before, he did not wait for the commissioner to invite him to sit.

Everything changes, he thought and said crisply, "You wanted to see me, sir?"

"Yeah, Paul. Relax, take it easy."

Regal responded by doing exactly the opposite. He nodded but continued to sit straight and stiff, imagining that this was how Dreyfus looked at his court-martial.

"What's new on the political front?" the commissioner asked, settling himself back behind his desk. "I haven't seen you in the paper recently."

"I stay out of politics, sir," Regal said. "Except when Patrice drags me along to something. But lately she's been busy planning that Storm Mountain extravaganza so we haven't had much time for going out."

"No, I guess not," the commissioner said.

To Regal, he seemed to be on the verge of saying something or asking Regal a personal question, but having trouble doing it. Finally, with a narrowing of his dark eyes, Gallagher visibly gave up the attempt and instantly clicked into an all-business mode.

"Joe Burton's been using up a ferocious amount of manpower on this Monogram Murderer," Gallagher said. "He's been taking men from precincts all over the city and we don't have anything to show for it yet. If it weren't for that damned chess game of yours, I'd be

ready to believe the murderer left town. Anyway, I've
been telling Joe he's got to unload some of the extra
manpower and today he came at me with an idea to use
video surveillance on all the streets in the target neighborhood. Sound familiar?"

"A little," Regal said.

"I thought so. Joe said it was your idea."

"That was nice of him."

Gallagher grinned. "I think he expected me to shoot
it down. The whole point, Paul, is that we don't know
when or even *if* this nut is going to kill again. And we
just can't keep the streets flooded with men on the off
chance that they'll run across him dumping a body. Camera surveillance sounds like it might cut our losses but
keep us in the game."

"Nobody was ever arrested by a camera," Regal reminded him.

"I know that," Gallagher answered impatiently. "And
nobody's ever going to get arrested anywhere else in the
city if we don't get our cops out of that damned big
chessboard of the Upper East Side." He paused as if
waiting for an argument, but Regal still sat straight and
silent and waited.

"Anyway," the commissioner said, "I've made contact
with Converse Security Systems. They're going to send
a man here to talk to you today. I want you to work this
out."

"Why me, sir? It's Burton's case."

"I know that but he's not very good at friendly, ex-
ploratory meetings. We want these people maybe to
help us, not to walk out cursing." Gallagher smiled.
"There are some advantages in having political skills."

"I wouldn't know, sir," Regal said stiffly. "There's a
problem with the cameras though."

"Naturally," Gallagher said.

"I've been thinking about this and we might be talking
about sixty or seventy cameras. Maybe more. It could
cost us a fortune. The manpower we're using, well,

they're already on the payroll. This might be an added starter and a budget-buster at that."

"Yeah," Gallagher said sourly, "I've been thinking about that too. Any ideas?"

"There's one possible out. Do you know anything, sir, about this Converse Security Systems?"

"I've run into the people once in a while. Their reputation is good."

"How about publicity? Do you think they'd be interested?"

"Who isn't? Except you," Gallagher said.

Despite his bitter feelings toward this man whom he felt had betrayed their almost-friendship, Regal smiled. "Maybe we could get them to cut their price if part of the deal was that if we nail this killer with their help we cover them head-to-foot with praise afterwards and tell the whole world that we couldn't have pulled it off without them? That might be worth more to them in the long run than some rental fees."

Gallagher suspended a pencil between the tips of his index fingers for a few seconds, then nodded.

"That makes a lot of sense, Paul. Here's what we do. You deal with these people and try to get their price down to the absolute bottom. Then let me know and I'll take it the extra step and see what I can con them out of." He shrugged. "And who knows? If worse comes to worst, maybe I can sandbag somebody into putting up the money as a civic donation."

"Fine, sir. Will that be all?"

Again Gallagher hesitated, but finally nodded and Regal rose and left the office.

Captain William Schmidt of the Communications Division's electronics section was a small lean man with rusty red hair and sharp darting eyes. There was a cautious foxlike look about him, Regal thought, but when he understood what Regal had in mind, Schmidt dropped any pretense at caution.

He rubbed his hands together and said eagerly, "I've

always wanted to do something like this. Putting an entire section under constant surveillance has tremendous possibilities. Naturally, it's not the same as having warm bodies on the scene, but in some ways, it might even be better. You can go back and reexamine tapes weeks and months later if you have to. I don't know though if I've got enough manpower in this division to ride herd on a gang of cameras working twenty-four hours a day. That's a lot of tape to look at, Inspector."

"I don't think it would come to that, Bill. It's unlikely that anybody's going to drop off a body during daylight hours, for instance. We're really talking about nighttime, and probably after midnight. What I need from you is how many cameras to put all these streets on tape."

"Take me a little while to work it out," Schmidt said. "I'll be in my office."

It was after 5 P.M. when Marv Isaacs of the Converse Security Systems showed up in Regal's office, listened to his idea, gave two hundred reasons why it couldn't be done and then, without even seeming to pause for breath, told Regal exactly how he would do it.

"I think the captain here"—Isaacs nodded toward Captain Schmidt, who was straddling a chair across the room—"has nailed it perfectly. Thirty-three cameras could do it." He started to speak again, but stopped as Joe Burton entered the office, leaving the door open behind him.

Regal did the introductions and Burton grabbed the only other chair in the office and pulled it up alongside Regal's desk.

"Explain to Joe just what you two have worked out," Regal said.

Isaacs nodded. "It's too big a job," he said, "to cover every street, every intersection."

"Tell me about it," Burton grumbled. He looked around and said, "This is a nice office, Regal. My furniture is falling apart."

"Chairs have a way of getting shabby when you keep

hitting people over the head with them," Regal said mildly and looked again toward Isaacs.

"What you want, basically, is to know every vehicle that goes into that section of town during the evening hours. It would be nice to follow every car for the entire time it's in the area, but if you think about it, that isn't really necessary. All you really need to know is what cars entered during the general time period, right?"

Burton said slowly, "I guess so. Yeah, that makes sense."

"Well, thank Captain Schmidt for figuring this out. All you need are cameras at about thirty intersections surrounding the target area. That'll get anybody coming in and it'll get them going out." He leaned back complacently, pulled a cigar from his coat, looked vainly for an ashtray and reluctantly replaced the cigar.

Regal opened a desk drawer, found an ashtray and pushed it over to Isaacs, who gratefully produced the cigar again and lit it. Burton promptly pulled out a huge black gnarly pipe, stuffed half a pound of tobacco in it and lit up, sending a billow of thick smoke across the desk toward Regal.

"Tobacco kills," yelled Jane Cole from the outside office.

Burton grinned. "You should fire that girl."

"I was going to until I found out you were the one who got her the job here," Regal said. "That makes her an untouchable."

"I'm glad you finally recognize my power," Burton said. "Tell me about these cameras," he asked Isaacs. "How would it work?"

"Every one of them has a built-in clock so the time shows up on the tape. So if you compare the entrance and exit times of vehicles, you'll be able to tell how long they took to drive through the area. Depending on where they exit the eight-block square grid, you could also tell what route they took, probably what street they drove down. That could help."

"What kind of picture would we get?" asked Burton.

"If anything happens, it'll probably be after midnight. Streetlights don't give a hell of a lot of illumination. Would a tape be able to make out a licence plate number, say?"

"Inspector, you wouldn't believe what we can do these days. Not only are the lenses better but so are the tapes. I'm not talking about the kind of tape you buy in a supermarket. With the equipment we have now, you can read a newspaper over somebody's shoulder from a block away."

Burton nodded slowly, reluctantly impressed.

"What do you think, Paul?" he asked.

"It sounds pretty good to me, Joe. It'll let you free up a lot of your manpower too."

"I'm still going to keep some people walking the streets," Burton growled. "Maybe I'm old-fashioned but I like to think that maybe a real cop, and not a computer, can get lucky and stumble onto the bastard and blow his fucking brains out."

"What about cost?" Regal asked Isaacs.

"My boss is working it out. You want the numbers when they come?"

Regal, remembering Gallagher's instructions to handle the first money negotiations, started to say yes but he was outgunned by Burton who bellowed, "Shit, no. Work that all out with the commissioner." Isaacs looked at Regal, who shrugged agreement.

"When could we have all this stuff?" Burton asked.

"If they work out the money and you get the vans, we'll have some of it in place tomorrow night. The rest by the end of the week." He shrugged. "We don't have that many cameras. I'll have to beg, borrow, or steal them."

"Theft is against the law in New York City," Burton said.

"The only thing that still is," Regal commented.

After everyone left, Regal was annoyed to hear Burton talking and joking in the outer office with Jane Cole.

Her girlish laugh echoed in the big room and he found himself wanting to go outside and tell Burton to get out and leave his staff alone to get some work done and he thought this was a curious attitude on his part.

He tidied his desk, then left and was mildly disappointed to see that Jane Cole had already gone. Had she gone some place with Burton? Maybe for a drink after work.

Who the hell cares?

As he went up the elevator to his apartment, he wondered if Patrice would be there.

She wasn't. A note by the telephone advised him that she would be working late at Storm Mountain and he should eat out or make himself a meal. Regal shrugged, mildly annoyed but not surprised, and rooted around in the refrigerator. He wondered if Patrice actually was working late at Storm Mountain and then decided that he really didn't care anymore.

Patrice was indeed working late at Storm Mountain. She was lying naked in a bed in one of the Storm Mountain model apartments. Next to her, also naked under a thin satin sheet, was Oliver Storm. Patrice had a swatch of fabric samples in her hand and was asking Storm if he had any preference.

"I've come to appreciate your taste," he said. "In fact, I think I like your taste more than any woman I've ever tasted."

Patrice smiled. "A woman does so like to be appreciated." She tossed the swatches to the floor and slid her hand under the sheet to rest on Oliver's groin.

"So warm," she said. "So lovely."

"So lonely," Storm said. He put his hand behind her head and pushed her gently down. She pulled back the covers, rubbed her cheek against him, grazed it with her lips, then closed her eyes and took him into her mouth.

"That's very nice, Patrice," Storm said, both hands moving instinctively to the back of her bobbing head.

"Don't stop. Don't even think of stopping."

Patrice moaned low in her throat as he continued gasping encouragement. Suddenly he stiffened and his fingers dug into the back of her skull and he moaned and spasmed. Slowly he eased his grip on her head, but she stayed in place, languidly licking him. Finally she looked up with a smile.

"Good?"

"Marvelous," he said.

"I love you," she said.

"Not as much as I am going to love you," Storm said. His voice caught as he pushed her back onto the bed, then bent her over and began licking the insides of her legs.

As he moved slowly upward, Patrice luxuriated in the lovemaking, rocking her hips up and down against his face. She groaned as the first surge of intense physical pleasure swept over her.

"Yes, Oliver, yes." Suddenly she gave a great shuddering gasp and ground herself against his face for a moment, then shrieked and tried frantically to pull away from him.

"No more, please. I can't . . . please . . . no more."

Storm moved over her and then she felt him enter her body and she wondered if it was true: was she really falling in love with Oliver Storm? That would be nice, she thought, especially if he really loved her too.

That would make everything much easier, much nicer. As she mused, her hips rocked automatically in rhythm with his and she felt a new sensation growing warmly deep within her.

She thought for a moment about Paul, wondering if he might ever dream that she was in Oliver Storm's arms at this moment. The thought gave her a twinge of guilt, quickly followed by an even stronger feeling of triumph and achievement, almost of revenge.

Then she stopped thinking about Paul Regal and concentrated on the steadily intensifying throbs of pleasure that spread through her body.

"Don't stop, Oliver," she gasped. "Please don't stop."

Oliver Storm grunted an inarticulate reply. He had no intention of stopping, not even if she begged him to.

21

Regal had lived on the Upper East Side for more than fifteen years but his nightly walks around the chessboard were bringing home to him how little he knew—or probably anyone knew—of his neighborhood.

The chessboard ran from Seventy-fifth Street south to Sixty-seventh Street, and from the East River Drive all the way over to Fifth Avenue bordering Central Park. He had always regarded it as all one homogeneous unit, all the same, but walking it every night now, he saw that it was a cluster of smaller neighborhoods. Up in the mid-Seventies where he lived, there were a lot more young people, and as he dropped down into the Sixties, there were fewer apartments, more townhouses, and many more chauffeur-driven limousines waiting in front of buildings.

Over near the river, there were real ethnic neighborhoods that he had never noticed before, with small delicatessens and groceries and street smells that cut sharply through the sour odor that lingered on New York's streets in the summer.

Does anybody really know his neighborhood? he wondered. Certainly not just by living there. You had to get out and study your neighborhood as if it were a strange town to get any feel for it, and the fact was he had never done that before. He was a good cop and a trained observer and he never even noticed what was happening around him.

And if I don't, who does? What do the simple folk do?

But the night's walks had changed that. He now knew where the kids hung out near the big hospital and he noted for future reference a place on York Avenue that looked like it might be housing an illegal gambling casino.

He found the bars that looked like pick-up joints and one that seemed to be doing a brisk business in drugs and he made a note to have the narcotics squad keep an eye on that establishment.

Under normal circumstances, he might have regarded his walks with some pleasure then, as an opportunity to get to see his neighborhood in a way that escaped most people.

But there was no pleasure in these walks. He was looking for a murderer.

Two nights after his meeting with the people from the video surveillance company, Regal skipped dinner and walked the entire chessboard before dark. The neighborhoods, he noticed, wore still another face before the sun set.

He realized that Burton must have made a good argument for his manpower because he saw uniformed policemen through the entire area. It was a rare block that did not have at least one patrolman on it and this was early at night. Up till now, the killer had dumped his bodies after midnight and Burton probably had even more men on the late-night shift.

Regal was also able immediately to spot the ragtag fleet of camera-bearing stakeout vehicles, which were parked at all the entrances to the area. Some of them were private cars of varied makes and ages, apparently illegally parked. Most of those had traffic tickets on them. Others were vans bearing a variety of identifications on their sides; they too appeared to be empty, and Regal was happy to see that even though he knew what he was looking for, he had not been able to spot any obvious signs that there were cameras mounted in the vehicles.

He also knew that three more vehicles, apparently taxis carrying passengers, were sweeping constantly through the streets, following predetermined routes that ensured an appearance of casualness.

Good enough, he thought, as, wearied by the long hike, he turned for home.

Now if only . . . if only what? If only he kills somebody so you can take a picture of him?

What a shitful way to make a living.

Meanwhile, the strange chess game continued. Every morning, the mechanical voice would recite a new move, and every morning, the calls were automatically traced. But they always wound up being made from a public phone, usually in Manhattan, but several came from Brooklyn and the Bronx, and that morning's call had come from the Port of New York Authority's PATH subway station in Jersey City, across the Hudson River.

"He hopped the tubes," Burton commented. "Count your blessings it was Jersey City. If it was Fort Lee, we'd start wondering if maybe the Mafia was involved."

"They don't have the Mafia in Jersey City?" asked Jane Cole, who was with the two inspectors in Regal's office.

"Between the Jersey City politicians and the Jersey City police, there's nothing left there for the Mafia," Burton growled.

Burton had been in headquarters on other business and had stopped in to see Regal on his way out. Off-handedly, he mentioned that he had managed to raise a little departmental slush fund money for Billy Abbott.

"What for?" Regal asked.

"So he can stop delivering those stupid flowers and sit home and play chess."

"He said he doesn't have to."

"I don't care what he said. I'm not going to feel right if our goddamned chess consultant winds up making a big mistake because he squashed somebody's fucking rhododendrons that morning and was feeling bad."

Regal smiled and realized there was no point in arguing. *Good. Let Burton lay some money on Billy.*

"Just be sure to tell him that the money didn't come from the Russians," Regal cautioned.

"Is he still on the Russians?"

"Worse than ever. You crammed his head so full of flap-doodle that he's convinced now every murder that ever happened in New York was part of a Russian plot."

"Good. As long as it keeps him interested."

There was no problem with keeping Abbott interested, Regal knew. When he had first taken over the game less than a dozen moves ago, he would complain anxiously about the game situation. "If I was playing the other side, I would have creamed me by now, you know. White passed up a beautiful sacrifice, the patzer. It was too complicated and long-range for him, I guess. It's an awfully dumb machine. It just can't improvise. Just a little longer."

"Then what?" Regal asked.

"I start sacrificing material to distract him. If I can get by the next few moves, we've got him. If it's a machine."

"And if it isn't?"

"Then you're dead."

That was early on, but soon Abbott was making his moves immediately, sometimes giggling as he gave them to Regal. Like most chess fanatics, he had become caught up in the game and hated his opponent with a lethal intensity. He wanted literally to kill the opponent on the other side of the board—and his conviction that he was playing against a computer program seemed to give him even greater determination to win. Abbott hated the very idea of machines playing chess.

"Why does that upset you so much, Billy?" Regal asked one day.

"It's immoral," Abbott replied with conviction. "It's a desecration of an art, turning it into a counting contest. It's like . . . like having sex with a mechanical woman, a toy that moves. It's a sin. Only the Russians would stoop to that."

"You think they're involved?"

"Of course they are. You heard Inspector Burton. But sometimes it surprises me, because chess is the only thing Russians are any good at and you wouldn't think they'd cheapen it this way. Maybe it's the Chinese. They're about as bad as the Russians, you know. They don't know shit about chess either, so they wouldn't care."

Abbott was clearly now in the playing groove. He was predicting the white moves accurately and responding immediately when Regal called him. "Hyper" was not strong enough to describe the young chess player's mood and he sometimes seemed to babble senselessly for a while after telling Regal what black piece they should move next.

Most of Abbott's diatribes were directed against the Soviet Union, especially Russian cab drivers, but he threw in occasional shots at the French, English, Germans, Arabs, and Jews too. "They're all against us, you know," he insisted. "Thank God they're all against each other too. Listen, what about a gun permit?"

"What?"

"I think I should have a gun permit. Just in case."

"I'll work on it," Regal said. "Permits take time in this town."

"All right, but if my father and I are murdered in our beds by the Russians, our blood will be on your hands, you know."

"At least you wouldn't have those maniac cab drivers to worry about anymore," Regal said blandly.

"Thank God for that."

Listening to the change in Billy Abbott's moods, Regal had begun having second thoughts about involving the young man in the strange game. It was apparent, even though Abbott might not admit it to himself or even know it, that he was becoming addicted to chess again. When Regal questioned him, he confessed with a combination of shame and defiance that he was spending most of his waking hours either endlessly replaying the current game with the Monogram Murderer or studying books on chess strategy that had been published in the past few years. His schoolwork had fallen off a little, he admitted, "but nothing serious. I can make it up as soon as this game is over."

Regal hoped it would be that easy. Increasingly, he felt that he was cold-bloodedly sacrificing Billy Abbott's hopes for a normal life. But what was the alternative? They dare not stop the game now.

Regal had almost given up studying the game position, finding himself increasingly lost and confused. Abbott's moves often completely baffled him, especially when he cheerfully allowed his opponent to sweep up one of black's bishops.

After they had lost the black bishop, Regal was going to ask Abbott if there was any hope for them in the game, but before he could, the young man gloated, "Is he blind or what? Just a few more moves and I spring the trap. I'm gonna crush this woodpusher. Death to all machines!"

But it was a human who died next.

Harriet Bailey had been unlucky all her life, as she never tired of telling her parents and sisters, her husband and children, and the few friends she still had. Her favorite phrase was "If only . . ."

"If only Mr. Tyson had stopped to think about who did most of the work in that office, I would have been executive secretary instead of Miss Mini Skirts. And then I would have stayed in that job instead of having to quit. The goings-on were shameful." Or "If only this building would go condo, we could buy this apartment and then sell it at a terrific profit."

"If only I had the time ... if only my children would appreciate what I have sacrificed for them ... if only this cold weather would go away ... if only my numbers would come in ..."

A plump faded blonde in her early fifties, Harriet had one obsession—the state lottery. Gambling as such held no great interest for her. She had been to Atlantic City once and had lost a total of forty dollars, most of it in the slot machines, and it had made her feel nervous and insecure. Too much noise and confusion.

But buying a lottery ticket that might mean millions of dollars never failed to thrill her. She would go to sleep at night thinking of all the things she would do if only this time she won. The first thing, she knew, would be to move from their small apartment on the west side of Manhattan to a split level on Staten Island where she had grown up. And she would sell the small used-furniture shop she ran on Ninth Avenue, with its stuffed crow in the window, and maybe find some nice business that she could run from her home.

It was her addiction to the lottery that proved to be Harriet Bailey's final piece of bad luck. Circumstances had prevented her from buying a ticket earlier in the day so she had closed down the antique shop early and rushed out to pick up a ticket at the newsstand several blocks away, stubbornly selecting the same numbers—all her family's birth dates—that she had played with no success at all for the last ten years.

"They're *bound* to hit one of these days," she explained to her husband. "Yeah, yeah, yeah," he responded wearily. "When tits give orange soda."

If only he weren't so crude. She often thought that.

She bought her lottery ticket and, if only it had not suddenly started pouring down rain, Harriet might have realized her dream.

But it did rain. It came down in torrents. Harriet stood in the doorway, cursing her luck. "If only I had thought to bring an umbrella," she complained bitterly to a young man who had ducked into the doorway to get out of the rain also. "Now I'm going to get soaked and my permanent will be ruined."

"Which way are you going?" he asked.

"Over on Ninth, three blocks down. I have an antique shop."

"That's the direction I'm going. If I can flag a cab, I'll drop you off at your place."

"That would be nice," Harriet said and looked up and down the street. "If only a taxi would come along."

"Here's one coming now," he said, waving his arm vigorously. "He's stopping. Let's go."

Taking her arm, he half carried her in a rush to the taxi, yanked open the rear door and almost tossed her in. He looked around hurriedly then got in beside her.

The cab driver did not wait for instructions but pulled away from the curb.

"Let's go to Central Park," the young man said.

The cab driver laughed—a curiously crazed high-pitched laugh—and Harriet thought, in a moment of rising panic, *They're going to rob me. My God, they're going to rob me.* She clutched her lottery ticket so tightly in her hand that it wadded up into a piece of damp cardboard.

"I want to get out at this corner," she stammered, reaching tentatively for the door handle.

"Forget it, driver. She's going to Central Park."

"Let me out," Harriet screamed. "I want out of this cab."

"You're making too much noise, lady," the man next to her said. He put his left arm around her shoulder, curling his hand so that it covered her mouth. With his right hand, he punched her hard in the stomach.

The blow seemed to trigger something in him. He punched her repeatedly in the stomach, grunting with the force of his blows.

The driver glanced at him in the rearview mirror, then looked away as if uninterested.

Inside Central Park, the driver said, "Any place special, sir?"

He laughed. "Over there. In that parking lot. Away from the light."

The cab stopped and the young man opened the rear door. Harriet Bailey was doubled over, both arms crossed in front of her stomach, her purse fallen to the floor. She moaned, as much from shock as from the pain.

He grabbed her by the hair and pulled her out onto the asphalt, then straddled her body, took her throat in his hands and began squeezing.

She writhed convulsively and beat at his hands for a few moments, then went limp. Her eyes bulged wide and unblinking and her tongue slowly sneaked out of her mouth.

It was fun. The horse wasn't any fun. But this was fun.

It was too easy. She died too quickly.

Maybe she's not dead yet. If she isn't, you can still hurt her some more.

That's a good idea. Maybe like this. Ooooh, I didn't know eyeballs were so gooshy. I think she's dead. She didn't even make a sound.

Next time, take the eyeballs out of somebody you know is alive.

I want to do that. I really want to do that.

Don't forget your knife. She needs an initial.

He opened a switchblade from his pocket and then sat down atop the body and carefully cut deep into flesh to carve the letter *R* on Harriet's forehead.

Now I have to kill some time.

Why not? You've killed everything else.

I hope the queen doesn't die this easily.

She won't. I'll see to that.

22

Harriet Bailey's husband had rather wished she had run away from home but when she had not telephoned by midnight to tell him that it was all his fault and if only he had been more sensitive to her needs she would have stayed, he knew something was wrong and called the police to report her missing.

The desk sergeant suggested that he call back in the morning and speak to Missing Persons. By the time he did get around to calling back, the body of Harriet Bailey had been found, stuffed between two parked cars on East Seventieth Street near Second Avenue.

She had been found while Regal was driving to his office so he did not hear about it until Jane Cole told him.

"Another body."

"Where?"

"It's one of ours," she said knowingly. "Seventieth and Second. A woman. Beat to shit and an *R* carved into her forehead."

"Fuck," Regal growled and stomped into his office.

He had been waiting for this shoe to drop. Ever since the killer had missed his victim and had to settle for that horse, Regal knew another murder was on its way. And this son of a bitch was no Jack the Ripper; he would not just stop killing and vanish one day. This one would kill until he was caught.

By phone, he learned that Burton was still at the crime scene. *No reason for me to be there now,* Regal thought. *I'm going to stay here and wait for this murderous bastard to call and try to get a rise out of him.*

He pushed around the morning pile of paperwork and then it registered on him. This new body had an *R* carved in it. An *R* for rook. But there had been no recent capture of a rook in the game. His stomach churned as he faced the possibility that the killer was perhaps changing the rules—anybody could die now . . . for any reason.

He forced the thought out of his head and looked down at the pile of reports. The first one noted that a taxicab which had been stolen the previous night was found abandoned in a little alley near Wall Street. The lights had been left on and there were traces of blood on the backseat. Police forensic crews had been at the scene.

Regal heard Tony Bolda walk into the outside office and called him inside where he handed him the report.

"Tony, check this out for me right away. See what you can find out from Forensics."

Bolda glanced at the sheet. "What should I be looking for?"

"We got another body up on the chessboard. I don't know. Maybe these are connected somehow."

Bolda nodded and walked from the office, still carrying the report.

He was back twenty minutes later.

"The cabbie is a Puerto Rican," he told Regal. "He left the rig parked on the street while he had a bite in that diner on Tenth Avenue where all the hacks eat.

When he came out, it was gone so he called his dispatcher who called the precinct."

"Cabbie clean?"

"Seems to be. There were people with him in the cafeteria and his movements are accounted for all night. The bulls checked him out when they found out there was blood in the cab. His book showed he made a couple of runs out to JFK and then bopped around midtown for a while before stopping at the diner. He didn't even bother to lock the cab and somebody just hot-wired it."

"Right in front of a diner? Didn't anybody see it?"

"That was during the damned cloudburst," Bolda said. "Nobody could see anything, I guess. Anyway, that's pretty near the same time the dead woman was leaving her store. One interesting thing."

"What's that?" Regal asked.

"The cabbie said that his gas tank was full, but when it was found this morning, the tank was almost empty."

"Did he log mileage? What did it show?"

"Yeah," Bolda said. "Whoever stole it put on almost a hundred and seventy-five miles. They didn't just park somewhere and let the motor run until it ran dry. The thief was driving somewhere."

"Okay. I'm going to stay here on the phones. I want you to go up and talk to Burton or his men and find out what's going on. Meanwhile, make sure Forensics tests the blood type in the cab against the dead woman's. Tell Burton we're doing it."

Bolda nodded.

"And keep me posted."

The inevitable telephone call came in at eleven o'clock.

The metallic voice said, "For-Inspector-Paul-Regal. Black's-last-move-was-stupid. I-play-rook-to-rook-one. But-I-have-killed-your-rook. Play-good-chess-or-more-will-die."

Even as the voice was grinding on, Regal was talking loudly over the message.

"Don't hang up. We've got to talk. Do you hear me? Don't hang up!"

The message stopped but there was not the automatic disconnect click that Regal was used to. Whoever was calling was staying on the line.

Now what the hell can I say to him? Regal thought.

He just let the words bubble out of him. "I think we should stop playing by telephone. We should meet and play. I'm going to win this game, you know. What do you say? Let's get together. I'll beat you easily, you know. I . . ."

He was interrupted by a muffled voice. It sounded like someone talking through a handkerchief and also trying to disguise his voice by imitating mechanical computer sounds.

"Do-not-insult-my-intelligence. The-game-goes-on. It-ends-when-the-queen-dies."

Click.

Regal slammed the telephone back down and ran outside to Jane Cole's desk.

"Did they get a trace on that call?"

She nodded. "Uptown phone booth. They're on their way."

"Maybe this time," Regal said. "I got the bastard to say something today."

"What'd he sound like?"

"I don't know. Young, I think." He thought for a moment. "Pull the tape and get it off to the lab. See if they can find out anything. And let me know what happens at the phone booth."

He went back inside and replayed the message again.

"Do-not-insult-my-intelligence. The-game-goes-on. It-ends-when-the-queen-dies."

Despite being muffled and distorted, the voice did sound young. It was high-pitched too, but that was probably from trying to imitate computer speech.

He played it again.

". . . when-the-queen-dies."

What the hell does that mean? The game isn't over

*when the queen dies. It ends when the king dies. What the
hell is going on here?*

When he called Billy Abbott with their opponent's next
move—rook to rook one—the young chess player broke
out into hysterical laughter.

"This is no goddamn laughing matter," Regal said
sharply. "The son of a bitch killed another person last
night—a woman this time."

"Oh, God," said Abbott, instantly contrite. "I didn't
know. I was laughing because I've got the bastard now.
He thinks we made a mistake but he's the one who made
a mistake. He just doesn't understand the kind of chess
I'm playing now. This game's almost over."

"We're going to win?"

"I guarantee it," Abbott said.

"I wonder what happens then?" Regal said.

"I don't know. Maybe he'll challenge you to another
game?"

"Maybe. Or maybe he'll react in some other way.
Billy, you're not telling anybody that you're playing this
game, are you?"

"No. I said I wouldn't and I won't. Anyway, I don't
want the people I know at school to even know that I
play chess, you know. I mean, I'm just William Abbott
to them and I want to keep it that way."

"He said something strange," Regal offered. "Actually a couple of things strange. He complained that our
last move was stupid."

"That's because *he's* stupid. The pawn move sets up
everything. You'll see."

"And he said the game wouldn't be over until the
queen is dead. Does that mean anything to you?"

"No. Goddamn Russian is talking through his butt-
hole," Abbott said. "We're playing pawn takes pawn.
Just play what I tell you and don't pay him any mind."

"I wouldn't if he'd just stop killing people," Regal
said grimly.

* * *

For lunch, Regal went to the small sit-down delicatessen around the corner from police headquarters and was surprised to see Jane Cole sitting at a small corner table.

She seemed equally surprised to see him, and when he asked, "Waiting for someone?" he thought he detected a moment's hesitation before she said, "No. Join me?"

He pulled out the other chair and sat facing her, conscious immediately that his long legs bumped against hers under the narrow table. He looked around for a waitress, but before he could find one, a chubby balding man dressed in white cook's garb hustled up to the table.

"So this is the boss, Lady Jane?" he asked in a thick Eastern European accent.

Jane nodded. "Inspector Regal. Inspector, this is Charlie, the owner. He's responsible for all those tuna salad sandwiches you eat."

Regal smiled and shook the man's hand without rising from his chair. "Nice to meet you," he said.

"These are busy days for you, Inspector, eh?" Charlie said and stared at Regal, awaiting an answer, and finally Regal said noncommittally, "They're all pretty busy."

"But these more than others," Charlie insisted.

What does this man know about our office? Regal wondered. *How does he know whether we're busy or not?*

It seemed as if Charlie had read his mind because the man said, "I can always tell when you're busy because Bagels doesn't come in that much."

'Bagels?' Regal looked at Jane. He could still feel his legs touching hers under the table.

"Tony Bolda," she said.

"My best customer," Charlie said. "And always bagels. Onion, poppy seed, whole wheat, always bagels. Every day. Just a couple of weeks ago, four bagels he bought for dinner. Four poppy seed bagels and we have more poppy seeds on our bagels than anyone else in New York. And two poppy seed bear's paws to go. What a man."

Bolda's nuts, Regal thought. *Who eats all those poppy seeds for dinner?*

He nodded. "We're thinking of starting an all-bagel hall of fame and Tony's one of the candidates," he said. He saw Jane smiling at him.

"Bagels is the best," Charlie said definitely. "Now you sit down, Inspector, and I take care of your lunch."

Without waiting for Regal to reply, he scurried away and Regal turned back to Jane.

"Does he greet everybody that way?" he asked.

"Only friends of Bagels Bolda's," she said.

"I didn't know Tony was so famous. I'll be nicer to him from now on." A waitress brought him a beer and after he poured it he noticed Jane staring at him with a quizzical look on her face.

"Something on your mind?" he asked.

"I was out again last night looking for Estrellita. No luck."

"Nobody's had any," Regal said glumly. "But maybe the Narcotics guys can come up with something."

"You know, Paul, I've never been able to make any sense out of the whole thing."

"What do you mean?" he asked, noticing that it was the first time she had ever called him Paul. It sounded easy and casual on her tongue.

"It's too easy for us cops sometimes," she said. "We just get in the habit of accepting what everyone else assumes are facts and we kind of get lost and stumble around."

He was silent, sensing that she wanted to talk this out, knowing that she would eventually get to the point by herself without any prompting from him.

She sipped at her own beer.

"Facts are one thing," Jane said, "but truth is another. The facts say that Pete had drugs on him . . . on his fingers, on his tongue . . . in his urine when he died, and everybody just kind of lies down and accepts that Pete was using drugs because you can't argue with the facts. But what do you do when the facts aren't true, Paul? I knew Pete better than anybody else in the world. He never used a drug in his life. Never." Her voice had raised and she softened it and leaned over the table, closer to Regal.

"Everybody has put that out of their minds," she said, and Regal knew, with a feeling of personal guilt, that it was somehow his fault too, that she was correct. "But Pete never used drugs. The facts are wrong. So now we have Hector Guzman giving Pete a tip on a new Panamanian gang. We try a raid and there's nobody there. Pete goes looking for Guzman and finds him dead. Then Pete goes looking for Guzman's girlfriend, this Estrellita who might have been Guzman's contact with the Panamanians, and Pete winds up dead. Why? What does it mean?"

This time she hesitated long enough for Regal to know she wanted him to answer. He shook his head. "I don't know. What do you think?"

"I think there really are Panamanians," she said. "I think Guzman gave Pete a good tip but somebody tipped off the drug dealers. And then I think somebody got Guzman for being a snitch. And I think they got Estrellita too. That's why nobody can find her. And then I think that Pete got in the way and they got him too. I know what some cops are thinking. That Pete was looking for Estrellita 'cause she was a little side piece of nooky for him. Well, that's insulting horseshit. Trust me, he didn't have to go looking for anything. And I don't think that Pete went up to Spanish Harlem by himself the night he got hit to try to make some kind of drug buy. He was too good a cop for that, too careful. He would have used marked money and a backup team, including guys from Narcotics."

"He went up there because he got a phone call that was supposed to be from me, don't forget," Regal pointed out.

She looked at him and her eyes narrowed. "Exactly. Everybody seems to have forgotten that."

"I never have," Regal said. "So what is the point?"

She opened her mouth, closed it again and looked abashed. "I'm still working it out," she mumbled evasively.

Regal eyed her in surprise, then slowly put down his beer. "Jane, don't give me that shit. We're not playing games. If you've got an idea, I want to hear it."

She looked up slowly, almost fearfully, and studied him for a moment. "I've wondered if maybe he was working on something that he didn't want to talk with you about," she said in a low voice.

Regal was puzzled. "Like what?"

"Like something he was afraid to come to you with until he had more evidence."

"Evidence of what?"

"Evidence that somebody . . . somebody on our side had gone sour," Jane said almost defiantly.

Regal felt a shock, almost as if she had slapped his face. His expression must have alarmed her because she looked at him with tired acceptance in her eyes. "It's just a thought, Paul. I've had a thousand thoughts in the past few weeks and this is the one that keeps coming back to me. I don't like it but it makes a nasty kind of sense. It's the kind of thing that Pete might have kept under his hat until he had something solid to give you."

Regal shook his head firmly but he felt the beer sloshing around just below his throat, threatening to reverse direction. Jane's suggestion was monstrous . . . but wasn't it exactly what Tony Bolda had said the night of the busted raid? Monstrous, maybe, but she was right: it did make a nasty kind of sense.

"Have you spoken with anyone about this?"

"Are you crazy? I wasn't even going to tell you but it just sort of came out. I feel better now that I've let you know. Maybe I can just put it out of my mind."

"Too late for that," Regal said levelly. "Once it's in your mind, it'll never get out until we find out the truth. As you said, not the facts but the truth. For what it's worth, I agree with you. Anybody could have splashed cocaine on Pete's fingers, lips. It's just the fact of that damned urine test."

"Somehow it's not true," she said.

As he looked at her, her eyes kept glancing away and he realized that she had not told him everything, had not unburdened herself of every suspicion.

Why not? he wondered. *This is as good a chance as she gets.*

And then the answer struck him.

She's holding back a little because she thinks I might be the one in the squad who's gone bad. That's the thing she hasn't said. I'm her number one suspect. Who else is there?

"I'm going to talk to Vincent Flaherty," Regal said.

"That devil? You wouldn't."

"I have to, Jane, if only for Pete's sake." *And for mine,* he thought, *and for whatever little faith you or anyone else might still have in me.* "It's a rotten thought that maybe someone's gone bad but it was a thought somebody else had too, and I shipped it on to Flaherty and I have to ship this on too. It has to be checked out and I'm too close to do it. It's Flaherty's job."

She shuddered. "I feel like standing under a shower for an hour and scrubbing myself. I'm sorry now that I ever said anything to you."

"Maybe so but you did and what's done is done. If it turns out that everybody in this squad thinks that somebody's gone bad and I'm the only one who doesn't think so, I don't want those suspicions to end at my desk because I'm thickheaded. Let Flaherty figure it out."

He finished his beer and ordered another just as his sandwich arrived. It was a monstrous construction on a poppy seed bagel, packed with tuna salad and standing three full inches high.

"If Charlies likes me so much, why is he trying to feed me to death?" Regal asked Jane.

She did not answer and he thought that she wanted to talk some more about Pete Muniz but he had had enough of the subject for one lunch.

"So how is Sarah?" he asked.

She sighed slightly, as if surrendering against her will, and answered, "She's been visiting my sister in Connecticut for a couple of days. It's good for her to get out of the city and I've been too busy lately to be much good to her."

"With your midnight prowling, you mean?"

She nodded, looking a little guilty.

"I've told you before, Jane. I'll tell you now. Be careful. There are some bad people out there. Do you still have your bodyguard with you?"

"Most nights," she said.

"A woman going around by herself, even a cop, is like a trophy to some of these bums," he said and hesitated. "If you've got to do it, at least call me. I'm a warm body; it might keep the dogs off you."

She smiled at him and he sensed a hint of flirtatiousness in her glance.

Warm bodies? Jesus, girl. Forget it. This is work, he thought. But he could not forget it himself and he hunkered down over his food and finished his sandwich without raising his head.

Finally he looked up. "I guess it's back to the salt mine. See what's happening on the chessboard."

"That poor woman," Jane said. "The press is going to go nuts with this one."

"I know. I'm glad it's Joe Burton and not me dealing with them."

"You live up there, don't you, Paul?"

"A half dozen blocks from where they found Mrs. Bailey. That doesn't make me feel good either. I still don't know why the nut picked me to call when this all started."

"The new tape is at the lab. I listened to it before I sent it down," Jane said.

"What'd you think of his voice?"

"He tried to make it deep but I think it was high and squeaky. I think it's a kid."

"Christ, the world is full of computer nerd kids. Let's

not let them start having murder as a special hobby," he said. "Did he sound crazy to you? Could you tell?"

She shrugged. "I couldn't tell anything. But he's crazy, of course. That's a given because sane people don't go around killing people for no reason at all."

"And if he has a reason?"

"You think he does?"

"I don't know. But somehow I think so," Regal said.

"I guess that's why you're the big inspector and I'm just a detective second grade," Jane said.

"And don't you forget it," he said, trying to end the meeting on a light note, even as he realized that he had rarely ever had a weightier lunch.

Regal insisted on paying for both their lunches, and after getting his change and being thanked profusely by Charlie for patronizing his establishment, he walked outside where Jane was waiting for him.

"Speak of the devil," she said softly, and he looked up to see Deputy Inspector Vincent Flaherty standing on the other side of the street waiting to cross in their direction.

Regal took Jane's arm and led her away back toward headquarters.

23

"I'm up at Homicide North, Paul." Tony Bolda's voice was sharp over a lot of telephone background noise. "That was a good guess on the cab. The blood matches. This woman, what's her name, Bailey, *was* in the cab."

"Are they sure?" Regal said. "A lot of people have the same blood type."

"No, the lab is sure. I talked to one of my friends down there. When blood is fresh, they can do a lot more tests than the usual Type A, Type B bullshit. Definite match. No questions."

"Is Joe Burton happy?"

"He looks like I puked in his coffee," Bolda said. "I think maybe he just doesn't like any suggestions that come from you, even if they're good ones."

"Might be, Tony."

"They found one little print in the cab, on the cigarette lighter. The rest of it was clean and they're trying to find out if the print belongs to the hack driver or the killer. And they won't let me in the room, but they're going over those TV tapes with a fine-tooth comb to see if they can spot the killer in the cab."

"Maybe we'll win one," Regal said.

"Yeah."

"If you see Burton, tell him to call me when he gets a chance. I won't bother him now."

"Sure, but don't hold your breath."

"One other thing, Tony. You know anything about this Mrs. Bailey?"

"No. She ran some kind of junk shop that she called antiques over on Ninth Avenue." He read off the address. "The bulls say everything else was normal. She and her husband made each other sick. She was a kvetch without any real friends. But no gambling, no drugs, no nothing. Just a victim."

"Okay," Regal said.

As he hung up the phone, he thought, *Just a victim.*

He wondered why there was such a rage seething inside him. *Because she wasn't supposed to die.* The killer had told Regal that his last move was stupid but had not captured a piece. So why did he kill somebody and carve them up with an *R* for rook?

In chess, he knew, rook was the common name for a castle. But what did Mrs. Harriet Bailey have to do with a castle? Or, since the police had already figured out the killer's first teasing clues, was the killer just picking people at random now?

If that's so, God save us, 'cause he's got eight million potential victims now. Maybe, he thought, he wasn't really angry; maybe he was just frightened.

Regal read reports for the next hour or so, then picked up the telephone again and called Deputy Inspector Flaherty's office two floors above his.

"The inspector wouldn't be in, would he?" he asked hopefully, after identifying himself.

"He's right here, Inspector," was the secretary's cheerful reply. "One moment, please." Regal grimaced and waited.

"Hello, Paul. What can I do for you?"

"Vince, I'd like to talk to you for a few minutes if you're free."

"Right now if that's convenient for you."

"It's not urgent, Vince," Regal said, his courage failing. "We can do it later if you're busy."

"Come on up. I bought a new coffee pot and you can help me christen it."

"On my way."

Deputy Inspector Vince Flaherty certainly did not look like the devil that Jane Cole called him. He was more like Santa Claus without a beard or moustache—a short, roundish man with a cherubic face and thinning white hair. He laughed easily and often and was fond of slapping people on the back, and if he could not reach their backs, clapping them on the shoulders, in a constant hands-on display of camaraderie and fellowship.

Despite all his efforts, however, he was the most despised man in the city's thirty-thousand-man police department, feared and mistrusted as someone who would send his own mother up the river for not paying a traffic ticket. He and the detested group of operatives who worked under him in Internal Affairs had brought an abrupt end to the careers of a number of New York City police officers, including some at the highest ranks.

It did not help his reputation either that on a few occasions, when department lawyers had recommended that an erring officer be allowed to resign quietly because there was not enough evidence of wrongdoing to convince a judge or jury, Flaherty was known to have bitterly protested each time, and around the department, from the rank and file up to the top brass, they truly believed that his motto was "Hang the dirty bastards. They're all guilty."

Regal had no personal fear of Flaherty, even if the IAD snoops were checking his bank records. They could check until the next ice age and they weren't going to find one crooked nickel that Regal had ever taken. But he hated talking to the man, hated giving any encouragement to an investigation of the personnel of his small tightknit squad. It felt like betraying men and women who trusted him, but common sense told him that it was a step he had to take, no matter how unclean it made him feel.

Besides, he thought, *none of this will be new to Flaherty. I know damned well that the commissioner rang him in to check on my squad after I mentioned Bolda's suspicions a few weeks ago. And right away, his shooflies started sniffing around Jane Cole, asking her too damned many questions. And then my bank account.*

So why be here? a small nagging voice asked him.

Because as much as I detest Flaherty, he's on the side of the angels. Cops ought to be clean.

As he entered Flaherty's office, Regal stiffened his back and determined to get it all over with as quickly as possible—like a mandatory trip to the dentist. Once seated beside Flaherty's desk, he declined the offer of fresh coffee and went straight to the point.

"I had lunch today with Detective Jane Cole, one of my staff people. As you know, she and Pete Muniz were ... well, good friends. She tossed an idea at me today that I didn't like but I thought you ought to know about."

He tersely outlined her theory that Muniz might have suspected that someone in the squad was tipping off drug dealers, and then noted hopefully that Jane had no evidence to support it. "She's just clutching at straws, trying to make sense out of Pete's death. But I can't ignore her suspicion. Especially after Tony Bolda had sort of thought the same thing a few weeks ago. I'm sure the commissioner told you about that."

Regal watched Flaherty's eyes for a reaction that would confirm his belief that the commissioner had rung Internal Affairs in already to investigate Regal's squad. But the white-haired man was a good poker player. He looked at Regal with an absolutely expressionless face that epitomized the concept of "neither confirming nor denying" and waited for him to continue.

"That's all I've got for you, Vince," Regal said.

"Nice girl, Jane," Flaherty said with a smile, bobbing

his head. "Good family. Paul, do an old man a favor and go over the whole business of Muniz's shooting with me, will you? I didn't investigate it, you know, and there are probably a lot of details I should be aware of."

It was all so kind and gentle and courteous . . . and so much bullshit, Regal realized. With drugs reported in Muniz's body, Flaherty could quote right now verbatim from the autopsy report. He probably knew more about the case than Regal did, and he was only asking just to see what Regal would tell him and what he might possibly leave out.

I'm a freaking suspect, Regal thought and then cheered himself with the knowledge, *Everyone's a suspect in this bastard's eyes.*

Regal swallowed a sigh and carefully described the entire sequence of events that led to finding Pete's body on a dark, shabby street corner in Spanish Harlem. He tried to remember everything, every fact, every detail, every rumor. Flaherty kept smiling encouragement and occasionally made a note on a pad in impossibly small handwriting. Regal wondered if he used a magnifying glass afterwards to help him read it.

"That's very helpful, Paul," Flaherty said. "Now if you would spare me a few more minutes . . . maybe we could go quickly over the roster of people who might be involved in something like this. Not that anyone is, of course, but we do have to look at everything, don't we?"

Chuckling indulgently, knowing that Regal would never give him agreement on that, he picked up a file folder that had been lying on his desk and began perusing it—not for the first time, Regal realized. He wondered whether the folder had been on Flaherty's desk even before Regal's phone call a short while ago.

"Do you really think this is necessary, Vince?" Regal asked desperately.

The older man looked up at him sharply, the smile still in place but the bright blue eyes cold and hard. There was a moment of silence as Flaherty studied him.

"Paul, no matter what anyone may say about me, I

believe in being loyal to one's men. But I don't believe in carrying loyalty too far. That's a disservice to ourselves and to the department and to the people. If someone is corrupt, he's a danger to everybody; and worse, he's a traitor, and God hates a traitor."

The Irish should know, Regal thought to himself. *You've had enough of them over the years.*

"All my men are clean," Regal said.

"I hope your people are as clean as a whistle but if there's a cancer there, we have to dig it out before it spreads. Right?"

"Right," Regal said with a resigned sigh. "I don't like it but go ahead and ask your questions."

For the next half hour, they went over the list of names in the folder—cops who had worked with Regal on drug cases in the past two years. Regal gave his candid appraisal of each of them, although several times he had to grit his teeth to answer candidly. He started to feel as if he were running a marathon through a pit of mud.

And always Flaherty came back to Pete Muniz. If he didn't use drugs, why were they in his body? And always Regal had the same answer. "I don't know, but he didn't use drugs."

Finally it was over. Regal said once more, "My men are clean."

"You've been very helpful," Flaherty said, standing to let him know that the interview was finished. "But it's no more than I would expect of you. After all, you're your father's son and he was a fine officer, a credit to the force, God rest his soul."

Flaherty beamed at Regal, who smiled feebly back, wondering if Flaherty knew that his father had detested him from the moment he went to work in Internal Affairs. With Regal's father, loyalty to the troops came first. He would have had trouble turning in a fellow cop if he had found him robbing a bank with a bazooka.

Regal returned to his office, feeling grimy and unclean but sure that he had done the right thing for Pete Muniz as well as for himself. But he said a silent prayer anyway. *Forgive me, Pop.*

He tried to avoid Jane Cole's eyes when he walked back in but she waved the *Daily News* at him.

EYES GOUGED OUT, screamed the headline that filled most of the front page.

MONOGRAM MANIAC STRIKES AGAIN, a subhead explained.

Regal snatched the paper from her hand. "How the fuck did they get that?" he demanded.

She shrugged. "People talk, I guess. Joe Burton called. He'd like you to call back."

Regal stalked angrily toward his desk, scanning the story. It was correct enough in detail, as far as he knew, but was written for maximum shock value. In a town not noted for exquisite journalistic taste, the *News* seemed intent upon setting new standards of sleaziness. Only deep on an inside page did the paper even bother to mention its own scoop of several weeks ago: that the killer was a chess player. And still no one had figured out that the game being played out every day on Page One of the *Times* was between Regal and the killer. *We must just have the stupidest reporters in the United States working here*, Regal thought.

Joe Burton was brusque on the phone. "You wanted to talk to me, Regal?"

"You busy?"

"Of course I'm busy. What the hell do you think I'm doing up here, planning a charity ball?"

"We'll talk later," Regal said, not wanting to engage Burton in any kind of argument. "When you get some more time."

There was a moment of silence and Regal could almost hear the gears whirring in Burton's skull.

"This have anything to do with this Mrs. Bailey?" Burton asked cautiously.

"No. It's just something about the Muniz shooting that I thought you ought to know. It can wait. Listen, how did the *News* get that business about the woman's eyes?"

"Some goddam blabbermouth down at the morgue, I think," Burton snarled. "If I ever find out who it was, I'll gouge out *his* eyes and stick them up his ass."

"Okay," Regal said. "Maybe we can get together later."

"All right," Burton said. "Hey."

"What?"

"You made a good catch with that stolen taxicab. If you hadn't figured out that maybe it was where Bailey was killed, it might have slid by us. We're looking for it now on all the tapes. We'll see if that stupid idea of yours works."

"Hope so," Regal said.

"Hah," Burton exclaimed and hung up with his usual abruptness.

"You're welcome, I'm sure," Regal murmured into the dead phone. He hung up and leaned forward, putting his head in his hands, thinking about the interview with Flaherty.

"Something the matter, Paul?" a soft voice asked. Jane was standing in the doorway, looking concerned.

"Just a headache," he said. "Here's your paper back. Wash your hands after reading it."

"I already did," she said, coming over to take it from him. "That's really filthy. It's bad enough that poor woman was murdered but those kinds of details . . . that's just gross."

"Well said," Regal answered.

She turned to leave and on an impulse Regal said, "Jane, stay a minute. Close the door."

She did as he asked and sat in the chair beside his desk.

"I saw Vince Flaherty just now," he told her.

Her face hardened.

"I had to."

"Did you enjoy it?" she asked, a touch of scorn in her voice.

"I don't think I deserve that," Regal said angrily. "I'm trying to find Pete's killer."

Jane hesitated, then nodded. "I'm sorry," she said. "It's just . . . well, my cop family always hated the Internal Affairs gang, the Vince Flahertys of the world."

Regal grinned. "He speaks highly of you."

"Oh, the divvil," she drawled in a deep Irish accent.

"Says he used to hold you on his knee."

"A pervert too."

"He was playing Santa Claus, he said. You were six years old."

"That was the year I stopped believing in Santa Claus."

"You're a hard woman, Jane. You never forgive and forget?"

"Never. I remember and I pay back. That's written on my family coat of arms."

"Mine, too," Regal said, suddenly serious. "And that's why I went to see Flaherty. Pete got shot and I can't believe anybody on this staff set it up, either willingly or unwillingly. But if somebody did, I want to find them out and that's Vince's job. That's why I went to him. It was the right thing to do."

She sat silent but then nodded her head slightly.

"Good enough," Regal said.

Jane got up to leave but picked up the paper before walking to the door. "I need this," she said.

"Lining your birdcage again?"

"It has a good horoscope. I need all the help I can get these days."

"We all do."

Something had been nagging at him all day but he couldn't focus his mind on it.

Some loose end, some piece of business, some . . . something that he was overlooking.

It finally registered while he was driving home, and he pulled off his usual uptown route and headed over to the west side of the city, looking for Harriet Bailey's antique shop on Ninth Avenue, on the opposite side of Manhattan from the deadly city street chessboard.

For that was the question. The killer had murdered Harriet Bailey and on the phone had called her Regal's rook. Why Harriet Bailey as a rook? Or was she just a random victim who happened to be handy?

He found the store and parked at a hydrant in front. There was a crudely lettered sign in the window: CLOSED DUE TO DEATH. A handful of people stared in the front window of the shabby shop as if they might be lucky enough to see another gruesome serial murder.

Regal felt dirty even standing by them, but he moved into the crowd and looked at the window.

Sitting on a perch made from an old log was a big stuffed black bird. A crow, he thought.

Also called a rook.

At that moment, he knew the killer must have once seen that stuffed bird too. Maybe he stood in exactly the same spot as Regal, smiling to himself, filing away the knowledge for future reference.

Regal walked back to his car. He would have to make sure that Burton's investigators had checked Harriet Bailey's sales records to see who her customers were.

When he got home a short while later, Regal found Pierre LeBlanc sitting in the living room, deep in a drink, while Patrice whirled about the room wearing a silvery white midlength mink coat.

"Darling," she said as Regal entered, her eyes shining with excitement. "Look what Oliver Storm gave me. Isn't this lovely?"

"Beautiful," he said in a flat voice. "And also very expensive from the look of it."

"Well, it's not ermine," she said defensively. "It's a bonus for the work we've been doing on Storm Mountain."

"Great," Regal said. "And did you get a fur too, Pete?"

LeBlanc grinned crookedly. "Well, actually I settled for a pat on the back and a hearty handshake."

"Don't worry, dear. I'll see that you get yours later," Patrice promised him with poisonous sweetness. To her husband, she explained, "Oliver saw this in a shop window marked down to half price and decided it would be perfect for me. So he bought it as an advance bonus on the work we've been doing for him. Wasn't that sweet?"

"If a man who buys discount clothing as a gift can be called sweet, then I guess it was sweet," Regal said disgustedly as he walked to the bar to pour himself a drink.

Patrice smiled at his back. "I knew you'd understand," she said. "Anyway, I'm off. Jacques will shave my head if I'm late for my appointment. Why don't you two darlings have dinner together?"

"You're not going to wear that coat out, are you? In August?"

"Darling, it's always the right season for a white fur. What do you think, Pierre?"

"Furs in August are tack-ay," LeBlanc said in a bored tone. "*Très* tack-ay."

"All right. Then I'll leave it." She tossed the coat over the back of a chair and Regal thought, *How like her. Her enthusiasms last for about a minute.*

"Bye." Patrice scooped up her purse and sped out the door without looking back.

And I just don't give a shit anymore, he thought. He looked over at LeBlanc. "Stand another of those?"

"Yes. Scotch, rocks, please."

As Regal poured the drink, he said, "My life's always full of surprises. 'Look at what Ollie Wollie gave me, darling.'" He handed the glass to LeBlanc, who hoisted it and said, "Here's mud in your eye."

"Mud or blood, all the same," Regal said. "Tell me, Pete, what am I supposed to say when one of these days she starts giggling about how Ollie Wollie is now buying her underwear and jewelry."

"You don't want my advice, Paul."

"Sure. I trust your advice. And your discretion."

"Well, I'm certainly no expert on love and marriage,

Paul, but if I were you, I'd start thinking about saying good-bye."

Regal grunted and flopped onto the white leather sofa. "More and more lately, that's becoming my idea too."

LeBlanc shrugged. "It's your call, Paul. I don't know what to tell you. If you wanted the truth, I'd tell you that I'm pretty sick and tired of Patrice Regal these days. I'm pretty sick and tired of covering for her. But fact-wise, I don't know a damned thing. She doesn't confide in me. All she does is order me around like a dog and pick fights with me. And I don't mean the kind of spats we used to have. I don't know about you two, but I'm about ready for a business divorce. This just isn't working anymore."

"That bad?"

"I'm not greedy, Paul. All I ever wanted to do was interesting work in a decent atmosphere. The money is nice and the big money is nicer, but it's not worth getting an ulcer over. I can always go back to fashion photography and make a buck. Or open my own personal design studio. My income would drop but so would my blood pressure."

Regal said, "Thank God, in a way, that I'm busy as hell at work. It keeps my mind off all this bullshit because I just don't know how to handle it. I know Patrice well enough by now to know that punching her out wouldn't improve things. And that's not the way I want to live my life anyway." He slugged away at his drink. "I feel like freaking Hamlet," he said bitterly. "I don't know whether to fight for her or walk out myself and so I just sit here waiting for her to walk out on me, wondering what's the right thing to do."

"The right thing for which of you?" LeBlanc asked.

"For the both of us, I guess. If I knew it was best for her, I could take a walk. But what if this little stupid Ollie Wollie house of cards she's building comes tumbling down around her ears? If I weren't here to help her, I'd feel like hell."

LeBlanc shook his head sadly. "For somebody who goes around shooting people for a living, you're a good guy, Paul."

"Haven't shot anybody lately." Regal suddenly drained his drink and sat up straight. "Screw it. You have plans or you want to have dinner with me?"

"Best offer I've had in a long while," LeBlanc said.

"Italian?"

"Anything but Chinese. I'm wokked out."

"All right. There's a place nearby with good food and large drinks. Patrice and I used to go there before she joined Ollie Wollie's fur coat crowd."

"Actually, the coat is rather nice."

"Oh, Oliver has good taste all right. He's already proven that." He paused. "Hasn't he?"

"I'm sure he has," LeBlanc said softly.

24

Patrice's visit to her hairdresser had been brief and from there she hurried to Oliver Storm's Central Park apartment where a burly bodyguard admitted her to the lavish duplex, picked up a telephone and announced her presence.

Dave Thornton, Storm's public relations adviser, joined the two of them a minute later, looking worried.

"Mrs. Regal, Oliver is having a political planning session and informal fund-raiser with some very influential people. It was supposed to be over an hour ago but you know how these things are. Would you mind waiting until the meeting breaks up?"

She stared at him coldly. "Keep out of sight, you mean?"

He blinked, then grinned. "Okay. Your words, not mine."

"Why? Everybody knows I'm in charge of the designs for Storm Mountain."

Thornton gave her a look of what could have been either admiration or pity. "Mrs. Regal, with your looks,

I'm just afraid that some people might get the wrong idea. Given the fact that it's nighttime, not noon, some might think that your relationship with Oliver is something other than strictly business and it could hurt. There's a very important Catholic bishop in there, for instance. It's my decision to make and I just can't take the chance, not now when things are going so well. So, please, wait in Oliver's office until they're gone."

"All right, but I don't like this," Patrice said bitterly. "I came over because Oliver said he wanted to see me and I don't like being hidden away. I have nothing to hide."

"Of course you don't," Thornton assured her. "But politics can be nasty business, as you know."

He ushered her into Storm's office, where she paced the room restlessly for a few minutes, paused to admire her reflection in one of the windows which looked out high over New York City, then sat down on a couch and theatrically tapped her foot, trying to curb her impatience.

A door opened and Storm's daughter, Marcie, walked in, stopping short with surprise as she saw Patrice.

"Hello, Marcie, how are you?" Patrice asked warmly.

"Oh, hello. I was looking for Dad."

"He's busy holding a political meeting." She smiled. "I guess all the women in his life have to wait. How's your vacation been so far?"

"All right, I guess," Marcie said grudgingly. She moved forward to perch on the arm of the sofa. "It's more fun here in the city than being stuck all summer at that dopey house in the Hamptons, surrounded by yuppies and gold diggers. And it's better than being at school. That's for sure."

"Your dad said you and Timmy loved it at Groton."

"No, *Dad* loved it at Groton. We hate it. The kids are a bunch of drears mostly and the teachers are all nerdos. The Kid and I would rather go to some school right here in the city."

"The Kid?"

"Timmy. He's twelve minutes younger than me, you know."

"It's funny," Patrice said. "I *know* that you're twins, but he's so much bigger, I just kind of think of him as older."

"No," Marcie said. "I'm older. And smarter. That makes me the boss." She grinned and her lips twisted oddly. Eyeing her professionally, Patrice thought that Marcie could be attractive if she could learn to hold her mouth in a composed way, instead of letting nervous energy jerk her lips about. The girl seemed sometimes to be snarling rather than smiling, her lips sometimes curling in rictus like those of a dog about to attack.

Patrice leaned forward and took the girl's hand. "I wish when I was a kid my family could have afforded Groton. You're lucky. The best school in the country."

Marcie seemed to shiver but let Patrice hold her hand. "The kids at St. Mark's and Andover and a few other schools might give you an argument about Groton being the best," she said. "They call us 'Rotten Groton.'" She shrugged. Again the twitch of the lips signaled an effort to smile. "Actually, who gives a shit? We have to be somewhere and Dad wants us there, so one more year in the Massachusetts boonies. It could be worse." Marcie pulled her hand free to scratch the side of her neck. Her fingernails left red lines in the almost transparent skin of her throat.

The door opened and Thornton stepped in, looking sweaty but happy. Secret meetings obviously were his idea of heaven on earth. "Sorry, ladies, but we're still at it. Not much longer." He ducked back out again before anybody could respond and Patrice sniffed with annoyance.

"We're used to it," Marcie said. "Timmy and I need appointments now to see Dad."

"Politics eats up a lot of time, I guess," Patrice said. "Look at the bright side. If he gets elected mayor, you get to live in Gracie Mansion."

"Would you love that?" Marcie said.

"Sure. Wouldn't you?"

"One place is pretty much like another. Do you think he has a chance of winning?"

"I don't really understand much about politics," Patrice said.

"The paper today said that this latest . . . what do they call it, Monogram Murder . . . that it's helping Dad's chances because he's come out so hard against crime." She paused. "Wouldn't it be neat if people who were so worthless wound up doing something good by helping my father get elected?" Before Patrice could ask exactly what she meant, Marcie said, "You two have a date tonight or something?"

"No," Patrice said, trying to maintain her composure at the impertinence. "I'm an old married lady, remember? Your father asked me to come over to talk about some final plans for the grand opening of Storm Mountain."

"A real blast, I hear," Marcie said.

"I hope so. Everybody from New York and from Washington and a lot of other places too. All over the world. I'm so excited, I can hardly wait."

"Well, we can but we'll be there. Why not? It's better than sitting around here and playing Scrabble." Marcie looked down at her nails, bitten almost to the quick, then said shyly, "You used to be a model, didn't you?"

"Yes, I was. I still do an odd job once in a while, just for the fun of it."

"Somebody gave me a big makeup kit once for my birthday. All kinds of brushes and tubes and stuff. Maybe . . ." She hesitated. "Maybe as long as Dad is keeping us both waiting, could you show me how to use those things?"

"I'd love to," Patrice said, really meaning it. Maybe this was a way finally to get close to Oliver Storm's daughter. So far, their relationship had been proper but distant and Patrice had the idea that Marcie did not care for her too much. This could change all that, she thought.

Marcie grinned crookedly at her. "It's in my room. Wanna come with me?"

They left the office by the back door and went down a hallway and up a flight of stairs to the suite of two bedrooms and a living room that was Tim and Marcie's own apartment. Tim was hunched in front of a large expensive computer in the middle of a sprawling expanse of stereo equipment and other electronic devices that almost filled one end of the living room. He wore gym shorts and a sleeveless undershirt and Patrice was surprised that his arms and shoulders were so muscular. She had thought him kind of a fattish boy. A heavy set of barbells was on the floor.

"On your feet, lardo. Say hello to Mrs. Regal," Marcie sang out as they entered the room.

Tim looked over, eyed them calmly, and nodded without standing. "Hi," he mumbled, then turned back intently to his keyboard. The large color monitor in front of him was filled with symbols that Patrice found absolutely unreadable.

"Don't mind him," Marcie explained, waving a hand. "He's busy playing with a new program. He'll mess it up anyway." She playfully messed her brother's hair as they walked by. He ignored the gesture, reached for a manual and began to thumb through the pages worriedly.

"He buys up a lot of junk out-of-date computer programs," Marcie said. "Then he tries to make them smarter."

"Can he do that?" Patrice asked.

"Sometimes. But sometimes he makes them dumber too."

Marcie's bedroom was already a mess with several panties and bras on the floor or tossed across chairs. "Ignore the litter," the girl said airily. "I have to keep my room neat at school so I make up for it when I'm home. Anyway, I like being a slob."

"Most teenagers do," Patrice assured her with more

warmth than she felt. "I know I did when I was your age. I'm still not much into housework."

Marcie eyed her oddly. "Is your husband sloppy too?"

"No. Paul's always going around picking things up behind me. I've told him he has the soul of an accountant."

"Timmy is a worse slob than I am," Marcie said complacently. "His room makes mine look clean as a whistle."

"What else are brothers for?" Patrice asked as Marcie cleaned off the top of her vanity by simply opening a drawer and sliding everything into it. From the floor, she produced a large case that opened up to expose row after row of makeup colors. She looked at Patrice and shrugged helplessly.

"I never wear anything but lipstick, but I feel sort of dumb having all this stuff and not knowing how to use it."

"This is a lovely set," Patrice said. "It's made in France. You'll probably never use most of these colors, but it's nice to have them anyway. Let's play with them for a while."

For the next twenty minutes, sitting side by side in front of a large vanity mirror, Patrice showed the teen-ager how to apply makeup in a skillful, subtle way. She showed Marcie how different tones of eye shadow could produce different effects and demonstrated how to apply lipstick with a brush, rather than simply smearing it on from a stick.

At one point, Timmy put his head around the door, stared in wonder for a moment, and went back to his computer.

Patrice was talking about mascara when Oliver Storm entered the room.

"Making a high-tone lady out of my little girl?" he chuckled comfortably.

"Hardly a little girl, Oliver," Patrice chided. "She's a young woman. A lovely young woman." She felt relaxed and confident in this setting. For a moment, she thought it might be pleasant to have a child of her own—not a big clumsy oaf of a boy like Timmy or a strange scrawny thing like Marcie, but a sweet pretty little girl who could be dressed in frilly clothes and on whom the secrets of cosmetics and fashion would not be wasted.

Still, she had never felt closer to Marcie than she did now. For these few minutes, at least, there had been . . . almost a sense of family between them.

Marcie looked at her father, her eyes wide and intent. "Does it look bad, Daddy? I just wanted to find out how to do it. The other girls are always putting on makeup and I didn't even know how until Patrice showed me."

Storm nodded his head slowly. "You look beautiful, Marcie. Patrice is right. You have grown into a lovely young woman."

Marcie smiled brilliantly at him and for the moment she really was beautiful, Patrice thought. Then the girl's lips gave an odd twitch and the illusion vanished.

"I'm sorry I kept you waiting, Patsy," Storm said. "That meeting took a lot longer than I had planned but I couldn't just throw them out."

"No problemo," Patrice assured him. "I know how busy you are. But Marcie and I aren't quite finished. Why don't you go downstairs and I'll be down in about five minutes or so?"

He gave her a look which let her know that she was calling this shot, but that she was doing it by his sufferance and she would probably have to answer for that later. Then he glanced at his watch. "Good. I have to call the coast anyway." He turned and left the room.

"Do you have any cold cream?"

Marcie shook her head. She looked sullen and abashed.

"Buy yourself a nice big jar. And a small jar like this to keep in your purse," Patrice said, delving into her own pocketbook. "There's nothing like cold cream for taking off makeup." She expertly removed the paint from the girl's face with cream and tissues. Marcie was silent, seeming subdued and withdrawn, allowing her face to be turned this way and that without protest or apparent interest.

"There. Finished," Patrice said. "Remember what I showed you. Experiment a little. But keep in mind about makeup; at your age, less is more. Better too little than too much." She leaned close and whispered in her ear. "Don't want to look like a bimbo."

Marcie nodded dutifully. "Thanks a lot, Patrice. I don't know, it seems like a lot of bother, but I'll fool around with them."

Patrice hesitated, then reached out for Marcie's hand, opened it up and turned it over. Puzzled, Marcie looked down, saw her short, gnawed fingernails and reflexively clenched her hand shut.

"I bit my nails too when I was your age," Patrice lied. "You should really try to stop. But in the meantime, buy some fake ones, stick them on, and put nail polish on them."

The girl studied her fingertips for a moment, then smiled widely. "Sure, why not? But what about The Kid? He bites his nails too."

"Timmy?" Patrice shrugged. "Boys can do whatever they want. Who cares what they look like?"

Marcie smiled even more widely. "So they say. Thanks again for the beauty lesson. It was really nice of you and I won't forget it. Tell Daddy that I'm going to bed. Timmy and I are getting up early to go out."

"I'll tell him," Patrice promised. "Good night, Marcie. You really are a beautiful young woman, you know."

"Yeah, sure," she mumbled, seeming embarrassed again. "Thanks again."

The computer screen was still lit up but Tim was not in sight as Patrice crossed the youngsters' common room. She could hear him moving around in his bedroom.

"Good night, Timmy," she called. She heard an answering grunt from the bedroom.

Patrice was smiling, pleased with herself, as she walked down the steps toward Oliver Storm's office. The boy was a stupid, sullen, hulking clod, like so many teen-age boys, but it had been fun working with Marcie to-night. With the right makeup, she was almost pretty. If only she could learn to keep her lips from twisting around in that strange, nervous fashion.

Her own lips twisted derisively.

Don't go overboard, Patrice. Marcie Storm will never be pretty. And when her face is all twisted up, she's down-right ugly. How could Oliver have had such a child? Their mother must have been some dog. No wonder she took the pipe. No. That was one of the stepmothers. Prob-ably couldn't stand to look at these two.

She wondered again for a moment what kind of chil-dren she and Paul might have had but dismissed the thought. It didn't matter. She was going to be with Ol-iver Storm and that was where she wanted to be.

She found him leaning against the edge of his desk, hold-ing a phone and listening intently. As she entered, he smiled and put a finger to his lips. "I absolutely agree," he said in what she recognized as his strong politician's voice. "Something has to be done."

He walked around behind the desk, reached under-neath and pushed a button. Patrice heard a click from the door she had entered and knew it was now locked against outside intrusion. She strolled with studied grace across the room to sit demurely on the couch, feeling a tingle between her legs.

Storm finished the call and hung up. He smiled and walked confidently toward her. He bent over, took her face between his hands and kissed her gently on the lips.

Patrice closed her eyes, pressed her hands against his and returned the kiss with fervor. He ended the kiss slowly and sweetly, then backed up until he was leaning against the desk again.

"Stand up," he commanded.

She obeyed silently, expectantly.

"Nice dress."

"Thank you."

"Take it off."

She smiled and slowly removed her dress, staring intently at him all the while.

"Don't stop there," he said when she was done, his voice growing thick. "Take off everything."

"Anything you say, Oliver." She complied gladly, exulting in her slavishness.

Storm had already removed his jacket. Now he pulled the tie from his neck and began unbuttoning his shirt.

When Patrice was naked, he beckoned her forward, then ordered, "Kneel down."

She did and he said, "Take off my shoes and socks."

She was surprised at the request but did what he ordered. *This is crazy,* she thought. *And what's even crazier is that I'm enjoying this. I love it.*

"And now what should I do?" she said, looking up.

He stared down at her.

"Anything you want," he said.

She smiled again, remaining contentedly on her knees. *What an absolutely lovely evening,* she thought.

Timmy Storm wandered into Marcie's room, a slim twisted hand-rolled cigarette burning between his fingers. He wore only his gym shorts. Marcie glanced at him, then resumed staring at her face in the triple mirror.

"What were you doing, learning to be beautiful?"

"Oooh," she squealed, "I learned so many things. I learned how to do my eyes and how to put on lipstick and mascara and so many things. I learned that I shouldn't bite my fingernails or the boys won't like me." She shook her head mockingly from side to side. "Have you ever heard such a load of shit in your life?" she said. She laughed and her mouth was twisted and vicious looking as she took the marijuana joint from Timmy and inhaled a long drag from it.

"I hate that woman," Timmy said in a flat voice.

Marcie pursed her lips again. "That's because you don't want to be pretty. That's because you don't understand how important it is to make the boys like you. If you're not pretty, Oliver Storm won't invite you over to blow him."

She laughed again and pulled Timmy onto the seat next to her. She jammed a brush into the makeup paints and started to paint wild purple lines around Timmy's eyes. He smoked the joint and watched her in the mirror, laughing all the while.

She jabbed the brush in again, and painted on him a broad thick set of matching purple lips, a nightmare from a Paris alley.

"Oh, look at yourself," she minced. "You will certainly be the belle of the ball at Rotten Groton, won't you? You'll have all the little boys with their balls in an uproar and that's what's really important, isn't it?"

He leaned forward and looked at his bizarre, garish face. "I don't know," he said in mock seriousness. "Something's missing."

Their eyes met in the mirror.

"Oh, yes," she said. "And I know just what." She took another brush, jabbed it into some red paint and drew a large red question mark on his forehead.

"Now, darling, you are dee-veen," she said. "Dramatic but understated; elegant yet simple. A vision of loveliness according to the gospel of Queen Patrice."

Timmy put the joint into an ashtray and stood up. "Still something missing," he said. She took a drag on the cigarette, then stubbed it out and watched him in the mirror as he slid down his shorts. He had an erection and he held it in his hand, very close to her face.

"How about making this dramatic and elegant?" he said. "Something worthy of dear sweet Patrice."

Marcie's lips writhed into her twisted smile. "Let Patrice get her own," she said in a dreamy voice, turning to face him.

25

From the restaurant, Regal was finally able to get through to Inspector Burton on the phone.

"This place is a zoo," Burton said. "We've got press vultures here from all over. 'Tell me exactly how the dead woman's eyeballs were plucked out,'" he mimicked savagely. "I'll tell you, Regal, we should put a bounty on these press bastards. Shoot 'em on sight, bring in their ears and you get a hundred dollars, no questions asked. I'm going nuts."

He sighed, and impulsively Regal said, "Sneak out, Joe. I'm only a few blocks from you. Come on over and have a highball."

Burton allowed as how he "might be able to do that," and Regal gave him the address of the small Italian restaurant. When Burton arrived, Pierre LeBlanc, who had been rational, calm, and good-humored all during dinner, suddenly decided—apparently on a whim—to act like a crazed fairy queen.

Regal introduced them. Burton gave LeBlanc a fish-eyed glare. LeBlanc gushed, his eyes wide with delight,

"Oh, I've read about you. You're always in the newspaper after you've dragged some miserable wretch off to the lockup." He held Burton's hand with both of his and announced earnestly, "You're my hero." Then he leaned closer to Burton. "Tell me the truth. Is it really as much fun in jail as they say it is?"

All this was accompanied by much eye-rolling, lip-smacking, and hand-fluttering. Burton looked toward Regal as if begging salvation. Regal laughed aloud and Burton glared at him. Clearly, in his mind, this was no laughing matter. And LeBlanc was still holding onto his right hand.

Finally, Regal said, "Okay, Pete, cut the crap."

LeBlanc grinned and let go of Burton's hand. "I'm sorry," he said to both men. "You told me once how Inspector Burton was ragging you for all the faggots you hang out with and I just thought I'd show him how the other half lives."

He grinned at Burton, who slid into a chair next to Regal. "Sorry, Inspector," LeBlanc said.

Burton cleared his throat and finally was able to squeeze out, "Think nothing of it."

"And now I'm off to the little boys' room," LeBlanc said. He frilled away from the table toward the men's room in the back and Burton looked at the other policeman and shook his head.

"Christ, Regal, I've got to hand it to you. You lead one hell of an interesting life. Is this guy real?"

"Real enough," Regal said. "He's my wife's business partner."

"Well, at least you don't have to worry none about her sleeping around. Not with Pierre . . . shit, I never even met a Pierre before . . . not with him on the job."

"That's reassuring," Regal said drily. "But don't take him for granted. Most of that swishiness is an act he puts on because it's expected of him. I think, when he wants to be, he's as straight as the two of us."

"You anyway," Burton said. "But if you don't mind,

when he comes back, I'm keeping my hands in my lap. So what's on your mind?"

Regal leaned closer and told him of Jane Cole's comment and his own subsequent visit to Vincent Flaherty. He mentioned that Bolda had had the same sort of suspicion just before Muniz's murder.

"So why tell me?" Burton asked.

"It's your case, Joe. I don't think there's anything to it, but if you see Flaherty's shooflies hanging around, I thought you ought to know what's going on."

Burton grunted approvingly. "Well, thanks for that but I think it's a dry well. I know Bolda and Jane and most of the guys who used to work for you and they're all good cops. I think you'd all be better off doing *real* police work but that's not my decision." When the waiter came, he stopped and ordered a bottle of ale.

Regal shrugged. "I don't think it's likely either. I've tried to make sure it couldn't happen. That's why we always tried to have somebody from Narcotics with us when we made a bust. Their guy got to be the arresting officer, whenever we could."

"Covering your ass?"

"Damn right."

"Why were you making any street arrests at all? That's not your assignment, is it?"

"No. Our job is . . . was drug intelligence. Try to find out who the big importers are and try to put the hammer on *them*, instead of the vendors. And that's what we concentrated on. But sometimes, we'd run across something and we just couldn't walk away from it. There had to be an arrest. And that's why I called in Narcotics. I never wanted one of my guys to be alone, facing some kind of opportunity he couldn't resist."

"You're talking about your own men. You're not a very trusting soul, Regal."

"Just like you, Joe," Regal said. "And that's why we're both still here. And for what it's worth, I think you're right. My squad should be working out of the Narcotics Division and not the commissioner's office.

Just another level of bureaucrats to fuck things up."

Burton's beefy features twisted into a wry smile. "But then our dear asshole mayor couldn't brag about his special crack antinarcotics task force."

He nodded thanks to the waiter who brought his drink and poured it ceremoniously into a glass.

"So how's it going on your end?" Regal said. "With Mister Monogram?"

"A couple of things. We've got our first sighting of the killer."

Regal leaned forward in his chair. "How's that?"

"Mrs. Bailey had a lottery ticket all rolled up in her hand. We checked with Albany and found out where she bought it. Some newsstand near her store. The owner remembered her and said she went out in the rain and stood on the steps of the store with some guy."

"Any description?"

"No. It was raining too hard and he couldn't see anything. Then he saw them in the street hailing a cab. And that was it."

"Did he say? Did it look like they were together?" Regal asked. He knew it was an important question because if the killer had been a friend of Mrs. Bailey's, their list of suspects had dropped from some four million to maybe a hundred or less.

"No such luck," Burton said. "He said it looked like they just bumped into each other getting out of the rain."

"Shit," Regal said.

Burton nodded. "My feeling exactly." He took a sip of his ale. He obviously found it acceptable because he tipped the glass and drained almost the whole drink. "We found one partial print on the cigarette lighter in the abandoned cab but one print is pretty much worthless. It doesn't belong to the cabbie though, so maybe if we ever get the bastard, it'll be another piece of evidence. And the lighter element had a little fleck of marijuana ash on it so the killer was smoking a joint sometime during the night. Maybe that pegs him as a young guy."

"Or an old pothead," Regal said. "Can I ask you something without your flying off the handle?"

"Try me."

"I went by Harriet Bailey's shop today. I was wondering why the nut called her my rook. There was a stuffed bird in the shop window—a raven, which some people call a rook."

"Good, Sherlock. So what?"

"So I was thinking that the killer must have been there or passed by to know about that rook. Have your men checked her sales records?"

"Good idea, but we did it," Burton said, with what Regal thought was remarkable calmness for him. "She didn't do much business. But guess who bought something there a few months ago?"

"Princess Diana," Regal said.

"No, but close. Oliver Storm. We found a receipt from his credit card."

Regal wanted to say "That's probably where the cheap bastard bought my wife's used fur coat," but instead he said, "Okay, that's it. Let's arrest Oliver Storm. He's the only guy who's getting any good out of these killings. They're helping his campaign for mayor."

Burton nodded slowly as if that thought had not occurred to him before. "Well, his turn will come," he said. "My men are questioning everybody we can find who ever bought anything there. When they reach his name on the list, they'll talk to him too. You never know who sees what."

"Speaking of which," Regal said, "what about the TV tapes? Tony said maybe they show something?"

"We've got a tape of the cab moving into the area and then another one of it moving out only six minutes later. The body got dumped on Seventy-second and it was our lousy luck that we didn't have one of our surveillance units rolling by right then."

"Doesn't the tape show anything?"

Burton sipped his ale and shrugged his massive shoulders. "License plate confirms that it was the cab they found down in Wall Street. And from what little we can tell, there was a driver and somebody sitting in the back. That's all." He put his glass down hard and said, "I hate this technology shit. They always promise you the moon and you wind up with green cheese. The tape quality is so bad because of the low light level that you can't really see much of anything."

"Shit."

"Schmidt and that guy from the surveillance outfit . . . what's his name, Isaacs? . . . they've got the tapes. They're as happy as two bedbugs humping. According to them, they'll be able to somehow enhance the images and get something out of it but I'll believe it when I see it."

He stopped speaking as LeBlanc returned to the table.

He stood behind his chair and said, "Maybe I should be leaving?"

"It's okay, Pete. We're pretty much done with business, anyway. Have some coffee."

"Merci," LeBlanc said and slid into his chair.

Burton eyed him warily. Regal noticed that the big cop's hands were indeed clasped together in his lap.

"Were you born in France?" Burton asked.

"Fuck no," LeBlanc giggled. "Cicero, Illinois. Al Capone's old hangout, you know."

Burton blinked and Regal laughed. "Pierre is really Peter White. LeBlanc is his stage name, so to speak."

"I'm a fraud, Inspector," LeBlanc told Burton gleefully and all the swish queen mannerisms were out of his voice. "I'm a con man. Pierre LeBlanc is an alias I picked when I first hit town. I learned the phony accent by listening to some French records."

"Why bother?" Burton said.

"It's the New York Me," LeBlanc said. "The people I deal with don't want to go to someone named Pete White. They want a Pierre LeBlanc, even if he was born in Cicero. It makes them safer. And usually they're women so it makes their rich husbands feel safe too. They don't mind paying the bill as long as they're sure the decorator isn't porking the old lady behind their backs." He snapped his fingers at the waiter and ordered espresso coffee for all.

"While I was in the men's room," he said, "I had a thought about these Monogram Murders. That's your case, isn't it, Inspector?" he asked Burton, who merely nodded.

"What's the thought?" Regal asked.

"All the bodies have been found on the Upper East Side, even though they were apparently killed somewhere else. Well, it just occurred to me that in five days we're going to have a major happening at Oliver Storm's newest venture—the Storm Mountain apartments—and that's up in this neighborhood too. I was wondering if the nut who's doing these killings might not get it into his brain to play some games at the opening of Storm Mountain. I mean, he must like publicity somehow or else he'd just be dumping the bodies in the river, right? Where could he get better publicity than by dumping a body at Storm Mountain? With the press of the world in attendance?"

Regal and Burton looked at each other for a moment. Regal said, "I doubt it, Pete. The security at the Mountain should be like security at the White House. Patrice told me that the vice president might even be there so we'll have Secret Service and FBI, as well as our own people and Storm's security personnel. Are they going to call them Storm Troopers, by the way?"

"Good idea," LeBlanc said.

Burton said, "I think the killer will probably stay far away from Storm Mountain."

"I don't know. He doesn't have to kill anybody there. Just drop off a body," LeBlanc said.

"It's something to think about," Regal agreed.

"I hear the mayor and commissioner might show up," Burton volunteered.

"Even if Storm is running for mayor?" Regal asked,

honestly perplexed. Politics always confused him.

"Especially for that reason," Burton said with the un-rivaled sureness of a policeman making a political judgment. "He has to show he's not afraid of him."

Regal noticed that Burton's hands were now out of his lap and back on the table. He had seemed to unwind in LeBlanc's presence.

LeBlanc smiled. "Maybe *Oliver* is the Monogram Murderer," he said. "He couldn't buy the kind of press coverage he got today."

"I didn't notice," Regal said honestly.

Burton said, "I thought you were one of his political buddies. That's what I heard."

"You heard wrong," Regal said. "My wife is doing a job for him; that's my only contact with him."

"He was in all the late papers and on the TV news," LeBlanc said. "Promising that when he's mayor, there'll be no more vicious murders like these cut-'em-and-label-'em jobs. I had the idea that his campaign was dying on the vine, but this latest killing has turned him into Tarzan again."

"The opening of Storm Mountain can't hurt either," Regal said.

LeBlanc shook his head. "No politics there. Not visible anyway. He said plenty of time for rallies later on."

Burton sipped at his espresso. "It makes sense," he said, "that the mayor and commissioner wouldn't show unless they were assured that they wouldn't be sand-bagged." He put down the cup. "I've got to go," he said. "Thanks, Paul, for letting me know about that business with Flaherty. I don't think there's anything there but it was better that you told me."

"Keep it under your hat, Joe. I haven't said anything to anybody—except Jane because she started it."

"Good enough." Burton nodded at LeBlanc, seemed to consider it for a moment, then said, "Nice meeting you."

"Maybe sometime we can go shopping together,"

LeBlanc said, and when Burton looked horrified, LeBlanc and Regal laughed aloud. Burton leaned forward and said, "Don't worry, Pete, I won't spoil your image."

"Could anyone?" LeBlanc asked.

26

Two miles north of where Regal was finishing his coffee, a slim, flashily dressed man oozed up behind Jane Cole as she was leaving a small Latino nightclub.

"You seek an Estrellita?" he hissed from the corner of his mouth.

Even as she nodded and answered, "Si," she glanced toward the nightclub door, wondering why it was taking Jose Colon so long to pay their bill. *Hurry up, Jose. Hurry up*.

"This Estrellita is not a Boriqueno," the man said with a smile as he pulled a cigarette from the breast pocket of his impossibly flashy silk shirt. He reeked of strong cheap aftershave.

Before Jane could answer, Colon stepped through the doorway and said, "No. Not Boriqueno. Panamanian perhaps."

The small slim man glanced up at the bulking Colon, who clapped an arm around the man's shoulders in a gesture that bespoke friendship and also contained the warning Don't try to run away or I'll wring your neck.

"I think I know of such a woman," the man said, his eyes flicking to both sides. "What do you want of her?"

"Where is she?" asked Jane.

The man smiled politely but said nothing. He had obviously made his decision that Colon was the one he had to deal with; Jane might just as well not have existed as far as he was concerned.

"My cousin was looking for her and he was killed," said Colon. "We would like to talk with this woman if she is the same one my cousin sought. We wish to find out who killed my cousin, who was a good man." Colon smiled all the while he was talking but not once did he lighten the grip around the man's shoulders, Jane noticed.

The slim man nodded. He began to talk in rapid-fire Spanish and Jane strained to follow the conversation, but even though her Spanish had improved remarkably in the last couple of weeks, she could not keep up with them.

"He says it may not be the same woman," Colon finally translated for her, "but out of the goodness of his heart, he will take us to her."

"Sure and I'm Peter Pan," Jane said. "How much does he want?"

The young man's name, he said, was Ozzie and the "goodness of his heart" indeed came with a price tag because the next few minutes were spent in haggling. Finally, Colon said, "He'll take fifty dollars," and Jane nodded and took the money from her purse. Colon hailed a cab and the three drove downtown near the area where Estrellita was reported to be living.

Jane looked up anxiously as the cab passed 107th Street—the street she had been told Estrellita lived on—but then it pulled onto 106th Street and, at the young Hispanic's direction, stopped in front of a shabby walk-up tenement.

Ozzie led them to a flat on the third floor. A radio was playing softly inside, apparently tuned to a Spanish-language station. Colon knocked but there was no answer. He knocked again with the same result.

"Does this building have a super?" Jane asked. Ozzie looked puzzled and Colon translated. Ozzie nodded hesitantly and said, "In the basement."

"You live here, don't you?" Colon said. Ozzie looked silently away down the hall and Jane said, "You two stay here. I'll get the super."

In the basement, the superintendent's apartment door was open, entry barred only by a screen door with several long rips in the screen. She banged on the door and a fat middle-aged woman wearing a man's bathrobe and slippers shuffled into sight.

Jane showed the woman her shield and said, "We want you to open an apartment for us."

"Something wrong?" asked the woman pointedly, but when Jane just waited silently, the woman shrugged and turned away. "I'll get my keys," she said sullenly.

She eyed Ozzie sharply when she got to the third floor. He avoided her gaze, staring down the hallway at nothing. The woman banged briskly on the door, but when there was again no response, she fumbled through the keys on a huge ring, tried one that did not work, and finally found the key that unlocked the door.

The radio that was playing was on the kitchen table, a cheap Japanese model ghetto blaster. Colon went to turn it off but Jane stopped him from touching the radio knobs.

The apartment was only a kitchen–living room combination with a small bedroom in the back and at first it seemed empty.

"Who lives here?" Jane asked the superintendent, who still glared at Ozzie. Colon walked into the bedroom.

"Just a young woman. Alone," the superintendent said.

"Her name?"

"I know only Estrellita."

Jane nodded and closed the door on the woman. "Find anything?" she called.

"There's a big Hefty bag in here," Ozzie yelled.

"Don't open it," Jane cried out but she was too late. She heard a choking sound from inside the bedroom. She ran inside and saw Colon with a pained look on his face. He pointed to the large heavy-gauge leaf bag in the corner of the room. He had opened the yellow plastic tie that had been used to fasten it.

Jane did not have to look inside to know what was in there. The unmistakable sweet-and-sour-pork smell of a decomposing body let her know that they had found Estrellita.

Regal was watching the eleven o'clock news. The murder of Harriet Bailey was still the main story, even though the television station chose not to talk about her plucked-out eyeballs, instead contenting themselves with a report that the body had been mutilated.

The report went on to mention the _R_ that had been carved in Mrs. Bailey's forehead, tying the killing in with the other three murders in the past month. The announcer breathlessly reported that police believed that "the Monogram Murderer" was carving the symbols for chess pieces on his victim's faces, then cut to a piece of tape of Inspector Burton saying he knew nothing about any chess player and, no, he wasn't yet prepared to say that all four murders had been committed by the same person, and, no, he was not inclined to say how the investigation was going, but, yes, as soon as police made an arrest they would announce it to the press, and now would they leave him alone because he had some (bleeping) work to do.

Actually, Regal thought, the television station handled the story pretty mildly. He had noticed that this seemed to be a pattern. The New York City television channels generally paid a lot more attention than did the newspapers to the city's public image and this manifested itself through a lot of strained reports—usually featuring film of children playing—that related how all of New York was just one big happy family.

The announcer smoothly segued into a piece about Oliver Storm, relating how his campaign drive in next year's mayoral election seemed to be picking up steam with this wave of murders. As Storm was interviewed by a reporter, Regal leaned closer to the set, wondering if he might be able to see Patrice among the people who stood in the background. He saw Storm's two kids before he realized what he was doing and leaned back in disgust.

Great, Paul. Stare at the TV. Maybe someday you'll get a glimpse of your wife while her boyfriend is being interviewed.

When the telephone rang, he was happy to walk away from the set. He only hoped it wasn't Patrice calling to tell him that she was going to be on the TV news, or that she was going to be late and he shouldn't wait up. Then he realized that his wife no longer bothered to call.

It was Jane Cole.

"We've found Estrellita," she said.

"Alive or dead?"

"Dead." She explained briefly what had happened and Regal said, "I'll be right there."

Twenty minutes later, the red light still flashing on the dashboard of his personal car, Regal double-parked outside the tenement building. A crowd of local residents had clustered outside the building, kept at bay by a half dozen uniformed policemen. Regal saw Lieutenant Davis of Homicide North walking up the steps and jogged to join with him.

Inside Estrellita's apartment, the smell was now sickeningly overpowering. Precinct men were already at work taking photographs and looking for fingerprints. Jane Cole sat on a threadbare sofa with a tall, strong-jawed young man who was murmuring in her ear. Regal was startled to feel a pang of disappointment.

"What have you got?" Lieutenant Davis asked crisply of the precinct lieutenant who was supervising the search of the apartment.

"Medical examiner just left and the body's gone off

to the morgue. He won't know for a while but he thinks she was dead maybe a month. We've got guys going up and down the halls trying to find out if anybody saw or heard anything but no luck so far."

He nodded toward Ozzie, who was sitting disconsolately on a hard-backed chair at the kitchen table. "This guy is the brother of the superintendent. He heard word on the street that Detective Cole was looking for a woman named Estrellita and he knew that his sister had rented an apartment to a woman by that name. Then they hadn't seen her in a while and he just thought he might make a payday out of it. I don't think he had anything to do with it. Anyway, it doesn't seem he'd lead cops here if he killed the woman."

"How'd she die?" Regal asked.

"Bullet in the head," the precinct officer said. "Just one, so far as we can tell."

"Any identification?" Davis asked.

"Nothing. The apartment is bare. Some clothes, that's all. Maybe we can trace her through those but I don't know."

"How long she been living here?"

"Five weeks. According to the super, some man rented the place from her. Paid two months' rent and said his sister might be staying here from time to time. He paid cash and he gave the name Jack Robinson. Interesting thing, though, the guy wasn't a Latino. He was a regular Yanqui, the super says. She figured the girl was his chippy."

"Got a description of the man?" asked Davis eagerly.

"Average height, thirties or forties maybe. Brown hair. Wore a suit. Always had sunglasses on. No mustache or other marks that she remembers. We'll sit her down with the Identikit artist but I wouldn't hold my breath. She only saw the guy once and I think she was half bagged then."

Regal walked away from the two men toward the couch where Jane Cole was still sitting with the young man. They rose as Regal approached and she shook her head angrily. "So damned close," she said. "So damned close, but too late."

"Good work though," Regal said.

Jane shrugged. "We just kept asking and asking about her. Finally somebody heard us."

She nodded to the young man who had stood politely waiting to be introduced.

"This is Jose Colon, Pete's cousin. He's a sergeant in the MPs at Fort Dix. He's been coming up here at night and helping me. This is my boss, Inspector Regal."

As the two men shook hands, Jane said, "It would be nice if you or the commissioner could send some kind of note to his commanding officer thanking him for his work."

Regal nodded. "I don't see why not. Jose, I'm glad to meet you and thanks for your help."

"It is more than a case to me," Colon said. "Pete and I were close. I think he's the reason I joined the military police, and if I don't stay in the army, I plan to join a police force somewhere."

"We're always looking for good men," Regal said, adding lamely for Jane's benefit, "and good women too."

"Thanks, Inspector, but not in New York. I don't want to bring up my kids in this city."

"You have children?" Regal asked.

"Not yet, but someday."

"You're married?"

"No," Colon said.

"Oh."

"Jose won't have any trouble getting married," Jane observed casually. "He's smart and honest and he's a good-looking guy, don't you think?"

"I guess so. Sure," Regal agreed.

"I think I'll fix him up with some of my friends the next time he's in town."

There was nothing to say to that and the three stood there awkwardly for a moment until Regal asked, "Have you given your statements yet?"

"Yeah," Jane said, and Regal called to Lieutenant Davis, "Okay if these folks leave?"

"No problem," Davis said distractedly. He was busy watching a detective search through the drawers of a kitchen cabinet.

"Can I give you both a ride home?"

"That would help a lot, Paul," Jane said. "It's been a long day and a long evening."

Colon, Regal was curiously pleased to find out, was staying with Pete Muniz's parents only about a dozen blocks away. Regal dropped him off first, shook hands warmly and thanked him again.

Over Jane Cole's halfhearted objections, Regal insisted on driving her to her apartment in Queens. Neither said a word for the first few minutes of the trip. Jane sat slumped beside him, her head back and her eyes closed. He was disconcertingly aware of the rise and fall of her large breasts under her tight silk blouse.

She opened her eyes and saw him looking over at her. "That was good work," he said quickly and looked back to the road.

"Not good enough."

"Time will tell. There may be usable prints. We may get a lead on the man who rented the flat. It's interesting that he wasn't a Hispanic, not one of the Panamanians. We don't know yet what we might find out, but whatever it is, it'll be because of you and Colon."

"I told you I was a good cop," she said and closed her eyes again.

"Tomorrow I'll talk to the commissioner's office about that letter for Colon."

"Let's just get the son of a bitch who shot Pete." There was a hint of tears in her voice and Regal reached over, found her hand and squeezed it. He left it there for the few blocks until he reached her apartment building.

"Here we are," he said.

She sat up with a sigh and reached for her purse. "Thanks for the ride, Paul. And the kind words. Keep it up and I may stop believing all the bad things everybody says about you."

He laughed and got out of the car when she did. "I'll see you safe inside," he said, waving aside her faint protest.

They were silent as the elevator took them to the fourth floor. The last time he had been here, he had come to tell her of Muniz's murder, and the recollection made him feel gloomy.

He walked with her to her apartment door. She unlocked it, then turned to him. "Thanks again, Paul. I wish...I wish..." Tears started to stream down her cheeks.

He pulled her against his chest and held her silently, patting her back while she cried tiredly for a few moments. Finally she pulled away, wiped the tears from her face with the side of her hand, then blew her nose vigorously on a tissue she rooted from her purse.

"I'd invite you in for coffee but I'm too tired," she said honestly. "Anyway, the place is a mess as usual. Is it okay if I stop at Homicide North before coming in in the morning? I could see if they need anything else from me."

"Sure," Regal said. "Take as much time as you need."

They looked at each other for a moment again and Jane said, "You know what I hope?"

"What?"

"I hope Estrellita was really dead for a month."

"Why?"

"Because I'd hate to think that someone killed her because they heard that Jose and I were out looking for her. I'd hate to be responsible for her death."

Regal shook his head. "The person responsible for her death," he said flatly, "was whoever pulled the trigger and shot her. Don't make yourself crazy."

She considered this for a moment, then nodded. "Thanks, Paul. I needed that."

"Good night, Jane. Sleep well."

She went inside and he waited until the door closed

behind her before walking slowly back to the elevator. All the way home, he wondered how he would have responded if she had invited him into her apartment.

The proper thing to do, he knew, would have been to politely decline. Would he have done that? He did not know.

When he returned home, he looked into Patrice's room. She was in bed with the lights out but he knew, with a spouse's sure sense, that she was still awake.

"I got called out on a knifing," he said quietly, not bothering to turn on the lights.

"When was that?"

"Around nine-thirty," he lied. He had been watching the eleven o'clock news.

"I got home around ten," she said. "I must have just missed you."

"That's the way it goes," he said. "Good night."

He closed her door quietly, wondering how many more conversations like this he would be having with his wife.

27

The previous day's coverage of the brutal murder of Harriet Bailey had been just a warm-up for the city's press. This day, the morning papers had the Monogram Murders splashed all over their pages, with main stories, speculative stories, feature stories on the victims, long think pieces by local columnists, editorials demanding that the police do something, everything, anything, just so long as it was swift.

Even the usually staid *Times* chipped in, running a story on the killings on Page One and, like the other papers, giving Oliver Storm and his anticrime campaign message a lot of space on the inside pages.

Regal wondered, reading the stories over breakfast at the coffee counter in a small neighborhood hotel, if it was just the savagery of the killings alone that made them so newsworthy, or if the press's zeal was intensified because the bodies had been found on the posh Upper East Side, one of the most fabled high-income residential areas in the world.

By the time Regal reached One Police Plaza, there

were a half dozen television equipment vans parked near the front of the building.

Commissioner Gallagher's going to have a busy day. And better him than me, Regal thought.

Gallagher was indeed already having a busy day. He was a few blocks crosstown, meeting with the mayor in his office, and it was not one of the mayor's better days.

"The whole damned nation is laughing at us," he screamed. "I want some arrests made and right away. I don't care if they're the right people or not. Arrest somebody, just to show that we're on top of this business."

"You don't mean that, Doug," said Gallagher, trying hard not to show that he was shocked to his flinty core. He had been around politicians long enough to know that, in private, they talked a lot of fire and brimstone, larded with profanity, but it was usually just locker room talk. This time he had the idea that the mayor might be serious and he found the whole thought of an arrest just for arrest's sake repulsive. He shook his head. "We make a cheap arrest and it doesn't hold up and then we'd look like fools."

"As opposed to?" the mayor snarled. "Grab some homeless bum. That's probably who the killer is anyway. Hell, do something. I've got so damned many citizens' committees on my back that I'm running them through here on a five-minutes-each schedule."

"Maybe I'll arrest Oliver Storm," Gallagher suggested sarcastically, unaware that two of his top officers had jokingly discussed the same thing the night before.

"Great," the mayor said. "What do we have on him?"

"Nothing."

"Arrest him anyway. The bastard's all over Page One with this damned story. Let them get a picture of him behind bars."

Throughout the entire conversation, the mayor had been standing behind his desk, leaning forward onto it with his arms. But now, his passion spent, he slumped back into his chair and covered his face with his hands.

Gallagher watched him silently. The threat of losing political power hit some people harder than others, he thought.

And this one's really facing a threat. Bigger than he even suspects.

Finally the mayor looked up, his eyes sad and soulful.

"What do you suggest, Dick? I've got to have something for these press bastards."

"Just stay cool is the first thing. If you panic, everybody in town will panic. Tell them that the police are doing everything humanly possible and that when the New York cops are on a case, it gets solved. I don't know why they're getting so bent out of shape anyway. It's only four people. Hell, in southern California they don't even start counting serial killings until they reach a dozen."

"That's California. Nobody cares about California except the people who live there and they don't give a shit either," the mayor said. "This is New York. Everybody cares about New York. Especially the people who don't live here." He looked triumphantly at Commissioner Gallagher as if he had just proved a scientific theorem by brainpower alone.

"We're in this alone," the mayor continued. "That bastard up in Albany just keeps clucking and shaking his head and calling press conferences and playing Hamlet. I won't forget him when the time comes. Please, Dick, tell me you're going to arrest someone today."

"I'll see what I can do," Gallagher promised, trying to look deeply concerned.

But he did not seem at all concerned when he talked to Paul Regal later that morning in his office and recounted the story. Regal sat stiffly, militarily correct, in the chair facing the commissioner's desk and listened. Once, there had been something close to friendship between the two men, but in Regal's mind that had vanished when Gallagher had called in Inspector Flaherty's Internal Affairs vultures to look into Regal's operation. He could no longer honor the man with his friendship;

the best he could do was to honor Gallagher's office with precise good manners.

And why the hell is he telling me all this anyway? Regal wondered. *Maybe he's already talked to Burton and Joe told him what we were joking about last night. And he wants to see if I'll tell him too. Well, screw the commissioner and his little loyalty test.*

Regal said nothing throughout the story and when the commissioner had finished and seemed to be waiting for an answer, Regal merely shook his head, and Gallagher said, "I think the man may be cracking under the strain. Maybe he's not cut out to be mayor." He searched Regal's face intently as if for a reaction but there was none there. Regal's countenance was as flat and unchanging as a plaster death mask.

After it was obvious that Regal was going to volunteer nothing, the commissioner said, "So what do you think, Paul?"

"About what, sir?"

"About everything. About the mayor."

"The mayor is politics and I don't know anything about politics," Regal said. "But of course arresting just anybody is . . . well, sir, as stupid an idea as I've ever heard."

"Why?"

"Obviously it's illegal, first. And second, because whoever is really doing the killings would promptly drop off another body, just to show us up, and then the shit would really hit the fan."

Gallagher nodded. "I've never seen him in a panic like this and Oliver Storm isn't helping things. I wish he would run his campaign on taxes instead of public safety. He's got the mayor running scared already and it's still more than a year till election day."

"Did you tell the mayor we've made some headway? That we've got some pictures on the TV tapes we've been taking?"

"I did not," Gallagher snapped. "He'd blab it to the press in minutes and our killer might just leave town.

We can just be happy that nobody's caught on yet to the chess game you're playing. Let's leave it at that. And until the mayor comes to his senses, I'm not telling him anything that might hinder this investigation. From here on in and until further notice, City Hall is just another one of our enemies."

Regal nodded his head in resignation. *What a way to run a city,* he thought. And this mayor was a gem, compared with some of them who had sat in that chair. Would Oliver Storm be any better?

Regal doubted it. The truth was that he *did* pay very little attention to politics or government but he had the firm suspicion that being mayor of New York City was not an honor but a sentence and few men survived it. The city was just too big, too vast, too unmanageable. The fact was, nobody could run New York. Only somebody with the ego of a politician would even dare to try.

"So . . . I just wanted to share this with you anyway," Gallagher said and Regal instantly wondered, *Why?* But he nodded and remained sitting stiffly in the seat.

"Do you have anything good for me?" Gallagher asked.

"Yes and no," Regal said, describing the finding of the woman presumed to be the missing Estrellita.

Gallagher listened, then said, "But there're still those drug tests on Pete Muniz. We catch his killers and it'll be a victory. But maybe only a small one."

"Why a small one, sir?"

"Because the autopsy evidence says that Muniz was a dirty cop. And we buried him with departmental honors. We get his killers, and if they tell the public he was a dirty cop, then we just get another black eye for covering it up."

"But he wasn't a dirty cop, and when we find his killers, we'll find out how they managed to make him look like he was taking drugs," Regal responded immediately.

"I hope you're right, Paul. We'll see. How's the chess game going?"

He doesn't want to think about Pete Muniz's killing. All he's worried about is the Monogram Murderer because that one hurts the mayor politically, Regal thought. *These people all suck.*

"Terrific, according to Billy Abbott," Regal said. "I got the killer's latest move this morning and when I called it in to Abbott, he was cackling like a hen that laid a dozen eggs. He's been slapping pieces all over the board, and to my eye, it looked like we're getting the crap kicked out of us. But he just tells me not to worry. Now he's going to make a pseudosacrifice of our queen."

"What the hell is a pseudosacrifice?"

"That means we offer the queen up for capture but the white player can't take it because if he does he loses."

"So then he won't take your queen," the commissioner said. "So what?"

"So if he doesn't, his position is weakened and we can win anyway. At least according to Abbott. We're going to win no matter what, he says. If that's so—and who am I to doubt him—this kid is really the chess genius everybody thought he was once."

"And what happens when we win?"

"God only knows, Commissioner. Maybe the killer will turn himself in. Maybe he'll go out and kill a lot of people out of spite. Who can figure a madman? None of these killings has made any sense from the start. Calling my phone and getting me involved has never made any sense either."

"In other words, we're just going to have to wait and see."

"Exactly, sir."

Gallagher blew air from between pursed lips. "Let's you and Burton make an arrest. Fast. It may be the only way to keep Oliver Storm out of jail, the way the mayor's going now."

"Maybe Storm belongs in jail," Regal said.

"Nobody belongs in one of our jails," Gallagher said, "and besides, he's not such a bad guy."

"Sorry, Commissioner, I really wouldn't know. We're not close."

Jane Cole came into Regal's office just before 11 A.M. and handed him a manila envelope.

"I just left Homicide North. Inspector Burton told me to give this to you," she said.

"How is it up there?"

"He's feeling the strain again," she said. When Regal raised an eyebrow, she explained, "Manpower. He's got leads now on the Monogram case and on Pete's killing, so he's dipping back into the precincts for men."

"And still no sign of our mysterious Panamanian drug dealers?"

"Nothing yet," Cole said. "Estrellita *was* from Panama though. One of Burton's guys tracked her down through immigration records. Estrellita Rollan. And she *was* Hector Guzman's squeeze. Hector's family identified her at the morgue. So she's the one Pete was looking for."

"I wonder if he ever found her," Regal said before realizing that it was a stupid comment, almost guaranteed to produce an image in Jane's mind of the two of them—Estrellita Rollan and Pete Muniz—meeting in the afterlife. He could tell that she had the same thought because a pained look crossed her face.

He glanced down and peeled open the envelope that Jane had brought him.

There was a simple white piece of memo paper inside. Written on it was a note from Burton:

> Regal. Thought you'd like to see the first pho-
> tos of our Monogram nut. Or nuts. Anybody
> you recognize? Air Force has them now. J.B.

"Look at these, Jane," Regal said. She came around behind his desk and stood beside him, her long firm thigh pressed against his arm.

There were two eight-by-ten black-and-white photos,

grainy, apparently reproduced from a piece of videotape.

The photos were of a yellow taxicab, clearly the one
stolen the night before and used in Mrs. Bailey's murder.
Both photos were taken from in front of the vehicle, and
in both, the driver was barely discernible behind the
glare off the windshield. All Regal could make out was
a small man, apparently with dark hair. A larger man
was in the backseat. In one of the pictures, there looked
to be some kind of lump next to the larger man.

Regal knew without knowing. *That's Mrs. Bailey,* he
thought.

Jane leaned forward to be closer to the photos. Regal
saw her bosom uncomfortably near his face.

"Not much to go on," she said. "You sure this is connected with that woman's murder?"

"Yeah. Burton's too careful to make that kind of mistake and you can see the cab's license plate here. That
matches the stolen cab we found with Mrs. Bailey's
blood all over it. So that puts her . . . or her body . . . in
this cab."

He pointed to one picture, then the other. "And this
guy in the backseat. Here he is, with that lump next to
him. I'd bet that's Mrs. Bailey. Maybe dead already, on
her way to being dropped off. And here, look, the man
has changed seats. He's on the right side here and the
left side later. People don't move around in their seats
when they're taking a cab. I think he dumped the body
and then sat on the other side leaving the area."

Jane squinted at the prints. "Not much to go on
though. I can't see the driver's face or anything. Just a
blur."

"There's an awful big thing to go on," Regal said.

"What's that?" Jane stood up and looked down at
him, her thigh pressing against his arm. He was terribly
conscious of it and he knew somehow that she sensed
their closeness too.

"There're two of them," Regal said. "Two killers."

She looked puzzled and he said, "Nobody who's not

involved is going to drive somebody and a body around in a stolen cab, then wait for him to dump a body, and then drive him out again. There're two of them."

"Damn," she said. "That makes it worse."

"No. It makes it better," Regal said. "We've got twice as good a chance now of catching them."

"Not from these photos."

"That's what they look like now. Burton's got an Air Force lab going to augment the pictures for us."

"Will that help? There's not much to augment."

"They've got cameras now that can read street signs from satellites ninety miles up. They've got computers that can take a picture apart and put it back together again. Don't forget, all those pictures from Venus and space probes; they're all put together by computers, just from numbers. I think we'll come up with something. And don't forget, when we do, we've got at least one fingerprint from that cab too. We may just be getting closer to this smart bastard."

"Bastards," she corrected.

Regal nodded, just as the telephone rang. He picked it up hurriedly, his arm brushing against Jane's legs, and the young woman walked back around the desk.

It was Patrice.

"Darling, fend for yourself for dinner tonight. I'll be over at the Mountain. I'm so excited I couldn't eat anything anyway. Oh, God, less than forty-eight hours now. I can't stand the waiting."

"It'll go fine, Pat. Relax."

"But, darling, this is so important. I've got to run. I probably won't be home until late. I may even stay over at the Mountain if it's too late but don't worry about me."

"I won't," Regal promised. "I know you'll be in good hands."

He sighed as he hung up the receiver. Jane eyed him shrewdly. Already there was more than the desk between Jane and Regal. Another barrier seemed to have been raised and the brief feeling of intimacy that they both had shared seemed to vanish.

"Your wife?"

"Letting me know she won't be home for dinner again. It would be simpler if she simply let me know when she *will* be home."

"I guess she's busy these days," Jane said in a non-committal voice.

"She's busy all right," he said, distracted from his thoughts about the Monogram Murders. He picked up one of the prints and stared at it blindly for a moment, then tossed it on his desk. "I hope the Air Force comes through for us."

"They will," Jane said firmly. "I've got a good feeling."

He wanted to say something smart, something flip, like, *You certainly do,* but he thought it would be out of place. It must have been written on his face, though, because Jane smiled at him, a curiously warm smile, and said, "I'll be outside if you need me, Paul." She looked at him for a split second longer than was necessary, then strolled from his office, glancing back once more at him before she walked through the door.

It was Tony Bolda who found the next bodies.

He called Regal late in the afternoon. "I'm in a tenement in the South Bronx with three dead bodies. I think we found the pineapples we've been looking for."

"Anybody I should call?" Regal asked.

"No. I already notified Burton, just so no one could go bitching later about us meddling. His guys are here now and I'm coming in."

"I'll wait for you," Regal said. He hung up and went out to Jane's desk.

"Tony Bolda's on his way in. He found three dead Panamanians."

"Pete's killers?" Jane asked excitedly.

"I don't know yet. We'll just have to wait and see." He paused, at a loss for words. "I hope so, Jane."

* * *

Tony Bolda arrived forty minutes later, eating a bagel, dripping melted butter on his expensive but soiled gabardine suit. A pair of sunglasses were hooked into his jacket pocket. Regal thought Bolda looked tired when he came into the private office, followed by Jane, and sprawled out on a chair. The daily racing form slipped out of his side pocket and Regal was not surprised. Bolda's love of the ponies was a running joke in the office, and it was well known that on any day off, you had your best chance of finding him at Aqueduct or Monmouth Racetracks.

Bolda picked up the paper and stuck it back into his pocket.

Jane stood in the doorway, listening, as Regal asked Bolda to tell them what happened.

"I was at the track last night, but when I heard that Jane found Estrellita, I sent word out through all my stoolies up in that area that I was looking for three Panama boys. I thought they might just be holed up nearby somewhere. Then I was up at the Two-Eight when I got a phone call giving me an address over in the South Bronx."

"Who made the call?" Regal asked.

Bolda shook his head. "A voice I didn't know." He looked over toward Jane as if it was necessary to explain it to her. "Obviously one of my stoolies wanted me to know but didn't want me to know it came from him. He might just have been afraid. Anyway, I went over there, found the building and these three guys were inside an apartment. Place smelled like hell. They'd been dead for a week anyway."

"How'd they die?"

"They all took bullets," Bolda said. "And there were guns all over the place. It's going to take ballistics to sort it all out but I think maybe . . . just maybe . . . they all shot each other in some kind of argument. Crooks falling out maybe."

Regal scowled. "The three men, they didn't mean

anything to you? Faces, names, nothing familiar?"

"No. Their faces were useless because . . . well, they'd been dead a long time. I checked them for wallets but they didn't have any ID."

"What made you think they were Panamanians then?" Jane asked from the doorway.

"There was a Panama City newspaper in the apartment. And the way one of them was lying I could see a tattoo on the underside of his wrist. It was a cross and a chain. I remember reading once that some of Noriega's bully boys in Panama had that kind of tattoo."

. "Does it mean anything?" Regal asked, and Bolda shrugged extravagantly.

"Got me," he said. "I may even be wrong about the tattoo but it just sort of stuck in my memory."

Jane spoke up again. "Tony, you said you thought they might have killed each other. Do you think instead that there's a chance maybe we've got a full-scale drug war starting in the city?"

Bolda pursed his lips and considered the idea. "I don't know," he said. "If somebody from Panama or anyplace else moves in and tries to take over some business, sure, we'll have a war. So maybe these guys were taken out by one of the Jamaican posses or some Colombian outfit. But I haven't heard anything about dealers getting antsy. It just looks like business as usual out on the streets."

"Maybe they'll all kill each other off," Jane suggested.

"What's the difference?" Bolda said with a shrug. "A new crew of peddlers would be out on the street in a day. They're like cockroaches in an old tenement. You can call in as many exterminators as you want, but two days later, they come crawling back. And the other cockroaches who use drugs, they're as happy as pigs in shit, and maybe someday we'll get lucky and they'll all die."

It was as worked up as Regal had ever seen Bolda get and apparently the lieutenant was himself a little embarrassed by his sudden outburst because he looked at his watch and rose from the chair.

"I have to get over to Homicide North and fill out a report. I'd better do that now."

"Okay, Tony. Good work."

Bolda nodded and walked heavily toward the doorway. Jane moved aside to let him pass and he stopped and told her, "Truth, Jane, I hope these are the bastards that got Pete. I wish we could have gotten them first but it's no loss to suffering humanity either way."

Jane reached out her hand tentatively and touched Bolda's cheek, both in gentle agreement and in a gesture of thanks.

But Regal was dissatisfied. Even if these were the men who had killed Pete Muniz, his death seemed somehow to be still unavenged.

It just wasn't clean enough yet and he did not want it to end this way.

28

It was six o'clock before Regal worked his way through the pile of paperwork on his desk, but when he left his office, Jane Cole was still at her desk.

She was filing her nails and Regal asked, "Sharpening them for the kill?"

"Something like that," she said. "Time to get out of here."

"Do you have to go straight home? Is Sarah waiting?"

Jane shook her head. "No. She comes home tomorrow. Why?"

"I just wondered if you'd like to have dinner."

She hesitated. "Only if it's Chinese and I pick the place," she finally said.

"Suits me. I hate making decisions."

Outside, they walked in companionable silence through the bustling streets of lower Manhattan's ever-expanding Chinatown. Regal was glad that Jane did not seem to demand a constant flow of chatter from him. She commented occasionally on a street sight but seemed mostly preoccupied with her own thoughts.

She stopped in front of several restaurants, glanced at the menus in the window, then pulled Regal along with her as she rejected the places for some private reasons.

The first three times he found it charming. The next three times he found it annoying. She looked again at the prices on the menu in a newly opened and lavish restaurant, whistled softly and started again down the street.

This time, Regal grabbed her arm "Not so fast. What's wrong with this place?"

"The prices are ridiculous. I've seen Japanese restaurants that don't charge that much."

"My treat so don't worry about the prices. It looks nice inside. What do you say?"

Reluctantly she nodded and obediently followed him into the restaurant, where they were seated in a corner booth. The food was worth the high price tag, and while they ate, Jane finally loosened up some and began to talk about some of her experiences on the bunco squad, including the time she was chasing a man whose suspenders snapped, dropping his pants around his ankles and halting his flight.

"The poor bastard fell flat on his face and knocked himself silly. So a *Daily News* car comes by and gets a shot of him lying there with his polka dot shorts that are almost as big as my dress. And wouldn't you know, the dumb son of a bitch wanted to sue me for assault. I never get over the gall of some of these guys. He's running from a cop and his pants fall down and he's lying there screaming about police brutality and demanding my badge number. I laughed so hard I almost wet my pants."

Regal laughed with her, feeling relaxed and at ease in her company. He had never been able to talk to Patrice about his work. She did not understand the life of a police officer, and once they were married, she no longer made any pretense of being interested.

Simultaneously and too soon for Regal, they noticed that a waiter was beginning to hover near their table and

Jane glanced at her watch. "God, almost nine o'clock. Finish up that plum wine and let's call it a night."

Regal wished they could stay longer but he obediently paid the bill and a few minutes later they were walking back toward police headquarters.

"How do you get home now?" Regal asked.

"IRT to Times Square, another subway from there."

"Hell, we can do better than that." Overriding her surprised protest, Regal flagged down a cab, pushed her inside and gave his own home address on Seventy-fifth Street.

"What are you doing, Paul?"

"I'm going to pick up my car and drive you home."

"I can make it faster by subway."

"Put a cork in it."

She subsided sullenly, muttering that all men were brutes who wasted good money and she had always known he would turn out to be vicious and depraved.

"I've never been depraved," he said. "I never had the chance. I've been deprived of depravity."

Jane giggled and fell against him as the cab swerved sharply to avoid a jaywalker. Then Regal fell against her as the driver wrenched the wheel back just as savagely in the other direction. Regal decided to tip the driver lavishly. He glanced at the hack license and saw the driver had a Russian name. He thought about Billy Abbott and changed his mind about the size of the tip.

At his apartment building, Regal was desperately tempted to invite Jane upstairs. But what would he do if she accepted? What would he say? What would she say? What if . . . ?

He led her down the ramp to the garage in the basement of his building and a few minutes later they were heading toward the FDR Drive.

They bickered amiably for the half hour it took to reach Jane's apartment building. Regal parked at the end of a bus stop and hesitated, unsure whether or not to turn off his ignition.

Jane gave him no help, instead sitting silently, watching him with a faint smile.

"Safe and sound," he said brightly. He turned off the motor. "I'll walk you inside," he said.

"Thank you." She let herself out and he locked the car, cursing himself for feeling as shy and awkward as a teenager again.

But what the hell am I doing here anyway? he asked himself.

They rode the elevator quietly up to her floor. At her door, before he could stumble his way into some kind of decision, Jane said, "Come in and have coffee if you have the time. I have a present for you."

His heart leaped. This girl was ten years younger than he was, a product of a different and far more open generation. What kind of present did she have in mind?

Her apartment was pleasantly messy with a number of toys scattered around the floor. Jane shook her head in disgust. "The place is a pigpen but at least I picked up my underwear. Make yourself comfortable."

He sat on the couch facing the television set. Magazines were strewn on the coffee table in front of him. A double picture frame was on the end table beside him, holding two color photos of Sarah. She looked pensive in one with a finger pressed against her cheek. In the other, she was grinning widely, her eyes dancing.

"Sarah looks just like you," he said when Jane returned from bustling about in the kitchen.

"Hell," Jane scoffed. "She's beautiful."

"You're both beautiful," Regal said. He paused. "And you're very lucky."

"I'll buy into that," she said. "You don't have any kids, do you?"

He shook his head, still staring at Sarah's photos.

"By design?"

He glanced at her and his lips tightened. "Not mine."

Jane shook her head sadly and got up to answer the whistle of a coffee pot in the kitchen. She returned with two cups on a tray and put them on the coffee table.

When she sat next to Regal, she said, "And now your present."

From inside her purse, she produced two fortune cookies.

"Here's your present. We never opened them at the restaurant."

He laughed, almost relieved, and broke one open. " 'You will encounter many new opportunities,' " he read aloud.

Jane extracted her slip of paper. " 'All men are savage unfeeling brutes.' "

"Let me see that," Regal growled, reaching for it. She laughed and handed it to him.

" 'Fortune favors your quest,' " he read aloud, then looked at her. She was very close to him. "What's your quest?"

"I want to be chief inspector by the time I'm forty."

"Why wait that long?"

"I need more experience."

"What kind of experience?"

"Police experience. I have enough life experience."

"Lucky lady," he said, a tinge of sadness in his banter. "Some of us never have enough life experience."

She looked at him for a moment but did not respond and they sipped their coffee in silence, Regal again realizing how awkward she made him feel. And how old. Coming up to the apartment, he had felt like a teenager. Now he felt like the most senior of citizens.

He finished his coffee and had no choice but to look at his watch, stand, and announce, "It's getting late. Time to go. Maybe we can do it again sometime."

"Maybe," she agreed. "It depends."

"Depends on what?"

She stood up also and looked at him steadily. "Are you getting ideas about me?"

He frowned. "That's a hell of a question, Jane. I mean, you're a beautiful woman, of course. Any man would . . . but I wouldn't want you to . . ."

"It's a simple question, Paul, and I'll take a simple answer. Yes or no?"

"You're putting me on the spot."

She reached up and grasped his tie just below the knot and tugged sharply three times, her eyes fixed on his. "Yes or no, Paul?"

He sighed in resignation. "I'm getting all kinds of ideas about you, Jane. Now let me out of here before I break out in hives."

She nodded thoughtfully. "I thought you were. I could tell by your sweaty palms. I'm glad because I'm getting ideas about you too."

His mind froze. He could not have been more startled if she had punched him in the stomach. He opened his mouth to speak but could think of nothing to say. She waited, still holding firmly to his tie, her smile slowly broadening.

"Jane . . . I . . . I don't know what to say," he finally stammered. He did not know what to do with his hands so he simply let them hang limply at the end of his arms.

"How about answering a few questions?"

"What?"

"How long have you been married?"

He had to rack his brain to remember the year he had married Patrice and count up the time since then. "Not quite eighteen years," he answered finally. "Why?"

"Eighteen years. That's a long time, Paul. Now tell the truth. Since you married Patrice, have you ever slept with another woman?"

He flushed but nodded. "A couple of times . . . twice . . . briefly. That's not something I've ever been proud of."

Jane nodded slowly. "So you're *not* a saint?"

"No. But I try not to be a sinner."

She nodded again. "People who have good marriages don't cheat on their husband or wife. You don't have a good marriage, do you, Paul?"

He shook his head silently, feeling a wave of sadness

break over him. Without conscious thought, his hands drifted up to rest gently on her shoulders.

Her eyes seemed to grow larger, engulfing him in their blue depths. "I've always thought you were something special, Paul, from the first day I met you. I think the time has come for me to find out if I'm right. Or if I'm just being a damned fool again."

She pulled down strongly on the tie and cupped her other hand behind his head, pulling his lips down to meet hers. Paul closed his eyes and surrendered blindly to the kiss, ignoring fragmentary thoughts of Patrice and fidelity and promises made eighteen years ago to man and God. For one stunning blissful moment, all that seemed to exist in life were Jane Cole's warm lips, Jane Cole's hand caressing his head, Jane Cole's body pressed firmly against his. His arms tightened convulsively about her, straining her even closer to him.

When they ended the kiss by some mutual subliminal instinct, Regal felt weak—but when Jane's head slumped in surrender against his chest, he felt strength flooding through him. A thousand thoughts were yammering in his head, a thousand questions urgently demanding answers, but he ignored them all to simply relax and yield to the contentment he felt holding her.

He also felt acutely lustful, he realized, but there seemed to be no urgency to this lust. It was simply there, waiting to be put to use when the time was right.

Jane drew a deep shuddering breath and pushed him firmly away. "A little more than I counted on," she said softly. "You'd better go, Paul. I'm a little woozy right now."

He looked at her with a puzzled expression. "Go? Jane, you're not playing some kind of game with me, are you?"

She smiled. "No, Paul. I gave up teasing in my senior year at St. Aloysius. But I know I don't want to rush headlong into anything. I did that once and lived to regret it. We have time. I think maybe we have something kind of terrific going on here. But let's not rush it. We're both carrying around a lot of baggage. A lot more than you know, even."

"And I'm a married man. Is that it? Shit, I feel like a heel."

She studied his face. "Do you feel like a heel on your wife's account or on mine?"

"On yours," he answered.

She smiled warmly. "Good. Right answer. That's because you're a decent guy, which is why I like you. Let's just go with the flow, Paul. I want you to stay but I know it's too soon so go home while I can still let you go. Please."

His answer was to pull her tight against him again and lower his lips onto hers, kissing her with a desperate intensity that he had not felt for many years. This time he was acutely conscious of time and place and the feel of her lips and the way her body was beginning to sag against his. She was his for the taking, he thought with exultation. *I can pick her up and carry her into the bedroom and she won't let out a peep.*

He broke off the kiss, gave her a long searching look, then lightly kissed her forehead. "Hell of an evening, kid," he whispered. "As I said, let's do it again sometime."

"I'm game," she whispered back.

He walked toward the door. When his hand touched the knob, Jane called his name.

He turned to her.

"Paul, I don't care whether you're married or not. I wouldn't care if you were the Pope of Rome. I want you right now but we'll both feel better if we wait. And someday you'll agree with me."

A dozen flip comments, dealing with self-abuse, cold showers, and incurable disfiguring diseases caused by sexual frustration, popped into his mind, but in the end all he did was nod slightly and leave.

It was after 1 A.M. when Patrice returned home. Regal was waiting for her in the darkened living room, sitting in his easy chair, nursing a highball.

She was startled to see him and reacted defensively. "Oh, Paul. Don't start anything. I'm exhausted. I've been working like a dog all night."

He said nothing, instead simply watching her as she hung up her coat and moved nervously about the room.

She spun around suddenly. "Why are you staring at me like that, Paul? Are you all right? Are you drunk or something?"

"Relax, Pat. I didn't feel sleepy so I decided to have a drink. When I finish it, I'm going to bed."

She eyed him suspiciously as she fussed with her handbag, putting her keys on the small table by the door. She went into the kitchen and poured herself a glass of buttermilk, a nightly ritual, and returned to the living room to sit and drink it with him.

"The Mountain looks just beautiful," she said. "Everything is falling into place. This is going to be the most fabulous event in New York since Truman Capote. I'm so proud of myself, I could just . . . just fly."

"You're flying. I can see that."

"I've never been so happy in my life."

"I'm glad, Pat. But I'm worried for you too."

"Why?"

"Are you planning to marry Oliver Storm?"

She jerked so suddenly that she almost spilled her milk. "Paul! What are you talking about?"

He ignored her outburst and said calmly, "I guess more important is, does Oliver plan to marry you?"

"Stop that this minute! I won't be badgered by you like this."

"Pat, no badgering. But give me a straight answer. Has he ever actually asked you to marry him? Or is he just stringing you along?"

She rose abruptly to her feet. "I don't want to put up with this insanity. Think what you want but keep your filthy accusations to yourself."

"There's nothing filthy about falling in love with somebody and marrying them, Pat. I just don't want you to be hurt by Storm."

She looked confused for a moment, then struck a hurt pose. "Do you really think that Oliver and I are having an affair or something?"

"Of course I do. Everyone who knows you does. You might as well have been carrying a billboard for the past few months. I know you think I'm blind, but please don't think I'm stupid. You said a moment ago that you've never been so happy. I believe you, Pat. I believe you're head over heels for Oliver and I'm glad for you. But I wonder what his plans are."

Her lips tightened. "If you must know, Oliver *is* in love with me. And he *has* asked me to marry him." She glared at him defiantly, but Paul only smiled back.

"I'm happy about that, Pat. He's the kind of man you deserve. He can give you all the things I never could or would. I think you two are perfect for each other."

"What kind of game are you playing, Paul?"

"No game. I'm tired of games. All we've had for too many years have been games. I'm just tired of it. I think it's time we both had the real thing."

Her eyes narrowed. "You're running around with another woman."

He shook his head. "I've met someone else that I think I could be happy with, Pat. Maybe even as happy as I was when you and I first got married. And you've met the same kind of person, at least if Storm is on the level. So now is the time to call it quits, don't you think?"

"I don't know what to say. You shock me, Paul. I thought you were happy."

"Sure you did. When you bothered to think about me at all, which hasn't been very often of late." He drained most of his drink. "Listen, Pat, I'm not trying to pick a fight or to cause you distress. This would have happened anyway, whether I met someone else or not. I'm not happy things turned out this way, but the simple fact is, we made a mistake when we got married. It's just that it got easier to keep doing it than to do something about it. Till now." He smiled. "Look at the bright side. Now you won't have to come back here every night when you'd rather be somewhere else."

He sipped again at his drink, amazed at how calmly he was conducting this conversation that he had dreaded for years.

Patrice eyed him warily. "Are you going to leave me, Paul?" She forgot to put a plaintive quaver in the question, he noticed—or maybe she simply didn't care enough to try.

"No rush," he assured her. "It's not as if we were actually sleeping with each other all the time. We've been only roommates for a long time now."

She put a hand to her throat. "I don't want a scandal," she said.

"You and Oliver won't have to worry. You've both got my best wishes. I'm not sure I want to wait until the election is over with but I certainly don't want to do anything that would embarrass any of us."

He could see her mind racing. "Paul, I want you to know that I have never been unfaithful to you. And Oliver Storm has never—"

"Stop it!" he cut her off. "Try to get it through your head that it doesn't matter to me. I'm not angry. I'm just sad. But don't annoy me with a bunch of calculating, transparent lies. I know Storm isn't your first lover, as a matter of fact. I don't know how many and I don't want to know. But you seem happy now and I'm glad for you. But no more lies."

He grinned. "Tell you what. You tell Storm that if he doesn't marry you, I'll name him as a co-respondent and ruin his political chances forever and ever." He smiled slightly as he realized she was mulling over the idiotic threat.

"Paul, I . . . I don't know what to say."

"Try good night," he told her. "I'm going to bed. I've had a busy night. I guess we both have. Sleep well, Pat."

He was at his bedroom door when she called after him, "You left your highball glass on the table."

"I know," he said and closed the door, feeling an enormous sense of personal freedom.

29

Regal slept fitfully that night, waking often, his mind shuttling back and forth between the scene in Jane Cole's apartment and his climactic marital conversation with Patrice. In a way, both memories filled him with apprehension.

He was a few minutes late arriving at his office, wondering as he entered how Jane would act toward him but her reaction was to show no reaction at all. She was on the telephone and gave him a cursory nod. He nodded back and walked briskly into his own office, determined to be cool and professional in all things.

An hour later he went to the men's room, and when he returned, Jane was standing by his desk phone.

"Creepo just called again."

Regal stepped toward the desk. "Play it back," he ordered, and Jane punched the buttons on the built-in telephone tape recorder.

"For-Inspector-Paul-Regal. White-plays-king-takes-queen. Your-queen-is-dead. You-lose, Regal."

King takes queen? Regal's jaw dropped. How could

his opponent make such a glaring mistake. Now the killer would be checkmated in just a few more moves. Regal would win. Only a novice could have overlooked the move, and the level of play thus far, whether by a human or by a computer program, had not been that of a novice.

"Play it again," he said and Jane dutifully complied. He listened and thought, *There's something else too. What is it?*

"You notice anything different about this call?" he asked Jane, but she just shook her head. "Sounds like the same son of a bitch to me," she said.

"Okay. Well, talk to the trace people and find out where this call was made from and then notify Burton and his people as usual," he said, all thoughts of last night gone from his head. "I'm going out."

"Where are you going?" she asked.

"To see a chess player."

Billy Abbott might have given up chess, but his father clearly had never forgotten those days of glory.

The elder Abbott's apartment, where Billy lived, was packed with display cases holding his son's chess trophies and framed photos of the chess genius playing matches against the greatest grandmasters from all over the world.

Billy himself answered Regal's insistent ring on the doorbell, and when he saw the policeman, he squawked, "What happened? Did he move?"

"King takes queen," Regal said simply.

Abbott stared at him. "I don't believe it," he said. "You must have made a mistake. White would never make that move."

"That's what I thought too, but he did. Why? Something's wrong. Is there something we overlooked?"

He searched Abbott's face and realized, to his own surprise, that he was waiting for advice from the young man.

Abbott grabbed Regal's arm and dragged him into the

apartment, toward a handcarved wooden chess table on the far side of the room.

"Overlooked? For Christ's sake, how can he overlook a forced mate? Knight to king knight six; bishop interpose; rook takes; queen interpose; rook takes. Next move mate. Finis. Done. We win. Checkmate. I told you he was a patzer."

As he spoke, he demonstrated the moves on the chessboard. "See?" he said.

"Yeah, I guess so," Regal agreed reluctantly. "I just wish I knew what was going to happen next."

"What do you mean?"

"Why did he make that losing move? It can't be that he missed it. He has something else on his mind and he's calling the game off. Why?"

Abbott started to speak but fell silent. "I don't know," he confessed finally. "I never gave any thought to what might happen after the game is over, you know. I just focused on winning."

For the first time since this whole business had started, Regal detected a note of concern in Abbott's voice and he knew he should cheer up the young man. *My problems aren't his problems*, he thought.

"Billy, you did something that Kasparov, even Fischer, couldn't have done."

"I know," Abbott said matter-of-factly. "I didn't want him to roll over and play dead though. I wanted him to keep fighting so I could crush his spirit."

"Well, he's given up and I don't know what comes next. But whatever it is, I doubt that I'm going to like it much."

The tone of his voice caused Abbott to glance up sharply at the policeman.

"You're really worried about something, aren't you?" Billy said.

"Yeah. Something's going on and I don't understand it."

"Well, let's look at this logically," Abbott said calmly, and Regal was touched by the young man's effort to lift him out of his sour despair. "Did he do anything different on the tape today?"

"I've been thinking about that," Regal said. "He said—Inspector Paul Regal. White plays king takes queen. Your queen is dead. You lose, Regal."

"Is that different from the way he usually talks?"

"Maybe. Same computerized voice, of course. But the business 'Your queen is dead. You lose, Regal.' That's different in a way. It's kind of making the whole thing personal. Up till now it's just been a chess game. But now, it seems to be him versus me. 'You lose, Regal.' That means something."

"What could it mean?" Abbott asked. "Think it through, man. The clock's not ticking and there's no time pressure. What could he mean?"

"I don't know, Billy."

"You sure you don't know this guy? What he said to you today . . . that *is* making it personal. Sort of between you and him. Now why should he do that?"

"I don't know."

"Well, you've got to keep thinking about it," Abbott said sharply. "He's talking about *your* queen and *you* losing. That's direct and it means something and you've got to figure out what and I can't help you. You know, you can't win a game if you start wallowing in doubt or self-pity. The tougher the position gets, the cleaner you have to think. That's what you have to do. And maybe you'll figure out why he's been calling *you* in the first place."

"I'll stay at it, Billy. Thank you."

"Okay. Anything else you want me to do?"

"No," Regal said. "Go back to school. Get your degree. Live your life, Billy. Live the kind of life you want to live."

"Yeah, sure," Abbott said uncertainly. "Well . . . you know the next move to put in the *Times*."

"Knight to knight six," Regal said. He thought a moment and added, "Maybe I'll wait a day or two. I don't think we have anything to lose at this point. If our chess player is going to do something, I think he'll do it whether we keep playing or not. Maybe he'll delay if we don't make the final move right away."

"Maybe. I just hope nobody else gets killed."

"I hope so too. But I don't think so."

"I don't understand the world," Abbott confessed. "Why do people do things like this? That's one good thing about chess. At least there's no bloodshed, no killings. No matter what you do to your opponent or he does to you, there's no shooting or stuff like that afterward. You know?"

"Billy, I've got to go. I'll call you again when I have any further news, let you know how this works out."

"Thanks. I appreciate that. And good luck, Paul. You're not such a bad guy after all, even if you are just a patzer."

"Most people are," Regal said. "You've got to be tolerant. You can't judge humanity by their chess-playing ability."

"Why not?" asked Abbott, sounding sincerely bewildered.

"It's against the law. Good-bye, Billy. Study hard."

Regal walked to the door, grinning to himself at Abbott's demented, obsessive outlook on the world, but the smile quickly faded as he looked back into the room. Billy Abbott had forgotten that Paul Regal even existed. He was sitting at the chess table, staring down at the pieces.

Regal softly locked the door behind him.

Driving back to Manhattan, his mind juggled what Billy Abbott had said. There was meaning in the killer's words.

King takes queen was a loser; the killer must have known it.

So why did he say, "You lose, Regal?"

The words kept repeating in his mind like a faulty phonograph record. It was white—the killer—who was losing, not black. Wasn't it? What was he overlooking?

For the first time since the earliest calls, Regal had the

feeling that the message was directed at him as a person, not just as a policeman.

But why? What the hell does it mean? Is there a message behind this message?

Regal felt a chill. Was he being directly threatened by an attack on his queen? Who could that be? Jane Cole? But who besides Jane herself would know of her new importance to him? Even Patrice knew only that he had met someone new.

Patrice! Could it be his wife who was under attack? Was that the meaning of the message?

Regal hurriedly called her studio and LeBlanc answered the phone. "Whatever it is, we don't want any," he announced in a harried tone of voice.

"Pete, this is Paul. Is my wife there?"

"She hasn't been in the studio today, Paul. She said she was going over to the Mountain to make sure everything is set for tomorrow night. Maybe you can find her there someplace." He hesitated. "Sounds important. Is it?"

"Pete, keep this under your hat but I have a nasty suspicion that someone might want to hurt her. I don't want to scare you but think twice about opening any packages, especially if they're addressed to Pat. And don't let anybody into the studio that you don't know. I'm going to try to get a cop on guard duty over there, just in case."

"Send a young handsome one," LeBlanc said, but after a split second, he said, "You're serious, Paul, aren't you?"

"Yes. It might be a bullshit stupid hunch and nothing more. I'll explain it to you later. Just watch your step, okay?"

He called the commissioner's office but Gallagher was out. After a momentary hesitation, he called the precinct closest to Patrice's downtown studio and talked the commander into sending over one of his uniformed men, promising to explain the request fully later on.

"For the moment, just put it down as acting on information received," Regal suggested. "I hope it's a waste of time but I don't know."

"Don't sweat it, Inspector," the captain said. "Just send me something in writing so my inspector doesn't jump my ass later."

"You've got it."

Next, Regal called Storm Mountain and asked for the head of security. After a long wait, a crisp voice identified itself as Greg Rafferty and asked what he could do.

"This is Inspector Regal. Is my wife there?"

"I saw her downstairs about ten minutes ago, arguing with somebody about a crooked mirror. You want to talk to her?"

"Yes, but first I want to talk to you. Are you already up to speed with your security setup?"

"Believe it," Rafferty said, but Regal detected stress in his voice. "We've even got a couple of dogs sniffing around, inspecting deliveries in case of a bomb. I guess we're like all cops. Paranoia's the name of our game too. Why do you ask?"

"This is for your ears only. Something has happened that makes me think there may be an attempt on my wife's life. I've already had a patrolman posted to her studio for security there. Is there any chance you can have someone follow her around there today, just to be on the safe side?"

"I don't see why not," Rafferty said slowly. "I have a few guys just sitting around looking dangerous. Can you tell me what this is all about, what we should be looking for?"

"Not really. It's confusing and a lot of it is classified. I can only tell you—and mind you, I'm counting on your silence—it has to do with the Monogram Murders."

Rafferty whistled softly. "I'll put a man on her right away. What about when she leaves here?"

"Can you spare the man to take her where she's going?"

"Sure."

"Do it then and you've got my thanks. I'd like to talk to her now if you can get her."

"May take a few minutes. Want to wait or should I have her call you? What's your number?"

"Have her call me," Regal said. He gave the number and hung up.

A minute later, the telephone rang.

"Patrice?"

"No. Greg Rafferty again. I just wanted to make sure your call was on the level. Sorry, Inspector, but you know how cranks are. Some of them . . . well, they're good liars."

"No problem. I understand."

"Hold on. Here comes your wife now."

There was a pause, then Patrice's voice asked, "Paul, is that you?"

"Yes, Pat. Listen, I don't want to alarm you but there's just a slim chance that somebody might be planning to hurt you somehow."

"Paul, what the hell are you talking about?" she said angrily.

"Dammit, I'm talking about the Monogram Murderer. Now listen, I've got a policeman at your studio and Rafferty has promised to keep a guard with you all day."

"I can't believe this," she said.

"You'd better believe it. This may be nothing, Pat, but it's for real. Don't take any chances and do what Rafferty's man says."

"What makes you think that I . . . ?"

"It's just a hunch, Pat, and maybe I'm talking out my ass. But humor me, will you?"

"All right," she said with a sigh. "Do you think I'm all right here?"

"I should think so," he agreed reluctantly.

"Then I'll get back to work." She paused. "Thank you, Paul."

Before he could respond she had hung up.

"Thank you, Paul"? Does she think I want a divorce so badly that I want her killed? Jesus Christ.

He leaned back in his chair and rubbed his eyes. He might be making a fool of himself but he didn't really have any choice. Still, the more he thought of it, the sketchier his reasoning seemed to be. Probably the message had an entirely different meaning than he had given it—or maybe it had no secret meaning at all.

Unless . . .

He called the protocol officer in the commissioner's office.

"Paul Regal. Any royalty in town right now? Or expected in the immediate future?"

"None that we've heard of. Why?"

"Just a dumb idea," Regal said. "Thanks."

Finally, he called Joe Burton. After a brief delay, the other inspector came on the line and snapped, "What's up, Regal? Make it quick."

Regal tersely outlined the latest chess move by the Monogram Murderer, explained its implications and outlined the steps he had taken.

"I don't get it," Burton said, "but I think you did the right thing. You're saying the guy is simply giving up on the game?"

"That's right. From here on in, it's an automatic win for our side."

"I don't like it. But maybe he has some other queen in mind."

"I'm hoping that's true, Joe."

"But still, the guy started it all out by asking for you by name, remember? I've never been comfortable with that. Somehow, Paul, this involves you. Shit, I hate mysteries. This Storm Mountain . . . that's opening tomorrow night, isn't it?"

"Yeah, and half the people there are going to be security guards," Regal said.

"You going to be there?"

"My wife has to be, naturally, and I promised her I'd go with her."

"Well, I may send a few people over too, just to be

on the safe side. The damned place is located in the target area anyway."

"I may bring some people too," Regal said.

"Don't trust anybody though, Paul. You be there and you keep your eyes open. Maybe . . . ah, forget it."

Regal said, "Maybe don't scare him off?"

"Forget about it," Burton mumbled. "It was just a stupid thought."

"Yeah, it was, Joe. There's no way I'm going to use my wife as a tethered goat to let this nut take a crack at her."

"Don't put words in my mouth," Burton snarled. "I said forget about it. I've got to go. Let me know if anything else happens."

He hung up abruptly as usual. Regal thought that Burton was embarrassed by what he had been about to suggest, but he couldn't be mad at him. Burton was a cop, a manhunter, and he wanted the killer so badly he could taste it. He would probably stake out his own mother as a target if he thought it would do the job.

His direct phone line rang. It was Burton again.

"Listen, Regal, I had a thought. Any chance we can use a policewoman as a double for your wife? Keep her safe at home tomorrow night?"

"Not a chance, Joe. This is the biggest event in her life. She'd walk barefoot through hot coals to be there. But I know what you mean. Thanks, Joe."

Burton grunted and hung up, and as Regal replaced the telephone, he realized there was nothing more he could do right now.

The game was all in the hands of the killer.

Or killers.

And what did he—or they—want with Paul Regal, anyway?

30

Jane Cole came into his office shortly after noon and Regal asked, "No lunch today?"

"No invitations."

He smiled. "You would've had one from me but... well, it's just been that kind of day."

She nodded. She was standing in the doorway so she could watch outside and see if anyone entered the office. "I didn't want to bother you, you've been on the phone for so long, but no good with the trace on the creep's phone call."

"The usual?" he said.

"Yeah. Street phone uptown, gone when our guys got there, nobody saw anything."

Regal shrugged. "It would have been too easy to nail him that way. It's not in our fortune cookies. Thanks, though."

Jane still lingered in the doorway, staring at him, and finally she said, "I just wanted to apologize ... about last night."

"Why?"

"I came on a little strong and I was awake most of the night thinking about it. I didn't ... well, I got to thinking that I was acting like a home wrecker and I didn't like thinking about myself like that. I felt a little cheap."

"Don't do that to yourself ... or me," Regal said, glowering. "There was nothing cheap about what happened. Actually, damn little did happen ... more's the pity."

"I just didn't want to cause you any distress."

"No distress at all. Last night made me think about a lot of things. I wound up telling my wife that it was time for us to split."

Jane gasped and put her hand to her mouth. She looked stricken. "Oh, God," she said softly. "It's all my fault."

"Horseshit," Regal said. "It was all my fault. Mine and Patrice's. Our marriage died a long time ago and it was just force of habit that neither of us ended it before this. I think I surprised her last night by making the first move but she surprised me too. She said that Oliver Storm wants to marry her."

"Oliver Storm? Holy shit. I mean we're talking real money now, aren't we?"

"Yeah. It's one of the few things that has always interested my wife."

"It wasn't anything I did?" she asked again.

Regal shook his head.

"Good. I feel relieved. I was having an awful lot of bad thoughts about myself last night."

"That's funny. I was having a lot of good thoughts about you last night."

"Paul, I don't want you to think I make a habit of grabbing guys by the tie and hauling them off to bed."

"You didn't exactly haul me off to bed. Just the opposite. You grabbed me by the tie and threw me the hell out before I could haul *you* off. But sure, I wonder about things like that. That was one of the things that had me tossing and turning. I mean ... you're from the sixties, a whole different generation than mine. You've probably got a different outlook than I do. You've been married. You were living with Pete. You—"

"Pete and I weren't living together."

"Okay. Sorry."

"But we slept together. That's true."

Regal shrugged. "I thought about that and, you know, I'm not being smug or acting forgiving because there's nothing to forgive, but I like you just the way you are. And whatever got you that way, then I'm in favor of it."

"We're going a little too fast," Jane said. "We haven't even . . ." She blushed.

"No, we haven't and I hope we rectify that sometime soon. But we get along. And we can talk shop and we can laugh and that's a hell of a lot better than I've had in the last eighteen years."

"I . . ."

"And don't talk. You had nothing to do with it. It's not your fault or anybody's fault." He grinned. "Now maybe we can get some work done around this place."

"Your wish is my command."

"I'll remember you said that sometime," Regal said and then immediately, his manner turning serious, he added, "I've put a guard on Patrice."

She looked bewildered and he said, "No, no. Nothing personal. It's just the phone message today. He said my queen is dead and I'm just wondering if maybe that means my wife."

"That's out of the blue, Paul," she said.

"I know. And maybe I'm overreacting. But I've been thinking that there has to be some reason why this maniac started right off by calling me. Why not the chief's office? Why not the local precinct? Why Paul Regal? Does it have something to do with Patrice? I don't know but I don't want to find out the hard way."

"Can you keep her under lock and key until we've got this guy put away?"

"Not much chance of it. I'll try to cage her tonight but tomorrow night is the grand opening of Storm

Mountain. I'll be there with her but there's no way I could keep her home."

He stopped as a thought took shape in his mind.

"Would you like to go to that opening tomorrow night?"

Jane looked shocked. "Are you kidding? Your wife would scalp me."

"She doesn't know you exist, Jane, although she will soon enough. But it's a great idea. I planned to have some extra police around anyway and what better than a beautiful lady cop?"

"Beautiful? Hah! I look like a wreck. My hair looks like a bird's nest. I don't have anything to wear."

"Make an appointment with the hairdresser. It's an assignment so you can visit him on office time. Buy a new dress if you need to. I'll pay for it."

"Oh, so you're buying me clothes already, are you?"

"Undies come next. I saw some great stuff in a window on Forty-second Street today."

Jane lifted her head in mock haughtiness. "Sir, what do you take me for?"

"For everything I can," Regal said. "Better yet. You just call the hairdresser. Do it now. Let me worry about what you'll wear. What are you, a size six?"

"You can always tell a married man. Six on the nose."

"Okay, get out of here."

When she left he called Pierre LeBlanc.

"Pete, you're still going to the opening tomorrow night, right?"

"Naturally. I'm going to wear a sandwich board telling the world that I'm the one responsible for anything visible that remotely looks to be in good taste."

"Will you be taking anyone with you?"

"I wasn't planning to."

"You mind escorting one of the people from my office? Detective Jane Cole."

"What does she look like?"

"A beautiful redhead. I think she'll need some help in the costume department."

"What does she dress like?" LeBlanc said.

"I don't know. Like a cop probably."

"Lor' luv a duck. We can't have that. She really beautiful?"

"Yes."

"What size?"

"A perfect six."

"I'll dress her," LeBlanc said. "I've got a friend who's a designer. He'll have something great for her."

"I knew I could count on you."

"Tell me . . . this Jane Cole . . . can I jump her bones?"

"I'd rather you didn't try."

"I figured that. I just wanted to hear it from you," LeBlanc said. "Does Patrice know?"

Dammit, he is clever, Regal thought.

"Patrice and I are splitting up. We talked about it last night. But she doesn't know anything about Jane."

"She'll hear nothing from me. But have this Jane call me."

"Right away," Regal said. "By the way, did the precinct send over a cop?"

"Yes, he's six foot seven and chews gum. He has muscles from head to foot. One of my assistants is enraptured."

"Male or female assistant?"

"I've never been sure," LeBlanc said.

"Hold on right now. I'll have Jane pick up this call."

"Okay. And Paul . . . ?"

"What?"

"Congratulations. It's long overdue."

"Hang on."

Regal had Jane pick up the call, briefly introduced the two, then backed out of the conversation and hung up.

And this is the way big decisions go, he thought. *Last night I tell my wife we should split up and today it's just another subject for idle chitchat with my friends.*

Well, about damned time, he told himself. For years he had been sure that Patrice was cheating on him, but rather than confront her and force a showdown, he had withdrawn into himself and kept her at bay with a cool smile. Perhaps if he had been more open and honest with her from the start . . .

He shook his head. No. Whatever his own character defects, Patrice had never played fair with him and she was even more unyielding than he was. In his heart, he could never forgive her for having cheated him out of the opportunity to be a loving father.

That caused him to wonder if Jane would be as attractive to him if she were not the mother of a young child.

He finally put it out of his mind by asking himself the unanswerable question that seemed to apply to so much of his life.

Does it really matter?

31

Regal was surprised to find Patrice at home when he returned just before seven o'clock.

For a moment he was touched by the thought that in a moment of danger Patrice had walked away from Oliver Storm and decided to rely on her large, protective, gun-carrying husband to shield her, but he was disabused of that notion as soon as he walked in the door.

"The designer delivered my new gown here. I was afraid if it went to the Mountain it might get lost."

She pointed to the garment, floor length with vertical ribs of silver sequins, hanging on the back of a closet door. He looked at it, then at her, but she had already turned away. She did not give a damn anymore what her husband thought about her dress.

And so marriages end, he thought.

But maybe he was not totally wrong about her desire for protection because she announced grandly that all her work at Storm Mountain had been done and she would spend the evening at home. She would even take care of dinner, she said.

"What would you like? Pizza or Chinese?" she asked.

"Pizza."

"Let's have Chinese instead."

"Fine. Chinese."

"But if you really want pizza . . ."

"Chinese," Regal said.

"What kind?"

"You pick it."

"That's a good decision on your part," Patrice said smugly.

When the food was delivered, they ate in the small dining room and Regal asked, "Did you tell Oliver about us?"

"We talked about it for a few minutes."

"And what'd he say?"

"I think he was surprised but relieved. This political campaign has really tied his hands and I'm sure he was worried that he might become involved in a messy divorce."

"A messy divorce is the last thing I want," Regal said. "And I don't see why there should be any problems." He smiled. "I don't have anything and you're welcome to all of it."

"Well, there's this apartment. It's in your name," Patrice said.

"You don't mean to tell me that you and Oliver want to live up here, renting five rooms on Seventy-fifth Street, do you?"

"Of course not," Patrice said, and Regal wondered if she had always lacked a sense of humor or if it just went hand in hand with her new social-climbing money-grabbing personality.

"Fine. So I keep the apartment. You go live in a penthouse somewhere. I'll live here. Hell, before long, you're going to be living in Gracie Mansion anyway. Mrs. First Lady."

Her eyes widened at the thought and she smiled broadly. "That will be nice, won't it?"

"That's why I think it's better if you and I dissolve

our marriage as rapidly as possible. Once you're free, there's no chance that Storm is going to wind up in the tabloids as Mister Home Wrecker. I wouldn't want him damaged politically."

"I bet."

"It's true, Pat. You and I didn't work out but I'll always wish the best for you. I'd like to have a friend in Gracie Mansion." He paused. "There's no question about Oliver marrying you, is there?"

She looked affronted. "None at all. Just as soon as it becomes politically practical. Why do you persist in thinking that he's just toying with me? He wants and needs a wife, not just a flat belly to jump in bed with. He's had plenty of those." She tossed her head indignantly.

"Well, you know us police types. Always suspicious of people's motives. Call it an occupational deterrent to social interaction."

"I'd call it being a pain in the ass."

"So what do we do next? I guess we get lawyers, right? We can keep living here together, if you want, until the divorce is final."

"I've already talked to one of Oliver's attorneys. He'll handle things for me and be in touch with you."

She certainly didn't let any grass grow under her feet, Regal thought, but said mildly, "Have him draw up whatever he wants. Let's keep it straightforward and neat and I'll sign it."

"You have to be represented by an attorney," Patrice said. "He told me that."

"Patrice, I *am* an attorney."

"You never took the bar exam," she said.

"No. But I can understand anything he writes. And just to touch all bases, I'll have one of the department lawyers check it for form. To protect both of us."

"Fine," she said. She wiped her mouth with a linen napkin. "So who is this new woman you're sleeping with?"

"Sorry, Pat, no cigar. I'm not sleeping with anybody."

"I'm not sure I believe that."

"I'm not sure I care what you believe," Regal said. "But it's true."

They stared at each other for a moment but the tension was broken by the phone ringing.

"Two things, Regal," Joe Burton began gruffly. "Those three dead guys *were* from Panama; we ran them down through Immigration. And one of the guns they had, well, it *was* used to kill Pete Muniz. I think we've cleaned up the Muniz case at least."

Regal was silent for a moment. "Partly anyway," he said. "I just wish one of those guys was still alive. I'd like to know about those narcotics traces in Pete's body."

"There're always loose ends," Burton said.

"Yeah, I guess so. But this whole damned thing just sounds... well, too convenient if you know what I mean."

"I wanted to hear you say that," Burton answered grumpily, "because I feel the same way. Three dead bodies and one hot gun and I just don't like the smell of it all. You know, Regal, you may make a cop yet."

"Thanks. Aaaah, let's face it. We've both had plenty of cases that were closed up with less than this. You're going to make the commissioner very happy. And the mayor, of course."

"Don't even mention his name to me. He's an idiot," Burton said.

"He's a politician. Same thing. You said there were two things. What's the other?"

"The Air Force came through for us. I'm sending a messenger over with new photos of that stolen cab. They did a good job on making the face of the driver more identifiable. It's a young white kid, apparently. The backseat passenger too, but you can't see him so well but maybe it's somebody you've seen around. We'll start showing the new prints around near Mrs. Bailey's neighborhood tomorrow. Maybe somebody will remember something worthwhile."

"The driver has a mustache, right?"

"Right."

"Try making up some prints with the mustache removed."

Burton was silent for a moment. "Not a bad idea," he said grudgingly. "I'll put the photo lab to work on it. But tomorrow. I'm tired and I'm going home. You got anything new for me?"

"Afraid not."

"Gotta go," Burton said and hung up.

"Same to you," Regal retorted to the dead phone and returned it to its cradle.

When he turned around, Patrice was standing in the middle of the living room, gazing about bemusedly, one hand at her chin. "That painting is mine," she announced. "And that one too."

"And I get all the Jerry Vale albums. And the pot holders and the dog."

"We don't have a dog," she said, bewildered.

"I know and this is all silly, Pat. It's a little early—or maybe late—to start splitting up property. Talk with your lawyer, tell him what you want and you won't get any argument from me. Now, let's drop it. Are you still planning to go to the opening tomorrow night?"

She stared at him as if he had lost his mind. "Of course I'm going to be there. I just bought a new gown to be there. I have to be there. No matter how many silly ideas you get in your head about murderers and things."

"Maybe you're right. Maybe it is silly."

"Has anybody threatened me?"

"No. But I've got a hunch that this Monogram Murderer has something against me." *It's funny*, he thought. *We're pretty sure now that there are two of them and we still keep referring to the one Monogram Murderer. I guess everybody wants his life to be simple.* "Anyway, I just don't want to take any chances that they reach me through you."

"Well, I'm not even going to think about it. Nobody

wants to kill me. And even if they did, they certainly wouldn't try it tomorrow night at the Mountain. That'll be the most heavily guarded place in the world."

"You're probably right, but I'm going to have extra cops there anyway. Appropriately dressed, of course."

"They had better be. No brown shoes at this affair." She looked at him belligerently for a moment but her expression softened when she saw the concern on his face. "Paul, really, don't worry about it. I've talked to Oliver. The Mountain is overrun with security people. We've even got all those cameras all around the place. The same ones you've got out on the streets."

Regal was puzzled. "How did you know about the street cameras? I never mentioned that to you."

"No, but I heard Oliver talking about them with his public relations man. Oliver is paying for your police cameras."

"Oliver Storm?"

"Of course, Oliver Storm. Do you think we're talking about Oliver Twist? I heard them talking about them. Oliver put up the money for the cameras. If they help catch the killer, Oliver's going to be able to take some credit for it. The PR man thinks that will really help the political campaign."

"I'll be damned."

"You didn't know about that?"

"No," Regal said truthfully.

"Well, there we are," she said brightly, but when he did not reply, she said, "I think I'm going to go to bed. I have to be at the hairdresser's early."

"All right. Sleep well."

"I don't expect to get much sleep. I'm too excited. But tomorrow's another day."

"It usually is," he agreed. "Good night, Pat."

Before she left the room, however, the doorbell chimed. It was a uniformed officer with a manila envelope from Inspector Burton.

Regal thanked the officer and took the envelope to the littered dining room table. The new photo enlargements showed a thin-faced youth with a rather large mustache behind the wheel of the cab. He looked to be of average height or perhaps somewhat shorter—but many New York City cabbies were shorter than the average native-born American.

The driver was wearing a cap of some type but not the usual hackie hat that cabbies wore. Perhaps a baseball cap. Dark hair apparently. The picture was still fuzzy and grainy but the features looked ordinary, regular.

Patrice stood behind him and looked over his shoulder, "Who's that?" she said softly.

"I don't know. Maybe the Monogram Murderer. You recognize him?"

"For a moment there he looked sort of familiar," she said, then turned away disdainfully. "I guess not. I don't know any people who wear baseball hats. Good night, Paul."

She touched his face with her fingers and went to her own bedroom and Regal looked at the next prints. They were blowups of the passenger in the back but even computer enhancement could bring very little out of the photograph. It was a man; that was about all anyone could tell.

He put the prints back in the envelope and shoved them away. As he poured himself a drink, he puzzled over Oliver Storm.

How had he gotten involved with paying for the police surveillance cameras out on the street? Had Commissioner Gallagher gone to him to ask him to pay? Didn't the commissioner know that he was handing Storm a big political bonanza?

He sat down with his drink and then chuckled to himself.

Of course, the commissioner knows. The bastard has made a deal with Storm. Gallagher knows this mayor's down the toilet and he's cutting his own deal. That's why he was so goddam interested yesterday in what I thought of Oliver Storm. The bastard has sold his boss out and gone to work for Oliver and he was hoping I'd join the parade. He sipped his drink. *All politicians are whores.*

He cleared the dining room table of the dinner leftovers and finished his drink before showering and getting into bed himself.

He was fast asleep when the private telephone line on his end table began to ring.

He shook his head to clear it, then picked up the telephone in the darkened room.

"Regal here," he said thickly.

It was a real voice this time.

"Your queen is dead, Regal. The game is over."

It was a real voice, not a computer's.

And the line went dead before Regal could say another word.

32

The morning newspapers moved the Monogram Murders off Page One so that they could trumpet instead that the killers of Narcotics detective Pete Muniz had been located. The *Post* said they had been gunned down. The *Daily News* said they had been slaughtered. The *Times* allowed that the three men had been found shot to death in a tenement.

The caveats that Regal and Joe Burton had expressed to each other the night before were not reflected in the tone of the newspaper reports, although Burton's own statement to the press stopped short of saying that the three slain Panamanians were definitely the ones who had killed the young detective.

When Regal arrived at the office, Jane Cole was already there.

"Is it over, Paul? With Pete, I mean?" She was holding a copy of the *News* in her hand.

"I don't know. It's too pat, too cut-and-dried." He shook his head. "I guess I don't buy any solution that doesn't clear up those narcotics found in Pete's system."

She reached out and squeezed his hand. "Thank you for saying that," she said. "I don't buy it all either. And now you'd better get upstairs. The commissioner wants to talk to you."

"Okay. Hey, I thought you were going to get your hair done. Your head looks like you're wearing a bird's nest."

"I've got a noon appointment. Don't worry. I won't embarrass you."

"That's the least of my worries."

Commissioner Gallagher seemed upbeat. "At least this one case is out of the way. I hope we get whoever killed the three Panamanians but it looks like we can close the file on Pete Muniz."

"Looks that way," Regal said reluctantly.

"It *is* that way," Gallagher said stiffly, picking up on the note of hesitation in Regal's voice. "I know what you and Burton are bothered about but that's because you're both perfectionists. Why would those men have the murder gun unless they killed Muniz?"

Regal shrugged helplessly. "I just wish I knew why," he said restlessly. "Maybe we'll know more when we get their killers."

"I'm sure we will," Gallagher said. "Why wasn't there a chess move in the *Times* today?"

Briefly, Regal filled him in on the move made the previous day by white, the Monogram Murderer, and on the curiously personal message he had left on the tape.

"I thought it would be best not to respond with our move for a day or so."

"Why?"

"Well, maybe we could catch this killer, first of all. Second, I don't know. Maybe seeing the move in the paper, with a checkmate coming in a couple of moves, might be enough to set him off on some kind of rampage. I thought I'd wait. And in the meantime, I've put protection on Patrice, in case she turns out to be his target."

Gallagher considered this for a moment, twisting the hair over his right ear.

"All right. I think you probably did right. You really think he might be aiming at your wife?"

"I don't know, sir. The killer called me last night at my house. No tape recording this time. And all he did was repeat that my queen is dead."

"What'd he sound like? Did you get it on tape?"

"No. I don't have a recorder on my phone and his voice was muffled. It was a man but I couldn't tell anything more about him. I called Joe Burton to tell him about it this morning."

"Well, Paul, you do what you think is best. We wouldn't want anything happening to Patrice, would we?"

"Thank you."

"Is she going to the Storm Mountain opening tonight?"

"Yes. I'll have extra men there and Storm's security people have been alerted too. Are you going there, sir?"

"I don't think so. The mayor might. You know, he's got to put up a good front, his city and all that, but I think I'll pass."

Sure you will, Regal thought. *You and Storm are already sleeping together; there's no need for you to be seen out in public holding hands.*

"Commissioner, you ought to know, in case it comes up: my wife and I are planning to get a divorce."

Gallagher leaned back in his chair. "Sorry to hear that. The usual police-work problems?"

"Something like that," Regal said. "And I think she and Storm might be getting married. That's in confidence, of course."

The information did not appear to surprise Gallagher, who simply nodded, and Regal wondered if the commissioner already knew of his wife's affair. Maybe everybody did. The private, reserved part of his nature cringed at the thought of being the subject of other people's gossip.

"If there's anything I can do . . ." Gallagher said.

"Thank you."

Jane Cole did not return to the office and Regal left early to go home and dress, locking the office up when he left.

The grand opening was to begin with cocktails at 6 P.M. and Regal arrived ten minutes early and was pleased by the thoroughness shown by security personnel who checked his identification and his invitation.

Inside, three musicians were installing themselves in a corner of the two-story main entrance hall and a catering crew was setting up long buffet tables in a large adjoining room.

Regal had not gotten all the way through the lobby when Tony Bolda, unusually dapper in a dark blue tuxedo, sidled over to him.

"Welcome to the Taj Mahal," he said with a mock bow. "I hear they're giving out harem bunnies as party favors."

"That should help sales," Regal said. "We've got other men around?"

Bolda nodded. "A half dozen guys from the precincts. I had to fight them off 'cause everybody wanted to see this place. And I'm impressed too."

So was Regal. Patrice and LeBlanc had done quite a job, he admitted. The deep purple plush wall hangings lent a dignified air to the entrance hall, contrasting with the hundreds of strategically placed tiny twinkling lights that gave the large room life and gaiety. The rugs, chairs, couches, and all the furnishings were low and tasteful. People were starting to arrive now and the musical trio began playing a medley of Cole Porter songs.

He saw Patrice walking toward them. The sequined sheath gown set off perfectly her model's figure and sculptured blonde hair.

Bolda whistled softly. "Your wife looks great, Paul. If Betty had looked half that good, we'd still be married."

Regal only grunted. This was neither the time nor the

place to disillusion his chief aide. His *only* aide.

Without saying hello, and totally ignoring Bolda, Patrice asked Regal, "Have you seen Oliver? I don't know where he is."

"Just got here. Haven't seen him, Pat."

"And where is Pete? He was supposed to be here an hour ago. He's getting absolutely impossible."

"Aren't we all?" he commented. She frowned at him and moved off, flowing smoothly across the pink marble floor as if she were on roller skates. Bolda wandered off restlessly, watching Patrice from across the room, while Regal went to the bar, ordered a drink, and watched the room begin to fill.

Storm appeared a few minutes later, trailed by his two children. In a well-cut tuxedo, Tim looked very sophisticated and very large, Regal thought. He was always surprised that the boy was so big. Marcie looked improbably mature in an off-white evening gown. Storm glanced Regal's way, gave him a brief wave and began shaking hands with a swarthy hook-nosed man wearing a gleaming white Arab robe and headdress. Patrice instantly materialized to stand demurely behind the two teenagers as Storm introduced them.

"A touching picture if ever I saw one," a familiar voice commented cynically at Regal's shoulder. "And who made over that wretched little girl? She looks almost human for a change."

Regal turned and smiled at LeBlanc. "Probably Pat had something to do with it. Speaking of which, she's looking for you. You're late."

"I'm always late. It's part of my mystique."

Regal looked past him, saw no one and said, "Where's Jane?"

"She ran off to the ladies' room. One question, one answer, no lies. You serious about this girl, Paul?"

"Yes."

"Good. I like her."

"Then keep your lecherous mitts off her."

"You wound me, sir. I am a man of great integrity. In

fact, I have integrity I haven't even used yet. Ahhh, and here is the lady in question now."

Regal turned and only by sheer will prevented himself from doing a double take. Jane Cole was wearing a knee-length black cocktail dress, festooned with rows of shiny black tassels that danced and swayed as she moved. Her flame-red hair was heavily curled and piled high on her head, with loose tendrils hanging down around her face.

She saw him staring at her and rolled her hips just a little more as she walked.

"Hi, there," she said. "How do I look?"

Regal shook his head. "You're a knockout."

Jane flushed with pleasure. "Pete insisted that I wear this dress. Why didn't you tell me you had friends like him?"

"Policemen never want to admit that they have friends like me," LeBlanc said. "Aren't you curious, Paul, why I didn't put her in an evening gown?"

"Well, yes, sort of."

"Because I wanted her in disguise as somebody's favorite floozy of the moment," LeBlanc said. "The dress cost two thousand dollars and it'll tell everybody right away that she's just some rich guy's party girl here to have a good time. So everybody will ignore her, nobody will guess that she's a cop and they'll all leave her free to work."

"Looking like that, no one's going to ignore her. Not any man anyway."

"Sure they will. Because their wives will be watching. Stop complaining. Would you rather she wore her uniform?"

"All right, all right, you win."

"I'm on Pete's side," Jane said, adjusting the spaghetti strap on one shoulder. "To tell the truth, I feel terrific. I was going to wear a long gown but this is the real me. Part cop, part bimbo. I love it."

"Well, don't love it too much. I'll bring you over to Patrice in a few minutes and tell her who you are. I told her we were putting some people here tonight so she won't be surprised. Just stick close to her all evening, even when she goes to the john. Pete, you can help by being Jane's escort and staying near Pat."

LeBlanc sighed in resignation. "I had better plans for the evening," he murmured, "but if that's what you want . . . yes, I'll trail Pat around, listening to her take all the credit for my work. I warn you, though. If she lays it on too thick, I may kill her myself. He saw the look on Regal's face and said, "Sorry, bad joke."

"Forget it."

Jane leaned toward Regal and said, "Paul, she doesn't know who I am, does she? I mean, you never mentioned . . ." The poised young policewoman suddenly looked apprehensive.

"No. I haven't told her anything about you, Jane. She has no reason to think you're anything but a detective on duty."

"Good. I don't want her sniping at me or anything."

"Don't worry about that. Just make sure nobody snipes at her. Probably nothing's going to happen, certainly not here tonight, but keep your eyes open."

"I will." She turned to look at Patrice. "God, she's beautiful," Jane said softly, almost in awe. "I wish I had those kind of looks."

"A bitch goddess. Believe me, child," LeBlanc said.

"And I prefer the cuddly redheaded kind of bimbo myself," Regal added. "She's on the move. Let's get her while we can."

They moved hurriedly across the room and intercepted her while she trailed along with Storm and his two children, greeting people in the lobby.

Regal turned his back to Storm's group and said softly, "Pat, this is Detective Cole. She's part of the extra security we laid on tonight. Pete's pretending to be her escort. Her assignment is to stick close to you all night, even when you go to the bathroom. Cooperate? Please?"

Patrice looked at Jane and said, much too loud for

Regal's comfort, "They are certainly making prettier policewomen these days. And your dress is darling. It's so ... so ..."

"Trampy?" Jane supplied.

"Not at all. It's cute is what it is. Like a little girl playing dress up."

"If you two are finished discussing fashion," Regal said.

"This is all unnecessary, Paul. Nothing is going to happen to me."

"That's the idea, Pat. Humor me. Just for tonight."

"Oh, if you insist." She eyed Jane again. "That dress looks familiar somehow."

"I got it for her," LeBlanc said. "I borrowed it from Mitzi Monroe. You know ... the singer down in the Village?"

"That's where I saw it," Patrice said. "I must say, you look better in it than that tramp did, by about fifteen pounds. Look, I'll be right back. I have to talk to the caterer."

"I'll go with you," Jane said promptly. "Don't mind me. If you have to, introduce me as an assistant at your studio."

"Good idea," Regal said. He turned to see Marcie Storm standing very close behind him, staring into his eyes, smiling.

She's a strange-looking thing, Regal thought. He nodded and looked across the room, then turned back to Patrice. "Look who's coming in. Hizzoner himself."

"Whoops, I'm off," Patrice said, even as Oliver Storm started across the room toward the mayor, who was flanked by a pair of bodyguards. She seemed to float serenely across the room, but moved at a jogger's pace, and·Jane trotted along behind her, the tassels on her dress swinging wildly.

"Have fun, Paul," LeBlanc said. "I think I'll stay with my date and go over and say something scandalous to· the mayor."

"Try not to give Patrice a heart attack."

"Don't worry about that. Women like Patrice don't have heart attacks 'cause they don't have hearts. They have tiny little electronic adding machines. Cut them, they bleed stock certificates."

He walked off and Regal returned to his former position at the bar. He glanced at his watch and sighed. It promised to be a long evening.

33

Regal almost wished the Monogram Murderer *would* show up, so that he could pull out his gun and shoot him and start a riot and a stampede for the exits in which hundreds of people who were too rich for their own good would get trampled to death and he himself would be booked for manslaughter, inciting to riot, and firing a weapon in a gawdy condominium lobby, and he would be sentenced to life in prison where he would train rodents to dance and would become known as the Mouseman of Sing Sing.

Anything to break the damned boredom.

He had spent the night leaning against the bar, nursing an occasional weak drink, watching . . . just watching.

His feet hurt.

Jane Cole had danced twice with LeBlanc and both times Regal had started out to cut in, but both times Jane had hurried away to stay close to Patrice.

Patrice was now seated at a table with Storm, talking to a group of what were obviously political types, and Jane was standing on the edge of the dance floor nearby.

She was alone and Regal started over toward her but this time he was intercepted by Marcie Storm.

"Hi there, Mister Policeman," she giggled, materializing beside him suddenly and tucking her arm under his. "This party is a drag. Twirl me around a few times?"

Regal thought briefly of explaining that he wasn't allowed to dance on duty, but before he could say anything, he found Marcie in his arms, swaying to the music of the combo, which had gone through Cole Porter, Gershwin, Rodgers and Hart, and Jerome Kern and were starting over again on Cole Porter.

Suppressing a sigh of exasperation, Regal began dancing with her.

Maybe Marcie had had too much to drink, he thought. She was dancing closer than close, clinging tightly to him and moving her body against his as they stumbled around in a slow foxtrot. When she looked up at him, she laughed, a jagged sharp-edged sound, and her eyes glittered and Regal belatedly realized that she was not high on alcohol at all but on some kind of drug. Cocaine, he decided with professional dispassion.

Looking about uneasily, he saw Jane watching them from the distance, studying them over a glass that hid the lower part of her face. Other dancers got in the way and then he saw Patrice on the floor, dancing with Oliver Storm—a close, intimate sensual movement that was almost public copulation.

He heard a snort and looked down. Marcie also was watching her father dance with Patrice and her lips were drawn tight in a disdainful expression.

Marcie smiled up at him. "They dance well together, don't they?" she said, moving her hips against his.

"I guess they do," he replied, feeling a strange trickle of sweat moving down his arm under his sleeve. Another sudden twirl by Marcie showed him her brother Tim standing on the sidelines, his arms crossed, watching them intently with a lazy smile on his face.

"But not as well as we could dance," Marcie whispered, "if you'd only loosen up. Come on, copper, relax." She punctuated the statement by pressing her thigh against his groin. "You've got to live each day as it comes, right?"

"Right," Regal said. *Is this little lunatic trying to seduce me?*

"And every night too," she said with another giggle. "Especially every night, right?"

"Sure."

When will this goddam music end?

"You know why they dance so well together?"

"Who?" he asked.

"Your wife. My father."

"Why?"

"Because they spend so much time fucking."

"I think that's enough, Marcie," Regal said stiffly, pulling back and separating from the girl.

"I think so too," she said just as the music came to a merciful end.

Shaking his head, Regal headed back toward his usual spot near the bar. He felt almost as if he had been raped by Marcie and he looked for Jane, wanting desperately to talk to her but she was once again not in sight.

Bolda ambled over. "This bash going to last much longer, you think?"

"Maybe another hour," Regal said. "These are the beautiful people and they go to bed early so they stay beautiful."

"Then the mayor's the most beautiful of all. He took off like a big-assed bird after five minutes of hellos."

"Just saving face," Regal said. "He only wanted to get his picture taken for television."

Regal glanced toward the front entrance and was mildly surprised to see Joe Burton standing near the doorway, looking about with his habitual scowl. Then his eye was caught by the somewhat incongruous sight of a plump middle-aged man wearing a dark brown suit entering the room—the only brown suit he had seen tonight. He stiffened with a grunt of surprise as he recognized Inspector Vincent Flaherty.

Behind Flaherty were two other men. Both, like Burton, were more appropriately attired in dark blue suits. Regal recognized them as men he had seen in Flaherty's office. IAD investigators.

"What the hell . . ." he heard Bolda mutter.

Regal suddenly sensed a new level of tension in the big room. He glanced around and saw Patrice and Marcie walking arm in arm down a hallway that he knew led to the ladies' room. Jane Cole was trailing along a short distance behind. On impulse, he walked off after them, with Bolda following.

By the time he reached the far side of the grand lobby, the three women were not to be seen in the corridor. He felt like a damned fool but he decided to wait outside the ladies' room and leaned against the wall.

Bolda stopped next to him.

"You're a good cop, Paul."

"Thanks."

"I've always liked working with you."

"Same here," Regal said, wondering idly why Bolda suddenly felt the urge to express camaraderie.

The ladies' room and men's room were next to each other and LeBlanc sauntered from the men's room, still holding a wine glass in his hand.

"Oh my God, a stakeout?" he said when he saw Regal, but he stopped smiling when Regal did not respond. "Is anything wrong?"

"I don't think so. I don't know. Patrice and Jane are in the ladies' room. Marcie too. I don't know."

"Hold this," LeBlanc said and gave Regal his wine glass. Then he walked briskly across the hallway, opened the door to the ladies' room and walked inside.

"Christ, he may be a fag but he's got balls," Bolda said.

"Or maybe he just spends a lot of time in ladies' bathrooms," Regal said.

LeBlanc came out only a few seconds later.

"They're not in here, Paul."

"Are you sure?" Regal felt his stomach start to churn.

"Of course I'm sure. They're not here."

Regal looked around, frowning. "What's down there?" He pointed toward a hallway that branched off from the main hall.

"Apartments," LeBlanc said with a shrug. "Dozens of apartments. And elevators up to even more apartments. But they don't work yet."

"No?" Regal said, as he heard the muted sound of an elevator motor. He ran down the hallway with Bolda following him. LeBlanc started after them too but Regal called out, "Get the security people."

They reached the bank of elevator doors and there were no indicators over any of them telling which was in use or which floor it was going to.

He pressed his ear to the closed doors, one after another, until he found the one that was working. He could hear its electric motor humming.

Frantically, he pressed the call button for the elevator, even as he looked down the corridor, hoping for LeBlanc and the security men who knew this place to catch up to them.

But there was no one in sight; the elevator motor kept running and then with an asthmatic whoosh of compressed air the doors of the elevator opened in front of him.

"What's going on, Paul?" Bolda asked.

"I don't know for sure," Regal answered. "Dammit, we don't know what floor the elevator stopped at."

He stepped through the doors into the empty car and looked at the control panel. There was a thick red smudge over the button for the eighth floor. He touched it with his finger. Lipstick.

"Eighth floor," he called out, even as he pressed the button. Bolda jumped inside just before the doors closed.

The elevator whirred quickly, almost noiselessly, up to the eighth floor, where the doors opened onto a broad corridor that seemed to stretch endlessly in both directions.

"You take that wing," Regal said, pointing to the right.

"What am I looking for?"

"Anything. Anybody. I don't know why anybody's up here," Regal said as he trotted off down toward the left. The main corridor branched off every twenty feet into side corridors. There were scores of apartments. How could he find the one he was looking for? And what was he looking for anyway? Bolda had asked him the question and all Regal had was not an answer but an instinctive feeling. *Find Patrice. Quickly. Before it's too late.*

He trotted swiftly along the main corridor, pausing at each intersection to listen down the side hallways. But there was nothing except the deep abiding stillness of an empty building, echoing in his ears like an empty conch shell.

In the third side hallway, he heard nothing and was ready to turn away when he saw something metallic glinting. He ran down the hallway, and outside an apartment entrance door he saw a woman's lipstick lying on the thick plush carpet.

From inside the apartment, he heard a muffled noise. *Nobody should be in these apartments. The place isn't even open for business yet.*

He moved to the door and heard the sound of a woman laughing—a high, excited barking laugh.

Marcie Storm.

He touched the knob and the door opened. Thoughtlessly, Regal charged into the apartment.

He tripped over Jane Cole, who lay doubled over on the floor just inside the door. Her skirt was hiked up and he noticed incongruously that she was wearing black panties. Her hands were pressed to her stomach, her mouth was open, her eyes shut. She was not moving. Was she breathing? Regal had no chance to find out because, horrified, inside the living room of the apartment, he saw Patrice.

She was being held from behind by Tim Storm, his thick arm looped around her neck under her chin.

Her feet were kicking frantically in the air and she was clawing with both hands at the arm that was throttling her. Her eyes were popping and her tongue protruded. The front of her dress was stained with blood.

Regal saw this and felt his breath catch involuntarily as he started forward, and then, rising up from the floor in front of Patrice as if she were some kind of grotesque plant, Marcie Storm burst forth, a knife in her hand, laughing loudly, insanely, as she slashed with savage rage at Patrice's breasts and belly.

She was laughing and cackling, "Die, queenie! Die, queenie!" and when Regal ran toward them, she saw the motion, spun, gave a strangled cry of surprise and hatred and lunged at him with the long thick-bladed butcher knife.

Regal threw up his left arm in defense and reached for the gun he was carrying under his left armpit. A searing pain exploded in his right shoulder and he reeled away from the young woman, his arm dropping uselessly to his side.

There was another slash of pain across the side of his face and then a blow to his chest as he staggered back.

She's cutting me to death. And my arm is paralyzed. This little bastard is carving Patrice and me to death and I'm not doing anything about it.

He heard a sound behind him. "Good Christ," a voice shouted. It was Tony Bolda.

Even as Regal dove toward Marcie, she was past him. He tried to shout a warning but Bolda was already lunging forward into the room, and as he reached Marcie, he hurled her against the wall like a stuffed toy and reached for the gun inside his shoulder holster. With a roar of anger, Tim Storm dropped Patrice, kicked Regal out of the way, and jumped at the detective. Regal saw Bolda pulling his gun out. Tim grabbed his hand and forced the gun toward the ceiling.

"Hold him," Marcie screamed as she scrambled to her feet and sprang forward, the knife waving in front of her like the antenna on some maniacal killing insect.

As Bolda and Tim struggled, the knife flashed. It thudded into Bolda's body, once, twice, before the detective back-handed Marcie across the face and slapped her away.

Tim Storm had his hand wrapped around Bolda's throat and was grunting as he tried to choke the detective.

Behind them, Regal saw, through his narrowing vision, Jane Cole seem to move a bit.

Then there was another shout ... from the doorway ... and the sharp report of a revolver being fired.

Tim Storm's head snapped back and he slid to the floor, pulling Bolda down with him. Regal could see a bullet hole neatly centered in Tim's forehead.

Crouched in the doorway, gun leveled, was Vincent Flaherty. His eyes were narrowed and his lips, normally fixed in a genial smile, were curled down in a ferocious grimace. He looked like a deadly, angry Buddha.

Regal crawled across the floor toward the spot where Patrice lay. With a strangled shriek of despair and rage, Marcie Storm ran across the room and flung herself at Flaherty. She had dropped the knife and now was clawing for his eyes with her fingers. Flaherty held her off with his left hand and, with his right, clipped her neatly behind the head with the barrel of the gun.

She dropped like a blood-filled balloon.

Regal reached Patrice. He saw a swarm of blue suits entering the room. He heard Joe Burton roaring something Regal couldn't make out, as he charged in with his men.

"Get a doctor. Call some ambulances," ordered Flaherty in a crisp voice as he straightened up and holstered his weapon. "Tell them to bring blood with them."

Regal looked around in pain and confusion. He saw Jane Cole stir. He looked down. Patrice did not move. Her eyes were wide open but her lids did not flutter.

She was dead. Patrice was dead. He held her in his arms but he knew she was dead. She had been cut and stabbed savagely in the chest but the blood no longer pulsed out with each heartbeat because her heart had stopped. Her eyes stared up at the ceiling and Regal followed her gaze and thought incomprehensibly that she would have been dismayed because there were drops of blood on the white plaster overhead.

He looked around in despair. Near the door, he saw Jane Cole helped to her feet by one of the detectives. She seemed groggy but he could see no wounds, no blood. Her eyes met his and she walked unsteadily across the room to him, then knelt beside him. She pulled the handkerchief from the breast pocket of his tuxedo and pressed it to his bleeding face wound.

"I'm sorry, Paul," she said, over and over. "I'm sorry. I'm sorry."

Why isn't Tony getting up? he wondered. *Get up, Tony. And why can't I talk? Why is no sound coming out?*

Bolda still lay sprawled on top of Tim Storm. Regal, holding Patrice in his arms, saw Flaherty move over to the detective and roll Bolda over, off Tim. Then Regal saw that Bolda had fallen onto a knife in the young man's hand. The bone handle of the knife still protruded from the detective's stomach.

Leave it alone, Flaherty, Regal wanted to call out. *Don't take the knife out. Leave it there.* He wanted to shout but no words would come out of his mouth.

Suddenly the room was silent.

Bolda's face was turning white and Flaherty leaned over him and said, "Ambulance is on its way."

"Too late for me," Bolda said. He winced in pain at the effort of speaking. "You were looking for me, huh?"

Flaherty nodded and reached down to pick up Bolda's gun from the floor.

"Too late," Bolda said. He coughed and a flood of blood came out of his mouth and nose.

Flaherty kneeled down and began whispering into Bolda's ear but the detective did not move. Joe Burton bent over on the other side of Patrice and bellowed to the door, "Find a fucking doctor out there. Hurry up."

Burton said something else but his voice seemed to be growing dimmer and dimmer.

I'm passing out. I'm passing out.

Regal tried to move to his feet but the movement caused a sickening pain to radiate out from his right shoulder and the room spun and disappeared.

34

Paul Regal woke up.

It was not the first time he had been awake. He remembered waking up before, maybe more than once. He remembered people talking to him but he could not remember what they had said. He remembered pain while he was awake and the pain was still with him when he slept again.

But now it was different.

He woke up and the pain was less and he remembered many things and the first thing he remembered was that his wife was dead.

He had opened his eyes to find himself propped up in a hospital bed, his right shoulder encased in bandages. There was something on the left side of his face too, probably more bandages. He thought about them for just a split second and then he remembered the opening of Storm Mountain, and he remembered his wife and he groaned in sorrow and closed his eyes.

Someone touched his hand and he looked up to see Jane Cole, standing alongside his bed, holding his left hand in hers.

"She's dead, Jane," he said. He remembered a time, not long ago, when he had not been able to speak. But now he could. "She's dead. Patrice is dead."

"I know, Paul. I'm sorry."

"I am too," he said evenly and went back to sleep.

He did not know how long he slept this time, but somehow the sleep had helped him grow accustomed to the idea that his wife was dead, and when he woke up again, it was to the sound of voices talking and, for some reason, he thought he would be interested in what they were saying.

He opened his eyes.

Jane was sitting on one side of his bed. Stomping back and forth at the foot of the bed was Joe Burton, who saw Regal's eyes open, surveyed him coldly, and shook his head.

"You look like shit," he said genially.

"I feel like shit, fried and stirred." Regal could talk well now. The words he wanted to say just appeared on his tongue the way they were supposed to.

"Don't go picking on Paul while he's lying here defenseless," Jane warned Burton.

"Defenseless? With you sitting there? Fat chance," Burton said and grinned toward Regal. "I thought you might be up to hearing the gossip but I can come back some other time if you want. I'm a busy man, you know."

"Sure he's busy," Jane said. "He's on television every six minutes. He's running for Pope."

"What can you do?" Burton said. "The media knows star quality when they see it."

"Sit down, Joe." Regal realized he had many questions and no answers. He did not remember how long he had been out but something about poison on the knife stuck in his mind. He did not know if he had heard that while he was awake one of the earlier times or if he had dreamed it. Maybe it would all get simpler after a while.

He wanted to ask Burton something. It took him a moment to remember what.

"It was definitely Oliver Storm's kids?" he finally asked.

"No question. The two little bastards even kept the tapes of that synthesized voice they were playing to you with the chess moves. That alone would have been enough to hang them but Marcie gave us all the rest. She was whacked out on drugs that night and Flaherty got her to tell the whole story."

"The brother is dead, right?" It was all still vague in Regal's mind.

"Yeah. Flaherty got him. It might have been better for Marcie if she got shot too. The way it looks, she's going to spend the rest of her life at the funny farm. In a cage, if they've got any sense."

It was all coming back now. All of it—the murders, the investigations, Patrice . . . a voice saying, "Your queen is dead."

"All . . . just for fun?" Regal said.

"No," Burton answered. "It was more than fun. We've been piecing a lot together these last four days—"

"What!" Regal interrupted.

"What what?"

"How long?"

"Four days."

"I've been out of it four days?"

"Yes," Jane said consolingly. "Do you remember getting stabbed?"

"A little."

"There was poison on the knife. Something like curare and it was mixed with amphetamines. The knife got you in some kind of blood vessel cluster . . . I don't understand all this medical jargon . . . but it got right into your bloodstream and paralyzed you almost immediately. You almost died."

"And Patrice died." It was not a question, merely a statement to reaffirm a fact.

"Yes."

"And I've been out four days."

"More or less."

Regal screwed his eyes tightly shut and took a deep breath. "Go on, Joe," he finally said in a hoarse voice. "You were talking about Marcie."

"Yeah. It looks like both of them have been around the corner since they were small kids. We've been talking with some of the servants and Storm's ex-wife and they had some hair-raising stories."

Burton stopped to light a cigarette. "There's at least a possibility that they may have had a hand in the drowning of their first stepmother. She was supposed to be a suicide. And a girl who used to go to Groton says Tim raped her one afternoon, while Marcie held her down. They told her they'd kill her if she talked and she believed them."

"But why people on the street? Why monograms and chess and me?"

"It was your wife, Paul. They knew that Storm and Patrice were getting serious and they decided to kill her rather than have another stepmother. She was the target all along. And they called you because they were snotty and spoiled little shits and they thought they were just too smart for anyone ever to catch."

"And the other people they killed? Those were just cover-ups?"

Burton shrugged. "You figure a nut. Maybe pretty much cover-ups. But they were going to show the police, especially you, how stupid we all were. And then when it started and their old man announced for mayor, they kept doing it because they thought they'd help him get elected and it would be fun to live in Gracie Mansion." He spat out the word again. "Fun. What an obscene word for these two sickos to use. And after they killed Patrice, they were going to kill one more, just to muddy the waters. Sweet kids, huh?"

"It was really four days ago?" Regal said.

Burton nodded.

"How come you were there that night?"

"Vince Flaherty called me and asked me to meet him there. Thanks to Jane, he had a line on Bolda and wanted help when he took him down."

"Tony? Jane? What are you talking about?"

Burton looked startled and confused. "Didn't you tell him?" he asked Jane.

Regal turned his head and saw her flush. "He really just came out of it," she said. "And I wasn't going to tell him anything if he wasn't strong enough."

"What about Tony?" asked Regal. In his mind, he again saw his second-in-command charge forward into the room and he saw him stabbed but the picture stopped there. What had happened next?

Burton shook his head sadly. "It was Tony who did Pete Muniz. And Hector, the kid that gave Pete the tip. And Estrellita and the three Panamanians. All of them."

"Oh, no," Regal said and looked away toward the window, toward the bright summer sun. "Why?"

"The gambling. He was over his head and he needed money and he turned dirty. Remember that drug bust that you guys had that went sour?"

"Yeah."

"We figure that Bolda tipped off the Panamanians. That he was already in their pocket."

"But he's the first one that suggested to me that somebody might be crooked on the squad."

Burton shrugged. "Maybe that was just to put himself on the side of the angels. Who knows? If you heard some other rumors about someone going south, you might be a lot less likely to suspect him if he was one of the guys who made the suggestion. I don't know. But he handed up Hector and the Panamanians killed Hector in reprisal. He hoped it was going to end there. But Pete wouldn't let go. He found out about Estrellita and went after her. Tony, it turns out, was squeezing Estrellita on the side. He had rented the apartment for her. When Pete found her, she must have figured out that Tony had turned on Hector. So she handed up Tony. Bolda knew Pete was going to see her but he got there too late. Pete had already gone. Estrellita admitted what she did and so Bolda killed her, then set up that phony meeting between Pete and you and killed Pete too.

"But the Panama dealers were anxious to get out on the street working and Bolda knew that if they got nailed, they'd drop a dime on him. He just couldn't get off the tiger. So he got rid of them too, dumped his murder gun with them, and hoped we'd drop the whole thing."

"Why didn't we?"

"Because Vince Flaherty was involved and he never drops anything. Jane saw to that."

"What do you mean?" Regal turned his head again to look inquiringly at Jane. She made a face and stared down at her knees.

"Boy, she really hasn't told you anything at all, has she?"

"No. I guess not."

"You want to tell him or should I?" Burton asked her.

"I'll tell him," Jane said. "Paul, I'm sorry, but I work for Vince Flaherty undercover in Internal Affairs. I have for four years since before I joined your squad."

"Oh, man," Regal said, squinting his eyes. "Why? Why?"

"Because it was my job. It's always been my job since I've been on the department. I hunt down crooked cops. I did it in bunco. When your new drug unit was formed, Flaherty had me pull strings to get put on it."

"You were spying on us?"

"No, no, no," she said, shaking her head for emphasis. "My real target was the regular narcotics squad. I didn't have enough background to get onto that squad without raising some eyebrows and maybe some questions. So we thought I'd work with you for a while, get some experience, then ask out because of 'personal problems' and get transferred to the Narcotics Division. It would be a better cover."

"Why Narcotics?"

"Because there'd been problems for a few years in

Narcotics with leaks and blown raids. Flaherty wanted to find the bad apple." She shrugged. "Maybe we did. Tony used to be in Narcotics. When he came over to work with you, the leaks from Narcotics stopped. And they started in your office. When Flaherty started looking at our squad, I told him to check Bolda."

"It sounds like you were hanging somebody for what might have been a coincidence," Regal said.

"It wasn't that. It was a lot of things. It was Tony's good suits. It was that he was a gambler. We always made fun of it in the office . . . Tony with his racing form . . . Tony with his lottery tickets. But it wasn't just fun. Tony would be out at Belmont standing in line at the hundred dollar window two, three days a week. He was broke, he was dirty and he killed Pete, and I'll be goddamned if I apologize to anyone for flushing him."

She stared at him and Regal turned away. *It's all happening too fast. Too much, too fast*, he thought.

"You did the right thing, Jane," he heard Burton say. "And Flaherty would have gotten him anyway. He got a search warrant and went through Tony's place and found safety deposit keys and records that showed Tony was playing around with big money. The afternoon just before the Storm Mountain opening, Flaherty took Bolda's picture up to the South Bronx. The landlady identified him as the man who'd rented the apartment for Estrellita." The burly inspector looked at Regal. "I'm sorry about it, Paul, but you had a bad apple in your barrel. It wasn't your fault."

Regal closed his eyes, feeling more than physical pain. "Tony was a good cop," he said. "He saved my life the other night. Marcie was going to gut me with her knife when he jumped in and got himself killed in my place."

"I know," Burton said. "When the chips were down, he finally remembered the way a cop is supposed to act."

"I guess I missed all the press coverage. What did you tell the reporters?"

"Nothing," Burton snapped indignantly. "This is dirty laundry we don't wash in public. Flaherty and I went round and round on it but it stays that Tony died in the line of duty, saving a fellow officer. We gave him a hero's funeral yesterday. Everybody was killed in a drug war between Panamanians and a Jamaican posse and that's where we leave it."

"The drugs on Pete. How'd that happen?" Regal asked.

Jane answered. "I know you don't like Flaherty but he's a good cop. He doesn't really want to hang cops. He just wants the department honest. After I swore to him that Pete never used drugs and you told him the same thing, he had one of our guys take some of Pete's autopsy specimens to a private lab. It wasn't drugs at all. Flaherty figured it out. The night he got killed, Pete was supposed to be in class, remember? But he never showed up. Tony found him in the office and pumped him and found out he was going to see Estrellita. So Tony bought him dinner. Bagels. Remember? You heard it from Charlie in the delicatessen. Poppy seed bagels."

"You're losing me. What the hell do bagels have to do with it?"

"Remember the poppy seeds. That's what they make opium out of. When you eat them, they break down in the body and wind up in the urine looking like traces of opium or heroin. It's just one of the things a longtime narc like Tony would know. He had figured it all out in advance. And then when he shot Pete, he just smeared a little smack on his mouth and nose, just to put icing on the cake."

She looked at Burton who said, "Anyway, it's finished."

It was still all too fast for Regal; his head was pounding from the tension.

"I guess that's best," he said dully. "Keep it all in the department. The mayor must prefer it that way too."

"He doesn't know anything about it," Burton said. "The commissioner is too smart to give that idiot damaging information. We're not doing it this way for the mayor's sake, Paul. We're doing it for our sake. Because we're cops and we have to live with each other. Even Flaherty agreed with it this time and you know how he feels about crooked cops."

"So Flaherty dragged you off to Storm Mountain and you just happened to follow me and Bolda to that apartment. What a crazy piece of luck."

"Well, there was more to it than that," Burton said. "You never saw the retouched photos of the cabdriver with the mustache taken out, Paul. I did, and as soon as I saw Marcie Storm it rang a bell. I was going after her, not Tony."

"How did they expect to get away with it?"

"Because they thought they were some kind of superbeing. Because they were twins, some kind of . . . I don't know . . . a German word that means a lot of things in one thing. They thought since they were twins, they were at least twice as strong, twice as smart as anybody else. Marcie went with them to the ladies' room but Tim popped up in the corridor and called Jane."

Jane related, "He said, 'Detective, come look at this.' I ran over to the corridor, and when I turned the corner, he coldcocked me. Marcie and Patrice followed me and then they had a knife at Patrice's throat and they just took us to that empty apartment. They had my gun and I was in trouble. The only thing I had was my lipstick. I wasn't functioning very well but I tried to jab the elevator button. I hoped you'd see it and then I dropped it on the floor outside the room. Thank God you had your wits about you, Paul. They got me inside the room and the big shit slugged me again. I guess they were going to finish me off after Patrice."

"Marcie told Flaherty that it was going to be a perfect crime. They had a rope ladder and everything just to confuse us poor stupid cops into thinking that the killer had escaped over the balcony railing," Burton said.

Regal sighed. "So many people dead because two spoiled brats didn't want their daddy to get married again. What a world."

Burton grunted agreement. "Played hell with Storm's mayoral campaign too. He's withdrawn from the race and they say he had a nervous breakdown. I can believe it. He was riding high and then his whole world comes crashing down on him. Nobody knows him today and last week everybody was sucking up to him." The burly inspector glanced at his watch and stood up. "Gotta run, Paul. Take care of yourself."

Regal lifted a hand weakly to detain him. "When I get out of here, do I still have a job?" he asked. "You hear anything around headquarters?"

Burton looked embarrassed. "Well, since you're going to be laid up for a while . . . well, the commissioner moved your operation over into Narcotics for the time being."

Regal nodded. "Good. That's where it belongs."

"And of course you haven't heard about Riley, have you?"

"Chief Inspector Riley?" Regal asked.

Burton nodded. "He just announced he's going out on early retirement. Health problems."

Regal smiled weakly. "Is it time for me to offer my congratulations?"

Burton looked both smug and abashed. "There's a chance I may get it," he said cautiously.

"That's good news, Joe. You're a good cop. You'll make a good chief."

Burton ducked his head like a small boy. "Well, we'll see what happens," he mumbled. "If I do get it, you know you've always got a job, Paul. You're a good cop too." He turned abruptly to the door. Half in, half out, he said, "Get well," and then left before Regal could respond.

There was a long silence after Burton's departure. Jane patted Regal's hand.

"He'll only be chief for a few years," she said. "You'll still get your shot, Paul."

He looked at her in surprise. "Don't be silly, Jane. I don't have a chance at chief inspector. Not anymore."

"Why not? With your record? You're a hero. You should see the newspapers."

Regal shook his head. "I don't think so. Pete was my guy and he got killed. Tony was my right-hand man and he was dirty. I was right in the middle of the Monogram Murders and my poor wife turned out to be the final victim. Even if her affair with Storm isn't made public, everyone knows it happened. I'm a walking stigma right now. They won't fire me, but they're not going to give me any promotions, either."

"That isn't fair!" Jane cried passionately.

He frowned. "Fairness has nothing to do with it, Jane. But it doesn't matter, you know. The only reason I ever wanted to be chief inspector was because it was my father's goal and because life with Patrice was . . . so empty. Now, the department just doesn't seem that important to me anymore. I'd rather build my life around you than around the job. Maybe around Sarah . . . maybe around more children."

He looked at her and she glanced down and he thought, *Regal, you're a goddam fool. She's got no interest in you at all. She's been smooching up to you because it was her job for Flaherty.* He felt sick to his stomach and shut his eyes.

"Is that a proposal?" he heard her say.

"It was," he said, eyes still closed. "I'm sorry."

"Don't be. I accept."

He opened his eyes and she was on her feet, leaning over the bed, smiling at him. She moved forward and kissed him hard. She brushed his right shoulder and the pain made him wince, but he ignored it and put his left arm around her and held her there against his lips for a long time.

"Paul, I love you."

He had waited a long time to hear those words. They made everything possible; all the problems would work out as long as those words stayed between them.

"And I love you," he answered. "But I've got one question."

"What?"

"That black underwear you were wearing at Storm Mountain? Did Pete LeBlanc give it to you?"

She stared at him in astonishment. "Are you crazy? That was mine. I always wear black underwear."

He sighed and closed his eyes. "Okay," he said. "I can live with that."

And then he went to sleep again.

This time his dreams were better.

Two days later, Paul Regal left the hospital, escorted out
a side door by Jane Cole in order to avoid what she
called "the rabid pack of reporters hanging around outside." She took him back to his apartment on East Seventy-fifth Street, propped him up in bed with two pillows
behind his back, and prepared him the first home-
cooked meal he had had in more than a year.

When he was done, she brought him all the newspapers he had missed while he was recovering in the hospital. He hated it but he read through them grimly,
doggedly, as if knowing the worst of it would somehow
ease the pain of all of it. It was even worse than he
thought, but when he had finished reading all the crime
stories, he found one more story which brought a smile
to his face.

It was in the *New York Post*, on an inside page just
in front of the sports section, and was headlined:

BILLY THE KID IS BACK

It related how Billy Abbott, "the young Brooklyn genius who was the scourge of the chess world as a teenager ten years ago," had announced that he was
returning to tournament chess and had predicted that he
himself would be playing for the world championship "in
no more than two years. Unless the Russians stall which
is pretty likely considering that they're all gutless patz-
ers."

It went on to quote Abbott as saying: "Let's face it.
The age of chess computer is here. Pretty soon one will
be challenging for the world championship. All the Rus-

sian cheating will be worthless then. The world needs me. I will play for mankind."

"Good for you, Billy," Regal muttered.

"What's that?" Jane asked.

"I was just saying a prayer," Regal said.

"For whom?"

"For the Russians. And for computers too."

She looked at him quizzically, then began to undress. When she was naked, she slid carefully in next to him, under the thin sheet.

"I think we've waited long enough," she said.

"Too long," Regal answered.

The next day, the final advertisement appeared on the chess page of the *New York Times*. It read:

THE CRITICAL POSITION

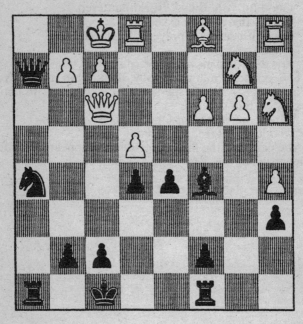

	White	Black
30)	. . . .	P×P
31)	Q×P	Q-N8 Check
32)	K×Q	N-N6
33)	B-R6	R×B
34)	Q-R5	R×Q
35)	White any	R-R8 Mate

Welcome back, Billy.   P.R.